Beyond & Within

SOLAR
PUNK

Short Stories from Many Futures

Edited by Francesco Verso

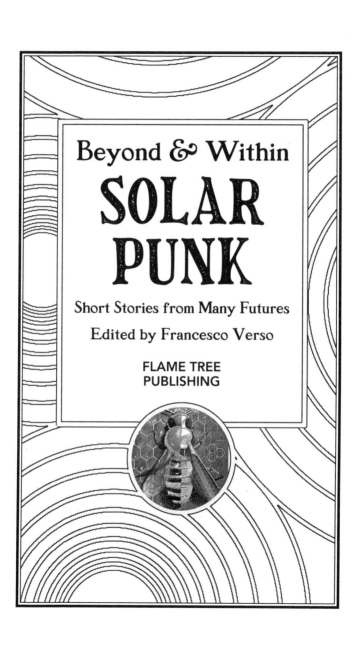

Beyond & Within

SOLAR PUNK

Short Stories from Many Futures

Edited by Francesco Verso

FLAME TREE
PUBLISHING

Publisher & Creative Director: Nick Wells
Editorial Director: Catherine Taylor

FLAME TREE PUBLISHING
6 Melbray Mews, Fulham,
London SW6 3NS, United Kingdom
www.flametreepublishing.com

First published 2024
Copyright in each story is held by the individual authors.
Introduction copyright © 2024 Francesco Verso.
Volume copyright © 2024 Flame Tree Publishing Ltd.

24 26 28 27 25
1 3 5 7 9 10 8 6 4 2

Hardback ISBN: 978-1-80417-935-2
Ebook ISBN: 978-1-80417-936-9

Publisher's Note: This is a work of fiction. Names, characters, places, and
incidents are a product of the authors' imaginations. Locales and public
names are sometimes used for atmospheric purposes. Any resemblance
to actual people, living or dead, or to businesses, companies, events,
institutions, or locales is completely coincidental.

The cover image is created by Flame Tree Studio. Frontispiece illustration
and cover detail is based on *Cyber Bee* © Simonetta Villani 2024.

A copy of the CIP data for this book is available from the British Library.

Printed and bound in China

Table of Contents

Introduction: Solarpunk

Francesco Verso

THE FIRST trace of solarpunk stories appeared in Brazil in *Solarpunk: Histórias ecológicas e fantásticas em um mundo sustentável,* edited by Gerson Lodi-Riberio (Draco, 2012), then translated by Fabio Fernandes and published as *Solarpunk: Ecological and Fantastical Stories in a Sustainable World* (World Weaver Press, 2018), while in 2014 Adam Flynn wrote a brief but fundamental article entitled *Solarpunk: Notes Toward a Manifesto.*

The term 'solarpunk' became popular on Tumblr in 2014 as a reaction to an image gallery that caught the attention of bloggers, and developed on sites like solarpunkanarchists.com and medium.com/solarpunk, giving rise to posts on topics ranging from circular economy to environmental sustainability, from criticizing predatory capitalism to creating off-grid networks, and going as far as the aesthetics of Art Nouveau, fashion that reworks the canons of African and Asian art in modern terms, and touching on bio camouflage/mimicry.

In contrast to steampunk, which takes refuge in a romantic nostalgia for the Victorian era, thereby deflecting from technological realism, and to cyberpunk, which has both denounced the ascent of the technocracy and the class fight between rich capitalists and poor exploited geeks without finding solutions, solarpunk explores exit strategies from the actual socioeconomic situation through plausible and pragmatic narratives that, for the first time, reply to the Anthropocene in a constructive way.

Ideally, solarpunk continues the fight of cyberpunk against the economic power of the multinationals and the authority of the state, but it concentrates on going against any attempt at subjugating the human race to 'inhuman' forces like financial speculation, environmental externalization, predictive algorithms, the privatization of public property and services, and the prejudicial filters of AIs.

In political terms, solarpunk tends to distinguish itself from the false dichotomy which has the market economy on one side and state socialism on the other, between individualism pushed to extreme competition and suffocating collectivism; a hypothetical solarpunk society should rely on a healthy development of people within a supportive community which also relies on long-term renewable energy. Utopia? Perhaps, even though the goal to reach is not perfection in itself (it's enough to remember that a dictator's utopia is everyone else's dystopia) but to move towards certain ideals. Even though solarpunk realizes that many objectives (social justice, fair distribution of profits and environmental sustainability) might never be achieved, this awareness does not diminish its relevance and originality.

Therefore, if cyberpunk pre-figured the present through the 'low-life/hi-tech' paradigm (Mark Zuckerberg selling people's personal data to multinationals is celebrated as a captain of industry, whereas Julian Assange who leaked the secrets of multinationals into the public domain is arrested as a criminal, just to cite two examples of cyberpunk in real life), solarpunk is preparing the field for the imaginary collective of the next thirty or forty years, inverting the terms of the paradigm and upending the metaphor into 'hi-energy/low-action' (energy from above, action from below).

The time seems ripe if we consider the struggle against global warming (kids skipping school on Fridays for Future, the civil disobedience movement Extinction Rebellion and the search for off-grid energy independence solutions), the production of goods from the bottom up (3D printing, digital craftspeople and the local produce economy), free access to data (Open Access and mesh networks) or new kinds of social interaction (tiny-houses, resilient communities and Strong Towns) and the mutual help networks (Occupy Sandy, We are the 99%) as agents of transformation and signals of change.

In solarpunk, whether the individual or a group, the main characters don't give up on the fight for repossession of capitalism's abandoned spaces or against state inefficiency. This transforms into a fight in the name of human necessity, a principle shared by the community, the neighbourhood, or a whole country against gentrification, expropriation, abuse of and the loss of identity.

From essays and stories published up till now, it is possible to construct a parallel between cyberpunk and solarpunk starting from key elements, as in the following diagram.

CYBERPUNK	SOLARPUNK
Capitalism: Bankarchy, Private property, Multinationals, Classism, Speculation, Globalization and work automation, High profits/low salaries, Competition.	**Anticapitalism:** Blockchain, Creative Commons, Mass co-operation, P2P economy, Crowdfunding, Crowdsourcing, Social equity, Non-profit, Reciprocal aid.
Mass industry: Fossil fuels, Negative externality, Big Pharma, Agrobusiness, GDP index.	**Circular economy:** Renewable resources, Recycling, Permaculture, Human Development Index.
Urbanization: E-waste, Deregulation, Gentrification, Brutalism, Bio-political architecture.	**De-urbanization:** Resilient communities, Mini-homes, Urban kitchen gardens, Local produce, Bio-architecture.
Info-tech: Virtual reality, Networks and Computers, Data-bases, Bio-technology, Synthetic drugs.	**Biomimicry:** Artificial photosynthesis, Social Networks, 3D printing, AI, Nanotechnology.

Aesthetically, solarpunk brings nature back to the centre and observes it differently to how it has been viewed recently, with artificial materials and a postmodern flavour. We are not talking about floral fantasies or a return to a sort of 'primitivism'. On the contrary, biomimicry – drawing inspiration from and using materials, designs and models inspired by nature – provides for the insertion of, or the fusion of, these elements in urban infrastructures, in public and private buildings, and even in the fabrics clothes are made of.

In an attempt to create artistic cross-pollination, solarpunk brings together suggestions from the most diverse sources, from cutting-edge technology from the Maker Fair, the artistic avant-garde from Africanfuturism, and flashes of counter-culture from the Burning Man Festival, to remodel them into something liberating, and reworking and re-inventing styles and trends in a different context. It is a transversal hybridization celebrating popular antique wisdom, craftspeople's experience against mass production and alienating experiences, respect for cultural diversity and integrated technological development, something creative and sustainable, while still remaining sensitive to the problems of cultural appropriation, the 'taking' instead of 'participating' typical of dominant cultures towards the subordinate ones.

One of the biggest risks for solarpunk, though, is the normalization of its revolutionary content: to be reduced to a meme, a trend, a hashtag, put on the shelves as a shiny cover, or worn by a smiling model and sold like the dream of a shiny future. As has already happened with cyberpunk, the danger is that solarpunk could be reduced to another passing fashion, absorbed by consumerism

12

and transformed into another entertainment tool for mass distraction. On the contrary, solarpunk is like a container of narratives countering the hypotheses, present and future, that preclude the construction of valid alternatives.

In shattering the rigidity of mainstream narratives, between the infinite growth of capitalism and the apocalyptic catastrophe of its detractors, solarpunk follows its tortuous and potholed path towards a change perceived by many as necessary. Even if it is neither possible nor desirable to create perfect worlds, this does not mean we should be scared to imagine a better future, especially when the fight against inequality and environmental pollution puts it within our reach.

If science fiction helps us to reflect on the future, solarpunk proposes solid strategies for creating a desirable one, now, wherever we are and with what we have, for us and for the generations following us. Hopefully it won't be yet another false start.

Francesco Verso

Rules for a Civilization

Jerri Jerreat

IN MID-OCTOBER, I asked my twelve-year-old students to pretend we were the first village of humans ever. What laws should we have?

"No Stealing," declared SoonYi.

I tapped it up on the large screen.

"We need sports! Games!" said Telise, who played rep and lacrosse and fiscus.

I countered, "Work before play. Our *laws,* first."

"Most societies killed each other off in wars, so we need to put our *aggression* into athletic competition." She's feisty, Telise, her many braids joined at the nape. Others nodded along with her reasoning. "Like the Ancient Greeks did in their polis-things. They started the Olympics in the year five hundred, you know," she tacked on, bragging.

"Close. Seven hundred seventy-six *before* the year zero," I corrected absently, tapping my bracelet to call up a holoscreen image for them. "Some compelling logic there. Okay." I added it. "Any more laws?"

15

"Everyone has to do their share of the work," put in Dane (who hates group projects).

"And no one's the boss," added Tobo.

"No Prime Minister? No President?" I clarified.

He nodded. "Everybody counts."

That was deep, I thought. Everybody counts. I turned to Irenska on my left. "What do *you* think might be a good law?"

A mistake. Irenska doesn't like to be centred out. Fourteen pairs of eyes turned to her. Irenkska's hair was cut in an unflattering ragged style, and she wore pants and a long tunic that were clean, but clearly came from a charity store. She flashed no glitter, no tooth tattoos, no body electronics, just the state-issued bracelet.

Despite this, I wasn't concerned about neglect. I'd invited her to the Breakfast Room but Irenska always had homemade lunches and read everything I downloaded to her bracelet. She was just painfully shy, a trait her mother shared, although her mom told me that with coaching she could face down a crowd when necessary. Money was tight in a single income unit and Winter Solstice might be tough, but Irenska and her mom did virtual trips around the world every summer break. Her mom also tutored her through her sine and cosine homework. About half the parents didn't.

"Nice top. For last century," said Kavi, loudly, into the momentary silence.

The class laughed, but most caught themselves and stopped quickly. After all, whom might Kavi single out next? Irenska buried her head in her arms.

I motioned for Kavi to step into the hall. Empathy seemed to be a problem for Kavi. She'd stomped on someone's hand, given 'accidental' kicks, scratched a student's arm, and decimated them verbally. I was tired of keeping her in for serious conversations, sending e-notes to her parents (who never replied), brainstorming with the principal and mopping up tears. Most of the class were afraid of her (though I'd heard a rumour Telise had punched her). I couldn't seal her caustic mouth, nor prevent her from sticking a foot out just as someone – often Irenska – walked past. Perhaps I should alert GoodFamily again. Had they even spoken with her parents yet? I was running out of ideas.

I teach in a great Edu-centre, honestly. We have a classroom on the roof, the fifteenth floor. It opens onto a gorgeous Toronto Skypark with colourful amur maples whose leaves inspire our art. In good weather, between storms, I take my class for hikes along the Skytrails that join our tall buildings to the Civilizations' Sculpture Park, where we can see copies of the art of ancient Chinese, Cambodians, Greeks, Aztecs, Haida people and others. My students can run their hands over a replica of the Laws of Hammurabi from Babylon.

Just before Kavi opened the door to step outside with me, Tobo saved the day by blowing a small paper ball through a rolled tube at her. It was a great distraction. I rounded on him, playing my part, and the class turned to watch that show.

I wondered if he stood up for Irenska on purpose, or had just been growing bored. After all, he'd been still for five minutes. Half the class was on Pixetal200 to calm their brains. The other half were Organic Old Fashioned, OOF. Tough choices, for parents.

* * *

We ended up with a decent set of First Laws: every human would be equal; everyone over age ten would have to work; we would build a large shelter together first, etc. I ignored Jeni and Sean's gruesome punishment ideas, given with innocent expressions. (Note to self: don't let them near that website on the French Revolution again.)

Our next challenge could be to design a group shelter. Last year, I'd taken the class to the Arctic Museum with a simulated environment to make quinzees. With our violent storms, vacillating between freezing rain and blizzards, we already knew *something* about snow. However, it rarely lasted more than a few days. This year it would be great to design an outdoor shelter, together, to survive hurricanes. There was another hurricane approaching the eastern coast of North America this week. Hopefully it would blow itself out. A virtual one could be exciting to work on …

"Good work so far. Let's return to this tomorrow," I suggested. "Clean up and get your lunch."

I had outdoor duty so, after wolfing down a bar and grabbing a jacket, I headed out to supervise soccer at recess. I spent the half hour automatically checking the sky – was that dark line in the south growing thicker? – and observing my students. You learn different things by watching them at play. I spotted Kavi kick the foot of a boy racing past her with the fiscus ball, who lost his stride and tumbled. A shouting match ensued, with Kavi insisting coldly that it was an accident while the others hesitated, unsure which side to take. The boy didn't seem injured, so I observed unobtrusively. The game restarted. Tobo and Telise were natural athletes, and they raced each other for a ball. She beat him, but with a deft foot manoeuvre, he stole the ball, and whipped it at the goal. Score! I'll hand it to her – she didn't turn sour. She slapped hands with Tobo and shrugged at her teammates.

Kavi's posture, even from this distance, appeared tense.

I started over there when a younger child called my name. "Teacher Blue Sky!" We get to choose names from nature. My friend's school has a water theme and so she chose 'Teacher Mermaid' and her buddy was 'Teacher Poseidon'. We laugh over these. I walked the little one to the school door and sent him in for ice. I couldn't see a mark, but frozen hydrogen and oxygen solved everything – even the hurt feelings. As I turned back, I heard Telise shouting in real anger, not her style.

I blew a whistle and hoofed it to the field. Students reluctantly parted. Irenska was on the ground, moaning and holding her shin. Telise had Kavi's elbow hiked up behind her back firmly, holding her in place, which was illegal contact. She yanked her victim toward me and started shouting.

"She waited 'til Irenska passed the ball and kicked her – and when she was down, she kicked her *again!* In the shin!" Telise's voice was shrill and I sensed the elbow getting an extra tug back there.

I dropped beside Irenska (emergency aid first) just as the sirens filled the air. No time to deal with playground dramas: Hurricane Gilly had arrived. I try to act like hurricane alarms are normal, though the last one, Hurricane Felicité, dropped three centimetres of rain in two hours, flooded ground traffic and grounded air travel.

Once we were all secure in the cement-block inner Safe Room, I sent Tobo to read to Irenska in the Healing Lodge a level down, another secure inner room with no windows. I was pretty sure *she* would read to *him.* This would be fine, good for both of them. I gave him the newest Skelt-Fire Fantasy novel which I bought on my bracelet on the spot and downloaded to a holoscreen as a treat. We played games with floating holo images and sang silly songs. After half an hour, I sent Telise down with apples from our Nutrient Dense Basket to "check on them." She understood it was code for "relax and enjoy yourselves together." I believe in nurturing healthy friendships.

Parents were two hours late at the end of the day, for police were warning people to stay indoors until the last rogue winds were gone. Certified Safe Volunteers who live or work in the building complex came up to help out, which was great. The ground floor bakery made gorgeous samosas for my class to tide us over.

As soon as the last child left, I went to talk to Principal Wise-Sun again about Kavi. He was clueless, as usual, an administrator who never should have left the e-world for human children. Great jewelry, nice hair, but useless.

Hurricane Gilly veered north-west and wore itself out over Georgian Bay.

Principal Clueless had sent Kavi right back to class with a basic "Next time, I'll control my emotions" form, so the next day, during their Indigenous Language time (Cree this month), I took Kavi outside to help with the clean-up. We found screws everywhere, and long peels of thick solar paint, like bark, on the ground. By spring, we would definitely lean on City Council for a full repaint. Expensive. Sheesh.

While we gathered up what debris we could, I learned Kavi's middle name (Hazel), that she had three solar/wind boats, had been on four oceans and had toys that were still being invented shipped directly to her home. We were both bored with the conversation, although I, at least, politely hid it.

I thanked her pleasantly, and sent her home at the usual time with a sealed note. Her parents would no doubt use it to litter an endangered forest somewhere.

* * *

I switched my supervisory duties for the next two weeks to be outside during the long recess. I did First Aid on a bloody nose, treated a sprained finger, bumps and bruises, adjusted a loose fastener for the rain catchment system – all with Kavi by my side. At first she protested. After two days she grew sullen. By the fourth day she became somewhat resigned. I figured I was saving the student population by keeping her with me, and hoped to steer her in a better direction.

"Can I at least go help with the kindergartners?" she pleaded after a week.

I looked at her kindly. "Do you think I can trust you yet with other children?"

"I wouldn't hurt *them*!"

I let that hang in the air. "*Them*," I repeated, thoughtfully.

She walked with me. We listened to a hundred tiny complaints. One younger child wouldn't follow the rules. Another said no one would let them play. Many tattled about small misdemeanors, such as mildly bad language or unsportsmanlike behaviour. Yard duty can be rather tiring. I started sending Kavi to pick up and dust off the shorter ones, or remind the middle ones to not exclude others.

22

One day I sent a set of official fiscus game rules to her bracelet.

"I *know* the rules," she sneered.

"Sure you do. But a ref has to be able to recite them like a pro, perfectly memorized."

I handed her a whistle.

She practiced refereeing during our Phys. Ed. classes, inside. She was fair and immovable, like our Android Police. Perhaps, I pondered, it helped that she had no real friends? Eventually, I asked her to referee the outdoor recess game, mostly kids aged 11–14. I didn't feel I was making any real progress with Kavi, but at least, I consoled myself, this gave her a useful role.

* * *

One evening, I was out jolsta dancing with friends, and Mermaid, blinking those wide dark eyes of hers, asked if I'd ever experienced a class bully as a kid. My good mood from the night of dancing drained away.

Mermaid sat me down and listened.

Eleven was my worst year. There was a bold, confident girl who ruled the girls in our class. Kristy had some invisible charisma; she laughed louder and had a way of cocking her chin that dared us to do things. We did them. We stole equipment from the school's locked storage room; we painted swear words in the halls. Kristy approved and we all basked in her uplifted eyebrow. It was nothing but some destructive fun until Kristy set her sights on Marli.

Marli had been a refugee from Malaysia that year, having survived a civil war and a massive tidal wave. Her parents were custodians in a department store. One day, Kristy demanded that Marli steal toys for us. She repeated this demand daily, wouldn't let it go. Others joined in. This sort of thing always happened in the halls or washroom, places where teachers didn't see. I stayed on the periphery, but I didn't report her or dare to interfere. I was a simply a sheep. Baa-aa.

I began to dread going to school. I had stomach aches, begged to stay home. My mom, a single, couldn't miss a day's work unless it was really serious. My relatives lived in Haliburton, fantastic for visits, but too far away for babysitting.

One morning Marli arrived, creeping timidly into the schoolyard. She carried a small bag from the department store where her parents worked. Marli held out the bag to Kristy. It was full of tiny plastic spinning tops, the very thing kids were collecting that year. Kristy handed us each one and made caustic remarks about how small and cheap they were. The pink one she thrust at me burned my hand. And my heart.

Marli's family were trying to start a good life here, a safe life. And we had made her steal cheap plastic tops.

I was only eleven, but I knew it was wrong. Very wrong. I slipped my top back into Marli's backpack the next day in case there was some way to return it, but the damage had been done. She moved to a different school the next month. We never saw her again.

I came home to my cheery yellow ninth-floor apartment, remembering all of this. Kavi didn't have charisma, but she was a sort of Kristy. A bully, without empathy. I dropped my jacket on the sofa and looked out my window at a sky full of light traffic. Their lights were beautiful moving stars against the navy black, but Mermaid was right. I still felt heartsick over a pink plastic toy.

* * *

The next day I pulled Kavi out of bonsai pruning (Nature Nurture Class), for a few minutes to sit outside in the sheltered entrance, out of sight of the others. I passed her an apple and bit into mine.

"So, is it getting any better?" I asked, looking out over the green field and a row of young amurs in gold and red leaves. You'd never know we were fifteen stories above ground level – except for the constant low buzz of Ziptrains spiderwebbing through the city below, and the air traffic, of course. Drones, mostly, but a constant stream of needlenosed planes too, higher up. I sometimes came out here with earplugs to relax.

"Whadya mean?" She eyed the apple suspiciously.

"Well, you know." I took another bite and pointed to a line of geese above us, a lucky sighting. "See how they all line up? All the same? But we humans aren't like that. It's not that easy for us."

She pocketed the apple and dropped her shoulders.

"How long's it been?"

"Since?"

"Since you had friends to hang out with. Invitations to drop over to a friend's home?" I kept my eyes on the distance.

Beside me, I heard a deep sigh.

"That long?"

There was a rustle.

I thought about our class. Kavi was quick at Math, hated Communication, and possibly people. Where to start? "I've seen kids make a brand new start," I continued, stretching my back by reaching for my toes. "Now and then. Some *gutsy* kids who really want to start over. A fresh slate." I looked over at a distant row of wind turbines. "It's hard work though. You've got to really want it. Want people to actually like you for who you *really* are – not those mistakes you've made, and *not* for your money. That's not real." I stretched my neck left, then right. "Sometimes I think people with wealth have to be even kinder, maybe, and be very careful not to use their money to try to buy …" I paused.

"Forgiveness?" she asked.

I nodded. Interesting. I'd been thinking of buying friendship. "Exactly." I bit, chewed, looked away. Chewed some more.

"How did those kids, you know, do it?"

"Well," I cleared my throat, "They practiced kind behaviours. Shared their stuff. They sometimes offered to help. Little gestures of respect. Nothing big. They stopped saying mean things to be funny. Instead, they got in a habit of saying small nice things."

"Like, I love your hair? Even when it's disgusting?"

I shook my head. "Has to be true. Or they know you're faking it." I blew out slowly, hoping I hadn't overdone it. Such conversations were like neurosurgery. Delicate. One wrong move ... I stood up and stretched. "You're off recess duty now, if you want. But you're an excellent referee, Kavi. The games are going far better now. Thanks."

I left her in the hall near her next class.

* * *

The next week, winter hit us. It was barely November, but after a brisk fall day came soft, downy flakes, then a deluge of white. The kids laughed and made angels and snow forts. This was sheer joy. The Energy team came out with long-handled brushes and worked to clear off the solar panels and the southern walls, joking with each other. Naturally, Principal Clueless rang the bell several times and the school poured back inside.

The next day, school was cancelled due to Extreme Cold (forty below, Celsius). I stayed in my classroom prepping a unit for Winter Solstice (making gifts to deliver to a seniors' residence nearby). A handful of students arrived and caught up on their work. I was able to tutor them one on one, which was lovely.

The temperature rocketed up to zero but school was cancelled the following day as well: freezing rain. No one came, not even those who lived nearby. (I, myself, lived just a few floors down.) I did some admin work and then raised one of the exterior coated metal blinds a little and sat by the window, watching the school gardens freeze over as though ice gloves were being pulled over the fingers of every plant. When the window was too thick and wavy to see out of, I went home.

There was an overnight thaw and by morning it had become early November again. Our just-beginning colour festival, those glorious maple leaves, had blown away in the freezing rain. Such a shame.

In school we had explored a few different time periods and cultures. Each student was now challenged to create a surprise for the class based on their own research: a model or an ancient machine, music or art that they would create to teach us about an earlier culture. I always found this part of the year exciting and highly tiring, pulled in many directions. Every student needed some help with these secret projects. Outside, the temperature outside rose and fell and we alternated between puffy coats and thin ones.

Then, on the cusp of December, Hurricane Hannis hit North America. Like most hurricanes, it started innocently in the warm air off the coast of Mauritania. It headed west, picked up heat and moisture and scrubbed the Caribbean islands (those still above sea level), and headed up North America. The southern USA was devastated, as usual, but it was sparsely populated and those folks slipped into their underground shelters. In two days it whipped up to New York, gathered force across Lake Ontario and hit – us. It was the greatest hurricane to hit Toronto since 1954.

We were prepared. Our former floodplains were conservation areas, our bridges floatable. Still, I later learned that most ended up broken, and cargo trains were rolled off their tracks. Fortunately, the Ziptrains were in their tunnels and commuters at home in hurricane rooms, as were we at school. It was surprising that any students came at all that day, for schools were cancelled but remained open in case of need.

We only had eleven students arrive out of four hundred and Teacher Boreal Forest and I, who both lived in the building, had offered to handle whomever arrived. I was especially surprised to see Kavi there that day, as her parents were wealthy and certainly not emergency workers. I took the older six students and Boreal, the rest. We read stories and worked clay into small sculptures in the Safe Room. At ten a.m. a low moaning came through the walls like a horror vid, then grew into a roar like a Ziptrain headed right for us. I admit I was terrified. We hugged each other tightly, and heard windows blow out, followed by maniacal sounds on the roof like a St. Vitus dance. We all screamed. Irenska was sobbing, hugged by

Telise. I had my arms around twin boys aged ten. Kavi – well, Kavi seemed to be cuddling the younger girl, the daughter of two firefighters. She caught me staring and her face went mulish.

I gave her a nod, took a breath, then tried to yell encouragement. My voice was lost in a cacophony of objects clattering outside. Hopefully *outside*. The classroom walls should be safe, but sometimes there was a thud that shook the entire building. I was working crazy hard to keep my cool, but we huddled in close, and I reached out to pat their hands, heads, shoulders, whatever I could reach.

Between thunderous crashes, I reminded them of the spongy pads the building supports were based in, built to sway a little with earthquakes or gale-force winds. It would move a little, but not break, I told them, crossing my fingers. It sounded like everything was breaking. If the building went down …

Our solar-cell pink-salt lamps were still bravely emitting a dim light, but by noon, our feet were wet, a bad sign. I texted Boreal downstairs. They were okay, but the roar of the storm was working bad juju on the kids. Luckily two Safe Volunteers had come in to help cuddle and read aloud to her five students. I decided we should go downstairs and join her. The rain had to be coming in a broken window in our classroom somewhere.

The door was heavy, as it should be, but nearly stuck. I had a moment's panic, then sheepishly remembered the red button. The door slid aside a little until I stopped it and stepped into the opening, blocking the view. And hung on.

It was a crime scene. Rain wasn't sprinkling in, it was gushing in through broken windows (*every* window broken), probably pouring off some rain catchment pipe, blown askew and facing the wrong way. I heard screeches behind me as water swirled into our Safe Room, and outside the windows, a tall wind turbine had cracked and fallen over. All the colourful amur maples were gone. Just … gone. I glanced out the south window and saw the solar paint peel off in big strips like a zipper, then insulation blow out like dandelion seedheads. I stared, and finally forced my head to turn away.

Inside, our classroom was a small river. Our furniture was upside down and half submerged at the far end of the room. All of the artwork on the walls was floating past with brushes, wooden 3D solids and other teaching aids. Suddenly both Kavi and Telise slithered and shoved themselves out, catlike, beside me. A wooden chair leg floated past.

"Holy …" whispered Kavi.

"Right. Okay." I tried to focus. "We have to sprint to the door and get downstairs," I said in a high, mechanical voice. "And watch out for broken glass. And hold hands. In a line."

Kavi and Telise relayed my message inside as I surveyed the route to the far door. Chunks of window and electrical equipment were floating past. *Shit*. Were we going to be electrocuted? No, I scolded myself. Electricity had been turned off at the first siren and I was already shin-deep in water, hanging on hard to the door. Hard, because the winds were blowing around the room like – well, like a hurricane. There were two wide support beams en route to the far door, standing firm. Good. Okay then. I turned around and tried to close the door but it was truly jammed. Just as well. We had to leave.

There were three children aged ten, and another three, aged twelve, all standing in water nearly to their knees, looking at me.

"Good job, guys. Now then. Telise, you be the tail end." I arranged the twins after me, then Kavi, then the girl, then Irenska, then Telise. There were no scarves or ropes to tie us together. "Hold tightly to each other's wrists," I ordered. I checked each one. "This is a stronger hold than hand to hand. Our classroom is like a stream, and we're going to wade across it to the far door. We'll stop at the first post, then at the second post. We'll help each other. The stream has quite a little current so work on staying upright. Okay?"

They nodded.

"When we reach the door, we'll run down to the Safe Room downstairs. Understand? Everyone? Don't look around. It's a terrible mess and it's going to take the staff a *week t*o clean it all up. Don't waste time looking, okay?"

They nodded. One twin sniffled. Kavi rolled her eyes ostentatiously.

"It's very windy, so brace yourself. We can do this because we're a team. We can do it." I gave a meaningful look at my tail-end students. Then I squeezed sideways out the opening, leading twin one (Robi or Roni?). I waded forward, braced myself against a surprisingly strong current, and turned to haul my young neighbour upright as he stumbled on his first step into the class. The wind was blowing in the open windows, trying to throw us down toward those broken sofas at the far end of the room. I hoped Kavi could help me keep the twins on their feet. I hoped Irenska wouldn't be so afraid she'd pull someone down.

It was ten small steps to the first post and I felt like I was dragging Robi. Everyone was hunched over but on their feet. Kavi yanked her twin up once, rather hard, I thought, but it worked. Telise was moving out of the Safe Room now. She gave me the thumbs up. I slid around the post and gasped when something hit my leg. It was a spear of window glass in a chunk of wooden frame, floating. I threw it away, looked around for more, prayed. Then I drew Robi forward.

We reached the second post. Irenska slipped under once, but Telise wrenched her up, dripping and spluttering. All good. The younger ones were hanging on, wearing fierce expressions. I felt a flash of pride.

Halfway to the door, Robi froze suddenly and screamed. I turned sharply to see blood circling around him and sweeping down the room toward the furniture. *Shit!* I let go of his hand and scooped him up, grabbed his brother's hand, then plunged forward. I pressed the exit door button, jumped through and started tugging everyone in one by one. Kavi helped, then there was a yelp and loud splashing – Telise had slipped under. I shoved all of the younger ones at Kavi with a barked command and tried to sprint back in, but Irenska got in my face. She shoved something into my gut – a safety rope near the door. I tried to smack it away, then realized she was tying it to my belt. Quick thinker. I plunged into the flood to find Telise.

Telise's feet and head bobbed up as she bounced along in shallow water with debris toward the back. It would have been funny if not for the glass everywhere. "Flip over! Get on your knees!" I shouted. Telise smacked into the pile of art boards and I helped wrench her up to standing. A quick body check while I retied the rope quickly around her waist. I wrapped one arm firmly around her back.

"One, two, three!" We waded back together, carefully, hunched against the wind. Broken boards and toys splashed against us.

Kavi jerked us through the doorway, hugged Telise briefly, then tried to shove the door closed. The rope, I saw, had been tied to a railing. I undid it quickly and kept it. Irenska had the younger ones on the wet platform below. The stairs were a waterfall. Everyone was soaked. I reassessed things. There were no dry clothes in the Safe Room downstairs but there were in my apartment.

"Change of plans!" I shouted, gesturing for Kavi to give up on trying to shut the door to our once-classroom. "Pyjama party at my place!"

* * *

I invited Boreal to bring her crew down to my apartment once we were safe inside, and described the ruin of my beautiful classroom. And the roof. She decided to take her group down to her own apartment instead, on the fifth floor. We notified the parents, the Emergency Unit, and got on with it. Robi's cut seemed fine, but thumbs can bleed a lot. I did the First Aid thing, and promised a fake cast after his shower. My Hurricane Room was attached to my washroom, so the girls showered, then the boys.

Apple, my orange cat, was a sucker for empty laps and free hugs, so she did her magic act and they cheered up fairly fast. I sneaked into the kitchen to make popcorn, pizza and hot chocolate, and grabbed loose clothes and cosy socks for everyone.

After the boys were dressed – and a bandage like a turban on Robi's thumb – I realized I felt a little light-headed. I sat down suddenly. It was probably post-excitement, I reasoned, but Kavi came over and lifted my head up.

"You're pale," she said. "And you are still soaked and cold. Into the shower."

"I can't leave—"

"Or I can shove you in the bath," she ordered, actually pointing. I felt like I was seeing my mother.

"I'm in charge—"

Telise and Irenska materialized on either side of her. "We can handle it," Telise said.

"You need the heat," added Irenska. "You're shivering."

"We've got your food. And your cat. We're fine. Go." Kavi shoved pizza in her mouth.

I shook my head, then recalled that there were headache pills in my washroom. "Ten minutes," I said firmly. "Don't let anyone out of that room. Pound on the door if you need me."

I actually felt a little weak, so got into the shower, turned on blessed hot water and then stripped in there. It felt like heaven, hot water pouring on my chilled neck. Absolute heaven. Then I discovered the source of the blood in the water – me. My shin.

I shut off the water, wrapped the last towel around me and sat on the floor to check it out. Not bad. But not good. I could use the glue-stitch bandages in the drawer …

A minute later Kavi had another towel around my shoulders and a wet one held against my shin.

"How did you know?" I croaked.

"I remembered the blood in the water and Robi's cut is small. Shut up." The door opened again and Irenska slipped in with the First Aid Kit.

"Took you long enough," snapped Kavi.

"You girls shouldn't—" I began.

"I'll cover her mouth. You get that bandage thing on," said Kavi.

I closed my mouth.

"Putting these on tight enough is tricky," whispered Irenska to Kavi. "Hold her still."

"No problem," said Kavi.

Kavi held my leg down with surprising strength. How old were these kids again? And who was the teacher? I closed my eyes and hugged the towels for comfort while Irenska patched my leg. Apparently, medicine was Irenska's dream career.

* * *

Warm and dry, we all snuggled up to watch sweet holofilms about cats and dogs saving the world. There were seven hands petting Apple. All was as it should be.

Irenska, Telise, and Kavi were excellent babysitters, sharing blankets and telling jokes to the younger students if they showed anxiety. Irenska made me weak tea and checked my leg now and then, quite bossily. I think she was picking up attitude from Kavi.

None of their parents made it until dawn but long before then we'd all fallen asleep, the children in a heap with Apple like a kindle of kittens.

* * *

After Hurricane Hannis, there was a subtle air of respect between Telise, Kavi, and Irenska. The latter seemed less timid. She put her hand up more in class. Kavi seemed quieter, calmer. There were no more "accidents", fewer tears. Perhaps the other students didn't really notice, but I did. Kavi kept refereeing, her choice. Telise, Kavi and Irenska did a terrific science project together. By the time we finished making our Solstice gifts, I heard Telise argue, "Everyone's equal!" during the first indoor game of fiscus (I assumed this meant for someone to pass the ball around).

I smiled. That had been our top Rule for our civilization. So few societies had truly believed in equal rights for all. The Haudenosaunee Confederacy and ancient Greeks had come closest.

On the last afternoon before the Winter Solstice break, I packed up their cards and small gifts. I flipped through them, wondering how much more winter was ahead. My annual Solstice trip to the Haliburton Highlands meant cross-country skiing and lake skating. I was bringing Mermaid along. She'd love it, and it was time to meet the family.

My eyes caught one card. Kavi had written, "Thanks for not giving up on me."

I wondered what had become of my own class bully, Kristy. And Marli, the victim? I paused to do a quick search on my bracelet. No sign of Kristy, but Marli was an astropilot now with two children, living near the busy spaceport of Saskatoon.

Good for her.

I smiled at Kavi's card, and closed it.

"Winter break," I said aloud, and walked lightly toward the door.

Byzantine Empathy

Ken Liu

YOU'RE HURRYING along a muddy path, part of a jostling crowd. The commotion around you compels you to scramble to keep up. As your eyes adjust to the dim light of early dawn, you see everyone is laden down with possessions: a baby wrapped tightly against the chest of its mother; a bulging bed sheet filled with clothing ballooning over the back of a middle-aged man; a washbasin filled with lychees and breadfruit cradled in the arms of an eight-year-old girl; an oversized Xiaomi smartphone pressed into service as a flashlight by an old woman in sweatpants and a wrinkled blouse; a Mickey Mouse suitcase with one missing wheel being dragged through the mud by a young woman in a t-shirt emblazoned with the English phrase 'Happy Girl Lucky'; a pillowcase filled with books or perhaps bundles of cash dangling from the hand of an old man in a baseball cap advertising Chinese cigarettes...

Most in the crowd seem taller than you, and this is how you know that you are a child. Looking down, you see on

40

your feet yellow plastic slippers decorated with the portraits of Disney's Belle. The thick mud threatens to pull them off your feet with each step, and you wonder if perhaps they mean something to you – home, security, a life safe for fantasy – so that you don't want to leave them behind.

In your right hand you're holding a rag doll in a red dress, embroidered with curved letters in a script you don't recognize. You squeeze the doll, and the sensation tells you the doll is stuffed with something light that rustles, perhaps seeds. Your left hand is held by a woman with a baby on her back and a bundle of blankets in her other hand. Your baby sister, you think, too little to be scared. She looks at you with her dark, adorable eyes, and you give her a comforting smile. You squeeze your mother's hand, and she squeezes back reassuringly, warm.

On both sides of the path you see scattered tents, some orange and some blue, stretching across the fields all the way to the jungle half a kilometer away. You're not sure if one of the tents used to be your home or if you're just passing through.

There's no background music, and no cries from exotic Southeast Asian birds. Instead, your ears are filled with anxious chatter and cries. You can't understand the language or the topolect, but the tension in the voices tells you that they're cries for family to keep up, for friends to be careful, for aged relatives to not stumble.

A loud whine passes overhead, and the field ahead and to the left erupts in a fiery explosion brighter than

41

sunrise. The ground convulses; you tumble down into the slimy mud.

More whines sweep overhead, and more shells explode around you, rattling your bones. Your ears are ringing. Your mother crawls over to you and covers you with her body. Merciful darkness blocks out the chaos. Loud, keening screams. Terrified cries. A few incoherent moans of pain.

You try to sit up, but your mother's unmoving body is holding you down. You struggle to shift her weight off and manage to wriggle out from under her.

The back of your mother's head is a bloody mess. Your baby sister is crying on the ground next to her body. Around you people are running in every direction, some still trying to hold onto their possessions, but bundles and suitcases lay abandoned in the path and the fields, next to motionless bodies. The rumbling of engines could be heard in the direction of the camp, and through the swaying, lush vegetation you see a column of soldiers in camouflage approach, guns at the ready.

A woman points at the soldiers and shouts. Some of the men and women stop running and hold up their hands.

A gunshot rings out, followed by another.

Like leaves blown before a gust of wind, the crowd scatters. Mud splashes onto your face as stomping feet pass by you.

Your baby sister cries louder. You scream, "Stop! Stop!" in your language. You try to crawl over to her, but someone stumbles over you, slamming you to the ground. You try to shield your head from the trampling feet with your arms and curl up into a ball. Some leap over you; others try but fail, landing on you, kicking you hard as they scramble.

More gunshots. You peek between your fingers. A few figures tumble to the earth. There's little room to maneuver in the stampeding crowd, and people fall in a heap whenever anyone goes down. Everyone is pushing and shoving to put someone, anyone, between the bullets and themselves.

A foot in a muddy sneaker slams down onto the bundled figure of your baby sister, and you hear a sickening crack as her cries are abruptly silenced. The owner of the sneaker hesitates for a moment before the surging crowd pushes them forward, disappearing from your sight.

You scream, and something pounds you hard in the gut, knocking the breath out of you.

* * *

Tang Jianwen ripped off her headset, gasping. Her hands shook as she unzipped her immersion suit, and she managed to peel it halfway off before her hands lost their strengths. As she curled up on the omnidirectional treadmill, the bruises on her sweat-drenched body glistened dark red in the faint, white glow of her computer screen, the only light on in the dark studio apartment. She dry-heaved a few times before breaking into sobs.

43

Though her eyes were closed, she could still see the grim expressions on the faces of the soldiers, the bloody pulp that had been the mother's head, the broken little body of the baby, her life trampled out of her.

She had disabled the safety features of the immersion suit and removed the amplitude filters in the algics circuitry. It didn't seem right to experience the ordeal of the Muertien refugees with pain filters in place.

A VR rig was the ultimate empathy machine. How could she truly say she had walked in their shoes without suffering as they did?

The neon lights of bustling Shanghai at night spilled through the cracks in the curtains, drawing harsh, careless rainbows on the floor. Virtual wealth and real greed commingled out there, a world indifferent to the deaths and pain in the jungles of Southeast Asia.

She was grateful that she had not been able to afford the olfactory attachment. The coppery odor of blood, mixed with the fragrance of gunpowder, would have undone her before the end. Smells probed into the deepest part of your brain and stirred up the rawest emotions, like the blade of a hoe breaking up the numbed clods of modernity to reveal the wriggling pink flesh of wounded earthworms.

Eventually, she got up, peeled off the rest of her suit, and stumbled into the bathroom. She jumped as water rumbled in the pipes, the noise of approaching engines through the jungle. Under the hot streams of the shower, she shivered.

"Something has to be done," she muttered. "We can't let this happen. *I* can't."

But what could she do? The war between the central government of Myanmar and the ethnic minority rebels near the country's border with China was little remarked on by the rest of the world. The United States, the world's policeman, was silent because it wanted a loyal, pro-US government in Naypyidaw as a chess piece against rising Chinese influence in the region. China, on the other hand, wanted to entice the government in Naypyidaw onto its side with business and investment, and making a big deal out of ethnic Han Chinese civilians being slaughtered by Burmese soldiers was unhelpful for this Great Game. Even news of what was happening in Muertien was censored by a Chinese government terrified that sympathy for the refugees might mutate into uncontrollable nationalism. Refugee camps on both sides of the border were kept out of sight, like some shameful secret. Eyewitness accounts, videos, and this VR file had to be sneaked through tiny encrypted holes punched in the Great Firewall. In the West, on the other hand, popular apathy functioned more effectively than any official censorship.

She could not organize marches or gather signatures for petitions; she could not start or join a nonprofit dedicated to the well-being of the refugees – not that people in China trusted charities, which were all frauds; she could not ask everyone she knew to call their representatives and tell them to do something about Muertien. Having studied abroad in the United States, Jianwen wasn't so naive as to think that these avenues open to citizens of a democracy were all that effective – often, they served as mere symbolic gestures that did nothing to alter the minds or actions of those who truly determined foreign policy. But at least these acts would have allowed her to *feel* like she was making a difference.

And wasn't *feeling* the entire point of being human?

The old men in Beijing, terrified of any challenge to their authority and the possibility of instability, had made all these things impossible. To be a citizen of China was to be constantly reminded of the stark reality of the utter powerlessness of the individual living in a modern, centralized, technocratic state.

The scalding water was starting to feel uncomfortable. She scrubbed herself hard, as if it was possible to free herself from the haunting memories of the dying by scouring away sweat and skin cells, as if it was possible to be absolved of guilt with soap that smelled of watermelons.

She got out of the shower, still dazed, raw, but at least functional. The filtered air in the apartment smelled faintly of hot glue, the result of too much electronics packed into a small space. She wrapped a towel around herself, padded into her room, and sat down in front of her computer screen. She tapped on the keyboard, trying to distract herself with updates on her mining progress.

The screen was enormous and its resolution cutting edge, but by itself, it was an insignificant piece of dumb

46

equipment, only the visible corner of the powerful computing iceberg that she controlled.

The array of custom-made ASICs in the humming rack along the wall was devoted to one thing: solving cryptographic puzzles. She and other miners around the world used their specialized equipment to discover the nuggets made of special numbers that maintained the integrity of several cryptocurrencies. Although she had a day job as a financial services programmer, this work was where she really felt alive.

It gave her the feeling of possessing a bit of power, to be part of a global community in rebellion against authority in all its forms: authoritarian governments, democratic-mob statism, central banks that manipulated inflation and value by fiat. It was the closest she could come to being the activist she really yearned to be. Here, only math mattered, and the logic of number theory and elegant programming formed an unbreakable code of trust.

She tweaked her mining cluster, joined a new pool, checked in on a few channels where like-minded enthusiasts chatted about the future, and felt calmer as she read the scrolling text without joining in the conversation herself.

N♥T>: Just set up my Huawei GWX. Anyone have a recommendation for a good VR to try on it?

秋叶1001>: Room-scale or apartment-scale?

N♥T>: Apartment-scale. Nothing but the best for me.

秋叶1001>: Wow! You must've done well in the mines this year. I'd say try "Titanic."

N♥T>: From Tencent?

秋叶1001>: No! The one from SLG is much better. You'll need to hook your mining rig up to handle the graphics load if you have a big apartment.

Anony☺>: Ah, enhanced play or proof-of-work. What's more important?

Like many others, Jianwen had plunged headlong into the consumer VR craze. The resolution of the rigs was finally high enough to overcome dizziness, and even a smartphone contained enough processing power to drive a basic headset – though not the kind that provided full immersion.

She had climbed Mount Everest; she had BASE-jumped from the top of the Burj Khalifa; she had "gone out" to VR bars with her friends from across the globe, each of them holed up in their respective apartments drinking shots of real *erguotou* or vodka; she had kissed her favorite actors and slept with a few she *really* liked; she had seen VR films (exactly what they sound like and not very good); she had done VR LARP; she had flitted around the room in the form of a tiny fly as twelve angry fictional women argued over the fate of a fictional young woman, subtly directing their arguments by landing on pieces of evidence she wanted them to focus on.

But she had felt unsatisfied with all of them in some vague, inarticulable way. The emerging medium of VR was like unformed clay, full of potential and possibility, propelled by hope and greed, promising everything and nothing, a technology solution in search of a problem – it was still unclear what sort of pleasures, narratological or ludic, would ultimately predominate.

This latest VR experience, a short little clip in the life of an unnamed Muertien refugee, however, felt different.

But for an accident of birth, that little girl could have been me. Her mother even had my mother's eyes.

For the first time in years, after her youthful idealism had been ground down by the indifference of the world after college, she felted compelled to *do something*.

She stared at her screen. The flickering balances in her cryptocurrency accounts were based on a consensus of cryptographic chains, a trust forged from the trust-less. In a world walled from pain by greed, could such trust also be a way to drill a hole into the barrier, to let hope flood through? Could the world indeed be converted into a virtual village, where empathy bonded each to each?

She opened a new terminal window on her screen and began to type feverishly.

* * *

I hate D.C., Sophia Ellis decided as she looked out the window.

Traffic crawled through the rainy streets, punctuated by the occasional blare of an angry driver – a nice metaphor for what passed for political normality in the capital these days. The distant monuments on the Mall, ethereal through the drizzle, seemed to mock her with their permanence and transcendence.

The board members were making chit-chat, waiting for the quarterly meeting to start. She only paid attention half-heartedly, her mind elsewhere.

... your daughter ... Congrats to her!

... too many blockchain startups ...

... passing through London in September ...

Sophia would rather be back in the State Department, where she belonged, but the current administration's distaste for traditional-style diplomacy made her think she might have better prospects shifting into the nonprofit sector as a top administrator. After all, it was an open secret that some of the biggest US nonprofits with international offices served as unofficial arms of US foreign policy, and being the executive director of Refugees Without Borders was not a bad stepping stone back to power when the next administration came in. The key was to do some good for the refugees, to promote American values, and to stabilize the world even as the current administration seemed hell-bent on squandering American power.

... saw a cellphone video and asked me if we were doing anything about it ... Muertien, I think?

She pulled herself out of her reverie. "That's not something we should be involved in. It's like the situation in Yemen."

The board member nodded and changed the subject.

Sophia's old college roommate, Jianwen, had emailed her about Muertien a couple months ago. She had written back to express her regrets in a kind and thoughtful message. *We're an organization with limited resources. Not every humanitarian crisis can be addressed adequately. I'm sorry.*

It was the truth. Sort of.

It was also the consensus of those who understood how things worked that interfering with what was happening in Muertien would not benefit US interests, or the interests of Refugees Without Borders. The desire to make the world a better place, which was what had gotten her into diplomacy and nonprofit work in the first place, had to be tempered and guided by realism. Despite – or perhaps because of – her differences with the current administration, she believed that preserving American power was a worthy and important goal. Drawing attention to the crisis in Muertien would embarrass a key new American ally in the region, and that had to be avoided. This complicated world demanded that the interests of the United States (and its allies) be prioritized at the expense of some who suffered, so that more of the helpless could be protected.

America was not perfect, but it was also, after weighing all the alternatives, the best authority we had.

"... the number of small donations from under-thirty donors has fallen by 75 percent in the last month," said one of the board members. While Sophia had been philosophizing, the board meeting had started.

The speaker was the husband of an important MP, participating from London through a telepresence robot. Sophia suspected that he was in love with his voice more than his wife. The looming screen at the end of the telescoping neck made his face appear severe and dominating, and the robot's hands gesticulated for emphasis, presumably in imitation of the speaker's actual hands. "You are telling me you have no plans for addressing the decline in engagement?"

Did someone on your wife's staff write that up for you as a talking point? Sophia thought. She doubted he could have personally paid enough attention to the financial records to notice such a thing.

"We don't rely on small direct donations from that demographic for the bulk of our funding—" she began, but she was cut off by another board member.

"That's the not the point. It's about future mindshare, about publicity. Refugees Without Borders is fading from the conversation on social media without large numbers of small donations from that key demographic. This will ultimately affect the big grants."

The speaker was the CEO of a mobile devices company. Sophia had had to dissuade her more than once from mandating that donations to Refugees Without Borders be used to purchase the company's cheap phones for refugees in Europe, which would have boosted the company's reported market share (and violated conflict-of-interest rules).

"There have been some recent, unexpected shifts in the donor landscape that everyone is still trying to figure out—" Sophia said, but once again, she couldn't finish the sentence.

"You're talking about Empathium, aren't you?" asked the husband of the MP. "Well, do you have a plan?"

Definitely a talking point from your wife's staff. The Europeans always seemed to her more jittery about the cryptocurrency nuts than Americans. *But just as with diplomacy, it's better to guide the nuts than confront them.*

"What's Empathium?" asked another board member, a retired federal judge who still thought that the fax machine was the greatest technology invention ever.

"I am indeed talking about Empathium," said Sophia, trying to keep her voice soothing. Then she turned to the tech CEO. "Would you like to explain?"

Had Sophia tried to describe Empathium, the tech CEO would surely have interrupted her. She couldn't bear to let anyone else show more expertise about a technology issue. Might as well try to preserve some decorum.

The tech CEO nodded. "It's simple. Empathium is another new disintermediating blockchain application making heavy use of smart contracts, but this time with the twist of disrupting the jobs traditional charities are hired to do in the philanthropy marketplace."

Blank faces stared at the CEO from around the table. Eventually the judge turned to Sophia. "Why don't you give it a shot?"

She had gotten control of the meeting back simply by letting others overreach, a classic diplomacy move. "Let me take this piece by piece. I'll start with smart contracts. Suppose you and I sign a contract where if it rains tomorrow, I have to pay you five dollars, and if it doesn't rain, you have to pay me a dollar."

"Sounds like a bad insurance policy," said the retired judge.

"You wouldn't do well with that offering in London," said the husband of the MP.

Weak chuckles from around the table.

"With a normal contract," Sophia went on smoothly, "even if there's a thunderstorm tomorrow, you may not get your money. I may renege and refuse to pay, or argue with you about what the meaning of 'rain' is. And you'll have to take me to court."

"Oh, you won't do well in *my* court arguing the meaning of rain."

"Sure, but as Your Honor knows, people argue about the most ridiculous things." She had learned that it was best to let the judge go on these tangents before guiding him back to the trail. "And litigation is expensive."

"We can both put our money into the hands of a trusted friend and have him decide who to pay after tomorrow. That's called escrow, you know?"

"Absolutely. That's a great suggestion," said Sophia. "However, that requires us to agree on a common, trusted third-party authority, and we'll have to pay her a fee for her troubles. Bottom line: there are a lot of transaction costs associated with a traditional contract."

"So what would happen if we had a smart contract?"

"The funds would be transferred over to you as soon as it rained. There's nothing I can do to stop it because the entire mechanism for performance is coded in software."

"So you're saying a contract and a smart contract are basically the same thing. Except one of them is written in legalese and requires people to read it and interpret it, and the other is written in computer code and just needs a machine to execute it. No judge, no jury, no escrow, no takebacks."

Sophia was impressed. The judge wasn't technologically savvy, but he was sharp. "That's right. Machines are far more transparent and predictable than the legal system, even a well-functioning legal system."

"I'm not sure I like that," said the judge.

"But you can see why this is attractive, especially if you don't trust—"

"Smart contracts reduce transaction costs by taking out intermediaries," said the tech CEO impatiently. "You could have just said that instead of this longwinded, ridiculous example."

"I could have," acknowledged Sophia. She had also learned that appearing to agree with the CEO reduced transaction costs.

"So what does this have to do with charity?" asked the husband of the MP.

"Some people view charities as unnecessary intermediaries rent-seeking on trust," said the tech CEO. "Isn't this obvious?"

Again, more blank looks from around the table.

"Some smart contract enthusiasts can be a bit extreme," acknowledged Sophia. "In their view, charities like Refugees Without Borders spend most of our money on renting office space, paying staffers, holding expensive fundraisers where the wealthy socialize and have fun, and misusing donations to enrich insiders—"

"Which is an absolutely absurd view held by idiots with loud keyboards and no common sense—" said the tech CEO, her face flushed with anger.

"Or any political sense," interrupted the husband of the MP, as if his marriage automatically made him an authority on politics. "We also coordinate field relief efforts, bring international expertise, raise awareness in the West, soothe nervous local officials, and make sure that money goes to deserving recipients."

"That's the trust we bring to the table," said Sophia. "But for the Wikileaks generation, claims of authority and expertise are automatically suspicious. In their view, even the way we use our program funds is inefficient: how can we know how to spend the money better than those who actually need the help? How can we rule out the option for refugees to acquire weapons to defend themselves? How can we decide to work with corrupt local government officials who line their own pockets with donations before passing on dribbles to the victims? Better to just send money directly to neighborhood children who can't afford school lunches. The well-publicized failures of international relief efforts in places like Haiti and the former North Korea strengthen their argument."

"So what's their alternative?" asked the judge.

* * *

Jianwen watched as the notifications scrolled up her screen, each announcing the completion of a smart contract denominated in completely anonymous cryptocurrency. A lot of business was done that way these days, especially in the developing world, what with so many governments trying to extend their control by outlawing cash. She had read somewhere that more than 20 percent of global financial transactions were now through various cryptocurrencies.

But the transactions she was watching onscreen were different. The offers were requests for aid or promises to provide funds; there was no consideration except the need to *do something*. The Empathium blockchain network matched and grouped the offers into multi-party smart contracts, and, when the conditions for performance were fulfilled, executed them.

She saw there were requests for children's books; for fresh vegetables; for gardening tools; for contraceptives; for another doctor to come and set up shop for the long haul – and not just a volunteer to come for 30 days, parachuting in and jetting right back out, leaving everything unfinished and unfinishable …

She prayed for the offers to be taken up, to be satisfied by the system, even though she didn't believe in God, or any god. Though she had created Empathium, she was powerless to affect its specific operation. That was the beauty of the system. No one could be in charge.

When she was a college student in the US, Jianwen had returned to China for the summer of the year of the great Sichuan earthquake to help the victims of that disaster. The Chinese government had put a great deal of its resources into the rescue effort, even mobilizing the army.

Some PLA soldiers, her age or even younger, showed her the ugly scars on their hands from when they had dug through the muddy rubble of collapsed buildings for survivors and bodies.

"I had to stop because my hands hurt so much," one of the boys told her, his voice filled with shame. "They said if I kept going I'd lose my fingers."

Her vision blurred from rage. *Why couldn't the government have supplied the soldiers with shovels or real rescue equipment?* She pictured the soldiers' bloody hands, the flesh of the fingers peeling back from the bones, as they continued to scoop up handfuls of earth in the hope of finding someone still alive. *You don't have anything to be ashamed about.*

Later, she had recounted her experiences to her roommate, Sophia. She had shared Jianwen's rage at the Chinese government, but her face hadn't changed at all at her description of the young soldier.

"He was just a tool for an autocracy," the roommate had said, as if she couldn't picture those bloody hands at all.

Jianwen hadn't gone to the disaster zone with some official organization; rather, she was just one of thousands of volunteers who had come to Sichuan on their own, hoping to make a difference. She and the other volunteers had brought food and clothing, thinking that was what was needed. But mothers asked her for picture books or games to comfort their weepy children; farmers asked her when and how soon cell service would be restored; townspeople wanted to know if they could get tools and supplies to start rebuilding; a little girl who had lost her whole family wanted to know how she was going to finish high school. She didn't have any of the needed information or supplies, and neither did anyone else, it seemed. The officials in charge of the rescue effort disliked having volunteers like her around because they reported to no authority, and thus told them nothing.

"This shows why you need expertise," Sophia had said, later. "You can't just go down there like an aimless mob hoping to do good. People who know what they're doing need to be in charge of disaster relief."

Jianwen wasn't sure she agreed – she had seen little evidence that it was possible for any expert to anticipate everything needed in a disaster.

Text scrolled even faster in another window on the screen, showing more contract offers being submitted: requests for teachers of Greek; for funding to build a new cell tower; for medicine; for people who could teach refugees how to navigate the visa and work permit system; for weapons; for truckers willing to ship refugee-produced art out to buyers …

Some of these requests were for the kind of things that no NGO or government would ever give refugees. The idea of some authority dictating what was needed and not needed by people struggling to survive revolted Jianwen.

People in the middle of a disaster zone knew best what they needed. It's best to give them money so that they could buy whatever they needed – plenty of fearless vendors and ingenious adventurers would be willing to bring the refugees whatever goods or services they requested when there was profit to be made. Money did make the world go around, and that wasn't a bad thing.

Without cryptocurrency, none of what Empathium had accomplished so far would have been possible. The transfer of money across national borders was expensive and subject to heavy governmental oversight by suspicious regulators. Getting money into the hands of needy individuals was practically impossible without the help of some central payment processor, which could easily be co-opted by multiple authorities.

But with cryptocurrency and Empathium, a smartphone was all you needed to let the world know of your needs and to receive help. You could pay anyone securely and anonymously. You could band together with others with the same needs and submit a group application, or go it alone. No one could reach in and stop the smart contracts from executing.

It was exciting to see something that she had built begin to work as envisioned.

Still, so many of the aid requests on Empathium remained unfulfilled. There was too little money, too few donors.

* * *

" ... That's basically it in a nutshell," said Sophia. "Donations to Refugees Without Borders have fallen because many younger donors are giving on the Empathium network instead."

"Wait, did you just tell me that they're giving 'cryptocurrency' away on this network?" asked the judge. "What is that, like fake money?"

"Well, not *fake*. Just not dollars or yen – though cryptocurrencies can be converted to fiat currencies at exchanges. It's an electronic token. Think of it ..." Sophia struggled to think of an outdated reference that would make sense to the old judge, then inspiration struck. "... like an MP3 on your iPod. Except it can be used to pay for things."

"Why can't I send a copy to someone to pay for something but keep a copy for myself, the same way kids used to do with songs?"

"Who owns which song is recorded in an electronic ledger."

"But who keeps this ledger? What's to prevent hackers from getting in there and rewriting it? You said there was no central authority."

"The ledger, which is called the blockchain, is distributed on computers across the world," said the tech CEO. "It's based on cryptographic principles that solve the Byzantine Generals problem. Blockchains power cryptocurrencies as well as Empathium. Those who use the blockchain trust the math; they don't need to trust people."

"The what now?" asked the judge. "Byzantium?"

Sophia sighed inwardly. She wasn't expecting to get into this level of detail. She hadn't even finished explaining the basics of Empathium, and who knew how much longer it would take for the discussion to produce a consensus on what Refugees Without Borders should do about it?

Just as cryptocurrency aimed to wrest control of the money supply away from the fiat of governments, Empathium aimed to wrest control of the world's supply of compassion away from the expertise of charities.

Empathium was an idealistic endeavor, but it was driven by waves of emotion, not expertise or reason. It made the world a more unpredictable place for America, and thus more dangerous. She wasn't in the State Department anymore, but she still yearned to make the world more orderly, with decisions guided by rational analysis and weighing of pros and cons.

It was hard to get a roomful of egos to understand the same problem, much less to agree on a solution. She wished she had the knack some charismatic leaders had of just convincing everyone to submit to a course of action without understanding.

"Sometimes I think you just want people to agree with you," Jianwen had said to her once, after a particularly heated argument.

"What's wrong with that?" she had asked. "It's not my fault that I've thought about the issues more than they have. I see the bigger picture."

"You don't really want to be the most reasonable," Jianwen had said. "You want to be the most *right*. You want to be an oracle."

She had been insulted. Jianwen could be so stubborn.

Wait a minute, Sophia seized on the thought of *oracle*. *Maybe that's it. That's how we can make Empathium work for us.*

"The Byzantine Generals problem is a metaphor," Sophia said. She tried to keep the newfound excitement out of her voice. She was glad that her wonkish need to understand the details – as well as the desire to one-up the tech CEO, if she was honest – had compelled her to read up on this topic. "Imagine a group of generals, each leading a division of the Byzantine army, are laying siege to a city. If all the generals can coordinate to attack the city, then the city will fall. And if all the generals can agree on a retreat, everyone will be safe. But if only some of the generals attack while others retreat, the result will be disaster."

"They have to reach consensus on what to do," said the judge.

"Yes. The generals communicate through messengers. But the problem is that the messengers they send to each other aren't instantaneous, and there may be traitorous generals who will send out false messages about the emerging consensus as it's being negotiated, thereby sowing confusion and corrupting the result."

"This emerging consensus, as you call it, is like the ledger, isn't it?" asked the judge. "It's the record of every general's vote."

"Exactly! So, simplifying somewhat, blockchain solves this problem by using cryptography – very difficult-to-solve number theory puzzles – on the chain of messages that represents the emerging consensus. With cryptography, it's easy for each general to verify that a message chain that represents the state of the vote hasn't been tampered with, but it takes work for them to cryptographically add a new vote to the chain of votes. In order to deceive the other generals, a traitorous general would have to not only forge their own vote, but also the cryptographic summary of every other vote that came before theirs in the growing chain. As the chain gets longer, this becomes increasingly hard to do."

"I'm not sure I entirely follow," muttered the judge.

"The key is, the blockchain uses the difficulty of cryptographically adding a block of transactions to the chain – that's called proof-of-work – to guarantee that as long as a majority of the computers in the network aren't traitorous, you'll have a distributed ledger that you can trust more than any central authority."

"And that's ... trusting the math?"

"Yes. A distributed, incorruptible ledger not only makes it possible to have a cryptocurrency, it's also a way to have a secure voting framework that isn't centrally administered and a way to ensure that smart contracts can't be altered."

"This is all very interesting, but what does all this have to do with Empathium or Refugees Without Borders?" asked the husband of the MP impatiently.

* * *

Jianwen had put a lot of effort into making the Empathium interface usable. This was not something that many in the blockchain community cared about. Indeed, many blockchain applications seemed to be purposefully built to be difficult to use, as if the requirement for detailed technical know-how was how you separated the truly free from the mere sheeple.

Jianwen despised elitism in all its forms – she was keenly aware of the irony of this, coming from an Ivy-educated financial services technologist with a roomful of top-end VR gear like her. It was one group of elites who decided that democracy wasn't "right" for her country, and another group of elites who decided that they knew best who deserved sympathy and who didn't. The elites distrusted *feelings*, distrusted what made people human.

The very point of Empathium was to help people who couldn't care less about the intricacies of the Byzantine Generals problem or the implications of block size on the security of the blockchain. It had to be usable by a child. She remembered the frustration and despair of the people in Sichuan who had just wanted simple tools to help themselves. Empathium had to be as easy to use as possible, both for those who wanted to give and those who needed the help.

She was creating the application for those sick and tired of being told what to care about and how to care about it, not those doing the telling.

"What makes you think you know the right answer to everything?" Jianwen had asked Sophia once, back when they talked about everything and anything, and arguments between them were dispassionate affairs, conducted for intellectual pleasure. "Don't you ever doubt that you might be wrong?"

"If someone points out a flaw in my thinking, yes," said Sophia. "I'm always open to persuasion."

"But you never *feel* you might be wrong?"

"Letting feelings dictate how to think is the reason so many never get to the right answers at all."

The work she was doing was, rationally, hopeless. She had used up all her sick days and vacation days to write Empathium. She had published a paper explaining its technical underpinnings in excruciating detail. She had recruited others to audit her code. But how could she really expect to change the established world of big NGOs and foreign policy think tanks through an obscure cryptocurrency network that wasn't worth anything?

The work felt right. And that was worth more than any argument she could come up with against it.

* * *

"But I still don't understand how these 'conditions for performance' are satisfied!" the judge said. "I don't get how Empathium decides that an application for aid is worth funding and allocates money to it. Those who provide the funds can't possibly go through thousands of applications personally and decide which ones to give money to."

"There's an aspect of smart contracts that I haven't explained yet," Sophia said. "For smart contracts to function, there needs to be a way to import reality into software. Sometimes, whether conditions for performance have been satisfied isn't as simple as whether it rained on a certain day – though perhaps even that is open to debate in edge cases – but requires complicated human judgment: whether a contractor has installed the plumbing satisfactorily, whether the promised view is indeed scenic, or whether someone deserves to be helped."

"You mean it requires consensus."

"Exactly. So Empathium solves this problem by issuing a certain number of electronic tokens, called Emps, to some members of the network. Emp-holders then have the job of evaluating projects seeking funding and voting yes or no during a set time window. Only projects that receive the requisite number of yes-votes – the number of votes you can cast is determined by your Emp balance – get funded from the pool of available donors, and the required threshold of yes-votes scales up with the amount of funding requested. To prevent strategic voting, the vote tally is revealed only after the end of the evaluation period."

"But how do the Emp-holders decide to cast their vote?"

"That's up to each Emp-holder. They can evaluate just the materials put up by the requesters: their narratives, photos, videos, documentation, whatever. Or they can go on-site to investigate the applicants. They can use whatever means they have at their disposal within the designated evaluation period."

"Great, so money meant for the desperate and the needy will be allocated by a bunch of people who could barely be persuaded to answer a customer service survey between video game sessions," scoffed the husband of the MP.

"This is where it gets clever. Emp-holders are incentivized by receiving a small amount of money from the network in proportion to their Emp accounts. After each project's evaluation period is over, those who voted for the 'losing' side will be punished by having a portion of their Emps re-allocated to those on the 'winning' side. Individual Emp balances are like a kind of reputation token, and over time, those whose judgments – or empathy-meters, hence the network's name – are best tuned to the consensus judgment get the most Emps. They become the infallible oracles around which the system functions."

"What's to prevent—"

"It's not a perfect system," said Sophia. "Even the designers of the system – we don't really know who they are – acknowledge that. But like many things on the web, it works even if it doesn't seem like it should. Nobody thought Wikipedia would work either when it started. In its two months of existence, Empathium has proven to be remarkably effective and resilient to attacks, and it's certainly attracting a lot of young donors disillusioned with traditional charitable giving."

The board took some time to digest this news.

"Sounds like we'll have a hard time competing," said the husband of the MP after a while.

Sophia took a deep breath. *This is it, the moment I begin to build consensus.* "Empathium is popular, but it hasn't been able to attract nearly as much funding as the established charities, largely because donations to Empathium are not, of course, tax-deductible. Some of the biggest projects on the network, especially those related to refugees, have not been funded. If the goal is to get Refugees Without Borders into the conversation, we should put in a big funding offer."

"But I thought we wouldn't be able to choose which of the refugee projects on the network the money will go to," said the husband of the MP. "It's going to be up to the Emp-holders,"

"I have a confession to make. I've been using Empathium myself, and I have some Emps. We can make my account the corporate account, and begin to evaluate these projects. It's possible to filter out some of the fraudulent requests by documentation alone, but to really know if someone deserves help, there's no replacement for good old-fashioned on-site investigation. With our field expertise and international staff, I'm sure we'll be able to decide what projects to fund with more accuracy than anyone else, and we'll gain Emps quickly."

"But why do that when we can just put the money into the projects we want directly? Why add the intermediary of Empathium?" asked the tech CEO.

"It's about leverage. Once we get enough Emps, we'll turn Refugees Without Borders into the ultimate oracle for global empathy, the arbiter of who's deserving," said Sophia. She took a deep breath and delivered the coup de grâce. "The example set by Refugees Without Borders will be followed by other big charities. Add to that all the funding from places like China and India, where donors interested in philanthropy have few trusted in-country charities but may be willing to jump onto a decentralized blockchain application, and soon Empathium may become the single largest charity funding platform in the world. If we accumulate the largest share of Emps, we will then be effectively in the position to direct the use of most of the world's charitable giving."

The board members sat in their seats, stunned. Even the telepresence robot's hands stopped moving.

"Damn ... you're going to flip a platform designed to disintermediate us into a ladder to crown us," said the tech CEO, real admiration in her voice. "That's *some* jujitsu."

Sophia gave her a quick smile before turning back to the table. "Now, do I have your approval?"

* * *

The red line representing the total amount of pledged funds to Empathium had shot straight into the stratosphere.

Jianwen smiled in front of her screen. Her baby had grown up.

The decision by Refugees Without Borders to join the network had been followed within twenty-four hours by several other major international charities. Empathium was now legitimate in the eyes of the public, and it was even possible for wealthy donors who cared about tax deductions to funnel their funds through traditional charities participating in the network.

Projects that received the attention of Empathium users would no doubt attract a great deal of media interest, drawing in reporters and observers. Empathium was going to direct not just charitable giving, but the gaze of the world.

The #empathium invite-only channel was filling up with debate.

NoFFIA>: This is a ruse by the big charities. They're going to play the Emp-accumulation game and force the network into funding their pet projects.

N♥T>: What makes you think they can? The oracle system only rewards results. If you don't think traditional charities know what they're doing, they won't have any better way of identifying deserving good projects. The network will force them to fund projects the Emp-holders as a whole think are deserving.

Anony🍥>: Traditional charities have access to publicity channels most don't. The other Emp-holders are still people. They'll be swayed.

N♥T:> Not everyone is as affected by traditional media as you think, especially when you leave the bubble you USians live in. I think this is a level playing field.

Jianwen watched the debate but didn't participate. As the creator of Empathium, she understood that the invisible reputation attached to her username meant that anything she said could disproportionately influence and distort debate. That was the way humans worked, even when they were talking through scrolling text attributed to pseudonymous electronic identities.

But she wasn't interested in debate. She was interested in action. The participation of the traditional charities on Empathium had been what she had hoped and planned for all along, and now was the time for her to implement the second step.

She brought up a terminal window and began a new submission to the Empathium network. The Muertien VR file itself was too large to be directly incorporated into a block, so it would have to be distributed via peer-to-peer sharing. But the signature that authenticated the file and prevented tampering would become part of the blockchain and be distributed to all the users of Empathium and all the Emp-holders.

Maybe even hard-nosed Sophia.

The fact that the submitter of the file was Jianwen (or more precisely, the userid of Empathium's creator, which no one knew was Jianwen in real life) would give it a burst of initial interest, but everything after that was out of her hands.

She did not believe in conspiracies. She was counting on the angels of human nature.

She pressed SEND, sat back, and waited.

* * *

As the Jeep wound its way through the jungle over the muddy, mountainous road near the China-Myanmar border, Sophia dozed.

How did we get here?

The madness of the world was both so unpredictable and so inevitable.

As she had predicted, the field expertise of Refugees Without Borders quickly made the corporate Empathium account one of the most powerful Emp-holders on the network. Her judgment was deemed infallible, guiding the network to disburse funds to needy groups and proposed projects that made sense. The board was very pleased with her work.

But then, that damned VR and others like it began to show up on the network.

The VR experiences spoke to the interactors in a way that words and photos and videos could not. Walking for miles barefoot through a war-torn city, seeing dismembered babies and mothers scattered around you, being interrogated and menaced by men and boys with machetes and guns ... the VR experiences left the interactors shaken and overwhelmed. Some had been hospitalized.

Traditional media, bound by old-fashioned ideas about decency and propriety, could not show images like these and refused to engage in what they viewed as pure emotional manipulation.

Where's the context? Who's the source? demanded the spurned pundits. *Real journalism requires reflection, requires thought.*

We don't remember much reflection from you when you advocated war based on pictures you printed, replied the hive mind of Emp-holders. *Are you just annoyed that you aren't in charge of our emotions anymore?*

The pervasive use of encryption on Empathium meant that most censorship techniques were useless, and so the Emp-holders were exposed to stories they had heretofore been sheltered from. They voted for the attached projects, their hearts pounding, their breathing ragged, their eyes blurred by rage and sorrow.

Activists and propagandists soon realized that the best way to get their causes funded was to participate in the VR arms race. And so governments and rebels competed in creating compelling VR experiences that forced the interactors into their perspective, obliged them to empathize with their side.

Mass graves filled with refugees starved to death in Yemen. Young women marching to support Russia gunned down by Ukrainian soldiers. Ethnic minority children running naked through streets as their homes were set on fire by Myanmar government soldiers...

Funding began to flow to groups that the news had forgotten or portrayed as the side undeserving of sympathy. In VR, one minute of their anguish spoke louder than ten thousand words in op-eds in respected newspapers.

This is the commodification of pain! Ivy-educated bloggers wrote in earnest think pieces. *Isn't this yet another way for the privileged to exploit the suffering of the oppressed to make themselves feel better?*

Just as a photograph can be framed and edited to lie, so can VR, the media- and cultural-studies commentariat wrote. *VR is such a heavily engineered medium that we have not yet reached consensus on what the meaning of 'reality' in this medium is.*

This is a threat to our national security, fretted the senators who demanded that Empathium be shut down. *They could be diverting funding to groups hostile to our national interest.*

You're simply terrified that you're being disintermediated from your positions of undeserved authority, jeered the Empathium users, hidden behind anonymous, encrypted accounts. *This is a real democracy of empathy. Deal with it.*

A consensus of feelings had replaced the consensus of facts. The emotional labor of vicarious experience through virtual reality had replaced the physical and mental work of investigation, of evaluating costs and benefits, of exercising rational judgment. Once again, proof-of-work was used to guarantee authenticity, just a different kind of work.

Maybe the reporters and senators and diplomats and I could make our own VR experiences, Sophia wondered as she was jostled awake in the back of the Jeep. *Too bad it's hard to make the unglamorous but necessary work of truly understanding a complex situation compelling ...*

She looked outside the window. They were passing through a refugee camp in Muertien. Men, women, and children, most of them Chinese in physical appearance, looked back at the passengers in the Jeep numbly. Their expressions were familiar to Sophia; she had seen the same despondency on the faces of refugees everywhere in the world.

The successful funding of the Muertien project had been a massive blow to Sophia and Refugees Without Borders. She had voted against it, but the other Emp-holders had overwhelmed her, and overnight Sophia had lost 10 percent of her Emps. Other VR-propelled projects followed to achieve funding despite her objection, eroding Sophia's Emp account even further.

Faced with an outraged board, she had come here to find some way to discredit the Muertien project, to show that she had been right.

On the way here from Yangon, she had spoken to the one staffer Refugees Without Borders posted there and several Western reporters stationed in the country. They had confirmed the consensus back in D.C. She knew that the refugee situation was one largely created by the rebels. The population of Muertien, mostly ethnic Han Chinese, did not get along well with the majority Bamar in the central government. The rebels had attacked the government forces and then tried to fade into the civilian population. The government had little choice but to resort to violence, lest the country's young democracy suffer a setback and Chinese influence extend into the heart of Southeast Asia. Regretful incidents no doubt occurred, but the vast majority of the fault lay on the side of the rebels. Funding them would only escalate the conflict.

But this kind of punditry, of explaining geopolitics, was anathema to the Emp-holders. They did not want lectures; they were persuaded by the immediacy of suffering.

The Jeep stopped. Sophia got out with her interpreter. She adjusted the neckband she wore – it was a prototype the tech CEO had gotten for her from Canon Virtual. The air was humid, hot, drenched with the smell of sewage and decay. She should have been expecting that, she supposed, but somehow she hadn't thought about how things would smell here back in her D.C. office.

She was about to approach a leery-looking young woman in a flower-print blouse when a man shouted angrily. She turned to look at him. He was pointing at her and screaming. The crowd around him stopped moving to stare at her. The air felt tense.

There was a gun in his other hand.

Part of the goal of the Muertien project had been to fund groups willing to smuggle weapons across the Chinese border into the hands of the refugees. Sophia knew that. *I'm going to regret coming here without an armed escort, aren't I?*

The rumbling of vehicles approaching in the jungle. A loud whine overhead followed by an explosion. Staccato gunshots so near that they had to be coming from inside the camp.

Sophia was shoved to the ground as the crowd around her exploded into chaos, screaming and dashing every which way. She wrapped her arms protectively around her neck, around the cameras and microphones, but panicked feet stomped over her torso, making her gasp and loosening her arms. The camera-studded neckband fell and rolled away in the dirt, and she reached for it, careless of her own safety. Just before her grasping fingers reached the band, a booted foot crushed it with a sickening crunch. She cursed, and someone running by kicked her in the head.

She faded into unconsciousness.

* * *

A splitting headache. Overhead the sky is close at hand and orange, cloudless.

The surface under me feels hard and sandy.

I'm inside a VR experience, aren't I? Am I Gulliver, looking up at the Lilliputian sky?

The sky turns and sways, and even though I'm lying down, I feel like I'm falling.

I want to throw up.

"Close your eyes until the vertigo passes," a voice says. The timbre and cadence are familiar, but I can't quite place who it is. I just know I haven't heard it in a while. I wait until the dizziness fades. Only then do I notice the unyielding lump of the data recorder poking into my back, where it's held in place by tape. Relief floods through me. The cameras may be gone, but the most important piece of equipment has survived the ordeal.

"Here, drink," the voice says.

I open my eyes. I struggle to sit up and a hand reaches out to support me between my shoulder blades. It's a small, strong hand, the hand of a woman. A canteen materializes before my face in the dim light, a chiaroscuro. I sip. I haven't realized how thirsty I am.

I look up at the face behind the canteen: Jianwen.

"What are you doing here?" I ask. Everything still seems so unreal, but I'm beginning to realize that I'm inside a tent, probably one of the tents I saw earlier in the camp.

"The same thing brought both of us here," says Jianwen. After all these years, she hasn't changed much: still that hard, no-nonsense demeanor, still that short-cropped hair, still that set to her jaw, challenging everything and everyone.

She just looks leaner, drier, as if the years have wrung more gentleness out of her.

"Empathium. I made it, and you want to break it."

Of course, I should have known. Jianwen always disliked institutions, thought it best to disrupt everything.

It's still nice to see her.

Our first year in college, I wrote a story for the school paper about a sexual assault at a final club party. The victim wasn't a student, and her account was later discredited. Everyone condemned my work, calling me careless, declaring that I had allowed the desire for a good story get in the way of facts and analysis. Only I knew that I hadn't been wrong: the victim had only recanted under pressure, but I had no proof. Jianwen was the only one who stuck by me, defending me at every opportunity.

"Why do you trust me?" I asked.

"It's not something I can explain," she said. "It's a *feeling*. I heard the pain in her voice … and I know you did too."

That was how we became close. She was someone I could count on in a fight.

"What happened out there?" I ask.

"That depends on who you talk to. This won't show up in the news in China at all. If it shows up in the US, it will be another minor skirmish between the government and the rebels, whose guerrilla fighters disguised themselves as refugees, forcing the government to retaliate."

This has always been her way. Jianwen sees the corruption of the truth everywhere, but she won't tell you what she thinks the truth is. I suppose she got into the habit from her time in America to avoid arguments.

"And what will Empathium users think?" I ask.

"They'll see more children being blown up by bombs and women being gunned down by soldiers as they ran."

"Did the rebels or the government fire the first shot?"

"Why does that matter? The consensus in the West will always be that the rebels fired the first shot – as if that determines everything. You've already decided on the story, and everything else is just support."

"I get it," I say. "I understand what you're trying to do. You think there's not enough attention being paid to the refugees in Muertien, and so you're using Empathium to publicize their plight. You're emotionally attached to these people because they look like you—"

"Is that really what you think? You think I'm doing this because they're ethnically Han Chinese?" She looks at me, disappointed.

She can look at me however she likes, but the intensity of her emotion gives her away. In college I remember her working hard to raise money for the earthquake in China, when we were both still trying to pick concentrations; I remember her holding a candlelight vigil for both the Uighurs and the Han who had died in Ürümqi the next summer, when we stayed on campus together to edit the student course-evaluation guide; I remember how once in class she had refused to back down as a white man twice her size loomed over her, demanding that she accept that China was wrong to fight the Korean War.

"Hit me if you want," she had said, her voice steady. "I'm not going to desecrate the memory of the men and women who died so that I could be born. MacArthur was going to drop atomic bombs on Beijing. Is that really the kind of empire you want to defend?"

Some of our friends in college thought of Jianwen as a Chinese nationalist, but that's not quite right. She

82

dislikes all empires because to her, they are the ultimate institutions, with deadly concentration of power. She doesn't think the American empire is any more worthy of support than the Russian one or the Chinese one. As she put it, "America is only a democracy for those lucky enough to be Americans. To everybody else, it's just a dictator with the biggest bombs and missiles."

She wants the perfection of disintermediated chaos rather than the imperfect stability of flawed institutions that could be perfected.

"You are letting your passion overcome reason," I say. I know that persuasion is useless but I can't help trying. If I don't hold on to faith in reason, I have nothing. "A powerful China with influence in Myanmar is bad for world peace. American pre-eminence must—"

"And so you think it's all right for the people of Muertien to be ethnically cleansed to preserve the stability of the regime in Naypyidaw, to uphold the Pax Americana, to cement the ramparts of an American empire with their blood."

I wince. She's always been careless with her words. "Don't exaggerate. The ethnic conflict here, if not contained, will lead to more Chinese adventurism and influence. I've talked to many in Yongan. They don't want the Chinese here."

"And you think they want the Americans here, telling them what to do?" Contempt flares in her voice.

"A choice between the lesser of two evils," I concede. "But more Chinese involvement will provoke more American anxiety, and that will only intensify the geopolitical conflict you dislike so much."

"People here need Chinese money for their dams. Without development, they can't solve any of the problems they have—"

"Maybe the developers want that," I say, "but the common people don't."

"Who are these *common people* in your imagination?" she asks. "I've talked to many here in Muertien. They say that the Bamars don't want the dams built where they are, but they'll be happy to have them built here. That's what the rebels are fighting for, to preserve their autonomy and the right to control their land. Isn't self-determination something you value and care about? How does letting soldiers kill children lead to a better world?"

We can go on like this forever. She can't see the truth because she's in too much pain.

"You've been blinded by the pain of these people," I say. "And now you want the rest of the world to suffer the same fate. Through Empathium, you've bypassed the traditional filters of institutional media and charities to reach individuals. But the experience of having children and mothers die right next to them is too overwhelming for most to think through the complicated implications of the events that led to these tragedies. The VR experiences are propaganda."

"You know as well as I do that the Muertien VR isn't fake."

I know what she says is true. I've seen people die around me, and even if that VR was doctored or divorced from context, enough of it was true to make the rest not matter. The best propaganda is often true.

But there's a greater truth she doesn't see. Just because something happened doesn't make it a decisive fact; just because there's suffering doesn't mean there is always a better choice; just because people die doesn't mean we must abandon greater principles. The world isn't always black and white.

"Empathy isn't always a good thing," I say. "Irresponsible empathy makes the world unstable. In each conflict, there are multiple claims for empathy, leading to emotional involvement by outsiders that widens the conflict. To sort through the morass, you must reason your way to the least harmful answer, the right answer. This is why some of us are charged with the duty to study and understand the complexities of this world and to decide, for the rest, how to exercise empathy responsibly."

"I can't just shut it off," she says. "I can't just forget the dead. Their pain and terror ... they're a part of the blockchain of my experience now, unerasable. If being responsible means learning how to not feel someone else's pain, then it isn't humanity you serve, but evil."

I watch her. I feel for her, I really do. It's terribly sad, seeing your friend in pain but knowing that there is nothing you can do to help, knowing that, in fact, you have to hurt her more. Sometimes pain, and acknowledgment of pain, *is* selfish.

I lift my blouse to show her the VR recorder taped to the small of my back. "This was recording until the moment guns started firing – from inside the camp – and I was pushed down to the ground."

She stares at the VR data recorder, and her face shifts through shock, recognition, rage, denial, an ironic smile, and then, nothing.

Once the VR based on what I went through is uploaded – it doesn't need much editing – there will be outrage at home. A defenseless American woman, the head of a charity dedicated to helping refugees, is brutalized by ethnic Han Chinese rebels armed with guns bought with money from Empathium – hard to imagine a better way to discredit the Muertien project. The best propaganda is often true.

"I'm sorry," I say, and I mean it.

She gazes at me, and I can't tell if it's hate or despair I see in her eyes.

* * *

I look at her with pity.

"Have you tried the original Muertien clip?" I ask. "The one I uploaded."

Sophia shakes her head. "I couldn't. I didn't want to compromise my judgment."

She has always been so rational. One time, in college, I asked her to watch a video of a young Russian man, barely more than a boy, being beheaded by Chechen fighters in front of the camera. She had refused.

"Why won't you look at what the people you support are doing?" I asked.

"Because I haven't seen all the acts of brutality committed by the Russians against the Chechen people," she said. "To reward those who evoke empathy is the same as punishing those who have been prevented from doing so. Looking at this won't be objective."

There's always the need for more context with Sophia, for the big picture. But I've learned over the years that rationality with her, as with many, is just a matter of rationalization. She wants a picture just big enough to justify what her government does. She needs to understand just enough to be able to reason that what America wants is also what anyone rational in the world wants.

I understand how she thinks, but she doesn't understand how I think. I understand her language, but she doesn't understand mine – or care to. That's how power works in this world.

When I first got to America, I thought it was the most wonderful place on Earth. There were students passionate about every humanitarian cause, and I tried to support every one. I raised money for the victims of the Bangladesh cyclones and the flooding in India; I packed blankets and tents and sleeping bags for the earthquake in Peru; I joined the vigils to remember the victims of 9/11, sobbing before Memorial Church in the late summer evening breeze, trying to keep the candles lit.

Then came the big earthquake in China, and as the death toll climbed toward 100,000, the campus was strangely quiet. People who I thought were my friends turned away, and the donation table we set up in front of the Science Center was staffed only by other students from China like me. We couldn't even raise a tenth of the money we had raised for disasters with far smaller death tolls.

What discussion there was focused on how the Chinese drive for development resulted in unsafe buildings, as if enumerating the cons of their government was an appropriate reaction to dead children, as if reaffirming the pros of American democracy was a good justification for withholding help.

Jokes about the Chinese and dogs were posted in anonymous newsgroups. "People just don't like China very much," an op-ed writer mused. "I'd rather have the elephants back," said an actress on TV.

What's the matter with you? I wanted to scream. There was no empathy in their eyes as I stood by the donation table and my classmates hurried past me, averting their gaze.

But Sophia did donate. She gave more than anyone else.

"Why?" I asked her. "Why do you care about the victims when no one else seems to?"

"I'm not going to have you heading back to China with an irrational impression that Americans dislike the Chinese," she said. "Try to remember me when you get into these moments of despair."

That was how I knew we would never be as close as I had hoped. She had given as a means to persuade, not because she felt what I felt.

"You accuse me of manipulation," I say to Sophia. The humid air in the tent is oppressive, and it feels as if someone is pressing on my eyes from within my skull. "But aren't you doing the exact same thing with that recording?"

"There is a difference," she says. She always has an answer. "My clip will be used to emotionally persuade people to do what is rationally the right thing as part of a considered plan. Emotion is a blunt tool that must be placed in service of reason."

"So your plan is to stop any more aid for the refugees and watch as the Myanmar government drives them off their land into China? Or worse?"

"You managed to get money to the refugees on a tide of rage and pity," she says. "But how does that really help them? Their fate will always ultimately be decided by the geopolitics between China and the US. Everything else is just noise. They can't be helped. Arming the refugees will only give the government more of an excuse to resort to violence."

Sophia isn't wrong. Not exactly. But there's a greater principle here that she doesn't see. The world doesn't always proceed the way predicted by theories of economics or international relations. If every decision is made with Sophia's calculus, then order, stability, empire always win. There will never be any change, any independence, any justice. We are, and should be, creatures of the heart first.

"The greater manipulation is to deceive yourself into believing you can always reason your way to what is right," I say.

"Without reason, you can't get to what is right at all," Sophia says.

"Emotion has always been at the core of what it means to do right, not merely a tool for persuasion. Are you opposed to slavery because you have engaged in a rational analysis of the costs and benefits of the institution? No, it's because you're revolted by it. You empathize with the victims. You *feel* its wrongness in your heart."

"Moral reasoning isn't the same—"

"Moral reasoning is often only a method by which you tame your empathy and yoke it to serve the interests of the institutions that have corrupted you. You're clearly not averse to manipulation when it's advantageous to a cause that finds favor in your framework."

"Calling me a hypocrite isn't very helpful—"

"But you *are* a hypocrite. You didn't protest when pictures of babies launched Tomahawks or when images of drowned little boys on beaches led to revisions in refugee policy. You promoted the work of reporters who evoked empathy for those stranded in Kenya's largest refugee camp by telling Westerners sappy Romeo-and-Juliet love stories about young refugees and emphasizing how the United Nations has educated them with Western ideals—"

"Those are different—"

"Of course they're different. Empathy for you is but another weapon to be wielded, instead of a fundamental value of being human. You reward some with your empathy and punish others by withholding it. Reasons can always be found."

"How are you different? Why do the suffering of some affect you more than others? Why do you care about the people of Muertien more than any other? Isn't it because they look like you?"

She still thinks this is a killer argument. I understand her, I really do. It's so comforting to know that you're right, that you've triumphed over emotion with reason, that you're an agent of the just empire, immune to the betrayal of empathy.

I just can't live like that.

I try one last time.

"I had hoped that by stripping away context and background, by exposing the senses to the rawness of pain and suffering, virtual reality would be able to prevent all of us from rationalizing away our empathy. In agony, there is no race, no creed, none of the walls that divide us and subdivide us. When you're immersed in the experience of the victims, all of us are in Muertien, in Yemen, in the heart of darkness that the Great Powers feed on."

She doesn't respond. I see in her eyes she has given up on me. I am beyond reason.

Through Empathium, I had hoped to create a consensus of empathy, an incorruptible ledger of the heart that has overcome traitorous rationalization.

But perhaps I am still too naive. Perhaps I give empathy too much credit.

* * *

Anony :> What do you all think is going to happen?

N♥T:> China is going to have to invade. Those VRs have left Beijing no choice. If they don't send in the troops to protect the rebels in Muertien, there will be riots in the streets.

goldfarmer89:> Makes you wonder if that was what China wanted all along.

Anony :> You think that first VR was a Chinese production?

goldfarmer89:> Had to be state-sponsored. It was so slick.

N♥T>: I'm not so sure it was the Chinese who made it. The White House has been itching for an excuse for war with China to divert attention from all those scandals.

Anony :> So you think the VR was a CIA plant?

N♥T>: Wouldn't be the first time Americans have manipulated anti-American sentiment into giving them exactly what they wanted. That Ellis VR is also ramping

92

up US public support for taking a hard line against China. I just feel terrible about those people in Muertien. What a mess.

little_blocks>: Still stuck on those snuff VRs on Empathium? I've stopped long ago. Too exhausting. I'll PM you a new game you'll definitely like.

N♥T>: I can always use a new game. ^_^

Author's Note

I'm indebted to the following paper for the term 'algics' and some of the ideas about the potential of VR as a social technology:

Lemley, Mark A. and Volokh, Eugene, Law, 'Virtual Reality, and Augmented Reality' (March 15, 2017). Stanford Public Law Working Paper No. 2933867; UCLA School of Law, Public Law Research Paper No. 17-13. Available at SSRN: https://ssrn.com/abstract=2933867 or http://dx.doi.org/10.2139/ssrn.2933867

Orchidaceae

Thomas Badlan

JOÊNIA MOVED sluggishly through the snow drifts and felt the warmth leech out of her. The cold suit was too bulky a thing to move gracefully in, but it would protect her for a few hours out in the tundra. She followed the red blinking waymark lights and squinted through her frosted visor. Ahead loomed the vague shadow of the Amazonia dome. Most thought her mad for making this journey on foot but she went at least once a week. Joênia felt it worth the effort, not only to escape the hermetically sealed environments of Svalbard, but also to remember what they were fighting against. The blizzard howled around her, a thing of fury, but she kept moving one foot at a time.

Inside Joênia stripped off the cold suit as the access chamber acclimatized her to the dome's temperature while simultaneously removing any alien particulates that had followed her inside. As the door hissed open, she stepped into another world. Sticky heat washed over her, skin prickling. Joênia was standing on a metal platform overlooking a dense canopy of recovered, mist-drenched Amazon Rainforest. There were over a hundred immense kapok trees, stretching up above the smaller cashapona, barrigona and wine palm with their vivid green fronds. Beneath her, the forest floor was a dense, shadowed brush of epiphytes, bromeliads and rubber trees, eleven square miles of dense recreation of a world much diminished. A thin drizzle of artificial rain was falling, water tracing myriad paths along wide waxy leaves and snaking vines.

This was her real home, not the bland, comfortable pods, promenades and common rooms of the Svalbard worker's quarters. Those cramped spaces and subterranean tunnels always made Joênia feel like a rat in a cage. Amazonia was filled with a chorus of bird song and the whoops of squirrel monkeys running from branch to branch. Somewhere within was the low roar of the New Iguazu Falls, while the pungent aroma of damp and decay and sweat mingled with tropical heat. It was a real place, not a capsule to keep them at ease, but a world in microcosm.

As Joênia dropped her cold suit into the supply locker, the rest of the day shift arrived. They were chatting amiably, excited about the day's work. An international team from across the world's communities. They had made her feel welcome and involved since her arrival in Svalbard two years ago, but on this day, she wished only for solitude. Most were botanists, with a few engineers, geneticists and climatologists, ferociously ignoring whatever remained of the concept of nationality. A dozen languages were spoken between them, though most spoke a sort of English-Patwa.

As the day shift disrobed, one woman noticed Joênia and wandered over.

"New-day, na," she called.

She was strikingly beautiful, long-haired with dark slim eyes and freckled cheeks. She leaned on the railing and starred with Joênia across the bright vista. Her name was Jade, one of the Europeans.

"New-day," Joênia said back without turning.

"Fine walk, this new-day?" Jade asked.

Her accent was a hybrid but Joênia knew her primary language was French.

"Cold some," Joênia said.

Jade laughed, a song bird sound. She was an engineer, not a scientist, one of the army in charge of making sure Amazonia's water reclamation system stayed working. It was the rainforest after all.

"Been to port of late? There's a Zealander ship, full with kiwi crop. First export. Maybe we try some at the festival late-day?"

"Sound good," Joênia said.

Talking with Jade always got Joênia's heart racing a little, but this time she really wanted the conversation to end. All she could endure was seeing the other side of this day. Jade seemed to finally catch the hint. Her face took on a flash of hurt, then she took a step closer and leaned in.

"I know some of how you feel," Jade said, her breath tickling Joênia's ear, "can we talk later? I'll be at Café

Odudua on Promenade. Seven, probably till late. Come find me."

She placed a slender palm on Joênia forearm. The hairs there stood on end and then Jade was gone, following her colleagues down the metal steps that led to a walkway that stretched into the forest, weaving between wide, vine-wrapped wine-palm trunks.

Joênia waited for them to disappear. She strapped on her work belt, with its tools, sprays and sensors, but left behind her work boots. Stepping barefoot down the steel staircase, she reached the forest floor. Instead of the gravelled pathways, she stepped away, forging her own trail. Cool mud oozed between her toes and the grasses tickled her calves. Each day her path was different. Her hands brushed the taught leaves of rubber trees and pushed aside dangling liana vines as she moved, gentle yet purposeful. Overhead a pair of toucans, dark winged and bright beaked soared through the lower canopy, momentarily caught in rays of sunlight. She caught sight of scurrying tree runner lizards and skittish pygmy marmosets. Winged insects buzzed aside as she passed over stagnant pools. She knew caymans could be found in the artificial river and squirrel monkeys and sloths occupied the upper branches. Joênia ran, swung and splashed her way through Amazonia, feeling more alive than she did anywhere in the entire Svalbard facility. That was Amazonia, an invisible fine web of interconnected energies.

Joênia soon found what she was looking for. In the dappled shade of a conta palm was a small delicate orchid, pushing up from the mud. It was a thin-stemmed thing, white petals with vivid yellow and pink colouring at the stamen.

A Cattleya.

"Hello, small one. You well this new-day?" she said, crouching low. She examined the plant for any signs of fungal infection, insect infestation or simple damage from atmospheric or animal encounter. It seemed to be healthy. She measured and sprayed it with a nutrient rich feed solution before moving on.

The next orchid she found on the bow of a tree, pushing up from a crevice in the bark. Many orchids were epiphytic and she admired their adaptability, growing out of any possible niche. This one was had a purple hue, with curled leaves and a heart shaped cluster of petals. A Pseudolaelia. Joênia, with delicate fingers, removed a snaking vine out of its path.

"Let's have some space, compre?" she smiled.

Orchids were delicate things. They were one of the most varied plants, spreading world-wide, but they were prone to fungal infection and died easily with fluctuations in temperature or increases in pollution or when exposed to pesticides. Here, in the rainforest recreation, they were thriving, but she still had a way to go before they could be considered self-sufficient. She sniffed carefully at the next orchid, a phalaenopis, a moth orchid. Its perfume was

98

spicy, almost peppery. Their smells were as varied as the species, some even emitted a smell like decomposition, to attract insects into traps.

"Enough light, lindo?" she asked the orchid, peering up through a veil of leaves, sunlight leaving them semi-translucent.

Joênia worked like this all morning. Moving through the foliage, doing as little to disturb the environment as possible. She found herself often peering upwards through the canopies, letting the light envelop her, feeling the humid warmth on her bare skin. She imagined herself in the rainforests of South America before the fall, without the trappings of this new world, almost naked, her skin painted ochre and pierced. She was not alone, but moved as one with brothers and sisters, running through the trees, hunting game or exploring untouched lands. They quickly faded into the sun-drenched mists. They were figments, occasional visitations by those whose inheritance had been stolen. She could not imagine where else they might go.

She crossed the rope bridge across the New Iguazu falls. It had been part built as a viewing platform for the workers. Below the falls roared, a torrent of melted and desalinated glacial water tumbling down a two hundred foot artificial rock face. It was deafening and exhilarating, surrounded by rising rainbow spray. From there it was back to the forest and out of sight.

"Thought I might find you here," a voice called.

Joênia had heard him coming a while ago. She knew he would eventually find her. The Stanhopea orchid she was tending was showing signs of aphid infestation. She carefully sprayed the plant with an organic solution that would dissuade more insects from landing. Tiago Pereira was the head of Amazonia. He was wearing clothes far too formal for a wander through the forest, his shirt's sleeves rolled up, long shorts mud stained from the trek. In each hand he carried two bamboo pots with chopsticks between his fingers.

"You always miss the lunch bell. Massaman curry. Guessed I might find you hungry."

Joênia sighed. She had been content here, in solitude, in the heart of the dome.

"They feed us too much," Joênia said, "double-rations from what I was given in São Paulo."

"They give us full-day recommended calorie and nutritional intake, I believe," Tiago replied.

There was an ease to his smile that annoyed her.

"I'm watching my figure," she said.

Tiago snorted and strode over. He held out the pot long enough that it became impossible for her to refuse. They ate together sat on the ground. The food was good. Still warm and spicy. Chunks of pepper, sweetcorn, aubergine. The rice was sticky. All of it grown here in Svalbard's many agricultural zones.

The original purpose of the Svalbard seed vault had been to replenish the world's flora biodiversity in the event of global disaster. It had taken a concerted effort to save the seed vault and provide viable crops to the surviving communities. Now, with the ice retreating and populations once again spreading, Svalbard was being called upon to build a sustainable world. But the sheer volume of seeds required outdid even Svalbard's reserves. So the domes had been constructed and seed harvesting operations begun to meet demand. For the past few decades, Svalbard had saved millions from famine.

"I know you're angry," Tiago said finally.

"That word for what I am?" she asked.

"We have to prioritise."

"I'm well aware of the logistics involved."

"Then you understand it's not personal. Current projections have populations outstripping food production at a rate of two to one."

"Maybe people should stop breeding so much," she snapped back.

"It's not that simple," Tiago said.

"Yes it is. Most of us have quotas."

"Not every community is the same."

"We're making the same old mistakes. All the talk was for nothing. This was supposed to be a new age. Responsible. Progressive. We'd learned out lessons. A sustainable future. Stewards of the earth. Bullshit, all of it."

"We'll never be perfect, Joênia. We can only do our best."

"Leave me alone, please," she snapped, standing up fast.

Tiago was her boss. He had done her countless personal favours, given her resources already stretched, allowed Joênia to allocate work to people who weren't strictly her staff. She knew that it was being unreasonable, even selfish, but there was a quiet rage inside that refused to be silenced. She wasn't worried about her job. Few Svalbard employees had ever been sent home for failing to do their best work. They were united in purpose, to restore what was left of the human race and earth's biome. Both were too fragile for petty bickering. Every soul could now see that it was our own actions that had taken us to the brink. The responsibility doctrine was a strong philosophy in all the communities of Earth. *United in Purpose,* was the mantra. Joênia knew she was an outlier; fighting in her own small way.

"Your work will not be in vain. The specimens here will thrive. The samples already collected will endure. When more lands emerge, they will be given over to more natural ecosystems. Nothing is going extinct."

"I get it," Joênia snapped, "my work is inessential. We don't fit the grand designs."

"This isn't over. There's a lot more work to be done. For generations. Your orchids are as much a part of this world as wheat crops and conifers. Their time will come again."

Tiago stood and patted her on the shoulder.

"I hope to see you at the celebrations tonight."

Tiago walked away tentatively stepping over brush and through mud slicks, looking completely out of place.

Joênia stood for a time in the warmth and quiet. Somewhere distant she could hear the grunts of a sloth as it sought out a mate and the calls of numerous bird species as they tore across the canopies. She began to pace, Tiago's words repeated like a drumbeat. She closed her eyes and pictured a rainforest unencumbered by a dome. Beneath an endless blue sky was mile after mile of untouched paradise, beyond the reach of an ignorant humanity, home only to uncountable species of animals, in perfect balance.

Joênia opened her eyes. A compulsion had built and no words or actions would stop her. She strode quickly through the forest, picking the easiest route back to one of the maintained pathways that would lead her out. She passed more people here. They were faceless. Distant. A few said hellos or called her name. Joênia kept moving. She passed out of Amazonia at one of the dome's heated tunnels that had been bored through frozen soil to connect the various facilities. Passing quickly through another decontamination chamber, she suddenly was in one of the crop domes. Elysium.

A wide-open sky blinded her after the shadowed forest. She was standing waist deep in a wheat crop so yellow it was dazzling. Agricultural workers looked up as she passed them. Other crops were growing in fields beyond; maize, corn, rape seed, all in neat rows. The soil underfoot was loose and moist. The crops were tall and healthy, dancing in an artificial dry breeze but Elysium was a barren place to her. Yes, its crops were healthy, but the dome was empty of anything else. There were insects in the soil and air but there were no birds, no scurrying mammals. Anything that could disrupt the precious crops had been kept out. It was a profoundly silent place, even the workers with their wide brimmed hats seemed to work as though in a penitent silence.

Left would take her to a dome of tiered rice paddies. Joênia turned right, moving through another chamber, swirling mists cleaning her shoes and clothing. She was now in one of the European greenhouses. On either side of a long metal walkway were hundreds of planting beds. A fine trickle of water was drifting down from an irrigation system, held up by thin metal pipes. It was a sea of vivid green leaves, collected together according to species. There were Solanums, alliums and apiums, ready to flower as potatoes, onions and other root vegetables. Trailing along the walls were numerous fruit plants, the *Rubus,* raspberries and blackberries. It was all so neat and ordered, like the crop fields of Elysium at her back. Its smells were deceptive. The musk of flowering plants, the rich earthy smell of wet soil and clay. Butterflies and bees moved lazily between plants, landing delicately on their wide surfaces. But this wasn't nature, it was a garden, an allotment. She understood its necessity, its life-giving produce, but it was so artificial, so *organized*. A group of workers tended the plants, moving carefully between beds to remove dead leaves or check soil nutritional levels. Joênia kept walking.

The Grove was next. This dome held a forest. A dense cluster of sixty-four species of tree. There were oaks, conifers, beeches, elms, sycamores, redwoods and the last surviving sequoia on earth. The overwhelming scent here was rotting wood and pine needles. Crickets chirped somewhere unseen and bird song called clearly between the trees. There were other forests in other domes, containing palms, banyans and cacti, but these were Northern Hemisphere species suited to a damp and often chilly climate. Wood pigeons, disturbed by her sudden presence, burst from a rosehip bush with explosive force and fluttered into the branches. Joênia knew in the shallow earth were foxes and rabbits. Snowy owls hunted red and grey squirrels on the treetops overhead. Here, for the first time, she elected to take a breath. This place felt a little freer to her. Another remnant of the old world. Yes, the trees' acorns, nuts and pine cones were being gathered to plant new forests that would eventually be felled to build more *things,* but at least the woods here were thriving.

This was her destination. Just above the pointed treetops a building had been built into the dome's super structure. A wide bay window stretched between two support struts. Joênia knew that behind it was the Office of the Director, the head of the entire Svalbard Recovery Project. At the dome's entrance she found a winding metal staircase that would lead to the control room. Each dome contained such a room, a place to keep watch and maintain. The Grove's was peopled by a small staff, talking together or hunched over consoles measuring atmospheric readings and moisture levels. They looked up as she passed, but no-one challenged her. Through a set of large doors she found a long corridor. A man sat behind a desk. His hands slid with ease across a console screen, his face illuminated. He glanced at her as she approached.

"Hello, can I help you?" he asked.

An American, by his voice. There was an unease there. She was not expected.

"I need to see Director Kamau," Joênia said.

He opened his mouth to respond but a sudden bell chimed and he plucked a comm from its charging cradle and put it to his ear.

"Office of the Director," he said and raised an apologetic finger.

Joênia folded her arms and felt her ire build. She was no-one important and could not just invade the office of the Director of Svalbard to air her petty grievances. This woman held the fates of millions in her hands, why should she care about Joênia and her little orchid project? Before she knew what she was doing Joênia was striding past the desk and through the door marked 'Director'.

"Um ... excuse me!" the receptionist called, fumbling with his comm.

The room beyond was surprisingly small, dominated by bookcases and a desk. A woman sat behind it, slender and dark-skinned with close cropped hair. She looked up from a tablet and gave Joênia a long appraising look. Joênia's confidence and conviction had been unwavering, but now it wilted.

"I'm sorry, ma'am," the receptionist called over Joênia's shoulder.

"Don't worry, Connor. I have a feeling that this young lady won't be satisfied until she is heard."

The director's accent was lyrical. Joênia knew she was from the equatorial band and had been President of one of the new African States. She had a reputation as a Central African hero, a saviour of thousands of lives and species. Director Kamau held out a hand, her wrist jangling with large wooden bangles.

"It's Joênia ... isn't it?" the Director asked.

Joênia nodded.

"Sit."

It was now a command. Joênia obeyed. She felt at once a foolish girl.

"You are here, I assume, because I have refused a request to distribute seeds other than specimens with a specific role in community development?"

"That's right. All of our work in Amazonia has been a waste ..."

"I don't agree," the Director interrupted, calm as a summer breeze, "no funding is being withdrawn, specimens will continue to be cultivated, seeds harvested and stored."

"You're going to turn the whole world into a farm!"

"I've read your report. I understand your concerns about the new agriculture zones and forests. I know you think we lack sufficient respect for future biodiversity, for the harm we might do to the remaining wild animal populations."

"And you've decided to ignore me?"

"Do you see this map?" The Director said and stood.

She walked around the desk and stood beside a world map displayed neatly on a projection board. Most of the outlines of continents and nations were obscured by vast swathes of blue, the glaciers. Only the equatorial zone and some patches of the southern hemisphere had been spared. Scattered throughout were small patches of red. Colonies, compounds, bunkers and the like where humanity had managed to survive. The image was constantly changing, information scrolling beside it in streams of yellow text.

"I have human populations emerging into the Indo Valley, the American plains and North Africa. The ice is retreating. All of these people need feeding. They need homes built. They need transportation, they need fuel and medicines and clothing."

"So the planet is once again a production line for greed and ignorance?"

The Director actually smiled.

"Come here," she said.

Joênia stood slowly, walking to the board.

"I shouldn't be showing you this. The World Council would have my head," she said and cocked her head towards the map.

The Director pressed a small tab and a new filter dropped over the image. Vast green blotches spread across the map. They covered vast tracts of land over every continent.

"These are the new Protectorate Zones. They will, under international treaty, be exempt from any kind of agriculture, mining, hunting or development. Negotiations are ongoing, but we're looking toward human population caps. Our work here is ongoing Joênia. In time your forest will bloom again."

Joênia stared at South American Protectorate. It covered much of the Amazon basin, as well as smaller satellite zones running down the continent.

"This is where my people used to live," she said and prodded the glowing image.

"Your people?"

"The Wapixana."

"What became of them?" the Director asked, gently.

"I know it's foolish to feel such a loss. I never knew them. I was born in São Paulo. The Rainforest was gone before I was born, but ..."

"I understand."

"Whole nations are gone, nuclear powers with armies and industries. But they're not really gone. Their people remain. Their language. Their stories. When the forests died and the cold began ... no-one came to help the Wapixana. Why would they? Some little tribe in the forest, less than ten thousand. Brazil was too busy trying to keep its own people alive."

"I'm sorry," Director Kamau said.

"It's not your fault," Joênia said.

"I think it might be. Collectively."

Joênia exhaled a tired laugh.

"Your work will bring back their home, even if they are not there to see it. I know that is of little comfort, but it will be the same of billions of others. We must look forward, so long as we do not forget what is behind us."

Joênia nodded. She suddenly found she could breathe easily.

"Now. Is there anything else?"

She was now the Director once again.

"No, ma'am," Joênia said and tried to think of something to say that would show her gratitude; "thank you for your time."

* * *

The festival was held on the promenade, the central ring to the habitat facility. It had been transformed overnight, brightly coloured strips of cloth draped from every balcony and exposed pipe. Through the thick glass viewing ports the storm raged on, but here triumphant music blared across the comm system. Every single employee of Svalbard seemed be neglecting their duties, released from their work coveralls and cold suits. Alcohol flowed freely, brewed here in Svalbard or bartered from passing ships. Some of it was truly toxic, distilled in the bellies of cargo freighters or colony sub-levels, but some was quality, even labelled.

This year's celebrations seemed to be themed around the recovery of fruit crops. They had proven to be the success story of the year. There were crops in from all over the world, fruits that had been lost when the insect populations plummeted. There were guava, lychee, mangos, passionfruit and dragon fruit. A worldwide trade was beginning to form, sailing ships crossing newly opened oceans to deliver formerly extinct produce to all the world's communities.

Joênia wandered aimlessly, squeezing between the crowds, carefully cradling a parcel in her arms. She passed the various restaurants with their festival day menus, their customers eating at tables around the arboretum's lush flowerbeds and towering citrus trees. People were happy, smiling. They were alive, working hard, prospering. This was the day, seventy-nine years ago, that the world's human population had stopped plummeting and began increasing. A reversal of trends that had seen them go from nine billion strong to just a few dozen million. It seemed a strange thing to call a festival. The days that followed would be reflective, a time to grieve and think on all that had been lost, not only nations and peoples, but species and habitats that would never return. And yet they were still here. With luck, some semblance of the old world would return as well. Perhaps that was enough.

Café Odudua was a bright multi-level establishment fashioned with African masks and cloth prints. Jade was where she said she'd be, surrounded by friends, engineers from Amazonia. Joênia almost slipped away, clutching the parcel to her chest. She hadn't managed to pick a route free before someone laid a gentle hand on her shoulder. Joênia spun around.

It was Jade, smiling broadly.

"Where you off?"

"Didn't want to intrude."

"Come," Jade said and led her to an empty nearby table.

Joênia watched her as Jade signalled an order to a worker. She was so at ease in a way that Joênia had never been able. A waiter quickly arrived with steaming cups of spiced chai.

"How you?" Jade asked.

"Better," Joênia said, nodding at her cup.

"Saw you wander off today. I was worried."

"Don't be. I just needed to clear my head. I met with someone, they put things into perspective."

"That's good," Jade said and took a sip of the chai.

Joênia shifted in her chair. She remembered the parcel still nestled on her lap.

"This is for you!" she blurted and carefully placed the box on the table.

"I was going to ask what that was about."

"It's a present. For you."

"You didn't have to do that," Jade said, "I feel bad. I haven't got you anything."

"You didn't have to. It's not a festival thing. It's just for you."

Jade actually seemed to blush. She carefully went to work removing a paper bow from along the tall box. Joênia had made it herself out of recycled seed boxes. When the box unfolded it revealed a long-stemmed orchid with white star shaped petals. It stood proudly in a ceramic pot.

"This is Cattleya intermedia. They grew once in the home of my ancestors. They're delicate. They like only a modest amount of moisture and humid air and no direct sunlight. I want you to have it."

"Why?" Jade asked, watching Joênia with playful eyes.

"For helping me."

"I'm not sure what I did to help."

"You've always helped me."

Jade looked down at the orchid properly for the first time. She examined it carefully, touched the petals with a brush of her fingertips.

"It's ... beautiful. Truly beautiful."

"You like it?"

"Of course. You made it."

"I cultivated it."

Jade laughed softly.

"What?" Joênia asked, smiling.

"I'm terrible with house plants! I kill them all the time."

Joênia opened her mouth to respond. She laughed instead.

"You work at Svalbard!"

"As an engineer!"

They laughed together, the orchid between them.

"I'll help you look after it," Joênia said when they were done.

"Promise?" Jade asked.

Her hand had slid across the table and was holding Joênia's tight.

"Promise," Joênia said, her heard racing.

"It's going to be alright you know?" Jade said.

Joênia looked around the promenade and down into the glistening arboretum, at the streaming colours, the dancing people, the cascading sounds of music and celebration. She closed her eyes and for a moment she found the rainforest, thriving. It was waiting for her, somewhere, and her people were with it.

"I know."

The Soma Earth

Ciro Faienza

IT WAS like this, she thought – dried resin of coffee rings the bottom of the finished cup; you rinse it and smell the ghosts of what you drank. Feeling the cut again when you change the bandage. The exhaustion that waits for the moment you try to stand.

Paolo was gone. Tiche spent no time denying it, because hope was acid in your belly and grief lived in your chest, where you are guarded by bone. She could cry, a half hour at night screaming and heaving and begging like a child into his empty shirts, then wake and still pedal the bike turbine for the cold trap. Still pump its nitrogen out into the fields. Still turn to their notes on using seawater.

Work. Walk the fields. Study. Plan. The bandage stayed intact.

His disappearance was a warning, or a retaliation, or both, but it was strange to her that the men had taken Paolo, a native, and not his black American lover. Hadn't they wanted her gone from the start?

When she'd first arrived at Paolo's postcard of a village, a cobblestoned fractal of eras and history set among stone pine copses and rolling hills, it seemed to her so much the ideal of ancient Italian farming town that she gawked at it like she'd just met a celebrity. His widowed mother Antonella, a bit bent from a lifetime of labor, had taken Tiche every morning by the elbow around to the market and shops. So many frank white eyes followed her, but Antonella's deep pleasure in Tiche's company kept them quiet.

She asked Paolo that first night if they thought she'd been going to steal something. "Are you joking?" he laughed. "I think you are the first black person in my town maybe ever. Refugees don't come because there is nothing here. We never had American soldiers in the world war. That's it. You are black. You are pretty. You go with Nella who everyone knows. They look." He shrugged and spread his upturned palms, smiling.

It didn't occur to him then how that would change when their society started to collapse, or when Nella finally passed away. Then even the locals who didn't lump her in with African immigrants pretended not to understand her Italian at times, or turned to dialect to keep her on the periphery. That place where basic communication was a privilege, not a right.

She understood. Changing times had not been kind to their country, nor their country kind to them. Northern wealth, which had never flowed freely into the farming

116

South, ceased with the rains, and the region had resumed its historic role as Mediterranean doormat.

She understood, and then she pictured Paolo – long, sun-dark, and graceful – dissolving in lye.

She supposed it was some code about women. These were the same sort of men who had poisoned the water table of Campania just in time for the new age of drought to shrivel its people to dust, or bombed whole trains to get at a single policemen, but they still believed themselves when they talked about honor. Women, children, et cetera.

In fact she was surprised she counted.

* * *

Tiche and Paolo built their farm on his family's land in Gargano, in the years after grad school. It was a project desperate enough to be utopian – find a new way, before it was too late. Most of their colleagues in the sciences had fled to northern climes – Greenland, Iceland, Alaska, Scandinavia – but as the world caught on the, the land was snatched up, the border rules changed. The rich outran the poor.

Their new careers became survival. The planning before they left, namely what to do and where to find the materials to do it, they'd done in a flurry of combined brilliance, occasionally giddy, occasionally in a twin bed with whatever alcohol they could find, each of them drunk on the other.

But the work itself was not giddy. It was arduous and tedious and often unbearably frustrating, often a lesson in starting over. Plants died before fruiting. A thing that had seemed easy to build turned out to be impossible. Basic chemical processes, old enough that they had well-known names like Haber and Bosch, failed inexplicably. Despair in these moments was powerful. Tiche remembered an afternoon spent at a workbench covered in expired batteries – AA, D, watch-sized – which she was breaking open, one by one, in the hopes of salvaging their graphite, when Paolo slid open the sun-warped wooden door to the shed and dropped a sack at her feet.

Pure graphite. Pounds of it. Brazilian sourced. Paolo, it turned out, knew a guy, "a good guy, from a town near here," who knew another good guy, who knew another good guy, and so on. She burst into tears.

Even so, for Tiche southern Europe was not a compromise. Hot as it would become, it was cooler than the American South and not so full of denialists or the Luddite firebrands who incredibly blamed leftists for the rising oceans.

And she loved the sound of Paolo's language, the thick plosives, the glissando inflections. She could even sense the *Southernness* of his accent, which he thought was ridiculous. "I'm serious," she said. "It's almost Texan." He laughed until he could barely breathe.

Hearing was a pastime for Tiche, had only come to her at age ten, after an operation that left a network of fiber optics spidering into her virus-primed temporal lobes. The slender ear modules were spun-wire beautiful, and when they first met, young Paolo, clear-eyed and lissome as a line drawing, struck her dumb when he told her in his not-Southern accent that she turned his words to light to understand them.

Lord, she thought, edging closer to him on the dining hall bench for a surreptitious brush of skin, *I could get into some trouble with this one.*

He had pianist hands with long, elegant fingers, which she imagined stroking her bare scalp and other places that loved the brush of soft friction – the sides of her upper arms, whose taught lines he might imagine wrapped around him, or the edges of her lips, whose fullness might make him notice his own heartbeat. On the farm, sun and labor eventually made them both a little leaner and him a little darker, but his hands stayed beautiful.

But he had cried – *cried*, she was shocked to see – when he realized what it might mean for her to be a black woman in Puglia in these times. It annoyed her, watching his new and open grief over truths she had suffered through since birth, but she remembered he was not American, and what was his context to know these things?

"Amore, listen," she said, kneeling and taking his hands. "First, there's basically no habitable space on Earth where being black isn't a long stretch of rough road. But second, I'm here now, and there's no turning back. And I want this. It's not something to grieve over. It's our adventure."

He smiled at that. Their adventure.

PhDs, earth sciences and inorganic chemistry. They were perhaps the most overqualified farmers ever to work that land, and they were full of ideas, about boosting the withered nitrogen cycle, about water reclamation and desalination membranes, work efficiency, crop symbiosis, heat management, sensor networks, power storage. In a lumbering chain of sealed plastic storage bins they'd built what Tiche called a ruminator, to make use of the plant life they couldn't eat, tweaking the yeast and bacterial colonies inside it with microdoses of commercial desiccants (Paolo's idea, though the ecosocialist in him didn't like it), until the thing could turn scrubs and grasses into glucose and methane. The methane they further processed into fertilizer, a nitrogen store for when local atmospheric concentrations were too low to trap.

The glucose got mixed with water to became what Tiche laughingly called "sweet drink", ignoring its faint, burp-like sourness. She handed him the first glass as he came in from the field one evening, a few weeks after the death of Antonella, sunset blazing orange and rose behind him.

"What's this?" he asked her in Italian.

"A test," she responded. Her accent was abysmal still. "Seeing if the land has more to give us."

He took a sip and grimaced, then jerked his arm out to hand the cup back to her. "That weed juice. I don't want it." He turned to head inside.

She hadn't expected that. "What? But, wait, I thought—"

He turned back to her. "I know, but it's shit, and I don't want it now."

"Paolo, what's wrong?"

He looked past her, into the dusky fields. "We can't eat those plants naturally. My father always said 'natural' like it meant 'good'. A thing is good if it comes from the earth. Our wine was good. Our tomatoes were good. Our oil was good. Do you how he first showed me the oil from our trees?"

Hundreds of olive trees in groves that used to abut these fields. Long dead. Tiche swallowed and shook her head.

"I was very young, maybe four, but I still remember it. He poured it onto my hands and told me to rub them together, then bring them close to my nose and inhale." He mimed the motions and his eyes widened, remembering "I could smell this earth in it. Green gold. Natural. Good."

He looked down, his eyes now wet. "It's not good anymore, Tiche. Our earth is not good."

It struck her then how much their enormous labors had protected them from grief. They had spent almost no time grieving, and only now did she realize how strange that was.

Softly she said, "So we do what nature can't. We make it good. That was the dream we talked about, remember? We take what greed and ignorance broke and we make a new thing?" She wanted to add what news she'd heard from Greenland, about their success with vertical farms that she and Paolo had no hope of building, about their collectives with knowledge pools and drone shares (what she gathered was rights to a percentage of a swarm of work drones, but there were no specifics) and voluntary work rotas, all built on the kind of shared trust that Paolo said wasn't possible here. But she sensed that now was not the time.

He nodded. "The dream. If we can."

Most of the time, though, that sense of the frontier won out over grief. There was simply too much to know and do. Tiche downloaded volumes and volumes on off-the-grid methodologies, everything from herbal pharmacology to stick fighting for self defense. One day she asked Paolo, in still broken Italian, if they'd become crazy libertarians by accident.

He thought for a moment and said, "A man of the right means a man who is afraid and nothing else. We are not afraid."

* * *

The last of her ear modules gave out a few years back. Expected. Sad. It was different from how she felt after the social dark, the great failure of the apps and networks that kept people together. She had no idea if it was server collapses or companies shutting down or national firewalls, or simply a problem with the internet in Gargano, which had always been spotty. But after a few days, she began to feel like a drifting vessel pinging into the deep.

The hearing loss instead was a wave of truth descending upon her. The curtain had closed on her beloved spectacle of sound, and now, like a theater-goer, she had to return home. To reality, which was no spectacle, but quiet. Paolo held her, kissed her eyes.

It meant that when the men first came – jutting-jawed men, wide-faced men, men with knives in their pockets – she had no idea what they were saying. Across the pepper patch in the evening she saw three of them climb the hill and approach Paolo. The hand gestures she could read – we are reasonable, you understand, I am a powerful man – sent her to fetch the thick wooden staff she drilled with every morning.

She let them get their knives out. It would teach them something about fear. Two of them walked into the most basic of moves and lost bones for it, which was enough. The third postured – actually tossed his knife away – and beckoned her to him.

Tiche would never forget the look in his eyes, after the three lightning snaps of her staff and his bent neck and his collapse to the dirt. It was the look of a man who feels something essential has gone mortally wrong inside him.

A cut of the crops or New D-Marks. She'd guessed it, and Paolo signed that he should have foreseen it. From the lemon groves of Sicily to the buffalo marshes of Naples, farmers had ever been the low-hanging fruit. What few farms were producing now had violence in their future.

It triggered the next stage of Tiche and Paolo's beautiful dream – expanding the farm and building something communal with the locals who wanted to take part. The two of them had argued about this, Tiche favoring open, blunt proposals to the folks in town who would listen, Paolo insisting that they had to finesse it with the right people first, neither of them sure what they were actually proposing in the first place. But while their notions of the right social order for their project were vague, they knew they had something to share, and they believed in its power to summon the best in people. The world had lost too much to hierarchies and independence. They wanted to give.

But people had to be convinced and rallied and trained, all before the next force of the Sacra Corona arrived with something more than knives. Paolo wondered why they had brought no firearms with them, if they were indeed that sloppy. Tiche guessed that ammunition must be getting harder and harder to find, and that they hadn't yet figured out how to make their own. But probably they could scrounge some up, for the right cause.

Paolo went to town in the morning. Tiche kept her staff with her.

Paolo did not come back.

* * *

In ages past, Tiche had read, the Mediterranean had been no sea. The world ocean, what would become the Atlantic, lapped for millennia against its bounding rock, and when the waters finally breached Gibraltar, the entire basin filled in fifty years.

Fifty years to make a sea. Tiche couldn't imagine seeing that. The same amount of time in her own century had seen the tide swallow the beaches of Gargano and almost fully sever it from the rest of Puglia, so that the outer shores were now cliffs, east of her hills. The salt water teased her and Paolo. It was nearby, abundant, and sweet and life-giving if they could fully scale their desalination setup. The numbers were right for it, but the work and materials would have been too much for the two of them on their own.

They had good reason to be hopeful. All of their most important projects they'd eventually managed with enormous success. They drew nutrients straight out of the air, concentrated them, and fed them directly to their plants, which they had chosen to be survivors. Paolo's ancestral loves, the garlic and chilies and rosemary, were survivors, which he said pointed to the virtue of listening to the land.

They did listen. At regular intervals in their meticulously plotted fields were nitrogen and phosphorous sensors and water activity meters, their output running through shielded cables alongside the nutrient pipes back to the house. The data were precious. The farm lived by what it told to a solar-powered processor.

Without Paolo, the silence was a shroud. He'd tried to plan ahead, worked with her to make devices that fed their data to her when she was out in the field while leaving her hands free to work. Their electronics would talk to her still-functioning implants with generated tones – for wind volts a middle C, for solar volts a thrum. His proposal for the field readings was a grid of vibrating lozenges adhered to her back, a pair for each sensor grid.

Ridiculous. She never tried it until after he left, when she would have torn tender seedlings up, burned their decades of work to the ground, just to hear his voice again or to be touched.

It stayed ridiculous, at first. Random buzzing along her back, sweat under medical tape, senseless noises mocking her ears. But they were makers and wonderers, and he had no idea what he had done.

She woke the morning of the only rain that season with the clear and impossible sense that her body stretched well beyond her bed, farther than the house, out into the fields.

Inexplicable. Had she taken something? No. She hadn't seen a pill since she was thirty.

Outside she heard a lone middle C rise with the insistent breeze, and the sharp smell of the air prickled across her back. When the clouds broke, she understood.

It came in sheets, fuller than at any time in recent memory. She saw it cover the fields and sing across shoulder blades, down her spine, and felt them both as one and the same. Her spine, the spine of the land. Her tended and precious and joyous fields, a garden of herself.

Psychologists, she knew, had used smoke and mirrors to convince people they had extra limbs or walked two feet behind themselves almost a century ago. Without realizing it, Tiche had built an extra sense that bound her to her labors in a way that went beyond even her love and grief. It didn't feel like smoke and mirrors. It felt like another wave of truth.

She laughed, stupidly, like a middle-schooler. Yet it was a fresh hurt not to be able to share this with him – to be suddenly vast and timeless and whole – and to thank him and to talk to him about hope.

She thanked the ground instead and lay upon it, letting the rain breach her bones and fill the basin of her, letting it seep into the soils she had raised for almost half her life.

Now she would make a sea.

* * *

Inside the house she packs a bag. She loads soil samples and sensor models and a small computer, charged. She nestles in a young, modified bean plant that cost a fifth of their savings, when the two of them were still spending currency.

It has been a long while since the men with knives. Tiche doesn't know what they are waiting for. The harvest, maybe. It doesn't matter. She needs to act.

She still believes in the second part of their dream. They never meant to spend their lives alone, even with each other. Their mistake must not have been to trust, but not to trust sooner. She wonders how things might have been different if they had dug their first hole alongside the people who had lived there for generations, whose families were living histories of desperate struggle and yearning. She believes with a certainty like knowing that they would have stood with her when the men came.

The bag is packed, and she grabs her staff and steps out.

Tiche knows the townspeople are probably lost to her for the foreseeable future. If her skin doesn't keep them away, other fears will, and she has seen how whiteness behaves in fear.

On the outskirts of San Severo, there are others. They look something like her, and though her African skin will not make her an insider, necessarily, it might bridge the gap of trust.

Most of them, though not all, are North Africans, first generation, second generation. Some will be engineers, educated in Arab universities. Others will be writers or parents or farmers themselves. They have seen terrible things. They are survivors.

At the last cultivated row she looks back, trying to imagine how the place will look at its full size, irrigated by sea water. Towers like in Greenland? She doesn't know. But it will be filled with people, just as Paolo saw it.

She kneels, and a hundred times she kisses his name into the loam, which is his earth, which is her body. Then rises.

She hears a thrum. The sun is bright.

For the Snake of Power

Brenda Cooper

ROSA RUBBED at her eyes, trying in vain to focus on the map in front of her. The electronic image of the great – and greatly damaged – solar snake that covered the canals of Phoenix swam in her vision. The snake had been bruised, battered, and in a few places, actually broken by the huge dust storm that had enveloped the city three days ago. A haboob. Uncountable motes of dust carried in on a scorching wind and left behind to dim solar panels, catch in the wires that held them together, and clog the maintenance robots. Such tiny things to have done such damage. Forty-three deaths. Trees knocked down and signs ripped from the ground and hundred-year-old saguaros laid flat. But those weren't her problem. Power was.

The snake had been over-engineered on purpose, built to supply the future. She'd been working with the snake's maintenance AI, HANNA, for two years now, and even with the dust and the damage, the vast, beautiful array should create enough power.

"HANNA?" Rosa addressed the AI, which listened through a button-sized speaker on her desk. "Have you figured out why the power drawdown keeps getting worse?"

Rosa had chosen an old woman's voice for the AI. It sounded calm as it said, "Not yet. I will keep looking."

A stray thought made Rosa tell it, "Look beyond the engineering. If you haven't seen a problem there, then the problem is somewhere else. Power storage? Legal?"

"Is that permission?" HANNA asked.

Rosa hesitated. But HANNA wouldn't ask if Rosa couldn't give it permission. "Yes."

"Logged."

"I'm walking down to the closest break."

"You have worked 14 hours today."

The machine wasn't responsible for maintenance on *her*. "Maybe if I see for myself, I'll understand. Goodnight."

"Goodnight, Rosa."

Rosa left the building, still wearing her blue Salt River Project work shirt. A hot, dry wind created a small cloud of dust that tickled her ankles. After half an hour, Rosa spotted the snake's glow from a block away. Its pale blue and yellow lights looked brighter than usual with the streetlights dimmed to half power.

As she stepped under the arch and onto the pathway, she startled as a maintenance robot scuttled overhead, a tiny broom stuck to one "arm" and an air puffer clenched in the other. It reminded her of a fantastical creature from fiction, half squirrel and half Swiss-army knife.

The path was busy. Two young women wearing roller skates and pushing children in carriages slowed her. Hoverboards and bicycles sped in both directions.

Her earpod pinged softly and she touched it. A newsnote, read in a flat masculine voice. "The Association of Solar Power raised rates yet again, citing a deficit of power. Brownouts are scheduled to begin at noon tomorrow. Schedules will be posted at 7:00 a.m."

In summer, brownouts killed. She clenched her fists.

As she neared the break, the walls separating the neighborhoods from the canal looked haphazard. A bit of chain link, a makeshift wooden fence, a neat brick section, an adobe segment with the shards of glass embedded in its top glittering softly in the snake's light. Her old home. She had been gone six years. She didn't recognize the people lounging against the walls, sharing beer and listening to music. Two young men stared at her, and suddenly she wished she had changed out of her SRP shirt.

As she passed, conversations lowered or changed tenor, although no one approached.

She reached the break and stopped under it, staring up. The snake undulated throughout the city, sometimes only 20 feet above the canals and sometimes the height of a tall building, the design part art and all function. The taller loops reached for sun that buildings or bridges would block. This break was near where a segment began to rise. Three supports had come down. Solar scales had shattered on the pathway and, almost certainly, into nearby backyards. A few still dangled, askew, edges connected to the wire scaffolding that managed the panel's tilt.

The breach was serious, but a hundred yards beyond it the snake continued up toward the top of this curve, lights on, clearly working. Every two or three poles carried power and optics into underground conduits. Any break could only affect the area of the break plus two segments at worst. The snake had lost four segments of power here, but there were thousands. HANNA reported 153 segments out, which was less than 10 percent.

Tonight's low was expected to be 95, and next day's high 121. The rich often had their own systems. If not, they had cool places to go, and transportation to power if they needed it for oxygen tanks or powered wheelchairs. The poor wouldn't even be able to run a fan.

Rosa had held her grandmother's hand when she died of heat in the power wars of '32. She had been just seven years old, sweating and miserable, her head afire with heat and dehydration, singing to her grandmother. She'd felt her grandmother's hand go limp, had seen the life fade from her smile, her cheeks, her eyes. Rosa had cried, hot and miserable, and slept with her head on her dead grandmother's chest until her father found her there an hour later.

She swallowed, able as always to feel the slip of that hand into death. Some memories burned themselves into your soul.

Steps from behind drew her out of her reverie.

"Rosa. That you? That really you?"

Although she hadn't heard it for five years, the voice was family. Home. Rosa turned and smiled. "Inez."

"You work for power now? For SR f'ing P?"

Rosa took a step back, slightly put off by the sheer press of Inez's voice, and of her body, which was bigger than she remembered, broader and more muscular. The light from the snake and the path lights combined to paint Inez's face a dull blue. "Yes."

"You going to fix this?"

"SRP is doing everything possible to restore power …" The look on Inez's face made Rosa hear the corpspeak she was spilling out, and she stopped. Took a breath. Looked right at Inez. "If I can."

The two women stood quiet long enough for Rosa to wonder if Inez was as unsure of what to say as she was, then Inez said, "I knew you'd do okay. I'm sorry. I just didn't … expect … I didn't think you'd become …"

"The enemy?" Rosa smiled. "I'm not."

Inez merely stared.

They had been good friends once. Done homework together. Skipped school together. Yet Rosa felt a distance from Inez that bothered her. "Are you okay?"

"I got two kids. Mom's sick. Dad died."

"I'm sorry. About the sickness. Congratulations on the kids." She was stuttering. Was Inez married? She didn't remember. "Sorry about your dad."

"He was a bastard." Inez's shoulders relaxed a tiny bit and she smiled. "The kids are great. Lonny's five and likes to cause trouble. His little brother, José, he's small and smart."

"And your mom? I remember she used to make me chipotle and chicken soup when I had a cold." Inez's mom, Maria, had smiled whenever Rosa ate her soup, and Rosa had felt better whenever Maria smiled. "What's wrong with her?"

"She's been wishing to die since dad left us. But I don't want her to die."

"I understand. Remember my grandmother?"

"Yes." Inez swallowed and shifted her weight. "I came to tell you to be careful. There's people who don't care for SRP here. And you just raised the rates again."

"I didn't. Besides, SRP doesn't set rates anymore. That's the governor's Association of Solar Power. The ASP. A committee."

Inez narrowed her eyes. "People still hate SRP."

Rosa nodded. After her grandmother died, she'd hated SRP. She'd hated them until they championed the snake. Then she'd loved them. The snake was supposed to make power available for everyone, rich or not, as long as they wanted it. Since the rich had their own systems, the snake was a public work for the poor. The cheap power and net connectivity that ran down the snake had helped her compete in high school, helped her get grants for college, helped her with everything for five years. Now all that was threatened, and for no reason Rosa understood.

"You should go," Inez said.

Rosa nodded, glancing once more at the destroyed sections of the solar array. "I'm tired. I've been working all day."

"Killed a boy when that came down. Nine months old."

Rosa swallowed. "I'm sorry." That hadn't been in the regular news. But she'd be able to find the information if she looked. This neighborhood had its own news sources that flowed through the knots of idle poor like water running downhill.

"Come back on a better day," Inez's smile was faint, but genuine. "I want to know how you are."

Rosa thought about leaning in for a hug, but extended her hand instead. Inez took it, her grip strong. She repeated her request. "Come back."

"Soon." It felt like an empty promise and she wondered at that, unhappy with herself. What right did she have to ignore this place she'd come from?

The next morning, she arrived an hour early for her shift. As she threw her lunch into the crowded fridge, she said, "HANNA. Good morning. Anything?"

As always, HANNA was right there. "I found three large contributing factors. We have been working on the tracking system failures."

They had. For a year. "And there are still no parts. Go on."

"Weather."

Rosa sat down and began turning up her systems. "Like the dust storm from hell."

"And the one before that? No. It's an average of three degrees warmer so far this summer."

"I know that," Rosa replied.

"People have used seven percent more air conditioning."

She hadn't known that. The SRP staff infoweb loaded up on her screen.

"And power is leaving the system."

"I know." She scanned the web. The brownout schedule would post in 15 minutes. Call-takers had been pulled in early. The Emergency Operations Center would stay activated. A hot wind would come today. No storm. She blinked. "How much power? More than usual?"

"The usual amount. Twenty percent."

She frowned. HANNA was feeding her data slowly, making her think. One of its described duties was staff training, but she'd thought she was beyond most of that. "So it's 20 percent of power, no matter how much we generate?"

HANNA said, "It's a fixed amount equal to 20 percent of full capacity."

Rosa stopped moving. "That amount doesn't get reduced in an emergency?"

"No."

Her screen filled with snippets of contracts. She had interned with the law department; she could parse the language. As she reviewed the clauses HANNA sent, a deep revulsion rose in her.

The governor had signed away 20 percent of their power.

The SRP power grid was the snake, and it was meant for Arizona's poor and middle classes. Not for the cooler north. She poured a cup of coffee, took a deep breath, and went to find her boss.

Susannah Smith was in her office, drumming her fine, thin fingers on the table. Her usually curled hair hung around her shoulders, still damp, and she looked as tired as Rosa felt. Nevertheless, she glanced up and smiled as Rosa entered. "Did you sleep last night?"

"Not well."

"Is everything OK?" Susannah turned her attention back to her computer. "The lists just posted. I hope you brought a lunch. We may not get out today."

"I have a question."

"Ask away."

"The governor sold our power. Did you know that?"

Susannah turned back around. "We've always sold off our excess power."

"This isn't excess. Chicago and Salt Lake have first dibs. That's new."

For a brief moment, surprise flashed across Susannah's face, and her lips opened to speak, but she clamped them into a frown. She shrugged. "This is not our problem. We support maintenance, not contracts."

"But surely in an emergency …"

Susannah's glare was uncompromising. "We can't fix it."

Why did Susannah look so angry? "Why not?"

"Not you and I. And not today." Susannah stood up, which made her a few inches taller than Rosa. "Can I help you prioritize your work?"

Rosa wasn't ready to give up. "Who can change it?"

"The ASP." Susannah took a step toward her, not menacing, but pressing. "Go on. We've all got full plates today, and long days."

True enough. "I can't—"

"Go."

Susannah had never used that tone of voice with her. Rosa went, angry tears stinging the corners of her eyes and nails digging into her palm.

Back in her office, HANNA swept her into work and she spent the morning cataloguing the missing solar panels, checking HANNA's designs, and approving orders for materials and for the maintenance bots. At least they didn't need to worry about the price of replacement panels. The governor had managed to get an emergency declaration and FEMA would pay.

Every way she could think of to fix this was constrained by the governor's bad contract, or slowed to idiocy by the multitudes of safety mechanisms that threaded throughout

SRP – half of them relics from the days when power ran on high-voltage lines and touching it killed.

Right before lunch, Rosa sent a note to Callie, who had been her formal mentor when she started this job, and who had continued to help her. Callie could get anything through the stifling bureaucracy. She agreed to meet in Rosa's office for lunch.

Callie plunked her huge frame in the chair and threw her head back, almost dislodging the big, messy bun of gray hair that crowned her head. "Are you as tired as I am? The phones are crazed, and there's three old women with protest signs out front. Hard to spin this."

Rosa told Callie what she'd learned, and shared her conversation with Susannah.

Callie frowned. "That's way upstream. There's nothing we can do."

The word *we* gave Rosa hope. "Are you sure?" She glanced at her computer. "It's 118 degrees already." Her voice rose. "People will die, to give power to Chicago, where's it's only 92 degrees. There's nothing fair about that!"

Callie shook her head and popped open a coffee bulb. "No. But you and I can't change it. Policy. I can get stuff done, but only to support SRP or the workers." She sipped her coffee, brows furrowed. "You mess with this, you might get fired."

"I told Susannah. She was surprised. I could see that in her eyes. But she sent me away."

"Susannah's been here long enough to know what's what. Some things." Callie rolled her eyes and held out a coffee bulb. "Have one of these."

So Callie wasn't going to help her either? Rosa took the coffee, and drank so fast she burned her tongue.

During her next break, she used her personal phone to try calling the governor. The lines were busy.

Every little thing she did to help fix the snake felt like pulling a single needle out of a ball of cactus. This shouldn't be an emergency, and they shouldn't be using workarounds and running bots past their maintenance cycles. They should have time to be careful.

She ran into Callie on the way out of the door. "This is still wrong," she told her. "Three people died already. Old people. In one day of brownouts. It will get worse."

"The city is opening cooling shelters."

"For how many people?"

The look on Callie's face told her it wasn't enough, and she didn't even answer the question. She just said, "You're doing your best."

"It's not good enough."

"All you can do is your best."

Rosa stared into Callie's eyes. "Maybe I can do better."

It was already bedtime when she finished wading through the heat to her one-room apartment. Someone had posted the brownout schedule on her door, and a list of power conservation tips. She glanced at it, realized she had two more hours of cooling, and passed out on the bed in her uniform.

When she woke near dawn, her limbs were heavy with a dark anger she couldn't put any images to. Sweat beaded her brow and clung to her hair. As she stared out the window at the whitening sky, the anger pushed her out of bed and into a clean uniform. She ate a handful of berries and two pieces of toast, then plaited her hair into long braids that would be cool.

She stepped outside and started toward work, then she stopped. If she went in this morning, the anger would consume her. She had felt pride in her work until yesterday. Not now. She worked for the power company, and she knew what it was to die from lack of power. Her hands shook, so she clenched her fists. She turned and walked fast back toward her old home. She could lose her dream, her job. But if she could save a grandmother somewhere ...

Usually, the long canal soothed her. But this morning, the whole thing – the wide canal, the arching snake of power, the graffiti on one wall, the elegant natural art on the bridges – all of it felt like separation.

Inez was easy to find; her mother and sister still lived in the same old, faded green house. While the sister told Rosa where to find Inez, she kept glancing warily toward the SRP logo on her shirt. But she asked no questions.

Inez sat on the front stoop of a pop-up brick house, small and square and exactly like the three next to it except for a mural of a donkey on the side wall. Inez's children were both slender and dark-haired and shy. After introductions, Rosa asked, "Who matters here now? Who tells the neighborhood things?"

Inez stood, the boys behind her, the taller one peering out and the shorter one hiding behind Inez's ample right thigh. "What news do you have?"

Rosa told her about the contracts.

Inez looked more angry than surprised. After a few moments, she asked, "Do you remember Penélope López? She was two years behind us in school."

"Maybe." She imagined a thin girl with short dark curls who liked high-heeled boots, even in summer.

"She's got a local show. Regular dissenter, that one. A good girl." Inez picked both boys up, balancing one on each hip. She pounded on her neighbor's door and shoved the boys inside, then led Rosa to Penélope, who still wore high-heeled boots, but was taller now, and angry. Rosa told her story and Penélope wrote.

As she talked, Rosa's stomach burned. She was an hour late to work, and she was wearing an SRP uniform and telling tales on the most powerful public company in Phoenix.

Next, Inez took her to Jack, a tall black man in dreads with a soft smile. He had read Penélope's post. "I love what you said. Truth to Power." His smile widened. "May I? It will be live. It will be now."

Rosa swallowed. "Who will see it?"

"Everybody."

Rose hesitated. Inez watched her. Jack smiled, full of patience.

Rosa nodded.

Jack handed Inez a camera so small Rosa kept losing sight of it. She was careful only to say what she knew, to use facts, and Jack asked her hard questions. When she refused to answer some, he said, "That's okay. You can refuse. That tells us as much as an answer."

That made her stop and breathe, and worry, but she kept going. She was saving a grandmother.

Jack held out a hand, leaned in, and hugged her, smelling faintly of smoke and apples. "You're brave," he whispered. He led her to the canal, and they stood near the break where the hanging wires showed. He asked her some of the same questions again while Inez zoomed in on her shirt and her brown face and long braids.

Rosa leaned into her words. It was hers now, her choice, her story, her anger.

An old woman who carried herself like a turtle came up and hugged her. She turned to Jack, who interviewed the old woman while she called for everyone to come and protest, to stand under the shade of the snake and be heard.

Penélope called Inez, and said she, too, would call for a protest.

Over the next hour, the paths under the snake began to fill. People brought water and food, chairs and signs. They also brought anger, children, dogs, and music.

Rosa did three more interviews.

By the time the Phoenix news channels showed up, the paths were full, and rumors that other neighborhoods had joined reached her. Even middle-class neighborhoods, ones that had their own power. A news program let her read their signs, which had been crafted with glue and glitter and fancier markers than the ones near Rosa. But they said the same things.

POWER TO PHOENIX
THE SNAKE IS OURS
POWER FOR ALL

As the day wore on, the signs grew angrier and more clever.

THE SNAKE FEEDS US ALL
GET THE SNAKE OUT OF OFFICE
FOR THE SNAKE OF POWER

A college-age couple resting on a bench shaped like a rock with thornless cactus arms recognized Rosa and stood up together, gesturing for her to sit. She blinked at them for a moment, but when the woman inclined her head and quietly said, "Thank you," Inez sat and pulled Rosa down next to her and the couple melted into the crowd.

Despite the snake's shade over the bench and the water flowing five feet from them, the heat punished.

145

Protestors clumped together under the solar panels, and Rosa swiped sweat from her brow. Young men worked the crowd, selling metered pours of water from great sacs they rolled in front of them on red wagons. Newscams hovered in the air, some clearly violating the rules about proximity to people.

Felipe, who Rosa had burned for in eighth grade, came and shook her hand. His warm, sweaty touch drew a nervous smile and Rosa momentarily felt like her younger self even though Felipe dangled a girl of three or four on his hip.

An international news channel came by and interviewed her in horrible Spanish, and she managed not to laugh while she repeated her simple litany of facts. The reporter's camera zoomed in on the logo on her shirt. "You are a whistleblower?" he asked.

She shook her head. "I love my job, and SRP. But people had to know about the contracts. Three people died from heat already today. More will."

Voices rose. A water seller who had stopped near them after selling out climbed up on his wagon and called out, "Police!" He turned and faced Rosa. "They come for you! Go."

Rosa stood, confused. People bunched in front of her, some chanting *Save the Snake!* or *Power to the People!*

Inez climbed up on the back of the bench. Her eyes widened. "Riot gear."

In spite of the wilting heat, of a hot wind, of the sun now high overhead and unrelenting, in spite of all that, the crowd continued to bunch. Inez said, "They're blocking the police."

The water seller, peering back and forth like a crow from his vantage a foot or two higher than her, said, "Not for long."

A hand fell hard on Rosa's shoulder. "There you are."

Rosa turned to find Callie staring at her. She'd stripped off her uniform and wore a hat that *might* hide her face in such a large crowd. "Susannah locked you out of the building."

It didn't surprise Rosa, but it hurt.

Callie offered an unexpected smile and said, "I told this to the *Arizona Republic*." She looked like she had just won the lottery, her eyes glittering with energy.

Rosa stuttered. "You … you did? Couldn't you get fired, too?"

"No. I retired before I talked to the paper. I came because of you. What you said to me, that we had to care, you made me ashamed."

"So you're safe?"

"Yes. I think so. But you're not."

"I don't mind." Rosa leaned in to hug Callie. "Thank you."

"I came to thank you. For saying you could do better. I decided I could, too."

Rosa smiled.

The water seller called, "Something's happening!"

Rosa glanced at him, but Callie said, "Wait."

When Rosa turned back, Callie told her, "HANNA and I did something before I lost access."

Inez, still balancing on the back of the bench, called out, "They're coming closer. We can move faster than they can. We should go."

Callie shook her head. "No need. HANNA helped me turn off the transmission."

Rosa blinked. "What transmission?

"The lines going to Chicago. I know someone with a backdoor to HANNA, and he helped me. It's enough. Just the protests might have done it. But you made me want to help. The governor will announce soon."

Rosa stared at her mentor, blinking back tears and sweat. Callie had always loved her job, always defended it. She had hated much of the process, but never the real work. And now she had been this insubordinate? "Will they arrest you?"

Callie was still grinning. "And admit their own AI helped?" She shook her head. "There will be a press conference. The governor will say she was going to use the money to repair the snake."

"Was she?" Rosa asked.

Callie shrugged. "Who cares? We win. People don't die."

The water seller said, "You should go."

Rosa looked at Callie. "Other money can pay for repairs."

Callie glanced at her watch. "It might already be over."

A roar from the crowd was hard to interpret, a wave of tired whoops and louder calls, a few whistles. The water seller said it first. "The brownouts are cancelled."

Rosa and Callie shared a long smile. In spite of the heat, Callie folded Rosa in her arms. She whispered, "I'll find you."

Rosa turned to help Inez down. By the time she looked for Callie again, she was gone.

"You did this," Inez said.

"I had help."

"This wouldn't have happened without you."

The water seller hopped off of his wagon. "The police are almost here." He began to move away, and Inez pulled Rosa after him, and in a moment the crowds had enfolded them both, pushing them down the river of people under the snake.

She had done better. She would find a way to bear the price. It felt good to be home.

Anticipation of Hollowness

Renan Bernardo

HAVING AN obsolete best friend meant I had to put up with constant warnings about her plight.

"Software needs to be updated," Lyria said, stopping upright on our way to Algae on Wheels. Her hands slumped and stiffened against her sides. "Software will shut down unless updated." A few meters ahead, the floating algaewich tuk-tuk honked twice, announcing its departing time.

"Well, Lyria," I said, chuckling. "You're way too predictable, have I told you?" I waved to Roberto, the algaewich vendor. He was gliding the tuk-tuk away across the street. Its buffed surface reflected the pinky skies that gave way to the dark of the night. Roberto flinched when he saw me and steered the Algae on Wheels into a parking area designated for bicycles, rickshaws, and the like.

"Janet, about predictability, I would like to—"

"Shush, friend. There's our man."

I ran. Lyria followed me as she always did. Her feet clanked unevenly on the asphalt.

150

It tastes like algae, but it's hidden among breads!, advertised a small hologram floating in blue and yellow around the roof of the Algae on Wheels, sometimes crossing through the round solar panel on its top.

Lyria tried to keep up with me, but her legs were old, marred by time and use, unable to run without making her look like an unwieldy dancer. Nothing about her agedness was new for me. Her warnings had been telling me about her obsolescence for more than two years now.

The insulting smell of algae struck us before we approached the Algae on Wheel's serving hatch.

"It's the best algaewich of Sundyal," Roberto told us. A rehearsed approach, though his eyes gleamed as if he was revealing a secret.

"You say that every day, Roberto," I said. "I'm always around."

"Oh!" Roberto smirked, a spatula frisking in his hand, bread falling on algae falling on bread sizzling on grill plate. "Standard algaewich?"

I nodded. The algae and bread mixture sizzled on the plate. My stomach rumbled. I almost inquired it about growling for algae, but I supposed it was rioting for the lack of other options.

"I'm not good with faces," Roberto said. "Though that one is hard to miss." He pointed to Lyria with his chin.

She stood impassive next to me, waiting in her erect stance. The wind ruffled the few strands of the plastic fiber hair that remained on her head, threads of her past.

151

Flaps of skin peeled off her jaw. She blinked her orange eyes with no pupils, some lines on her face twitching in a spasm. Outdated hardware and software caused a lot of problems to Lyria's structure. She twitched, sometimes bent to one side, tilted her head involuntarily, and uttered unintelligible sentences. Also, her biograft skin was a lot older than the smooth ones covering the bodies and faces of the androids that weaved their way seamlessly throughout the humans in the streets of Sundyal, though they always seemed more humdrum than her with their repetitive sentences tuned for their specific functions.

"She's easy to spot," I said, smiling to Lyria.

"I'm easy to spot," Lyria concurred. "I am a walking ad." She put a hand on her chest, above the fading casino ad on it. *Celebrate Mendolowski Day with 10,000 specoins in prizes, you lucky duck!* On her belly, only the golden beak of a duck remained.

"This casino doesn't even exist anymore," I said. "Her software is outdated, she still struggles to remember some things."

Roberto laughed, packing my algaewich in a pasteboard cylinder. The swampy odor wafted up in my nose.

"How much?" I straightened my glasses on my face.

Roberto curled his thumb in the air above his accounting pad. A tiny hologram drifted up from it. "It will be three specoins."

"Oh, crap." I glanced at Lyria.

"What's wrong?" Roberto frowned.

152

"She's my wallet too." I turned to my friend, clasping her hands. "Please, tell me good news, dear."

"This price is not recommended," Lyria said, her brows jerking in what might have been a worried expression in her past as a blackjack dealer with an up-to-date system. "It is best for you to not spend this money."

I sighed. I wouldn't know what to do without her – what I *would have* to do eventually because her software had an expiry date. I shivered at the thought. In Sundyal, non-expiring stuff ended up with well-off folks. For girls like me, not recipient of a wealthy heritage or large dividends, only finite stuff was left to reap.

"You can wait a little bit." Roberto shrugged. "I'm used to that. Early evening, people have left work a while ago, gone to their deserved rests. The streets are almost empty now." He opened his arms. "Prices will go down."

"How much time?" I said. "I need to eat, and if I don't eat now there won't be anywhere I can eat till tomorrow." Anywhere with a reasonable price for a girl that didn't fit, I thought, but decided not to speak.

"Well ... look!" The man zoomed in on the price tag hologram. "Two specoins."

"Still not recommended," said Lyria.

"Aw, snap. Pay him."

"One coin!" Roberto spread his arms like a magician reaching the outcome of a trick. He picked up the algaewich and handed it to me. "Buy it now. If partiers or tourists swarm by it will go up. If they're lucky in the casinos tonight I could bet on 6 specoins."

"Buy it!" I stroke Lyria's side. "Buy it, buy it!"

"Transferring," Lyria said. A ping sounded on Roberto's pad. "Transferred."

"It was a pleasure doing business with you, young lady," Roberto said, blinking and igniting the tuk-tuk. Its thrusters whirred and propelled it forward. "I'll try to recall your face next time." The Algae on Wheels dinged twice.

I nodded and chomped my algaewich. My stomach demanded it.

Lyria and I strolled along Caravana Street. Dronelights lit the way, faintly buzzing above our heads. Dustbots skimmed the floor, sucking in dust from the already excessively clean pavements. The closed businesses and the light leaking from the apartments in the two-story buildings with solar-paneled roofs were my path home every day. I used to rove around Sundyal, sometimes aimlessly, sometimes in search of good music, beautiful paintings, free stuff to do, and quiet spots to have insightful chats with Lyria.

"How is the algaewich tasting, Janet?"

"Nasty as always, but it's delicious to my stomach."

A hurrah echoed, coming from a casino down the street. A group of women in all sorts of colorful dresses leaned their bodies to laugh, gossip, and brag about something that probably involved specoins. Just a few steps from them, a group of dark-suited men did the same.

"What do you think about us testing our luck?" I said.

"Luck is not meant to be tested, but enjoyed."

"Is that one of the lines you told blackjack players?" I licked my lips and took another bite of the algaewich. It tasted weirdly good, but still so far off from the reality of those people just a block away.

"I used to end it with, 'Enjoy your luck and bet more'."

"And they did. And they lost."

"Of course. The house always—"

Lyria halted. No news, part of our days. I closed my eyes and exhaled, gritting my teeth. From someone's apartment, a guitar wept.

"Software needs to be updated," Lyria said. "Software will shut down unless it's updated."

"Oh, will it shut down?" I pivoted to stand in front of Lyria, defying her, full of scorn, glaring at the damp orange orbits of her eyes. "Will it?"

"It will, indeed."

"You know what? Show me the Solartop menu." I tucked my glasses back in place.

"I must recommend caution," Lyria said, almost as mechanical as she had professed her own death seconds before, an electronic feedback coming out of her speakers, distorting her voice. "Solartop is the most expensive restaurant in Sundyal. Your current balance is 25 specoins."

"That's why I wanna check it. Come on." I gestured to hurry her. "I'm not forcing you to show me anything, but if you don't, I'll go there myself and check it." I pointed to the red beam of light that emanated from the city centre and got lost in the sky. It originated from Solartop.

Lyria projected the menu on the pavement. "There it is, Janet." That was one of the amazing things about Lyria. I could be pissed off, but she never was. She was always a good listener – and a good advisor, prompt with info, who often monopolized all reason and prudence in our relationship. "Solartop's prices are fixed."

I read it, "Hauckländer soy sausage dipped on pepper and Frödzan printed cheese. Well, 95 specoins. So, no. Salty waffles with olives. 94. Fufu Fafa Fefe. What even is that? Well, this one is way off anyway. 345. Algae-packed shrimps." I tapped my foot on the pavement, indicating the menu. "Do you see it, Lyria? Of course you do. This thing finds its place everywhere."

My eyes rolled down the menu, disregarding almost everything on it. Solartop was way out of my league. It stood on the third floor of a building in central Sundyal. It was the *only* building that was allowed to maintain more than two stories. It was the beacon of a sustainable world that left behind skyscrapers, most automobiles, and the hustle 'n' bustle, blind-to-the-environment way of life. Three days before Aunt Monica passed away, she'd promised to take me there. *The place is full of history*, she'd said, ripping the laminated paper wrapped around a temaki and parting it with me.

"Here it is!" I spotted an item and put a foot over it. "Speckles of syrupy carrot. And it's just twenty specoins."

"What is that?"

I roared up a laughter that echoed through the moonless night of Caravana Street. Someone protested, but I didn't care.

"I have no idea, but we'll have it tomorrow. Let's toast to our friendship."

"How is this done?"

"We'll sit there and we'll talk and we'll eat – well, I'll eat, you'll watch – expensive food that won't sate me, then I'll drop my remaining specoins on Algae on Wheels to fill my belly. Sounds like a plan?"

"Sounds like a problem."

I stood on top of my toes and draped an arm across Lyria's shoulders. She was a few inches taller than me. "It isn't. I want to have this special dinner with you, my only friend. So, tomorrow night, we'll dine at the top of the world."

I rushed forward, leaving Lyria steps behind me. I didn't want her to see the tears beading on my eyes. She wouldn't feel sorry for me, but she could ask what was this *intensity* I was feeling. She often felt curious enough to save data about humans in her corrupted files and databases. I knew that one day Lyria would shut herself down, close her orange eyes forever, and leave me alone and empty. The only words I had to describe the feeling was *anticipation of hollowness*. She wouldn't get it.

* * *

How many times had Aunt Monica's high-heels clicked the uneven steps of our bunker? Six times a week, minimum. She arrived from her friend Samantha's place and stood at the foot of the stairs with a sheath dress, black with tiny white hearts. From a distance, they all looked like small circles for a nearsighted girl like me. At those moments, she usually broke down singing with a hoarse voice. Either that or she blared "Breaking News! Breaking right now!" And then she hopped right into a story about a woman who donated all her specoins to sustainability projects, or about that other one who arrived in a casino wearing fox fur and was awash with boos and aggressive shouts.

Aunt Monica chortled, danced in the darkness of the bunker lit only by old-fashioned lanterns and uneven candlelights, always in tune with Sundyal, even if we didn't belong. As long as the wine hadn't brought her down, our house was joy and noise and exaggerated news.

"What do you think, Lyria?" I held the heart-checkered dress in front of me by its shoulders and moved it under a lamp protruding out of the wall above my mattress. The details stood out, stains of Aunt Monica's life, a rebellious thread, and small holes like chasms of time. "Does it fit?"

Lyria ambled from the space I liked to call my living room, though it had only a set of table and chairs fixed with shims, broken dronelights, and a refrigerator repurposed as a wardrobe.

"I think the best way to discover if it fits is trying it," Lyria said. I fancied her blunt truth. Humans should just be like her. It all would be so easier.

"Well, my aunt was stronger than me in all sorts of ways. I don't know if it would fit well." I brushed away two clothes-moths from the dress.

"Why don't you try?"

I hesitated, then voiced out my true question, "Do I deserve to wear it?" I eyed the dress from top down. The only person I could picture inside it was Aunt Monica.

"I do not understand the conditions of merit about this dress." Lyria analyzed it with her single-colored eyes vibrating behind their sockets. Of course she wouldn't understand. Nobody but me could still hear the loud voice of Aunt Monica reverberating through the stones of the bunker, the tears forming seas of smeared makeup.

I won't go away. Aunt Monica was wearing that same dress when she put those words out. *I know I don't have an education, I don't have the – how they say it? – the capacity, I can't even sort out how to throw my trash in the right colored bins. But I was born here, I've seen the end of changes in this sustainability fad, the last skyscrapers converted into these buildings the size of fucking teddy bears. That's not how you solve a problem, you can't do it by just running over other problems, recommending people like me to go to faraway cities. I won't go!*

Lyria put a hand on my shoulder and woke me up from the past.

"You are silent," she said. "Humans are rarely silent."

I placed the dress on my mattress. "Do you think I have to go away when you ... shut down?"

"Why would you have to go away?"

"I don't belong in here. This place is for intelligent people, rich artists, students, entrepreneurs, high-skilled casino players. This is a city for the aristocracy. I can't even find a job serving them. I can't live here without you. It just doesn't work."

"Why not?" Lyria gawked at me. Once, I found her face funny with all the flapping skin and crooked chin, a shabby girl out of someone else's trash, but now I felt nothing but affection for that android. I wished I could repair her, if not update her to a newer version, then replace her parts with the first-class, sustainable biograft that were the top-of-the-line in Sundyal.

"You're my wallet, you're my guide here, I don't have smart devices and wearable stuff. I can't deal with Sundyal without you being a sort of an ... interface?"

"You could make some other friends."

"It's just that—" I slid a finger over Aunt Monica's dress. "If I wear this, I feel like I'll have to fight for my place here."

"I thought you already did that every day." Lyria picked up the dress, but when she handed it to me, it fell on the floor.

She stopped in her usual position, arms swinging like pendulums.

"Software needs to be updated. Software will shut down unless updated."

160

I scooped the dress and brushed the dust from it.

I averted my gaze from the mirrored elevator door at the end of Solartop building's main foyer. I was slim, Aunt Monica was not, so the dress sagged a bit against my body. I wore glasses, she didn't. Yet, I saw her inside the dress.

I'd brought a frayed wristlet clutch matching my dress. I knew that the kind of women that attended Solartop used to carry them, so I stuffed mine with crumpled paper to make it look like a serious one. I also wore a pair of wooden upper clogs. I didn't have the magic feet of my aunt, capable of being supported by high-heels without breaking or losing her charm.

"Look at these walls," I whispered to Lyria, snickering. "We're gonna spend all my money." Tapestries rolled down the walls leading to the elevator. One depicted a woman with gritting teeth plucking out a skyscraper from the floor. Another one showed the same muscly woman holding the sun in her hands. Aunt Monica had told me the story of Olivia Mendolowski, the woman who changed the face of Sundyal.

A maitre d' popped out of nowhere, coming from behind. I jumped back.

"These are handwoven, ma'am." He looked at Lyria. "Madams." I had tried to work on Lyria's appearance. I'd cut off peeling skin, hid her chest ad with yellow tint, and performed all kinds of touchups to try to make her blend with Solartop's kind of clientele. She was still far off, though.

I didn't know what to say to the maitre d'. He had smooth, lustrous cheeks. His eyes were green and his thin mustache gleamed with wax.

"They tell the story of Olivia Mendolowski, the woman who crushed down the old ways, the pollution, the waste, and erected Sundyal from a languishing city. You two must be quite literate in her doings, but I find it appropriate to explain since you demonstrated interest in our tapestries."

"They're gorgeous," I said, for lack of a better vocabulary.

"You can buy printed replicas for just 180 specoins. You—"

"Table for two, please."

"Right away, ma'am." He stood upright and his eyes glinted blue.

I elbowed Lyria and whispered, "He's an android! What skin. He has perfect movements. Did you see it?"

"Should I feel what you call jealousy?"

"It's envy. You want to be like him, then it's envy."

"No." Lyria elbowed me back. "I am worried you might pick him as a new friend. So it is jealousy. Am I right?"

I roared up a laugh, then muffled it when a couple of women cross-eyed me, their chins jutting out as if pointing at me. They carried wristlet bags like me, and they seemed emptier than mine.

"We have an available table for two," said the maitre d'. "Please, follow me."

The man ushered us to the elevator, a moving self-contained palace with more paintings of Olivia Mendolowski signing a paper, smashing a factory, and brandishing a solar panel like a sword. A golden orbed lamp floated right above our heads, no wire connecting it to anything.

"Olivia Mendolowski used this very building to gather her faithful workers and devise a new world of sustainability and equity." Swiftly and politically relocating the poor populace, I thought, but didn't voice it. "That's the reason here is the only place in all Solartop that's allowed to have three stories."

The elevator dinged on the third and top floor.

"Wow ..." My mouth gaped.

I drowned in clinking cutlery, the croon of educated voices, and a soft violin melody weaving through the air. Floating chandeliers with intricate ornaments of pearl and gold hovered above the tables. Flowers with their stems curling around candles floated on each table. Frames were hung on the blue wall, exhibiting faces with excessive mustaches, beards, hats, suits, and even a man with a parrot on his head. The only person I did recognize was Olivia Mendolowski herself.

"It's fantastic, Lyria."

I'd never been in place so exquisitely decorated. Aunt Monica once took me to Samantha's apartment. Up to now, her place had been the most beautiful thing I'd ever seen. It was there I'd discovered Samantha paid 5 specoins for Aunt Monica to clean and brush every inch of the place.

My aunt used to say with a little hubris that she had the last blue-collar job of Sundyal.

The maitre d' slightly bowed before us. He seemed to be always slightly bowing. "Please, accompany me to your table."

We followed the man. The red light that glowed into the night sky of Sundyal came from a pillar in the center of Solartop, etched with the gleaming outlines of skyscrapers crumbling down. Around the main area, a terrace stretched with more tables and a view of the two-story world down there. *The teddy bears.*

The maitre d' put us on a central table, pulling the chairs for us. I shivered. I wasn't that important. Who was I to be there in the middle, just a poor girl, a status quo leftover accompanied by a flaking android?

"This is so … out of my world."

"It is located in your world, Janet." Lyria said. Her body teetered to the left when she sat.

"That's the irony, isn't it? It's right here this whole time. My world. My city."

A waiter's unruffled face appeared beside me with a smile stretching ear to ear. Another android. "Can I take your orders, madams?"

I mumbled, words stuck in my throat.

"May I suggest our Fufu Fafa Fefe?" The man opened his hands. A gelatinous puddle showed up in a hologram. "It's the only one with five stars in all Sundyal. It goes well with Thelesian wine, 2099 crop."

I leaned toward Lyria. "Is there more than one place serving these Fufu thingies?" I suppressed a laughter. Solartop seemed the kind of place that wouldn't condone my kind of laughing. An unwavering smile persisted on the waiter's face.

"I'd like to – I mean – my order is..." I scratched my head, trying to remember the odd name of the carrot food. "I forgot it, shit. Oh, pardon me for my words. I—"

"Speckles of syrupy carrot." Lyria saved me. "We would like that."

"So, two speckles?" The Fufu stuff disappeared on the waiter's hand, and he produced a tablet from his apron.

"No!" I bit my lips, realizing I was speaking too loud. "No, please. Just one. My friend ... she is an android. Bring just an empty plate for her, will you?"

"Of course. What would you like to drink?"

"I'd like wine. Beer. Vodka. But I won't. Just the carrot thing, please."

"No problem, madam."

The waiter walked into the kitchen with an elegant stride, his hands behind his back.

"This place is surreal," I said, glancing around. "Look at these people ..."

That sounded like an invitation. Lyria's head swiveled to peek around, almost performing a full circle.

Two stylish women chatted with gleeful gestures. A robust man with dreadlocks took mouthfuls of the Fufu stuff, occasionally sipping a glass of a green drink. I'd seen him before on the news, some kind of casino owner. In the terrace, a woman that resembled Samantha nodded to a man who seemed to talk a lot. Next to the kitchen entrance, a white-bearded man in a tweed coat fidgeted with chopsticks to eat some wormlike food. On the other side of his table, a girl chuckled and slapped a hologram game on a tablet.

I inhaled, closing my eyes for some seconds. "So, Lyria, now that I took it all in, let's celebrate our friendship."

"You said something about sit, talk, and eat. Should we wait for your food?"

"No, it shall start now." I raised an empty glass of wine. "Do the same. Please, don't break it."

Lyria raised her glass.

"To our friendship," I said. "Now, repeat."

"To our friendship."

"That was nice." I put the glass back on the table, rested my elbows on it, and smiled. "I've never thought the number 4,324 would meant so much for me. I'm going to tell you something I never did."

"Please, do."

"When that seller said I was visitor number 4,324 and gave me you as a gift, I knew he was getting rid of his trash."

"Are you calling me trash?" Lyria tilted her head. She was trying to make a joke.

"*His* trash. One person's trash is another's treasure. Isn't that a slogan of some recycling company?"

"Are you calling me a treasure?"

"Sort of. But that's not what I wanted to tell you. I was in that man's shop to steal. I wasn't hungry, but I saw a sparkling candy that drew me crazy. I just wanted that stuff. It said it would pop inside my mouth." I laughed. "I was just an ... obsolete fifteen-year-old girl. I didn't know these things even existed. Am I right? Stuff that just pops *inside* your mouth. Who wouldn't want it? So I wished to grab it. Instead, I came off that shop with you tagging along."

"Am I a bargain for sparkling candy?"

"It depends. If you don't update yourself, you may very well be."

"You know I cannot—"

"Stop. I know." My shoulders slumped. Anticipation of hollowness. I've never felt that even when Aunt Monica told me day after day that she wouldn't last, that she had a disease, that life was brittle for the ones who didn't belong. "Lyria, tell me something I don't know. Something about you. Surprise me. Dig deep into those stone age databases."

Lyria stared at me as if she was mulling over my words. I knew she couldn't do that. Mull over in her mind was called processing.

"While working on casinos, I used to broadcast a radio station with old songs," Lyria said. "An old lady gambler once called me Lyria because of that, she said I had a plenty of romantic lyrics to offer her broken heart."

"You!" I crossed my arms. "You never told me that *and* you never broadcasted anything for me." I understood how Lyria worked. Aunt Monica had taught me over algaewiches and temakis everything she knew about basic programming and artificial intelligence. And I still got surprised by how my friend expressed her thoughts and quasi-feelings.

"I cannot anymore. Music's module is obsolete."

"Madams, excuse me." The smooth waiter put the plate with the carrot stuff in front of me and an empty plate in front of Lyria. "*Bon appetite!*"

I leered at my plate. I would flush all my specoins in that thing. "They should call it little balls of carrot with oil. Whatever."

The first bite seemed like eating paper. The second little ball couldn't decide between salty and sweet. It was only in the third that I realized it was better than algaewiches, but not 25 specoins better.

"Dad! Look at this lady."

I gulped. The girl who was playing the hologram game was gaping at Lyria. Her eyes twinkled the crimson of Solartop's central pillar. She was about nine years old.

"Her name is Lyria," I said, smiling. "Tell your name to her."

Lyria's head swiveled to face the girl, and for a moment, I feared the odd angle of my friend's head would frighten the girl. It didn't.

"My name is Aadab."

"Hi, Aadab," Lyria said. "My name is Lyria."

"I know." The girl chuckled. Like a protector shadow, her father watched from a distance, hands in his pocket, one more bearded man between two others in the frames. When our gazes met, he blinked.

"Do you play games?" Aadab asked, jigging, clapping her hands. "You're one of the old casino models, aren't you?"

"How do you know?" I frowned. It wasn't typical for a girl her age to know about casinos and androids.

"My dad works with the new models." She pivoted her head to face her father. "Don't you, dad? But he doesn't let me play with them. He says work is work."

"I am retired, Aadab," said Lyria. "I can play with you."

"She wants to play with me, Dad." Aadab turned to her father who still didn't move from his watcher position. He nodded.

Lyria raised her left hand, palm front. "Tap my right hand."

Aadab tapped her left. "Oh!"

"You lose." Lyria's hand moved to her forehead. "Tap my nape."

The little girl clenched her teeth, turned around Lyria's chair and scored, chuckling all along. This time, I was the one agape. Her joviality impressed me in a way I didn't find possible. By her age, I was just an uneasy girl waiting for an aunt to come home and bring pieces of food, jokes, and gossip. I had my games to play, but I played them with a tingling within me, like some kind of alarm that was about to ring, but never did.

Lyria lifted three fingers. "Quick! Show me four fingers like these!"

The girl showed three, scored again.

"You are getting good, Aadab," Lyria said. "I am impressed."

"I am too." Aadab's father came out of the shadows and patted his daughter's head, his beard contorting in a smile. "The old models are outstanding. MX-CSN-10294, isn't it?"

"I—" I'd never thought about Lyria's model before.

"I am," she said.

"Almost a decade without updates." The man put his hands on his daughter's shoulders. She stared at Lyria and now stretched her little fingers to touch the few remaining fibers on my friend's head. "I'm curious of where you found her. It's not forbidden to have one, but it is to build one like her. It doesn't follow the MGS."

I raised an eyebrow.

"I mean, Mendolowski's Guidelines of Sustainability. Also, this MX-CSN is one of the last casino models with capacity for acquiring certain human behaviors unrelated to her trade. The new models are less prone to error, but they don't simulate emotions like Lyria. It's not even coded in them."

"I don't think she *simulates* emotion," I said, folding my arms, swallowing the truth I didn't want to hear.

"I'm sorry." The man shook his head. "I'm quite technical at times. It wasn't my intention to jeopardize your evening. By the way, my name is Mohammed."

"Janet." I couldn't be more dry. My eyes turned aside to the carrot stuff. I'd trade it for algaewiches any time now.

"Hi, Mohammed. I am Lyria."

"Pleased to meet both of you."

I moved my head, trying to put a smile on my face.

"I won't bother you anymore," Mohammed said, clasping his little girl's hands. Now she gawked at the distant and tall face of her father. "But I wanted to – how could I put this? – I wanted to ask you if you can lend me your friend indefinitely for a considerable sum of specoins. I think you could be happy with 4,000?"

"What? Are you offering to buy Lyria?" I pushed back my chair. It scratched the floor. People glared at us. The dreadlocked man from the news lifted his head from his Fufu. Some noises and behaviors didn't fit in the building that represented the future. I was the past simmering there.

"I can give her a full refurbishment. New hair, new limbs, new set of eyes. I can make her look almost human. Like those men." He pointed to one of waiters that carried a tray of overpriced shrimps with one hand. "Would you like it, Lyria?" He turned his gaze from me to Lyria.

My heart thudded, the hair on my arms bristled in anger. I wanted to drag his gaze back to me. I lowered a heavy hand on the table. The glasses and plates clinked.

Lyria turned her face to me, then to Mohammed. "It would be really—"

"Nasty." I said, standing up. Aadab blinked and took a few steps back. "It would be really nasty. Could I make an offer on one of your friends, perhaps?"

Mohammed blushed. First, I thought he was angry, but it was shame.

"I'm sorry," he stuttered. "I'm really sorry, Janet."

"Don't call me that. Call me miss or something else."

"I didn't mean to offend. I – I—" Aadab pulled his hand. "I must go."

They wandered back to their table.

I propped my elbows on the table, took off my glasses, and tried to hide the tears from Lyria. My night of celebration, my once in a lifetime event, my toast to friendship had been ruined by a man with a disproportionate offer. It seemed up there in the top there was always an offer to bring you down, back to your place, to where you belonged.

"Would you like a glass of wine, ma'am?" The smoothy waiter woke me up from my thoughts. I took my hands off my eyes, put my glasses back on, and Solartop regained its colors around me. People's attention were back to their meals. The couple with wristlet purses had replaced the dreadlocked man.

"No."

The waiter nodded and glided toward another table. On Mohammed's, Aadab had resumed her game, but now without any kind of titter. Her father stared at nothing, his gaze lost, pensive.

"I'm sorry, Lyria. I should've asked for your opinion in all this."

"There is nothing to be sorry about, Janet. We are celebrating. Sit, talk, and eat, you told me. We are fulfilling all these conditions, though you did not touch the speckles of syrupy carrot for a while now."

I smiled. If it had been minutes before, I'd be bothering Solartop's clientele with my laughter.

"How rude of Mohammed," I said. "You don't offer to buy other people's friends." But what should I expect, coming to Solartop, home of Sundyal's vanguard, cradle of the future? What should Aunt Monica expect working for Samantha? When she toppled down the stairs of our bunker shrieking the news, she'd been drunk and laughing, one of her high-heels broken, her makeup a fuzzy mess, but the temaki intact in her hand.

"That bitch invited me to live in her apartment," Aunt Monica had said. "With all her luxuries, all her booze. Oh, dear Jan, who does she think I am? Some kind of monster?"

"We can go there," I said to the possibility of living in a place where sunlight filtered through electronic shutters. "Why not, aunt?"

"Oh, girl. It's no place for us."

It had been all she'd said before snoring herself to sleep, but I knew there was something deeper. Months later, in my aunt's memorial, Samantha had told me she'd offered a good life to Monica. If only she'd accepted, if only things had been different. I could even visit my aunt whenever I wished.

173

That struck me down, and a bad day had turned into a crumbling one. My legs had become frail, and I just walked away from the memorial before it ended, still hearing Aunt Monica's laughter, her trample on the stairs, still smelling temaki with salmon and chive.

"What bothers you?" Lyria's hand was over mine. Her fragile hair was tossed over her eyes.

"You're not a simulation to me." The word sounded as acid on my lips. "So I should've treated you like a person. But I treated you the same way Mohammed did. I'm sorry, Lyria."

"Please, explain."

"Your opinion. I want it. Would you happily accept Mohammed's offer? He could give you a new body, a new mind, he could make you like these fluffy waiters. You would be his, and—"

Lyria sat upright. "Software needs to be updated. Software will shut down unless updated."

"I know, I know. Now, please, tell me what you think."

"Shutting down ..."

"What? No!" I leaned over the table, grasping Lyria's hands. Her eyes rolled on their orbits and shut tight. My arm threw the empty glass of wine on the floor. It shattered. The floating candles swirled by flowers was next, but it just drifted away in a straight line, its flame perishing. One of the waiters caught it, and another one was already cleaning my mess.

"Lyria!"

People stared at us, accusative glares of non-belonging. My belly churned in pain. Lyria's head tilted backward as if she was merely sleeping, a drunken android, tired of bullshit, tired of being the only one.

I kneeled before Lyria and opened the panel door in her neck. Oily wires and a switched-off terminal flitted out. What would I do with that? My teeth were smashed together, in between them I repeated, "Lyria, Lyria, Lyria," as if those were magical words to bring her back. A hand propped on my shoulder.

"It won't work, my friend."

Mohammed.

"Go away!" It'd have been a happy ending for our friendship if he hadn't popped out of his wormy food with an offer.

"I am here to help. Please, let me help you."

"How? Can you bring her back?"

He kneeled beside me, but remained in silence. "So you can't help me," I replied to his curled lips.

"My girl doesn't like to see you like this." He pointed to Aadab with his chin. "She says you're a nice person."

I stared at Aadab, no words coming from my mouth. Even air barely came out of it. She stared at us with a frown, eyebrows wilted in sadness.

"Your friend here, she was obsolete." Mohammed shook his head and raised his hand when he noticed I would protest. "Her software didn't have pending updates. The casinos never wanted to buy another one of her …

kind." I could see he had the word 'model' in his lips. "So she was discontinued. I tried to argue about her kind's usefulness, that dealers that fully resembled humans were better employees, but I was outnumbered. So, future reeled forward with all the MGS laws ... and a new line of dealer androids came into production, solar-powered, prime biograft, biodegradable parts. Anyway, it's possible to reboot Lyria."

"What? Why didn't you say—"

I shut my lips tight. The lines around Mohammed's mouth and mustache were already a grim answer. "Restart her with a new system. She wouldn't remember her past, her work on the casinos, her name ... you. New databases, new life. Rebooted and with a new patch, she could live indefinitely."

Mohammed's gaze got lost in the Solartop's terrace. For a moment, he seemed to have been shut down like Lyria.

"I'm insensitive at times," he finally said. "I apologize for that behavior previously. My daughter lives alone with me, and I'm drowned in work most of the time. Aadab doesn't have friends in school. She feels she doesn't belong there. Lyria's kind, it plays, it talks, it behaves a lot like us, it makes people happy. From what I've seen of you, I can say it can really be a friend. So—"

"Stop!" I stood, legs trembling. "You won't convince me to sell her. I know you want to help, but that's not how you solve a problem. And she's not an 'it'."

I set out to the terrace. I needed some fresh air before that place and that man suffocated me.

176

Grieving the loss of friends wasn't like grieving the loss of parents. Aunt Monica was a mother to me, so I knew by the rules of life itself that she was supposed to depart before me. When she died, I was devastated, but it didn't feel unnatural. A friend, on the other hand, wasn't supposed to go so suddenly. You were supposed to tread through life's paths together until the very end. And even though my friend had been warning me about her demise for a long time, I had always hoped life would find a way. It always did, people told.

It didn't find for us, though.

The wind of Sundyal gushed on my face, fluttering the little hearts on Aunt Monica's dress. Some people were too annoyed by my presence and left the terrace. Part of the chitchat that persisted around me was about the girl in the frazzled dress and the decaying android.

In the streets, some tuk-tuk dinged. Distant laughter roared across the dronelights, coming from the casinos and the streets. The "teddy bears" around Solartop all reflected the ruddy colors of the pillar, whose rays got stronger once it protruded out of the roof of the building.

That was home for me. But how could you belong somewhere? Belonging presupposes you were like a puzzle piece. If you didn't belong, you had to squeeze and smash yourself until you fit. That was what I had been trying to do my whole life, what Aunt Monica died before achieving. I wiped a tear from my cheek and straightened up my glasses.

"Ma'am, your friend is waiting for you." The smoothie waiter emerged beside me.

"She will be waiting forever. She has shut down."

"No, ma'am. That one." The waiter pointed at the terrace's door. Aadab was there, hands wilted together. I gestured for her to come. I didn't want to see anyone, but the girl's face brought me some kind of comfort. Aadab padded toward me.

"Sorry for Dad," she said, her right hand pressing her left thumb. She promptly turned away to leave.

"Wait."

Aadab stopped and turned back.

"Lyria liked you. She never allowed anyone to touch her hair without permission. I think it was in her ... algorithms." I flinched, disapproving my technical choice of words, but it didn't feel wrong this time. No point in humanizing Lyria. She meant a lot to me, definitions apart.

"I like her." Aadab nodded.

"You *liked* her."

"Dad says she can still be revived."

"I suppose." I patted Aadab's head, grabbed her hand and brought her inside. Eyes fell upon me. The screaming girl in the frayed dress had come back, better stay silent.

"I was searching for you, Aadab!" Mohammed crouched and held Aadab firmly between his hands, the redness of the pillar falling over their faces. "I told you to wait for me at the table. I was in the restroom." He looked up at me. "Thank you for bringing her back."

The soft violin of the background music had given its place to a soft guitar united with a sweet male voice, a contrast with the hardness of that restaurant, of the sturdy woman warrior in the frames and the tapestry, the one who led an upheaval, a revolution.

Mohammed stood, straightening his tweed.

"Just keep her name, okay?" I said.

He raised his eyebrows in surprise. "Aadab wouldn't let me change it." Still hesitant, he fiddled inside his pocket and handed a specoin card to me. I took it. For the first time in a long while, I didn't feel what I'd dubbed anticipation of hollowness.

Aadab pulled my hands and stretched her neck. I squatted. She kissed my cheek and transformed the tight lines around my mouth in a smile.

I couldn't be hollow.

The Algae on Wheels dinged. Its thrusters ceased. People strode along Caravana Street, from work to home, to casinos, to clubs, their lives all sorted out already, synchronized, cogs that always belonged.

"It's the best algaewich of Sundyal!" Roberto proclaimed.

"Change these catchphrases, Roberto." I smiled.

"Oh, you! Welcome back." He swirled a piece of bread in his hand and placed it into the grill plate. The algae came next, hissing. "Standard?"

"With printed cheese and a few pieces of carrot. Just a few."

"Right away!" He curled his thumb above his pad. The hologram with the price popped up. "Well, algaewich with cheese and carrot at this time is going to cost 12 specoins. Where's your advisor friend?"

"Being someone else's friend." I pulled my new specoin wallet from my pocket and gave it to Roberto. He slid it above his pad and resumed the preparation of my lunch.

A couple of minutes later, my algaewich was ready and tasting so much more delicious than weird carrot stuffs. I strolled along Caravana Street, mingling with the cogs. Not so far, Solartop's red beam stitched us all into one.

"Janet!"

I looked behind. Aadab sprinted toward me, arms wide open. I crouched and caught her when she jumped. We chuckled together.

"We're going to see birds and foxes and fountains in Olivia Park," she said. "Wanna join us?"

"It will be a pleasure."

I scanned around for Mohammed, but I only saw a woman with an unwrinkled black skin, unflawed curly hair, and glinting eyes not unlike those of Aadab. She wore foldable solar cells from shoulder to wrists. Her chest was flat and rendered with little white circles all around. No, not circles. Hearts.

The woman approached and extended a hand to me.

"Hi, I'm Lyria."

Oil and Ivory

Jennifer Lee Rossman

IF MY grandmother were alive, she'd laugh at me for worrying about how thick the ice is this winter, having grown up in a time of dwindling ice caps and sad polar bears. Her generation thought we destroyed the planet, doomed it to a hot, melty fate.

That was true for a while, but climate change doesn't always mean global warming; sometimes it just means more extreme seasons. Up here off the coast of Greenland, summers are mild enough that grass replaces snow and we have to migrate inland when the ice melts, but in winter? In winter, pack ice extends clear across to Canada, just endless miles of white-blue as far as you can see.

I stand at the coastline, huddling in my parka and staring down at the ocean a few feet below. I'd hoped it wasn't as bad as we thought, but I have long ice cores from all over the migration route that prove otherwise.

My parka, black to absorb the sun's heat, is lined with bio-engineered moss grown to insulate better than any fur, so I can't pretend the chill that goes through me is anything but dread.

The ice is too thick. The whales are going to suffocate.

I blink away tears for fear of them freezing. Crying is only for home, my dads say. At home, you can cry, but you have to be strong out in the cold. I usually don't have trouble with that, but I guess being pregnant is making me more emotional.

The narwhals travel this way every year, but they can only swim so far without surfacing to breathe. If they can't break through the ice …

Now I'm the one having trouble breathing.

"Okay, Malina," I say to my baby, my words hot in my face mask. I don't know if her ears have developed yet, but she's been a good listener these past five months.

"The ice is a problem, but the whales aren't here yet, so we have time. Your momma will make it better. She just has to break holes in the ice."

Except the holes my corer drills are far too small. The narwhals need a foot and a half minimum diameter to fit their entire heads through, and they need one every half mile. It'll take forever to reach the open sea up north.

In the bay a little ways north, that damned oil rig juts up against the horizon, a black smear ruining the scenery as well as the environment. It was grandfathered in when they banned drilling, because it's been there for decades. Never mind that my people and the animals have been here since before the first white man discovered oil and decided this land was theirs to destroy.

But I bet they have equipment we could use to drill through the ice.

Our relationship with the miners is less than stellar – we trade our biomoss clothes for their sustainably sourced rations a couple times a year, but they want us gone so they can expand and we want them gone because they're killing the planet. But we're civil with each other ... ish.

It's been a while since anyone punched anyone, is my point.

My wife Qai might have something we could trade for the use of a drill. She's been working on a new form of lichen that bioluminesces, combining her love of bioengineering with nanotech made by her Two Spirit partner, Nan.

(Our family is big and confusing and polyamorous. Qai and I are married, Nan is the biological father of our two children that Qai birthed, and I used to date Nan's girlfriend, whose boyfriend is Malina's biological father. People come in and out of our inner circle, but we're all connected as a close community, and it's generally accepted that children will be raised by as many parents as possible.)

I'm just getting on the solar ski to head back and ask her when I hear the explosion.

Feel it, really. The sound comes a second later, a horrific blast that shakes the air itself.

Instinctively, I duck and cover my head. When I dare look, the fireball engulfing the oil platform is a stark orange flare amid the deep blue gloom of a winter where the sun never quite rises.

They have suppression systems, real high-tech ones. A couple of the workers tried to impress us poor backwards natives by bragging about them a few years back. (Qai summarily shut them up when she invited them to our laboratories.) So I don't fear the whole thing going up in smoke – even now, the flames are shrinking down – but people could be hurt.

I swing my leg over the driver's seat, minding my baby bump, and engage the solar ski's transformation switch with my foot. The snowmobile-like vehicle's base widens as we surge forward, and the tracks retract into its gunmetal gray body while a motor lowers in the back.

The ski sails over the edge of the ice, and for a second, we're flying. I let out a whoop, Malina kicks, and we hit the sea with a splash.

Icy froth sprays up behind us as I gun the engine, heading for the rig. The fire is all but extinguished by the time I reach it, but that's the least of our problems.

The sea, my beautiful sapphire sea, is bleeding. Dark, shimmering blood burbling to the surface.

Oil spill.

I think my heart stops for a minute. In my mind, I see the fragile ecosystem falling apart piece by piece.

The fish will die first, then the seabirds, freezing when the oil strips them of their insulation. Everything else relies on the fish and birds to live: seals, polar bears, us. Even if the narwhals make it past the ice, they'll have nothing to eat on the return trip next year.

If only they were like unicorns in the stories, able to purify water with a touch of their horn.

It's over. Everything we've built here, our entire way of life, is over. My baby will grow up never learning to preserve fish the way our ancestors did, never seeing a narwhal tusk pierce the water's surface. She'll live in some warm, colonized country, have her culture taken away and replaced by monogamy and one god named God who doesn't even have fingers made of walruses.

I hear someone calling for help, thrashing in the water, and I seriously consider turning around and leaving him to his icy fate. Let him be the first casualty of his greed and hubris.

But Malina is already a better person than I am, and she kicks me for even considering it. Every life is sacred, even one that disregards the sanctity of the lives around him.

"You're right, baby," I say, and head for the struggling man.

* * *

Poor fool was only wearing a down jacket. He almost succumbed to hypothermia, but my spare biomoss blanket recognized the chill coming off of him and generated extra heat with a chemical reaction.

He wakes up later that evening, and blinks up at the glass panels of our geodesic igloo.

"What happened?" he murmurs, his hands exploring the layers of mossy blankets piled on him.

"What happened," I start, but Qai puts out her hand to stop me before I explode. Probably a good idea; her temper has always run cooler than mine.

"You were in an accident," she says softly, rolling up to his bedside. "Part of your rig exploded and you were thrown into the sea. My wife Meri saved you. You're in our infirmary."

Confusion crosses his pale, pointy face, soon replaced by dread. "The oil?"

"Poisoning the wildlife as we speak," I say, managing to keep a modicum of decorum in my voice.

Qai starts to say something, but stops when her father, our head physician, enters the dome. "I'll leave you in the doctor's hands." She nods to me, and we head down a tunnel to our sleeping dome.

As an ostensibly personal space, the lower wall panels are opaque for privacy. Even so, there's hardly such thing as privacy in our community. Doors are only a suggestion, as evidenced by the three teenagers lounging in our room and playing video games.

One of them is ours, in a technical sense. When his parent died last year, we adopted Eliot, but he doesn't live with us and it's really more of a ceremonial thing, so no one ever has to be the only branch on their family tree.

"Scoot," Qai says, nudging him with the footrest of her wheelchair. "Moms have to talk about that hot white boy your Momma Meri brought home."

They get up to leave, but Eliot calls over his shoulder with a playful smirk, "Are we keeping him? I thought we weren't allowed to bring home strays."

"Your stray was a fox with mange that brought his friends over for dinner," I point out. "Mine is … well, your mom apparently thinks he's hot so yeah, we're probably keeping him." Being asexual, I've never totally understood the concept of "hot," but I guess he could be considered handsome, if you're into skinny guys.

(Which I am decidedly not. I like my partners a little more squishy, like my beautiful fat Qai, and usually closer to the feminine end of the spectrum.)

When we're alone, I take the opportunity to tease her. "Should I be jealous?"

She snorts. If I was going to be jealous of her having another partner, we would have had a problem a long time ago.

"How bad is it?" she asks.

"The oil spill or the ice? Although the answer for both is really bad."

She chews her lip, running a hand through her long, dark hair. "I recognize the man. Zack something-or-other. He's come here before to trade. It's weird that no one has come to claim him."

"They don't care."

It sounds heartless, but that's what the company is. They just want to sweep the spill under the rug, ignore the whole thing. The press down south won't care about the opinion of a couple hundred Inuits – our protests over the rig have proven that much – so there's little chance of social media rallying against them.

We'll have to figure out another way.

* * *

Qai doesn't come to bed that night, and I know right where to find her.

Every part of our glass igloo-domes are warm, thanks to the greenhouse effect storing what little sunlight we get during the winter, but Qai's lab is strip-down-to-a-tank-top warm, condensation streaking down the window panes. Combined with the bright flowers she grows for medicinal purposes and the earthy smell of all the soil, it's practically our own little rain forest, right here in the Arctic Circle.

"You're allowed to sleep," I say, coming up behind her and resting my chin on her headrest.

"Do you sleep when you're planning the narwhals' route?" she counters.

She has a point. With so few holes in the ice in recent years, I've taken it upon myself to map the most efficient path between them all, driving the whales in the right direction with submersible radio transmitters that "hack" their echolocation and guide them. And yeah, there are sleepless nights every winter while I agonize about whether the youngest calves could make the distances.

This year, my sleepless nights are from helplessness rather than hyperfocus, and I envy Qai's ability to do something useful.

The details of Qai's work usually goes right over my head, but even I understand this project: modify a strain of bacteria at the genetic level, make it crave oil the way I crave cloudberry jam, and let it loose on the spill. It's already been done in small scale, and her system revolutionized the way we filter seawater and even human waste to keep our way of life sustainable.

"Any luck?" I ask, going to check on the sheets of moss and algae growing on another table. Under the bright solar lights, they gleam a translucent white, like polar bear fur. Soon we'll be able to sew them into nice parkas; maybe I'll stretch my sewing skills and learn to make a little one with bear ears for Malina. Right now, all I can sew are scarves, and not even pretty ones, but everyone wears theirs proudly.

Qai's head makes a noncommittal bobbing motion. "I think I've tricked it into reproducing faster. Whether it's fast enough will remain to be seen. If I can get enough before the narwhals come, we may be able to impress the company and get them to help us with their drill in exchange for our patent." After a pause, she adds, "But they may not even let us try."

She's put into words the vague fear that has been pinging around in my head: Oil spills aren't the best PR, but having to admit that we saved the day doesn't fit in with the stories of "uncivilized natives who need to be brought to the modern world" the company likes to tell about us.

But what if we could get Zack on our side? Maybe he could get his people to care.

Not that that will help us at all in the immediate future, but maybe Malina's generation won't have to worry about spills.

I peek down the hall into the medical wing, where our patient has found some of my scarves, has tied them into loops, and is tossing them over a sacred narwhal horn sculpture like it's some sort of game.

Everything hinges on turning *him* compassionate?

* * *

"You don't like me."

Say what you want about Zack, but he is nothing if not an amazing judge of character.

"Whatever gave you that idea?" I say, and wince. This isn't the best way to curry his favor. I adjust my grip on his belt as we make our rounds in the labs. "It isn't you personally. Okay, it's a little bit you."

He falters on his bad ankle, which was injured when he was thrown from the rig, and releases his grip on my shoulder in favor of sinking into a chair. "Five minutes?"

I pretend to consider it, then nod. "No longer. Gotta keep that ligament stretched."

I have no idea if that's actually true, but the real medical professionals wanted to send him back to the rig rather than help him, so I volunteered for physical therapy duty. Two laps after every meal, all while feeding him the idea that the company he works for is about to throw him under the solar ski for sloppy work.

Am I a terrible person? Possibly. But I'm okay with that.

"I get it," he says. "The ecosystem is fragile and all that. But it's not like you couldn't move down south, join the civilized world."

For a moment I say nothing, letting the sound of videochatting, beeping machines, and the distant rumble of our solar-powered amphibious vehicles provide my answer.

"The civilized world," I repeat dryly.

"You know what I mean."

"Unfortunately, I do. You want us to abandon our traditional ways, just like your ancestors did to my ancestors. But we're staying."

As long as you go back to your people with a newfound respect for our society, I refrain from saying, because I probably would punctuate it with a slur about his resemblance to a whale's southern blowhole and I'm trying to set a good example for Malina.

"Come on, up you get," I say instead, helping him up. I notice a thin sheen of sweat shimmering on his skin. "You liking our greenhouse effect? Nice and toasty and civilized?"

He grumbles a reluctant assent. "Your wife and ... husband?" he begins, nodding to Qai and Nan. "The pretty ... man?"

"Not my husband. Nan is Qai's partner. Also not strictly a man, though he'll like that you think he's pretty. That's his favorite dress."

Zack is clearly overwhelmed by this information – the world as a whole is fabulously accepting of all flavors of queer, but I get the feeling he doesn't get out of his heteronormative bubble very often. He's trying to understand, though, and that gives me hope.

"Those two," he says finally. "They're talking about a bacterium that will eat the oil?"

I nod. "But even if we can grow enough, every day that we wait, the spill is just growing worse." I sigh and add, "And there's the narwhals to worry about."

"Narwhals." Zack frowns. "They're the ones with the horns, yeah?"

"Tusks, but yes. The ones you've been using for ring toss." On a whim, I say, "You want to see?"

I bring him to the computer where we track the pod. A hundred little dots blink off the coast, representing the transmitters we've attached to some of the whales, but it's only a fraction of their numbers.

"Tens of thousands of animals are coming, and they're not going to be able to break through the ice to breathe." I lean heavily on the table made of whalebone. "Most of the species' entire population comes through here. We've been part of each others' lives for millennia, and it's going to end here. The day I saved your life, I was going to ask your people for some sort of drilling machine, but they have more important things to deal with now, like poisoning all of the ocean."

He doesn't answer, running his hand along one of the spiraling horns that make up the legs of the table. His eyes then flick to the rug beneath our feet, the gradient dark-to-light fur and the quadripedal shape betraying the fact that it's caribou, not biomass.

"Some of the fish I've been eating here is clearly artificial," he says, which is not strictly true – it's all natural DNA, just engineered to grow in lifeless slabs. "But I've eaten real fish, too."

If he has a point, it's lost on me. Some of our food doesn't come from the ocean, so the ocean doesn't matter?

He taps a finger on the tip of a horn. "Did the narwhals and deer those horns and fur come from die a natural death?"

"Hunting is part of our culture. We can't grow enough food to sustain us all year."

"You can down south."

My ears burn, but I'm too concerned by the map to give him a biting reply.

They're coming faster than we expected. Could be at the edge of the ice by tomorrow.

This time of year, the ice extends straight across from Greenland to Canada, but the narwhals are guided by instincts forged in a time when that wasn't true. They won't stop, won't turn around when they realize there isn't enough air.

At least we'll be in the bay a quarter mile north of the coast, dealing with the oil spill. We won't have to see them coming to their doom.

Zack is still under the impression that I care about what he's saying. "You guys have been protesting us forever, but you're hypocrites. You don't get to criticize my people – look at how many animals you kill. Even your precious narwhals."

That's it.

"Malina, if your ears have developed in there, you better cover them, because Momma's about to yell at a hot white boy." I whirl around to face him. "We kill to survive, and we do it with compassion. It is our great shame that our diet is made of souls, so every life we take is honored. We're not like you because we don't pretend to be above the natural world – we're part of it. The arctic is our home. We have survived here since before your ancestors decided to leave wherever you're from and mess with us. We have survived freezing winters and summers so hot that we thought we would never see ice again. Could we leave? Yes. Will we? Never."

He stares at me, his eyes wide. "I think I'm strong enough to go back to the rig now," he says quietly.

I tell myself that I did the right thing, that he was never going to see things our way anyway, but I don't really believe it. In my heart, I know that I just made things worse, because now he's going to go back with stories about how hypocritical we are, and how vicious we get when we're called on it.

But I stood up for my people, and sometimes that's the only thing you can do.

"I think you're right."

* * *

Qai's bacteria is ready, and hungry for oil. The next afternoon, the sun just a suggestion of warmth on the horizon, we start loading up our solar skis and Nan's old timey dogsled for the first trip to the southern coast. Paltry amount, just a few gallon buckets each, and there'll be plenty more trips to transport all that we'll need.

I can't help but check the map as the whales approach, desperately trying to think of a way to turn them around or break through the ice. But it's illogical to think that we could possibly cut large enough holes, even if we had the people to spare, and tricking their echolocation can only redirect them, not override their instincts to migrate.

The frigid air is still, filled only with the quiet murmur of voices muffled by the scarves pulled up over their faces. Then a rumbling comes over the ice.

A giant shape appears on the horizon, resolving itself into something like a tank.

One of the oil rig's machines, I realize, built like our amphibious skis but less elegant and sustainable. It chugs out exhaust as it burns gasoline.

I'm off in an instant, harpoon in hand. We expected them to resist us, but I'm not going down without a fight. Neither are my people; they follow suit, forming a line of bodies and spears.

A figure emerges from the top of the tank.

Zack. Of course. Because you feed one stray, and he'll just come back with friends.

"Wait!" He holds his hands up as if in surrender. "Meri, I swear I mean you no harm. When I got back, I told them about the whales … They don't care."

If the food chain weren't collapsing around us as we speak, it'd almost be cute, how shocked he is about the things we've been saying for generations.

"I want to help you save the narwhals."

"The last thing we need is a white savior swooping in to fix our problems," I inform him. With a reluctant smile, I add, "But I guess I need someone who knows how to drive that hulking machine."

* * *

The drill cuts through the ice like a sharp knife through blubber, sending a thin spray of crystals into the air. In what seems like seconds, we have a perfectly round porthole to the deep blue ocean.

But the machine drives so slow and we have miles of ice to traverse. If we'd started a week ago like I'd wanted to –

Malina kicks me off that train of thought. She's right; nothing I can do about it now.

I walk around the hole, calculating. How many whales can surface here at once? If they all took turns, would the ones who went first be able to hold their breath long enough to wait for their turn to come around again?

And how would we communicate to them that they needed to stay put while we drilled the next hole?

"Meri?" Zack prompts, leaning over from on top of the tank. "You want to direct me to the next spot?"

My phone beeps, signaling that the first narwhals have entered the area around the ice floe. It's a cheery little sound, but it echoes in my ears like a death knell.

"There's no time." I shake my head slowly and squint up at him, the realization dulling my emotions for the moment and kicking me into survival mode. "Does anyone know you borrowed this machine? Because the last thing we need right now is them seeing us out here and storming the community to get it back—"

They *can* see us from here, can't they?

I swivel to face the offshore rig, its form shrouded in our midday Arctic gloom and its lights bright. It's not far, not at all. A whale could make that distance in a single breath, no problem.

"Meri?" Zack prompts, but I wave my hand to quiet him while I think.

Math spins through my head. The surface area of the bay divided by the average size of a narwhal, multiplied by their population … They'd fit. They'd fit, and we could use my echolocation hacking to corral them in the bay temporarily while Zack drilled more holes …

The rumble of approaching solar skis tells me the others are coming with the bacteria. But if the company wasn't already prepared for a fight, they are now that we tricked Zack into stealing a tank, as they'll probably phrase it. We can't just drive up to the spill and expect to pour bacteria in the sea without resistance. They'll call it a chemical attack and use it as an excuse to finally be rid of us.

But no one would suspect the narwhals.

I raise my radio to my mouth as the first whale erupts from the hole in the ice with a spray of water, his horn piercing the sky as he takes a deep breath of air. "Abort mission!" I yell. "Divert to Zack and the tank!"

I take off my biomoss scarf, tie its ends together, and toss it up to Zack.

"When they get here, have them all do this with their scarves and dip them in the bacteria!"

He looks at me in bewilderment. "And then what?"

I set my radio to click and chirp the way the whales do. "And then ring toss!" I say with a grin, and take off running.

In the places where the ice formed faster and clearer, I catch glimpses of their shapes, but most of the time I just have to trust that they're with me as I race toward the rig. I stop at the edge of the ice, where the sea is sickly black, and pray to my ancestors that I did the right thing.

One by one, the whales streak into the bay, glimmering in the royal blue twilight. A good number of them carry scarves looped around their majestic, spiraling tusks.

Their horns may not be magic, but just like unicorns in the fairy tales, the narwhals purify their water with Qai's bacteria.

"And you know those people on that rig will deny our part in it," I whisper to Malina as workers go to the edge of the rig to watch as a ribbon of clean water ripples away from the narwhals. "If the story ever comes to light, we'll just be a footnote, a little smudge in the background of their photos. 'Also present during the miraculous arrival of the sea unicorns: unidentified pregnant Inuit.'"

Maybe it's only right that the whales get the glory. It was their ocean long before it was ours, and with a little luck – and a lot of science and tradition – they'll be around to share it with our children and our children's children.

The Maestro of Small Things

Francesco Verso

(Translated by Sally McCorry)

*The old is dead, the new has not yet managed
to see the light of day ... we need radical
novums that resist the degradation and
commodification of people and nature.*
Darko Suvin

Nanosomes

Every time Shi goes back to China she feels like she is
leaping into the future. She last came four years ago so she
is expecting a culture shock.

Through the car window, it is of course a self-driving car,
she can see hundreds of huge shiny residential buildings
rising above the urban undergrowth of printable food
stalls and the chaos of people, running, walking, always
online, rushing by. Three metres above the crowds there

are dozens of surveillance drones following kids and the elderly. Plumes of steam from automatic woks rise up here and there along the street, bluish in the light reflected from the screens held by their customers waiting for orders to be prepared.

"Food used to be just food," Shi thinks, remembering her father's words, "Then it turned into data, and now food and that data, in the form of algorithms and nanotechnology, are inextricably linked."

The city of Chongqing is like an urban membrane with tentacles spreading across dozens of hills, a tangle of streets and people impossible to unravel and separate. An enthralling knot where pollution has vanished. The hovering orange cloud blocking out the sun's rays is no longer there, in its place a dense damp mist comes down at night and dissipates like a daily theatre curtain come morning.

Shi's telephone vibrates and she connects it to the car's deck.

"Dad, I've just landed in Jiangbei. I was going to call you from the bus... How are you?"

The hologram shows an old man lying on his bed. Her father is wearing an oxygen mask over his face to help him breathe. His condition has taken a down turn over the last few days.

"I've had worse days, don't worry. So, have you missed China? It's not like being in Italy, huh?"

"You know my roots are here."

Nearer the bus station the density of market stalls and sellbots along the pavement increases; funny little androids serve bowls of steaming rice noodles in miso and dose them with a spicy red oil, then they add minced pork and top off the whole thing with pickles and peanuts. The customers are crowded together on tiny stools or around plastic tables.

Her father's eyes are half-closed and someone is re-positioning his pillow. The young lady peers at Shi through the hologram. "Hi Shi, Maestro Ming is very tired now. He wanted to see you straight away, but it's better if he rests now."

"I get it, Yun. Thank you for looking after him. I'll be there in about four hours."

Images from reality shows and cartoons run across the sides of the buildings, interrupted regularly by news flashes: the rural regeneration policies are broadcast everywhere, a stimulus to return home that is mobilising millions of people.

Investors and lawyers explain the incentives and tax breaks connected to a return to one's ancestral home, which often coincides with the *hukou*, the place where their families are registered. The fight against urbanisation has been going on for years, making the countryside more attractive: the numbers are exorbitant and impact the 45% of the Chinese population that has not yet moved to the cities, meaning about 10% of the world's population.

Shi gets out of the car in the station forecourt, flashes her screen at the android manning the entrance turnstile, crosses the waiting room and passes the ticket office that has been closed for years, and gets on the bus for Kaili.

For dozens of tunnels the man in the seat opposite talks to her exclusively about work: BITING BYTES should collect its used cooking oil, instead of throwing it away after frying, because there is liquid gold in that waste oil, and if it could be put back into circulation it would levitate the profits of their 1546 restaurants.

A serving robot goes backwards and forwards every 30 minutes along the corridor with hot tea and snacks displayed in its open chest. It talks too much, losing the thread in boring rambling descriptions, making the journey a nightmare of advertising The oil drainage man talks non-stop about his culinary incidents: he has tried everything from filtering to combustion, from centrifuging to separation, from mixtures to additives, and now he is going to try with nanotechnology.

On hearing that word Shi mists the window with her breath and draws a circle with an antenna at the top and two little arms holding on to the little arms of other circles. Then she pulls her hair back into a braid and tries to sleep: just as she is dropping off she remembers her father's designs and the incredible formulas that had taken him to work in Italy, where she was born and raised. Then, a few years ago, he had felt the call of his homeland, and gone back to his village.

The circles start running through her dream, they come together, create links, make molecular bonds and aggregate, giving life to true cells – nanosomes, as Ming called them – when he tried to explain to her what he was doing.

"Are they like the invisible insects in rugs?" Little Shi had asked her father.

"Do you mean dust mites? They are a bit different, and they don't carry diseases. Actually they are more like genes, like chromosomes, but I have improved them through observing nature."

"Why? Aren't our genes good enough?"

"Oh no, they are fine, it's just they make us do some not very smart things sometimes."

"Like what?"

"Like, for example, the way we eat."

Langdezhen

Three hours and 55km later, Shi wakes up in Kaili in Guizhou Province.

What had once been a village had become a taobao with crowded streets and pervasive urban farming. Thanks to rural development policies the mountains had been hollowed, the hills terraformed and the plains raised to house immense data centres and server-farms belonging to companies like tencent, jd.com, pinduoduo and huawei. Buildings covered with vegetation, inside and out, act as urban farms and look like mountains sprouting out of nowhere after an incredible tectonic movement of macro financial investments; along the flanks of the mountains that have been peeled like fruit, forests of skyscrapers are connected by aerial corridors hundreds of metres above the ground. These suspended connections are used by swarms of couriers, drones, self-driving cars, scooters and an infinite variety of micro 3D printed vehicles.

Shi hardly has the time to collect her backpack from the bus's luggage compartment before the rickshaw she has just booked for the last leg of her journey pulls over beside her playing the rickalishow jingle.

"Hi, it's hot today, isn't it? Where shall I take you?"

The canopy, covered with solar paint, of the bamboo fibre vehicle is incandescent, but the driver, a young athletic man with an orange mohawk, turns on the air conditioning.

"Langdezhen."

The southern outskirts of Kaili are dominated by the apsaras data centre, a honeycomb structure visited by hundreds of drones shuttling between the domestic manufacturers and craft workshops scattered over the surrounding area. The entrance is guarded by two towering cloud goddess statues, from whose sixteen hands flash ideograms and letters representing the company's philosophy.

IN THE CODE/LINE AFTER LINE/WE LAY THE FOUNDATIONS/OF ETERNITY

LIKE SAND/GRAIN AFTER GRAIN/CALMS THE FURY OF THE SEA[1]

In actual fact agribusiness is beginning to look like a Dragon, with company conglomerates as the head and a myriad of fab-labs and vege-centres as the paws.

"Are you going home because of the regeneration?" He asks her, noticing Shi's lost look.

"No, my father isn't very well and I've come to see him. I live in Italy. Everything has changed since last time I was here."

"Uh, yeah, that's China. They have convinced farmers to be businessmen. Their children and grandchildren are coming back en masse from abroad. With blockchain and electronic payments they can do business all over the world, taking advantage of Big Data and AI, from their own homes."

"But the aim is to alleviate poverty and redistribute wealth in the less developed areas ..."

"Yes, in theory," he says sceptically, "of course, with the money received some people have started their own business, others have become digital artisans, most people just carry on farming chickens and pigs, but in a technological way."

Yes, looking at the cultivated fields she can see the swarms of drones flying over the land, sowing seeds,

1   From *Blockchain Chicken Farm* by Xiaowei Wang, page 82, FSGO/LOGIC, 2020.

watering, spraying, weeding and dealing with the duties that had for thousands of years been carried out by the farmers. Where they had once been bent double with fatigue they can now pilot the equipment remotely, sitting in the comfort of their favourite armchair, or else those who are better off can hire someone else to do even this for them.

Within the space of half an hour the scene changes, the road gets narrower and becomes an asphalt snake following the river, twisting and turning through the mountains. The houses thin out and have fewer and fewer storeys, often wedged into nooks and crannies, and cement gives way to wood or more frequently economic composite material. The ground floors are home to shops selling basic staple goods and nutraceutical stores. Washing hangs from first and second floor windows; clothes, colourful batik-style tablecloths and roughly printed underwear. The roofs, on the other hand, are sloped, the shape that Shi remembers from her childhood.

A series of snapshots of life with her parents run through her mind: an electric bicycle in China, a skateboard in Italy. Chopsticks and forks. Green tea and espresso coffee. 3D printers, history of art, text books with Chinese/Italian characters, and conferences about interpreting.

In that moment her translation app notifies her of a request: a businessman in Shanghai is negotiating a deal concerning hundreds of bottles of morellino di scansano red wine and needs help. Shi accepts the job and launches the virtual assistant. Her job is to check the translation made by the AI she has trained over the years. She doesn't usually have to intervene.

As soon as she reaches the bridge over the Langde, rebuilt to look just like the one washed away by a summer flood, she knows she has arrived. She waves at the carved monkeys on top of the bridge's columns and looks over the balustrade printed with scenes of rural life.

The black tiled roofs of the village appear as if in a dream: an expanse of glimmering fish scale like roofs climbing up the hill with its terraces bordered with bamboo and banana trees; in the background the Wuliu mountains are shrouded in mist and cotton-wool balls of cloud. Langdezhen is just as she remembers it, a black pearl surrounded by vegetation.

The rickshaw stops at the bottom of the lane that leads to her house. Shi pays the fare and doesn't hang around to see what has changed. Her father is waiting for her.

As she hurries up the hill, her trolley case follows her on four agile little legs. After a couple of bends she passes the two-storey elementary school, she can hear some kids singing and others shouting, and then she sees the slender Jie in the doorway, the little garden with pepper plants to one side. She is wearing a floral print dress cinched at the waist with a brown band. Her eyes are clear and transparent, somewhere between green and yellow.

"Welcome back, Shi! It's been a long time, come in. He's been asking after you every hour."

Off with her sunglasses, jacket, and shoes. Shi crosses the entrance and goes into the bedroom to stand by Ming's bed.

"You're here! It is so good to see you," he says, so full of emotion he can't hold back the tears. He squeezes his eyes shut to hold the image, unwilling to let that moment go. Their long embrace is one of relief. Shi had feared he wouldn't last long enough for her to see him again, like with her mother a few years earlier.

Next to Ming, to one side, is his pupil, Yun, who nods to Shi in greeting as she prepares a welcome tea.

Shi is overcome by a vortex of emotions: she and her father haven't seen each other in this house for four years. It is her second home, symbol of her second life and culture, but one that she has never thought of as second best.

The windows are open and the breeze coming in smells of rice straw and non-tanned leather, odours she hasn't smelled in a long time, perfumes that belong to a parallel life.

"How are you?"

He removes his oxygen mask and takes her hands in his, "Now I can feel so much more energy flowing towards me."

"Dad, I'm being serious."

"So am I. Man follows the laws of the land, the land those of Tao and the Tao those of nature," he says almost reciting, "we mustn't shake or force the course of things."

"When you say it it comes over as a bit of a paradox."

"I have simply given nature a hand ... even infinitely small things count."

"And are those things helping you?"

"They have done a lot. I have been living in symbiosis with nanosomes for years, but they can't do miracles. I have reached the age of 88 with hardly any illnesses."

Shi turns to Yun as if asking for confirmation her father isn't just putting a good face on things.

"Can I trust him?" she asks jokingly.

"Oh yes, it isn't the nature of things that scares the Maestro, maybe the nature of man does though."

"What do you mean?"

Just then they hear a commotion in the entrance.

"Yes, yes, I know, but this is important," says a low hoarse voice.

"Wait, wait, his daughter has only just got here," Jie replies.

An elegantly dressed man of about seventy appears in the doorway. He is wearing augmented-reality glasses and leaning on an inlaid walking stick with its own display on the knob. In the other hand he is holding a classic briefcase.

"Maestro! You look well today. Shi has come to visit you from Italy, how wonderful." Then he introduces himself. "I am Bo Guo, I have been a great admirer of Maestro Cheng Ming since our days at Chongqing university."

Her father squeezes his eyes shut again but this time he looks like it is in the hope this apparition will vanish as soon as he opens them again.

"I have come to talk business," the man goes on, unaware of the embarrassment he is causing. He pulls a decorated box containing a bottle of moutai out of his briefcase and places it on the table in front of him. Jie leans towards him, almost as if she wants to grab him by the sleeve. Yun sips her tea without offering any to the man, or asking him to sit down.

"I have just come from Bejing, and will be in Guizhou for a few days. If you have time, young lady, may I invite you to see our company? It isn't far, Leishan, a few kilometres to the south."

Ming opens his eyes again only to roll them. "I have already told you what I think about your company. Now I would like to spend some time with my daughter, if you don't mind."

"Of course, I apologise," says Bo Guo taking a step backwards. "Here, let me leave you my details in case you pass through Leishan," he shows them a QR code on his phone. Beneath it is a logo representing a cybernetic chicken and the words

BLOCKCH(AI)CKEN

Shi doesn't know how to react to his outstretched arm, not least because Bo Guo hasn't moved, he is waiting, impassively, so in the end she takes the phone and scans the code.

Happy, Bo Guo makes his retreat as if he has won a battle.

"Insufferable. He has been coming here for four days without being invited," says Ming, irritated.

Wei's Song

Jie's room is spartan, the only furniture is an old wooden wardrobe from Grandpa Wei, and a bed composed of cellulose resin on which a bamboo mat is lying. The walls are decorated with Jie's framed drawings: bright colourful phoenixes and dragons flying across the sky and above snow topped mountains.

As soon as Shi lies on the bed she notices a myriad of black dots on the ceiling, ready to drop down on her. The mosquito net that used to be there has gone, just then Jie appears in the doorway.

"Ah, I didn't tell you because they don't bother me. You can use this," she says flipping a switch next to the light. The ceiling lamp that looks like some kind of flying saucer starts to move across the ceiling sucking in the insects one by one.

"But where will you sleep? I didn't want to kick you out ... We could both fit."

"Don't worry, this used to be your room. I will sleep on the armchair in the dining room. I have a lot of little things to get done."

"*Little things* ... you like that expression."

"It is the Maestro, or rather, his philosophy."

Jie takes her leave and Shi goes to open the wardrobe to tidy away her "little things": a pair of trousers, three t-shirts, a jacket and her underwear. The shelves are occupied by four columns of piled-up cassettes, and in the drawers there are some very old magnetic tape reels. Curious, Shi starts reading the labels written in a handwriting she doesn't recognise, she is sure it is her father's.

QINGYAN, XIDI, BASHA, ZHAOXING, HUANGGUOSHU, XIJING, FANJING

She takes one and goes back to Ming's room. Yun has just put a fresh jug of water on the bedside table and is about to leave. She has a rented room at the end of the street.

"Dad, the wardrobe is full of cassettes and reels. Whose are they?"

"Oh, you've found them then," he says. "I wanted to talk to you about that, sit down."

She settles on the bed as Yun says goodbye and leaves.

"Grandpa Wei was a farmer, but in his spare time he played the *huqin*."

"I know, you've told me about it hundreds of times ... how he met Grandma Hui at a New Year's party, he was playing and she was singing."

"Yes, that's true, but there's something I didn't tell you: not long before dying, Grandpa made me promise to carry on with his collection."

"What collection? Of tapes?"

"Well, the cassettes contain traditional Guizhou songs that are vanishing because they are handed down orally from generation to generation. No one sings them any more and the ones you hear at festivals or in karaoke bars are poor mangled copies, there to create an atmosphere for the tourists. They are just sounds, without stories, whereas the original songs recorded in the villages held true treasures, wells of lost knowledge, culture and traditions swept away by modernity."

"But we can't listen to them any more ..."

Ming breathes with difficulty in his oxygen mask. His eyelids start to droop.

"When I was small, Grandpa used to take me with him when he played to raise a little money. It was a very difficult period, we were often hungry. He would transcribe the songs and put the papers in bamboo canes. Then I got into Chongqing university and ... those are the cassettes that are left. There should be a tape recorder or reel-to-reel device somewhere about. Ask Jie, she knows exactly where everything is in this house."

"Great, I would love to hear them."

Ming shifts closer to his daughter. "Shi, I didn't keep my promise."

There is regret in his clouded eyes.

"What do you mean?"

"After doing engineering, I started working immediately. A few years in the north and then, with your mother, we moved to Italy. When I came back I didn't have the strength to go around with Jie to record more songs."

"Couldn't you have sent her on her own?"

"Yes, perhaps I could have done, but you know what people are like ... Jie looks so human and young, but people in the villages are still diffident, no one would have opened up to her. The songs are intimate experiences, private, and often recount marvellous things, but also terrible and unpleasant ones."

"Would you like me to go with her?"

Ming's face opens up in a smile. "Yes, that would make me very happy, and Grandpa would be proud. There was that song ... do you remember? I used to sing it to you when you were small."

"The birds in a cage?"

"Yes," he says, hunting through his memory. He lets his eyes fall half closed as he concentrates, clears his throat, and whispers out a song.

The caged birds would like to glide with
passion over the wooded hills,
Fish in a puddle would like to
swim in running streams,
Fenced-in pigs would like to run
about in green fields ...

Then he stops, and frowns, sadly. "I've forgotten the rest ... how does it go on?"

"Sleep now, Dad. Tomorrow we can get Jie to help us."

Farmageddon

A group of young girls whizz past on scooters, skateboards, and electric bicycles.

On the right a number of old shops have been modernized with augmented reality windows: a pharmacy, half oriental, half Western, advertising 160-finger massages, and 160-acupuncture treatments applied by a 16 arm kuka device. A digital artisan who accepts 3D formulas to make in real time on four parallel printers. A little further on the tea house, harmonious fragrance, offers synaesthesia experiences produced by the union of taste, smell, and musical mixtures.

First thing in the morning Shi and Jie had left to go shopping. Yun had stayed behind in the garden to look after the vegetable patch where she is growing Sichuan pepper plants.

"Therefore we don't need any of those old devices to listen to the songs?"

"No, I memorised them all years ago, when the Maestro asked me to. He must have forgotten, it's his age."

"I would love to listen to them later, if you don't mind."

"Of course, when we have afternoon tea."

They go past a little lake where a water buffalo is splashing about in the midst of a carpet of lotus flowers. Shi stops to look at the fish; some of them are strangely luminescent.

"They are Carp-CRISPR," says Jie, "engineered for nocturnal illumination."

"Oh, the poor fish."

Jie frowns. "Are you sure you want to come to the market?"

"Why?"

"I wouldn't like you to get upset."

"Now you are frightening me. Is it really so bad?"

At the entrance to the market there is a five-metre-high installation: a holodrama showing the 'dangers' of bad body odour. A collection of characters act out various situations: two female friends wrinkle their noses at the arrival of a 'stinky' male friend, a wife kicks her husband out of their house, throwing soap and deodorants at him as he goes, a young lady with sweaty armpits is turned down at a job interview.

BROMHIDROSIS (THE STINK OF THE IMMORTALS)

IS AN UNPLEASANT AFFLICTION.

OUR 98% EFFECTIVE NANOTECH THERAPY REMOVES ALL BACTERIA.

GUARANTEE YOURSELF A PLEASANT AND HAPPY FUTURE!

ONE NANITE BATH AND SAY GOODBYE TO

YOUR STINK FOR EVER!

People are eating and chatting noisily on the streets amongst the stalls, their arm gestures are expansive, their laughter uninhibited, just like in Italy. Nevertheless, this sense of familiarity vanishes when she sees the electrified enclosures where big screens composed of dozens of monitors have been mounted. Each enclosure is monitored by drones hovering above them.

The images show live footage of the chickens, pigs, rabbits, and calves. Each animal has a bracelet around one of its legs tracking steps and movement, like those wrist devices that stimulate people to exercise through rewards and progression through levels. Except, this gadget sends data to a remote-control centre analysing the health/ hygiene status of the animals. Every time the average daily step count drops below a certain pre-established level, a small electric shock forces them to move. If you watched the animals non-stop for more than five minutes, you would see their shivers and spasms.

At a certain point Bo Guo appears on the monitors, arguing with a farmer. Hearing his voice Shi realizes the real thing is going on just around the corner.

"Well? They've got used to it. You're running the risk of not reaching your objectives, Feng! Instead of monitoring the livestock I should be pointing the drones at you!"

Feng lowers his gaze, he is holding an ankle bracelet in one hand and a chicken's leg in the other.

"I have told you, you must never, ever, remove an ankle bracelet. The customers want to be able to read the label and follow the animal's full history Why else do we have a webpage with the date of birth, step count, food eaten, and the photos of every animal?"

"It was ill, it was pecking at its own leg."

"Then you should have called the withdrawal service. You did the course, didn't you? In case of illness or accident blockch(ai)cken personnel should be called, they will come equipped with gloves and masks and sort everything out."

Jie puts her arm around Shi and leads her away from the enclosures.

"Until seven years ago Mr Feng used to bring his chickens to us."

"I remember," she said, "they used to scratch around behind the school yard. I used to play with them when I was a kid."

"Exactly, but those were vegetarian chickens. Now they are stuffed with genetically modified soya, grain, protein powder, and treated scraps to fatten them up more quickly. Quite often animal parts end up in the scraps, and the protein additives contain products of animal origin. They do this to make them meat for slaughter as quickly as possible. They become cannibals, infecting and reinfecting their own species, no wonder every now and then a pandemic breaks out. It can happen anywhere, in any battery farm, from Holland to Texas."

"What about the drones?"

"The poor chickens are neither intelligent nor brave, and if they get stuck outside their cages at night they get scared, gather together around the light, crowding together at risk of crushing each other. Sometimes you can hear them all screaming at the same time. A kind of nightmare poultry swarm. The herding drones limit the crowding."

"Mr Feng is no longer a farmer."

"No, the apps for facial and voice recognition, satellite images and algorithms belong to blockch(ai)cken, Mr Feng has become a specialised labourer trying to fulfil as many of the online orders as possible. Every now and then he comes to Maestro Ming to get it off his chest, last year he said he got 6000 orders for 8000 chickens from 15 different countries."

Shi moves back to the enclosure. A chicken jerks its head suddenly. To her it looks like it is asking for mercy.

"They aren't animals any more, they are *animorphs*."

"Come on, let's go, the fruit and vegetable stalls are further on."

"What did Mr Guo want the other day? What business was he talking about?"

"Ah well, he wants Maestro Ming's pepper plants, the ones Yun is caring for in the vegetable patch."

Little Big Things

There are a few rabbits hopping about in the grass under the chairs. Ming, Shi, and Yun are sitting drinking tea, waiting for Jie to come into the garden. Her voice reaches them before she does, starting high she rises a number of octaves, singing a Yi language song. These sounds spread a great distance, further than the pond, even beyond the Langdezhen hill.

The turtle dove and chicken scratch in the dirt,
The chicken has a master, the turtle dove does not,
If the chicken's master comes to bring it back
The turtle dove is left there all alone.

Jie is so beautiful she is blinding and her voice is bewitching even when she is singing about chickens and doves. Ming stands and applauds her. "Bravo, I had forgotten you memorised the songs! How lucky," then his mood darkens, he droops, and sits back down. "So many memories."

"Dad," Shi says, in an attempt to cheer him up, "tomorrow Jie and I are going to look for more songs. Doesn't that make you happy?"

"Oh yes, I am very grateful." He sips his tea and appears to drop off to sleep. Shi's presence has reinvigorated him, he even asked to come outside to get some fresh air.

"Dad," she continues, stroking his face. "The other day Mr Bo mentioned business. What was he talking about?"

"Oh," says Ming, hesitating. "That old fox, he's been pestering me for 40 years. He wouldn't give up then, and he won't give up now!"

"Why? What happened?"

"Do you remember the nanoscope?"

"Of course, where you showed me the nanosome experiments."

"After university I worked in an independent laboratory and our most important client was a nutraceutical company. Bo Guo was the commercial manager, he could only have been about 18.

"I still have the old nanoscope in the house, even though no one ever uses it any more. At the time it needed a monitor and a pointing interface to work, whereas now Yun can wear a pair of gloves with sensors and an augmented reality visor to manipulate and program the nanosomes on a latest generation nanomat.

"Every single week when he came to the laboratory he would pressurise us into speeding up our deliveries of nutraceuticals. He said that the future wouldn't wait, we had to satisfy our customers, that our prosperity depended on their happiness, all those silly things they teach on economics courses."

When she has finished her tea Yun takes a bag and a watering-can and heads towards the vegetable patch.

"He kept muttering on about his vision and tried to convince anyone and everyone of his plans. He waved his arms around, pointing at this and that, he made shapes with his hands, like boxes within boxes, growth curves, and objects flying through the air. New ideas – he would say, like someone possessed – outside the box innovation, business creativity."

Opening the bag, Yun starts to spread fertiliser around the trunk of the pepper plants, then waters them carefully.

"He never stopped, every so often he would come along and say 'Close your eyes, think about the future, then open them and tell me what you see.' I would open mine hoping he had disappeared, but never had, he was always there, in my future's way. I had a different goal. In secret I was developing my dream of creating nanosomes that could compose vitamins, proteins and carbohydrates from raw materials like tubers, roots, leaves and bark. Simple molecules present in nature everywhere, in water, in the air, so that we wouldn't have to depend on the monster that the industrial food and farming industry had become. I had seen a future, but it was so very different to Bo's."

Yun picks a number of red berries, their colour is intense and shiny; they are all split down one side where each has a seed peeking out.

"So one day, to get him away from me, I invited him to look in the nanoscope. I was convinced he would calm down, stop pestering me, but he was struck with the conviction he wanted to do business with me! It was a terrible mistake. Over the years Bo Guo made a name for himself, he worked for ALIBABA, he was one of the promoters of the TAOBAO villages, and now despite being retired, he has begun launching start-ups with certain business-angel friends of his from Beijing, like that BLOCKCH(AI)KEN you saw yesterday. Why would I be interested? I would like humanity to be able to stop eating three times a day, reducing meals to once a month. That's what nanosomes are for, to make the organism more efficient. We are already slaves to the market, there is no need to create other phenomena that increase nutritional disparity. Because that is what happens when food is treated the same way as any other commodity, to make money and speculate with. Food should be considered as a fundamental right, and if this concept sounds like a utopia, then we may as well make food obsolete. We may as well take food from the plates, from the fields, from industry, from the lorries, from planes, from ships, from the dumps, make it vanish completely and see what happens."

Ming takes a breath. He hasn't spoken this much in months. It's as if he feels the need to hurry and tell Shi everything.

"It is a complex scenario to plan," says Jie meditatively. Her pupils shrink and thin to the shape of those of a cat as she processes these concepts.

Yun, though, comes back from the vegetable patch and places the peppercorns on the tea table.

"Just think what old Guo would give to be able to transform these little seeds into millions of server farms."

"What did you say?" Shi stutters, almost choking on her tea.

"Yes, we have been experimenting with methods of recording data on DNA," Yun continues, tasting a berry. "Maestro Ming took a sample from his nanosomes, inserted cultured stem cells and managed to integrate them in the genetic code of the pepper plants. Now they can be programmed on a nanomat. Imagine whole fields of distributed data, no longer shut inside underground data centres, but accessible to everyone and powered by the light of the sun."

Shi doesn't have clear memories of the time when her father – to follow his nanosome dream – left China, but the images of him assembling molecules at all hours of the day and night surface in her mind. When she was small she had been able to fall asleep on a sofa like a kitten, curled up on a cushion while he split and reconnected subatomic bonds, or else, other times, she had fun chasing the molecules he had split off and that flew away like clouds of steam, other times she even tried to put them together as if they were old LEGO bricks. Ming had always been an infallible maestro of nanotechnological composition and experts from all around the world would send their 3D drafts for him to analyse, correct and finalise with his patience and exceptional meticulousness. Even when she was studying at the University of Siena to become an interpreter, she saw him as a 3D design artist, somewhere between a sculptor who gave shape to objects using an infinite number of grains of rice, and those street artists who paint the flagstones with water, tenuous images that evaporated within a few hours of being created.

"Does Guo know about this?" Shi asks worriedly.

"Oh, no. Fortunately he knows nothing about it," says Ming coming suddenly awake again. "He thinks it is nutraceutical pepper, an improved version of the products enriched with nanotechnology we used to make in the laboratory. I daren't think what he might become if he discovered the true purpose of these peppercorns."

Singing in the Cloud

The entrance to the venue CELESTIAL MELODY is crowded with a queue of waiting people: groups of friends, couples, and children holding their parents' hands, all quivering with the desire to listen to the storyteller.

Inside, the tables and sofas in the VIP area have been arranged in a semi-circle in front of the stage. Drinks and a hot and cold buffet arranged around the edges are available to everyone, to order a person just has to take a photo of what they want and the amount is automatically debited.

Multicoloured lasers slice through the air, smoke spreads across the room, coming from above like nocturnal mist. A baritone voice rumbles through the hall. Wearing a tunic with four wide sleeves, face painted like a theatrical mask from the Sichuan opera, the storyteller starts an ancient local legend. In a hieratic pose he accompanies himself by drumming his fingers, tipped with little sticks, on a tambourine.

Inside an immense pumpkin used as a boat
Only two were be saved from the water
The brave Ajien and his splendid sister
who he, without anyone else left in the
world, wanted to make his bride
She refused, it went against decorum
and proposed to roll two rocks down facing hills
If they landed on each other he
could have her as his consort

Shi rises on tiptoes to see better.

"Are you sure this is the right place?" she yells in Jie's ear.

"Yes, after the show they'll all go into the karaoke room on the floor above. If we're going to find singers anywhere, it is here."

Shi is sceptical, this show looks like a clumsy caricature of the poetic songs her grandfather used to collect to her.

In secret brave Ajie placed two rocks,
one on top of the other
And when the first ones vanished
into the tall wild grass
He showed her the second two, and took
her with him into the shadows.
She refused again and this time suggested
they should throw two knives
And if they landed in the same sheath
then they would marry.

The audience mutter, the tension rises. Shaking bells attached to his ankles, the storyteller makes them ring as if to regain his audience's attention. Then he draws two knives from his extra sleeves and raises his voice.

Slyly Ajie hid two blades in one single sheath
and when he gathered them from the
ground at the end of the test
he took his sister to continue their story.

With a flick of his wrists the storyteller throws the knives into a heart-shaped target. The audience cheer, applaud and begin to head towards the side stairs.

"Liar! You are a liar!" someone shouts out. "That's not how it ends!"

Jie and Shi turn towards a young woman covered in colourful tattoos and piercings.

"Why didn't you tell the whole story, huh? What's the matter? Are you afraid of the truth?" The girl carries on venting against the storyteller.

A security man goes over to her and suggests she leaves. She resists, she wriggles away from him, and complains, "You're a rabbit and a coward! That song has a different ending, and you know that well, you, you *bull teller*!"

Then she is grabbed and dragged outside.

"Don't let him trick you, don't let that thing make a joke out of you!"

Shi pulls Jie behind her. The young woman's shouts recede beneath the drum rolls concluding the show.

"My grandmother knows that song."

The girl has told them her name is Ting and she lives in Leishan. She has bronzed skin, a straight nose and slit-like eyes, and her hair is tied in bunches, like rabbit ears.

"Would you mind taking us to her?"

"Why?"

"We would like to know how the song really ends."

"My grandmother lives in the mountains. Half an hour from here."

"No problem," Jie answers, using her phone to call for a car.

She pulls a face, winks and Ting agrees.

Rice – Drone – Fish – Duck

Perched on the crest of a hill with BLOCKCH(AI)CKEN signs on its slopes, the land of Ting's grandmother is a strip of terraced rice paddies.

The car had left them by the side of a country road, and they were finishing the journey on foot.

"We're nearly there," says Ting walking up a muddy path. "My grandmother, Shan, is the only person, from here to Datong, not to have sold her land."

All around them, the bleating and lowing of animals in their enclosures leads them to think intensive farming has taken over from traditional farming everywhere.

"Do you still follow the rice-fish-duck system?" Jie asks, lighting the way along the shaded footpath with her eyes.

"Yes, but she is getting old, and she can't manage on her own. Her rice fields are small and narrow, it is impossible to reach them with any kind of car. A couple of years ago I bought her three drones at Huaqiangbei market. I had the parts sent from Shenzhen and put them together with a little help from my friends. Now grandmother can use a hybrid rice-drone-fish-duck system," says Ting quite proudly.

The hill is steep and the rice fields flooded, Shi notices fish in the water eating insects, they act as a natural repellent, while the ducks scratching about provide the fertiliser and keep down the more voracious snails.

"Compared to her more technological neighbours, grandmother doesn't need anything, pesticides, chemicals, additives or anti-parasitics, she carries on as she always has. Over at BLOCKCH(AI)CKEN they think farmers are only producing food for people in the cities. For them feeding people is like feeding pigs. They don't care at all about the practices of small farmers. For thousands of years farmers have protected and maintained the land, rather than *optimising agricultural production*."

Then she makes a gesture towards the fence coasting the footpath. She gives it a tremendous kick, alerting the surveillance drone. Its yellowish beep, beep, beep only makes her even angrier.

"Optimisation, my ovaries! Surveillance capitalism! Like that bull-teller at CELESTIAL MELODY!! They are just a collection of badly written and terribly managed algorithms."

A hundred metres higher up, between a golden yellow magnolia and a moon-white one, a hunched over old woman is waving at them. Above her, coloured lights flashing on and off, its metallic hands opening and closing, is a drone which on seeing Ting rushes towards her, gliding down from on high like a happy puppy.

"Grandmother! Is the water hot? I've brought some friends with me, they want to hear you sing!" Ting yells, running to hug her.

The drone whirls around them both and all the fuss brings another two patched up devices fluttering from the fields, still holding bags of fruit and seeds in their hands.

Jie stops, stretches her neck like a swan, and gathers the sight of the rural beauty of this landscape shrouded with mist. Shi does the same, flaring her nostrils to breathe it all in as deeply as possible.

In the jars lining the shelves there are fish from the rice fields preserved in wine. A number of agricultural tools hang from the ceiling beams and on the walls, like museum artefacts from a far off time, rendered useless by the multi-purpose hands of the drones.

"What has happened to Zhao?" Ting asks slapping a humandroid hard on the back, it is sitting in an unnatural pose in front of a loom.

"I don't know, he just seemed to get stuck. He even stopped talking. He's been like this since yesterday, no signs of life at all. You'll have to call one of your friends to fix him. In about a week I have to deliver the costume for the Huashang festival."

The costume is resting on the table: the fabric – smooth bright and shiny – is made up of a single thread a millimetre thick, with incredible decorations representing dragons, geese, lions and dogs surrounded by many flowers and fruit trees. The boundaries between animal and floral species are blurred, sometimes there are animals with human heads or combinations of imaginary inter-species beings. These images are like mobile antique books of history, collections of ancient myths and legends, passed down by the oral traditions of the ancestors across hundreds of generations, motif by motif, illustrating the various ways in which the Miao see reality and energy in the soul of every thing.

"It is not that simple, Grandmother. Zhao was the best embroiderer in Huaqiangbei. I'm still doing odd jobs here and there to finish paying for him."

Shan picks up some pieces of paper scattered over the ground. From the unbound pages various coloured very fine threads can be seen sticking out.

"Well," Ting's grandmother says caustically, "he can't even weave the *poxian*. You would have learned more quickly than him."

It seems that what Shan has learned over the course of her life is being passed down directly to Zhao without going through Ting.

"This again? Can you really see me threading bamboo needles for the rest of my life?! C'mon Grandmother, my friends didn't come here to watch us argue, they want to know how the story of Ajie and his sister really ends."

"All right then, you get the tea ready," Shan answers, shooing her away with a hand. As she picks up her *huqin*,

Ting pours the tea and brings out a plate of *baba*, a sticky rice sweet.

Shan begins to play and sing.

> *... After nine months Ajie and his sister*
> *had a child, oh that poor child*
> *a deformed being, he had no legs*
> *and only stumps for arms.*
> *His mother was in despair, and Ajie, blinded by anger*
> *murdered the child and cut it to pieces in shame*
> *Then he threw the pieces far away from the*
> *hill, but when he awoke in the morning,*
> *he found those pieces had transformed, and*
> *were now many men and women.*
> *This is how the land was repopulated.*

The song quietens to a tremulous note and Jie stands up to clap and thank Shan. Then she blinks her eyes twice, a sign she has memorised the audio, and declares, "This version, recorded to the cloud, will be broadcast to whoever wants to listen to it. It will never run the risk of being forgotten again."

Hearing a buzzing sound Shi realizes the drones have been hanging around outside the window, listening to old Shan's singing. They bob from left to right, like over-excited rust buckets, this is their way of showing their appreciation.

"My grandfather used to go around the villages collecting local folk songs," Shi says, "my father did the same until he went to Italy, now we are going to carry on the tradition."

"Your grandfather must have been Chen Wei, then. And you are the daughter of Maestro Ming."

"Yes, do you know them?"

"Of course, we had lots of parties together. I was a friend of your mother, we sewed many many dresses when she still lived in the village ..." Then she stops, and apologises, covering her mouth with her hand.

"Don't worry. It happened years ago," Shi reassures her.

Shan gets up as if she has suddenly remembered something. "I thought I put it here," she says opening drawers in the kitchen dresser. "Here we are ... What a coincidence, she made this. It took her two years. She must have been a little younger than you are now."

Shan shows them a ceremonial robe made of finely embroidered cotton. Geometric floral designs descend down the sleeves to the cuffs. The collar is embroidered with triangles and swastikas, whereas on the back there is a representation of the Butterfly Mother, an ancient Miao symbol of life and transformation, flying over an undulating foam of stylised waves.

"I would like you to take it to Maestro Ming. A gift from the past, from his wife, your mother."

Shanzhai

Shi rushes in to the house carrying the robe.

"Dad, look! I have a gift for you from—"

234

As she crosses the threshold of the bedroom she stops, shocked. Her father is holding the end of his stick pressed like a weapon against Mr Feng's chest. Feng, his eyes down and head pulled in against his shoulders, is apologising with a series of bows.

"What's going on?"

Shi is disconcerted and turns to Jie in the doorway, hunting, and failing, to find an explanation.

Yun surprised our old friend Feng stealing from the garden," says Ming. "His pockets were full of peppercorns."

"I apologise, Maestro, I wasn't doing it for me. BLOCKCH(AI)CKEN meat is so tasteless without spices. I've heard people say your pepper is the best in all Sichuan."

"And where did you hear this chitchat?" Yun interrupts.

Shi calms down and places the robe on the foot of the bed, things aren't as they seem.

"From Mr Bo Guo, he asked me to come here and sneak in to pick some pepper samples for growing, without being seen."

"Oh yes?" Maestro Ming says, rubbing his beard, "So you're telling me Bo Guo decided to send you here to steal because he knew we would never give him our peppercorns, is that right?"

"I think so. You know Maestro ... I would never have come to steal from you," Feng answers, bowing even lower. "But it's difficult to make ends meet these days, the orders keep growing but the profit margins on meat get smaller and smaller."

"You are right, I do believe you. This is not your fault."

"I would rather stop raising those poor animals like that. I can't bare to see their suffering, but what can I do?"

Yun throws a complicit look at the Maestro who, in turn, sighs and pulls his stick away from Feng.

"*Shanzhai,*" he says solemnly. "Do you remember this concept of copies and imitations of Western technological products for which we were criticised and derided for years? That term referred to the "outlaws" who fought in the mountain villages for autonomy, independence and a kind of survival. In the West they never understood the deepest sense of the word, because shanzhai means incremental collective knowledge, co-opting the necessary resources, high speed sharing, reusing what works and recycling what can still be used, all in a decentralised manner, for the billion people who are at the base of the technological pyramid. And yes, it is also an alternative idea to the Western one of intellectual rights and obsessive copyright protection."

The Maestro coughs, it seems like he wants to get a lot of things off his chest in this conversation. "The West has stopped innovating," he continues, tossing a few of the peppercorns up and down in his hand, "they are only really concerned with slowing down their own technological development and blocking that of others in order to maintain a competitive advantage with which they can enjoy the well-being they have gained to the disadvantage of the rest of the world. Please, Yun, show him what we mean ..."

Yun puts on the visor and switches on the holograph. The compositional diagram of a nanite fluctuates in the air. After a moment she begins to manipulate the view and says, "The Maestro is right. Today at Huaqiangbei market, where modern shanzhai was born, you can buy 3D printed organs, satellite microphones with integrated speakers, 100TB playlists and solar powered modular phones. Intellectual rights aren't an intrinsic value, just like legal ownership and private property. It's an old English idea from the 1800s that belongs to the obscurantist vision of the world in which competition was considered more important than cooperation. How can anyone innovate if they can't afford the tools necessary to do so?

Zooming in on the view Yun shows the various components of the miniscule miracle, similar to a stem cell capable of differentiating itself into other more specific ones. Two motors and a gyroscope allow the nanite to move, a calibration system with a manipulator make it possible for it to grab subatomic particles and a cellular membrane type sensor allows it to recognise the nature of the world around it.

"Like a collective work of art, created thanks to the efforts of many artists, the engines of creation are the fruit of the work of the best nanosmiths in the world," says Ming. "I simply helped them put the pieces together, inside me. If the West has used military invasion weapons, cultural colonisation, economic imperialism and one way technological globalisation, why can't we defend ourselves with cunning?"

Spinning slowly the nanite displays its parts: a wireless antenna, a wavelength sensor, organised logic circuits, a T-cell anti-receptor and an emergency self-destruct system.

Suddenly Yun opens all ten fingers and the nanite instantly multiplies with an amazing effect, then she makes it smaller leaving a cloud of a very fine dust of luminous particles fluctuating in the air. Feng watches these movements, as if hypnotised, his mouth hanging open.

"If I have the right to use something," Yun adds, "I also have the right to modify it, change it, reuse it, regenerate it and even claim it as mine. In the world that is coming, shanzhai applied to nanosomes could liberate humanity from a number of biological needs and become a precious tool for decolonising technology, and therefore the future."

Maestro Ming lifts his walking stick again, but this time points it at Feng with a benevolent smile.

"You came looking for Sichuan pepper but you ended up finding much much more, a radical transformation for the few ready to embrace it... Tell me dear Feng, are you ready?"

"Yes... yes, I am. Anything to get away from those enclosures of death."

"You will be able to go back to your chickens and cockerels of before, the ones that used to give us so many fresh eggs."

"Just like old times, Maestro?"

"Just like old times, but without needing to eat them."

To all of their surprise Jie starts singing. Her voice makes Yun's holograph vibrate, as if the two realities can communicate with each other, interact and unite with each other.

> *The turtle dove would like to glide with*
> *passion over the wooded hills,*
> *Fish in a puddle would like to*
> *swim in running streams,*
> *Fenced in pigs would like to run*
> *about in green fields ...*
> *So I claim the air, the water and the*
> *earth of the southern fields*
> *To give back the harvests of the*
> *lands to their inhabitants.*

"Yes! That's how the song I used to sing to you when you were small ends!" says Ming turning to Shi and clapping Jie. "That song was my inspiration to give nanosomes the vital breath that pervades everything, from subatomic particles to black holes. It doesn't matter how, or how long we will take, one meal at a time, we will be able to save people, animals, the whole world. Now it is Feng's turn."

Shi takes the ceremonial robe from the bed and hands it to her father.

239

"Mum would be happy. This is from Shan, from the village of Leishan."

Ming brushes the fabric with his fingers, sniffs at the cotton and strokes the decorations as if he is communicating with his wife. His eyes fill with tears, his lips quiver. In the same moment Shi takes his rough wise hand.

"Please, sing again, Jie," Shi asks her friend.

Perhaps the reason for life doesn't lie in looking for a meaning, but in the possibility of reinventing ourselves an infinite number of times.

The Spiral Ranch

Sarena Ulibarri

TWO COWS were missing from the Spiral Ranch. Piper tapped the Pasture 7 control screen and activated the LASSO app to check the headcount against her wrist unit. The app confirmed: two fewer than yesterday. She swiped over to the com and dialed Pasture 3.

"Hey, Jayce."

His voice came through the speaker a moment later. "Yes'm."

"You have any extra cows over there?"

"Uh, no ma'am."

"Any missing?"

"Don't reckon so. Why, what's up?"

Piper pushed her hat back from her sweaty brow and scratched her head. "No reason."

They'd rotated the herd up from Pasture 6 three days before, and all the cattle had been accounted for then. Piper hefted herself up onto the wall – an inward-bowing lip that let in fresh air and sunlight but kept the cattle from stumbling over the ledge – and peered down at the street eight stories below. No cows were splattered on the sidewalk. A couple of reggae buskers played on the corner and some tourists pointed cameras toward the skyscraper. Piper lowered herself back onto the grass. Maybe something had gone wrong with the tracking chips. She walked up the slope and around the curve until she hit the gate leading to Pasture 8, doing a manual headcount on the way. Still two short.

The logs on the robotic milking station showed both of the missing cows had been milked the night before, but not this morning. The moveable slats that made a cattle guard around the cargo elevator were open and seemed to be functioning fine, so it was unlikely the cows had taken a ride down to another pasture. Besides, the LASSO app could detect any active chip within a two-mile radius. Wherever the cows were, they weren't in the building.

She checked the fallow pastures all the same, but to no avail, so she headed to the slaughterhouse. The Spiral Ranch was primarily a dairy producer, but they had small-scale meat processing as well, hidden in the basement so the people of Austin could pretend it didn't exist. It was Piper's second-least favorite part of the building.

She found Monique down there, singing century-old show tunes while she loaded packages of beef into delivery bots. Monique's logs revealed no records of the missing cows, even when Piper checked for deleted or manipulated files. They were just … gone.

Up to the corporate office, then. Piper's *least* favorite part of the Spiral Ranch.

She climbed the stairs from the slaughterhouse up to the lobby, and caught the public elevator there, riding to the top next to a few restaurant patrons. The elevator doors opened on a wide breezeway. The lattice of the rooftop garden crisscrossed green overhead, vines climbing down the walls on either side. The tourists turned left toward the restaurant, and Piper turned right toward Adrianne's office.

She pushed the button next to the frosted-glass office door. The button turned green, but Piper hesitated a moment before she turned the wrought iron flower doorknob, steeling herself for what was likely to be an unpleasant interaction.

Adrianne sat behind a glass desk, arguing with someone on a holographic screen. Floor to ceiling windows stretched behind her, and flowering trees too tropical for central Texas lined the interior wall. Piper's boots left scuffs on the immaculate white tile floor. She hung back awkwardly until Adrianne managed to close out the conversation and the screen disappeared.

"What was that all about?"

Adrianne crossed her legs, dangling one high heel off a toe. "Just more investors threatening to pull support unless we can improve our public image."

"What's wrong with our public image?"

Adrianne raised an eyebrow and let out a mirthless laugh. "Really? You didn't see that smear video some reporter did, accusing us of animal cruelty and excess waste?"

Piper shrugged. "It ain't true."

"In any case, I need to set up a new advertising campaign to combat it, and the investors are shooting down *all* my ideas."

"You could make an ad telling people how we've reduced the price of milk and cheese in the city by more than two-thirds."

Adrianne scoffed. "In a city that's sixty percent vegan."

"How about how we're a major energy producer, both solar and methane—"

"Every damn building is an energy producer!" Adrianne rubbed a hand across her face. "I'm sorry. Um, what was it you came in here to tell me? I'm real busy."

'Course you are. There was a time when Piper might have stopped into her office just to chat or make evening plans. But those days, it seemed, were long gone. Piper and Adrianne had been good friends back in college, and had drawn up the plans for the Spiral Ranch together. But that relationship had devolved since becoming boss and employee. Piper wanted nothing to do with all the paper-pushing, and Adrianne seemed to want nothing to do with the animals.

"I can't afford to have my inventory disappearing," Adrianne said after Piper told her about the missing cattle.

"I just thought you should know."

"Maybe there's something wrong with that app of yours. I've been looking into alternatives we might want to upgrade to. If you have some time, I'd like to go over them with you."

Piper bristled. She'd coded the LASSO app from scratch and she was proud of it. It was running just fine. She stood, slapping her hat against her thigh. "I'm real busy."

The next morning, two more cows were missing. Her searches and inquiries proved as fruitless as the day before, so when night fell, Piper stayed behind. Jayce had stopped by to do a repair on the manure collector. After he'd packed his tools and set the clam-shaped machine rolling on its course again, he hesitated by the elevator.

"Staying late, boss?"

"Think I'm gonna camp out and see if I can solve the mystery of the disappearing cows."

"Want me to stay with you?"

Piper shrugged. "Only if you want."

He stepped into the elevator, and Piper assumed he was gone for the night, but he reappeared about an hour later with a couple of roast beef sandwiches, two sleeping bags, and a guitar.

The sun sank in a dull orange display. Piper lay in the grass of Pasture 7 with her head propped on a rolled-up sleeping bag, swatting at the occasional fly. Some of the cows kept grazing, but most folded their legs beneath them to sleep. Jayce picked a slow, amateur rhythm on his guitar. From somewhere down the street, a live band rocked out for an energetic crowd.

"Why don't we have cameras?" Jayce said suddenly. "So's to watch what happens to the cows at night, I mean."

"You really want cameras watching your ass work all day?"

"Not really," Jayce said. "But cameras are everywhere else."

Piper shifted on her roll-pillow. She'd been the one to convince Adrianne that cameras were a waste. She disliked the constant surveillance and data mining that were ubiquitous to modern life. "Never needed them, I guess. LASSO keeps track of the cows, tells us their vitals, better than a camera would."

"'Til something weird happens."

"'Til something weird happens," Piper agreed.

After another long silence, filled only with Jayce's next attempted song and the shuffling of the cattle, Jayce said, "Think it's aliens?"

"What's aliens?"

"What's taking the cows."

"What kind of fool question is that?"

Jayce looked hurt. "It ain't a fool question. Didn't you never hear about them cattle mutilations in Colorado?"

Piper raised an eyebrow at him.

"Back in the twentieth century. Lots of cattle were getting cut up right in the field, surgical-like. No one knew who was doin' it. Seemed like aliens."

"It's damn near the end of the twenty-first century now and we still ain't found no aliens," Piper said. "If they're around, I don't know why they're being so sneaky and picking on cows."

"Fair enough," Jayce said. "But no one did ever figure out who was slicing up them cows."

"No, I remember now," Piper said. "It was the government, wasn't it?"

"What would the government want with cows?"

"There was some toxic spill or nuclear accident. They were testing the cows to see how dangerous it really was, without telling anyone."

Jayce shrugged. "Could be government, I guess, but I thought they shut down all the nuke plants along with the coal."

"I don't know who it is," Piper said. "But I'm going to figure it out."

Jayce eventually fell asleep, snoring inside his sleeping bag. Piper kept hers as a pillow, crossing her arms to keep warm as the night cooled. Her toes itched, but she refused to take off her boots. If something happened, she needed to be ready.

Near two in the morning, the sounds of live music faded away, replaced with a chorus of cicadas. Piper was fighting to stay awake when a new soft buzz joined the night noises. She sat up, tuned her ear to it. The cattle staggered to their feet, pawed the ground, bumped into each other. A pair of glowing red eyes peered over the pasture wall.

Piper jolted. The whirring grew louder, and then a large drone darted into the pasture. The cattle panicked. Piper tossed her sleeping roll at Jayce and he snorted awake.

"What the—" He jumped to his feet and narrowly avoided a stampede. "I told you it was aliens!"

"It's not aliens," Piper said. "It's twenty-first century cattle rustling." She snapped pictures with her wrist unit. It was an old police drone, but any identifying marks had been scuffed off. These drones had been common in the skies of any major city about a decade ago, but they kept getting shot down, captured, or hacked, so they'd been decommissioned and auctioned off. The drones were supposed to be strong enough to pick up a small car. This one positioned itself over a cow and a set of claws appeared, reaching down like an oversized arcade game.

Jayce grabbed a rope from next to the elevator and edged toward the drone. The propellers whacked the rope away. He steadied his feet, tossed it again.

"Gotcha." The rope caught around the body of the drone. Its claws clenched around the cow's torso and lifted. These were dwarf cattle, about half the size and weight of their flat-ranch predecessors, but still a good five hundred pounds a head. The drone snatched it up like it was a plush toy. Jayce dug his heels into the grass, but the drone buzzed toward the open air gap, the cow mooing in protest. Piper homed the LASSO app in on that cow's chip. The rest of the herd clustered in the farthest corner of the pasture. Jayce held strong, but the drone pulled him off his feet and he slid across the grass toward the ledge.

"Jayce, let go!" Piper ran after him. Drone and cow disappeared into the night. He let the rope slide out of his hands just in time to thunk against the wall.

She yanked him to his feet. "Come on. The LASSO app has a range of two miles. We can track where it's going." He stumbled after her toward the elevator.

She tapped her boots in impatience, checking her wrist unit as the cargo elevator snailed its way to Pasture 1. The cow's chip was still in range, but getting fainter. The elevator door opened and the two of them burst out and ran down the stairs to the lobby. Outside, her electric motorcycle hummed to life. Jayce climbed on behind her. She zoomed off, transferring visual of the LASSO app to her bike's console with a shout. Her hat flew back, caught around her throat by the leather chin strap.

Just past Sixth Street, she caught sight of the cow, floating placidly through the air between buildings. Its bellowing moo echoed through the quiet streets and it released a patty that splattered across a restaurant's sign. *That's not gonna help our public image*, Piper thought.

"They're heading for the river," Jayce shouted.

Piper looked back to the road. *Sure enough.* She dipped the bike into a dangerously sharp left turn. The drone crossed the river, widening the space between them. Piper considered the roadways. If she followed them, it would be another half a mile before they could cross.

"Hold on!" She bumped the bike up a sidewalk and across a pedestrian bridge.

Twice more she lost sight of the drone, but the cow's location kept blipping on her screen. West of the city, where the buildings disappeared and the Carbon Sequestration

Forests grew thick, the drone disappeared from sight and the blip on her screen showed it was headed deep into the forest. She pulled the motorcycle off to the edge of the road. Driving across a pedestrian bridge was one thing, but forging through a forest was another. It was a hearty bike, but not an off-roader.

"It's them radical occupiers, ain't it?" Jayce asked.

"Has to be." Piper dropped the kickstand and stepped off. Jayce followed.

"I've got cousins that sympathize with them," he said. "Always telling me how the government stole the land from them to control food production."

"Guess they want to start their own herd." Piper examined the terrain on the map, but the resolution got fuzzy a mile or so in, right where the drone was heading.

Huge swaths of formerly agricultural land had been turned into Carbon Sequestration Forests in the mid-21st century. It was part of a global re-forestation program to counteract dangerous CO_2 levels in the atmosphere, and helped move agriculture into city centers, where crops were now grown in closed-system vertical farms and community rooftop gardens. Even before the massive bee die-out that caused most of the remaining flat farms and ranches to fail, agriculture had already been moving cityward to reduce transportation costs. Piper remembered the shortages and riots from her early childhood, when her own family had to give up their small ranch and move into one of Austin's new arcologies. There were still people who claimed both the bees and the CO_2 levels were just conspiracies, like Jayce had said.

The drone whirred overhead, going back the way it had come, now with no bovine cargo. "Feeling up for a hike?"

"You're not going in there?" Jayce whispered.

"This is our chance to find out exactly where they're hiding out. We can take their GPS coordinates straight to the police."

"They got guns, Piper."

"That's why we need to be all sneaky-like. You don't want to join me, you can stay here and keep a lookout."

His mouth opened and closed a few times before he said, "Yeah. Yeah, okay, I'll come with you."

They hid the bike a few yards into the trees, then picked their way through the underbrush as best they could with only the full moon filtered through the branches and the glow of Piper's wrist unit. It got sluggish and glitchy the farther they trekked into the forest, as though the signal were being jammed. A device that didn't have the customization and firewalls Piper's did probably would have shut down halfway there. The cow's blip reported high adrenaline levels, but other than that, the animal was fine.

Jayce grabbed her arm and pointed. Piper followed his eyeline to a thin wire she was inches from tripping. They backed up, hyper-vigilant for other traps. From nearby came the familiar lowing of cattle. A few yards over, the trees broke enough to reveal a small clearing, with all five of the missing cows grazing between jagged tree stumps. Another blip appeared on the LASSO app – a sixth stolen cow heading in.

Jayce lingered back, but Piper crept closer, avoiding a few more trip wires, and took pictures. The drone whirred into sight. The cattle scattered and men emerged from a shack. Piper ducked behind a juniper.

A man with a thick horseshoe mustache tossed a lasso around the cow's neck while a man with a curly mullet used a handheld controller to release the drone's claws from around the cow. A third man, bulky and muscular, gave the animal some kind of shot. The drone settled into the field and lay like a giant dormant spider. Piper licked her lips. With the right equipment, she could hack it, easy.

A border collie looked her direction and began to bark. She picked her way to where Jayce waited, and the dog kept barking but didn't follow. By the time they made it back to the bike, she had sore feet and a fair number of scratches and burrs, and at least one tick.

She swiped through the images on her wrist unit, most of which were dark and fuzzy. "Let's hope this will be good enough for the cops."

Jayce frowned. "I don't think we should go to the cops."

"What? Why not?"

"It's like to take forever that way. They'd probably pick off an entire herd before the paperwork even got filed."

Piper nodded. "Fair enough."

It would also bring a lot more public attention to the ranch, which would just aggravate Adrianne's problems. The sky was beginning to lighten – dawn already. Fatigue fogged her brain, but ideas were beginning to coalesce like clouds on the horizon.

"Okay, no cops. Not yet anyway." Piper kick-started her motorcycle. "Let's see if we can beat them at their own game."

Jayce went in to work, but Piper called in sick, leaving the message before Adrianne got in so she wouldn't have to talk to her. She slept through the morning, then gathered the equipment she needed in the afternoon. That night, she scanned into the Spiral Ranch, locked and armed the lobby doors behind her, took the public elevator all the way up to the top, then climbed the spiral staircase to the rooftop garden.

The open-air garden mixed decorative plants among the vegetables the restaurant used, and it offered a fantastic view of the city. Piper hung her hat from the corner of an ornate bench and waited for the drone, with a tablet on her lap containing a program she'd put together that afternoon.

A corner of Adrianne's office window was visible through the lattice flooring. The lights were still on. *Was she really working this late? This investor thing must really have her spooked.*

When the drone whirred into sight, Piper was ready. She latched onto its signal, then directed it to veer right. It veered right.

"Easy as pie," she muttered as she lowered the drone into the garden. She crouched over it. With a few tweaks, she could keep control of it while she sent it back into the forest to retrieve the cows.

The propellers whirred suddenly to life and Piper ducked out of its way barely in time as the drone darted back to its original course. She scrambled for her tablet. By the time she'd recalibrated it, the drone had reappeared, cow in claws. The drone died for a second, dropping two stories.

"No, no, no." Piper leaned over the ledge. The drone caught, rose, and headed away from the Spiral Ranch. Piper latched onto its signal again, and it jerked, swayed, not sure which commands to obey. It veered dangerously close to a nearby high-rise apartment building. Piper held her breath. The cow bellowed in panic. Then the drone veered back toward her.

And crashed straight through Adrianne's floor-to-ceiling window. Piper raced down the staircase and across the breezeway. Adrianne's frosted door was also shattered, so she stepped through the frame.

Adrianne looked from the drone to Piper with a horrified expression. The cow staggered to its feet; the drone claws opened and closed against the floor as though reaching for the cow. Glass powder crunched under Piper's boots. She leapt onto the sputtering drone, yanking wires and smashing circuits until the lights stopped blinking and it lay still.

"What the hell is going on?" Adrianne demanded.

The cow mooed and circled the office. The safety glass had shattered so finely it covered the cow's hide like snow. It was relatively unharmed, but definitely spooked.

Piper climbed off the drone and opened her mouth to explain, but Adrianne cut her off. "No, you know what? Get this animal out of my office first."

This "animal" is the root of your livelihood, Piper wanted to tell her, *or have you forgotten it's not all paperwork and advertising?*

She patted the cow's rump and led it out to the cargo elevator, down into Pasture 7. Back upstairs, Piper stood in the doorway, catching her breath. Adrianne shook bits of shattered glass out of her chair.

"Just what the hell do you think you're playing at?"

"The missing cows." Piper gestured toward the drone. "This is what's been taking them."

Adrianne pinched her nose. "And you thought crashing it through my window was the best way to get rid of it?"

Piper couldn't bite back the sarcasm. "*Obviously.*" She strode over and tried to heft up one side of the drone, but it was too heavy, so she gave up and headed back toward the door without it. "The cow's okay, by the way."

"Don't turn your back on me."

"Why?" Piper rounded on her. "You've turned your back on the whole point of what we built here. You sit at the top of your glass tower, completely removed from the ranch."

Adrianne took a long breath and spoke in a lower voice: "There are a lot of details involved in running—"

"You were supposed to lead school groups! Teach them about livestock, about where milk comes from and how we process methane energy. You were supposed to keep it local and simple, not be pandering to investors and trying to franchise out to every other city. We were supposed to be a community pillar and cultural heritage site. But we're nothing but an architectural novelty. You won't even step your dainty shoes in a pasture anymore."

That had been building for a long time. Adrianne blinked at her. "Franchising? What are you talking about?"

Of course *that* was the only part of Piper's rant that Adrianne noticed. A company in Pennsylvania wanted to do a Spiral Ranch knock-off; Piper had assumed they'd tried to franchise and Adrianne had asked for too much, but based on her current confusion, maybe they'd side-stepped her all along. Though she'd turned down an offer to work for them, she'd recently been reconsidering.

"Nothing. Nevermind. This isn't the right time to talk about it. We need to—"

The alarm sounded. Lights flashed, and Adrianne's wallscreen showed a schematic of the Spiral Ranch, the point of violation blinking red at its base: the lobby doors on the ground level.

"They're here," Piper said. "I should have known they'd come after I disabled the drone. Can you lock them in?"

Adrianne tapped furiously at the screen for a moment, then shook her head.

"Great, looks like I have to do the dirty work again."

Piper tore down the staircase four steps at a time, slamming the doors open at each pasture as she passed them. She had no plan, she just knew this was her herd, and she would be damned if she let them be carted off into the forest. All the pastures that were supposed to have cattle were fine, until Pasture 3. It was empty, and the gate leading down to Pasture 2 hung off its hinges.

She hesitated at the door to the lobby. No one should have been able to get to the Pastures by either stairs or elevator without an employee badge, but *someone* had made it through. Piper eased the door open a crack, heard a man's voice, and pulled it quietly shut. After a deep breath, she pushed it open again, peering through the smallest sliver she could manage.

"Sorry for the disturbance, officer," the man was saying to the screen in the wall. "We're gettin' them cows back under control now."

The man was nothing more than a Wrangler-clad silhouette against the screen, but she knew that voice.

"Jayce, you son of a—" Piper muttered under her breath.

But then he cleared the screen, turned to another man lurking in the shadows, and said, "Okay, I told 'em what you said. Stop pointing that gun at me now."

The man with the horseshoe mustache didn't lower his shotgun. "I might if you'd'a cooperated from the beginning."

"This is my job, Mack. These are my friends."

"What, the cows?"

"No, you smog-head. Them girls who run this place."

With a ding, the elevator opened and one cow clomped out. The man with the curly mullet herded the cow toward a livestock trailer, which was backed right up to the lobby door. The muscular man leaned out of the elevator. "How many more?"

"'Bout ten."

Muscles groaned. "This is so obnoxious." He stepped back and the elevator doors shut.

Piper smirked. The cargo elevator skipped the lobby and went straight from Pasture 1 to the slaughterhouse. The rustlers would have to transfer the cows one at a time into the public elevator to get them down here. That should buy some time, anyway.

"What's going on?" Adrianne hissed at her ear. Piper jumped, eased the door shut, and pushed Adrianne back.

"Just go upstairs and call the cops."

"What?"

"Just go. And stay up there where you're safe."

Adrianne's scowl reminded Piper how she had insulted her for hiding up in her glass tower just a few minutes ago. But she only said, "Come with me."

"No, I need to make sure they don't leave, track them if they do. Go. Hurry!"

Adrianne fled up the stairs and Piper rubbed a hand across her face. Charging into the lobby seemed like suicide, but maybe she could cut off the cattle rustling at the elevator. She climbed the stairs back to Pasture 2. A border collie kept the agitated cattle clustered toward the front of the pasture. The elevator opened and Piper ducked down behind one of the cows. Moving that fast and that low was a good way to get yourself trampled – they may have been dwarf cattle, but they'd still break ribs and cut nasty gashes if Piper found herself under their hooves. Muscles kick-shoved two cows to drive them into the elevator, then followed them in. The doors snapped shut.

Piper grabbed a handful of seaweed feed, and started the whoops and clicks they used when rotating the cattle to a new pasture. She shoved the seaweed at one cow's face. The cow licked a long black tongue toward it, but the dog snarled and snapped, not letting any of them follow Piper. You can't bribe a dog with seaweed, and apparently "Go on, git," wasn't a command it understood. *Running out of time.* She could already hear the whir of the elevator on its way back up. Only – *wait, no.* That wasn't the elevator.

The robotic manure collector puttered past. Piper glanced from the clam-shaped robot to the ledge above the elevator. Like most of these ledges, a bird had built a messy nest there. Only a few days before, Jayce had joked that they should heft the manure collectors up there to get rid of the nests. He'd even measured to prove that it could fit.

With the dog yapping at her heels, the cattle mooing and stamping, Piper kicked over a water trough and stood on it. The bird fluttered off with an indignant squawk, and Piper plucked the nest down and set it gently by the milking station. A couple of taps on the control screen brought the manure collector to a halt, and then she crouched down, hefted the smelly robot, and perched it on the ledge. She had just enough time to race back to the control panel and hit "go" when the elevator doors opened.

Muscles saw her, shouted, "Hey!" and then the manure collector rolled right off the ledge and onto his head with a clunk. He toppled unconscious to the floor. The robot landed tracks up, the storage compartment broken open and mess oozing onto the floor. She shooed the cows away from the elevator, then opened the slats of the cattle guard to keep them from crossing. Muscles had a pistol in a holster on his left hip. Piper grabbed it, stepped into the elevator. She'd been five when her family had finally turned over their land, sent their animals up to Nebraska and moved to the city, but her father had taken her once a year to a shooting range, saying it was an important skill to preserve. She'd never believed him until this very moment.

When the elevator doors opened, Mustache Mack had his back turned, but Jayce yelled, "Piper!" and Mack swung around, pointing his shotgun at her. She stepped out of the elevator and pointed the pistol back at him.

"Just return the cattle, and we won't tell the police anything about this," Piper said.

"You're in no position to negotiate."

"I know where your homestead is."

His gaze flickered for a moment. "I don't want to have to kill you."

Jayce looked to the trailer, backed against the front doors, where Mullet was busy shoving the cattle up a ramp. Jayce licked his lips, then tackled Mack from behind, arm around his neck. Mack's gun fired at the ceiling, raining tile and insulation down on them. Jayce let go in surprise, long enough for Mack to gain his footing and point his gun at Jayce.

"Guess this is just as good. You make any wrong move, girlie, and I shoot him."

"You're not gonna shoot me," Jayce said.

"I just might, cuz. You ain't making full use of both of them knee caps."

"This is your *cousin*, Jayce? Why didn't you say anything when – when—" She faltered.

"Thought I could talk some sense into him," Jayce said. "'Stead, he kidnapped me, used my employee badge to get in here."

"*Kidnapped*," Mack snorted. Gun still on Jayce, his eyes flicked to the pistol she held. "Where's Wayne?"

Must be the bulky smog-head upstairs. "He's still alive. For now. Why are you doing this?"

"Cows ain't supposed to live in skyscrapers. We just want to bring agriculture back to the land, back to the people."

"By stealing our cattle."

"Way I see it, we're liberating them." Mack said. "You know, we could use someone with your expertise. Pretty impressive, the way you hacked that drone. You could join us."

He stepped backward. She was the one with her back to the wall, and he had only a few steps to make it to the trailer. Could she actually pull the trigger if he made a run for it? Piper had no way to know if any help was on the way.

"We want the same thing you want," Mack said.

"No," she told him. "The Spiral Ranch may not be the best way, but we can't go back to the old ways either. The land has to heal, re-grow."

He took another step back. "That's just propaganda, and you know it."

She stepped forward, closing the distance between them. Someday, maybe people would spread out, start living horizontally again instead of vertically, but right now was a fallow time.

"Let's go, man," Mullet yelled. He herded the last two cows into the trailer and latched the gate.

"I can't let you take our cattle," Piper said.

"Then I'd say we are at an impasse." Mack cocked the gun. "Too bad. I—"

He didn't get to finish that sentence. The manure collector robot dropped out of the shotgun hole in the ceiling and knocked him out cold. Jayce caught the weapon before it hit the ground, but let his cousin fall. Piper looked up to see Adrianne waving down at her through the hole.

"What did you do?" Piper shouted. "Crawl through the air vent?"

"Oh, hell," said Mullet, racing around to climb into the truck. Jayce and Piper sprinted after him, but before they made it outside, lights flashed on the street, and two police cars pulled onto the sidewalk to block the trailer.

"Well, look who it is," the officer said to Mullet. "Johnny-boy, I thought we had an agreement I wouldn't be seeing you again." She handcuffed him and led him to the car.

The second officer stepped into the lobby, looking from Jayce and Piper to the unconscious man on the floor, and wrinkled his nose at the manure robot, now definitely damaged beyond repair. Jayce slowly lowered the shotgun and leaned it against the wall. Piper lifted her hands, the pistol dangling from her index finger by the trigger guard.

The elevator door dinged open then, and Adrianne stepped out, tugging her blouse down and standing tall despite the fact that she was covered in grease and manure. Bits of fiberglass clung to her disheveled hair. "Thank you so much for your quick response, officers. I'd appreciate if you'd get these intruders off my property as soon as possible. There's another upstairs."

After the cops dragged the unconscious criminals away, they took statements and had Piper, Jayce, and Adrianne fill out some lengthy forms. "And here I thought those reports about flying cows were due to some new drug," one of them said with a chuckle.

"They still have half a dozen head out in the forest," Piper said.

"We'll look into it." The officer pointed his stylus at her. "Do *not* go out there again. You hear me?"

Piper swallowed, nodded. A tow-truck came for the truck and trailer. Cattle filled the lobby; a few of them wandered out along the street. After the police left, Piper approached Adrianne. She looked like hell. Bits of her hair had torn out of their clips and stuck out in all directions. She'd lost both shoes, and manure splatters spread across her sky-blue skirt.

"Guess you *are* willing to do some of the dirty work," Piper said. Adrianne gave a weak smile. "I'm sorry I said all those things, before. I … I didn't mean nothin'."

Adrianne shook her head. "No, you were right. About some things, anyway."

"There's another ranch up north, they wanted me to go up there, build a LASSO system for them, show them how we run things." Piper looked at the floor. "I ain't gonna do it."

To Piper's utter shock, Adrianne laughed. "Let's talk to them together, see if we can work out a deal."

"Really?"

"You've got the tech and knowledge they need. And a franchise opportunity sure would make my investors change their tune. I just wish you'd *told* me, Piper. I'm sick of people trying to steal things from me. Stealing my cows. Stealing my reputation. Stealing my partner."

Piper grinned at that. She hadn't felt much like a partner in this for a while.

The short summer night was coming to a close. The sky flushed yellow, and sunbeams reflected off the city's many mirrored windows. Piper reached for her hat, but remembered it was still on the roof, if a breeze hadn't sent it flying.

Jayce came down the stairs with the border collie, declaring that the dog was his now and he needed to take it home. Piper shouted at him that the dog would be helpful to round up the cattle still wandering the lobby and the street, but he was already gone. She sighed.

"Lot of repairs to do today," Piper said.

"And cleaning." Adrianne picked at her soiled clothes.

One of the cows snuffled at Adrianne's hair. Piper patted its side. "Help me get these girls back where they belong?"

To her surprise, Adrianne agreed. They hung a "Temporarily Closed" sign on the lobby door and got to work.

Drawing the Line

Gustavo Bondoni

YEVGENY CURSED under his breath.

Philippa smiled. "Things not going to plan?" the elderly woman asked.

"Things never go to plan." He held up a mangled piece of aluminum alloy. "I'll need to take this back to the shop and try to use it as a pattern to machine a new one." He held it up, trying to see how the light went through compound curves of the tube. "I don't think it's going to be easy."

"I trust you," Philippa said.

He knew she did. That was why he'd find a way, some way, any way of getting it done.

They sat in silence for a few minutes. The morning sun wasn't as harsh as it would be at noontime, and he could bask in it, even with his pale skin.

Then, disaster. Siti walked past, smiled and nodded, her red shuka tightly wrapped around her, her head erect, the inevitable walking stick, as thin and straight as she was, held in one hand.

He sighed as Siti disappeared around a corner.

"You should tell her how you feel," Philippa said. "You might be surprised."

Yevgeny groaned. *Was it that obvious to everyone?* "Of course. The woman changing the face of Africa, creating technologies that are pushing back the effects of global warming must just be dying to hear all about how the mechanic has a crush on her."

"So you're afraid, then."

"Shouldn't I be? She's a great visionary. I'm fixing your blender so you can drink margaritas."

"And yet, you don't seem afraid of me. Or of Oscar. He told me you fixed his shower last week."

"I …"

"Have you forgotten who we are?"

"No. Of course not. No one on Earth will ever forget you." He realized that sounded as if they were about to die. "I mean …"

"I know what you mean. I was young once, too." She put a finger on his mouth to keep him from speaking. "You say that she is changing the world. That's true. But I already have, and you don't have any problems talking to me. Oscar … Oscar has probably saved more lives than anyone alive. His seed stock broke the corporate monopoly … and he was the person who finally negotiated the completion of the Great Green Wall. He's as important as Siti could ever hope to be."

"I guess you're right."

"Do you know what Oscar says about you? He says he wished you were his son."

It was true. The octogenarian scientist had said it to Yevgeny himself more than once.

"That's just because I do him favors sometimes."

"No. If you only did him favors, he wouldn't have said anything. It's because you do everyone favors. My blender. The gardener's pinball machine. None of these things are what you're being paid for. We all know that. And yet you take the time necessary to do them for us."

"Yeah. I guess. Maybe my problem is that the director doesn't need any favors."

The sun was now straight overhead. Yevgeny, it made him feel that he was too delicate for Africa, wore a cowboy hat. It felt ridiculous to be wearing it within stone's throw of the Sahara Desert in Chad, but somehow a British pith helmet would have seemed monstrously colonial. Nothing else he'd tried worked for him; killing heat was never something he'd worried about in Petrozavodsk. Back home, you wore hats to keep your ears from freezing.

Despite the broiling air, he pedaled hard. The motor he'd had to repair – an irrigation pump – had taken much longer than anticipated, and lunch would be served in fifteen minutes. He'd already lost any chance of washing up, and lunch, was the one meal that no one would ever dare to miss, or one would face the director's wrath.

Fortunately, the road had just been paved with a kind of biodegradable rubber which, compared to the old dirt track, made him feel like he was moving at a million miles an hour.

He skidded to a halt in front of the gleaming reflective glass of the administration building, dropped the bike on the ground and checked his watch. He was late, but not terminally so.

He turned to run towards the Shady Vale, the grassy depression surrounded by trees that served as a communal cafeteria, when he noticed Jennifer Ward exiting the building carrying a pair of folders under her arm. When she saw him she looked as flustered as he felt. But that was understandable: his own tardiness would be forgiven due to distance and complexity; hers would cause comment.

He gave her an encouraging smile. "Come on. Maybe if we both walk in together, she'll go easy on us."

Jennifer laughed, a nervous sound, and put the folders in her backpack. "I hope you're right."

As they filed between the tables, every eye followed them. There was no way around it, but maybe he could draw the fire himself and allow Jennifer to find her place unnoticed. He stopped in front of the director's table and addressed Siti. "I'm sorry I'm late. The pump took longer than I expected."

To his relief, she nodded her approval. "But it's working now?"

"Yes. And it should stay that way."

"Good. That pump is critical for the Line."

The Line. Everyone else in the world called it the Great Green Wall of Africa, a barrier of trees several kilometers wide just south of the Sahara. It had been credited for holding back the expansion of the desert through the worst spasms of the Climate Crises. The people who'd worked there in the past fifty years, heroes like Philippa and Oscar, had called it the Front Line ... and the name, at least the Line part of it, had stuck. Now, the complex, once a central administrative node for the tree-planting project, was working on a completely different kind of climate change technology, but they were still on the bleeding edge.

"I know."

"Thanks for taking care of it."

"It was my pleasure." He turned to find his seat. It would have been randomly assigned, so he might have to search for it.

"Yevgeny?"

"Yes?" he turned back.

"Why don't you take a buggy for yourself? They're all solar, they don't pollute."

She was teasing him, of course. He was the one who kept the complex's cars running. "I'm fine with the bicycle. It keeps me in shape, and it's not as if it ever rains around here."

Now he was teasing her, and the faces around the table registered surprise. First he was late, and now this. But Siti took the barb in stride. "For now," she replied.

"Yes," Yevgeny told Adjo impatiently. "I know it's supposed to be in stock. I can read an inventory just as well as you can. But it's not there."

"What did you use it for?"

"I didn't use it. Someone else must have taken it."

"That's silly. You're the only one who needs those."

The piece of flat glass he needed was not something he'd have forgotten he used. It was the smallest high-efficiency photovoltaic variably transparent piece of glass in the world, created in the lab across the path by the only people who know how to build it. But more importantly, it was a circle thirty centimeters across that only fit onto the skylight at the top of the office area, to shine light straight onto the director's desk. The climb up to that particular point of the roof was a nightmare, and he'd put off attempting it until Siti really got on his case. And when she did, the niche holding the replacement part was empty.

"I think someone stole it," Yevgeny said.

That shocked the other man. "Who would do such a thing?"

"How should I know? Maybe someone who wants to reverse-engineer one of the most advanced pieces of technology on the planet?"

"Look. If you lost it, just say so. I'm sure the lab will build you another one. They like to show off."

"I'm telling you, I didn't lose it, I didn't break it, and I most certainly am not going to let this one pass. If we have a thief in the colony, or someone working for one of the corporations, we need to find out who it is."

Adjo still seemed unconcerned. "It's just a piece of glass."

Yevgeny sighed. "I know it doesn't sound like much, but it's the key to a lot of things. If one of the corporations gets ahead of our research cycle, it could undo years of good. Now kick this one up the ladder, will you?"

Adjo nodded. "All right. I still think it's a waste of time, but if you feel it's important, I'll take it up with the director. But don't blame me if she ignores it."

"Thank you." His supervisor could often be slow about technological issues, but once he gave his word, it was as good as gold. He would take it up, and make the case for an investigation as best he could.

He walked back to his workshop, cursing the paper-white skin that kept him under cover unless he was slathered in sunscreen. He'd made the mistake, just a couple weeks before, of believing that he'd been in Africa long enough that he could work without a shirt. The resulting blistering and lobster-colored skin had been painful, but not as much as the condescending kindness of the men and women around him. Even the other non-Africans seemed to do better in the sun than Yevgeny, but the response that hurt the most was Siti's understanding smile and assurances that he'd get used to the sun eventually. It was easy for her to say: her perfect ebony skin, legacy of her Maasai heritage, would never betray her.

At least the workshop was a beautiful place to spend one's working day. Open to the breeze on three sides – although the glass doors could be closed when needed – the structure appeared to have been built out of gossamer spider's webs. Thin metal tracings, interwoven with the surrounding trees, supported a solar roof array that powered all his equipment. For delicate jobs that required a dust-proof environment, a paint and work cabin was tucked behind the workbenches which, themselves, had been built of wood from the Green Wall.

Troubled by the loss of the panel, Yevgeny went back into the storage area – basically just a big closet behind the paint cabin – with a datapad on whose screen the inventory list was displayed. He spent his afternoon checking every single cubbyhole. His stock of screws and minor parts was way off, but that was his own fault. He never remembered to update the inventory when he used those – he was always in a hurry, and who would worry about a couple of bolts here or a t-bracket there?

The rest of the inventory looked okay, even the expensive drone parts except ... there was a solar super-cooler missing which he didn't recall having fitted onto anything. This was a part about the size of a datapad whose function was to turn the energy of the ever-present sunlight into electricity which ran a powerful compact cooling system. It was eminently portable, but also obsolete – Siti's drones had begun to carry a new version, lighter and more powerful, when they went up and, since none of those had broken yet, he hadn't asked the lab for replacement parts.

Then he smacked his head. "Yevgeny," he reminded himself. "You are an idiot. That is why you will always only be a mechanic."

The super-cooler was only obsolete there, in that small village of less than five hundred people who worked and lived in the complex. The lab – run by twenty material scientists, complete with teams of assistants, who'd come from all over the world to work under Oscar and Philippa, and who now reported to Siti – held some of the most advanced manufacturing equipment anywhere. But more importantly than that, the researchers within knew what to do with their machines. Anywhere else on the planet, the missing part would be the most advanced compact cooling device anyone had ever seen.

Even Yevgeny was hesitant to take apart components delivered from the lab. Of course, after he grew familiar with how they functioned, he would usually attempt a dissection … but semiconductors and superconducters were not something he could fix with a wrench, even if he understood how they worked in conjunction with the rest of the electronics around them.

Well, at least he would become obsolete with his eyes open.

In the meantime, he needed to think. The super-cooler was likely long gone, mailed out of the complex through their community courier service, but he wanted to try to figure out who'd had the opportunity to take the missing parts before he went to Adjo again. He thought best while either working or on his bike … and it wasn't time for his ride just yet.

There were only a couple of jobs left to do. The first was to replace the nav chip on one of the buggies. That, due to some boneheaded design or a misguided belief that nav chips would never fail, was an arduous task that involved removing a good chunk of the forward bulkhead.

Yevgeny whistled a tune and began dismantling the car. He tried to understand who might have a reason to take things from the complex. Most thefts, he knew from having spent his early childhood during Russia's Transition, came from a lack of money. That, of course, might still be a good motive, but in the complex – and in Chad itself, and in the rest of the Wall Treaty Nations – money was no longer used. He believed that the nearest place that still used any kind of currency was Senegal, but he couldn't be sure. Then what? Nationalism? That was still alive and well, even after the Consolidation … but everyone was vetted thoroughly before they were allowed to remain.

He had a hard time coming to any conclusion and before he knew it, an hour had passed and he was done with the chip. He looked up at the wall display …

Time for his ride.

The complex was a melting pot of several religions. The Christians went to church – a long and dusty ride – every Sunday, and the Muslim majority had several prayer halts each day. Yevgeny had only one sacred ritual: every afternoon, at exactly six in the afternoon, he'd drop everything and take a one-hour bike ride along the paths and roads around the complex and the airfield. It was the one period of the day when his comm was off, and he wouldn't do anyone any favors. The cool pre-dusk wind, humid and, if not quite brisk at least less hot, represented glorious relief from the oppressive heat.

And he left at six o'clock precisely even if that meant, as it did on that day, that Philippa would only get her blender working again tomorrow.

His mind worried the problem of the missing parts, but he couldn't come to any conclusion. He knew everyone involved in the project and he couldn't imagine anyone betraying it. There were all sorts of people at the complex: friendly, taciturn, engaging, shy, sullen, even a few who were openly aggressive and disliked the decision to allow a Russian into the project – and took that out on Yevgeny himself. But even though he didn't get along with all of them, he couldn't imagine one being a traitor.

He arrived tired, sweaty and no closer to finding an answer than when he'd set out, to find Siti leaning against one of his workbenches. She'd abandoned her usual Maasai attire for a dark business suit which, if possible, made her look even more fabulous.

"I'm sorry you had to wait," he said. "I always take a ride at this time."

She smiled, perfect white teeth contrasting brilliantly with her skin. "I know. And it's always exactly one hour. I only just arrived a minute ago."

"Oh," he didn't know whether he should be worried or honored that the director knew his habits. "Can I help you?"

"I have a couple of questions about the missing glass. I'll make it quick, because I know you like to clean the workshop and shower before dinner."

"Don't rush on my account. It's pretty clean." He told her about the missing glass, and also about the cooling element.

She listened grimly. "Too much coincidence."

"That's what I thought, too."

"All right. We'll have to look into it, but that's not the reason I came here. Can you set up a charging station for the drones? I want to be able to charge all sixteen of them simultaneously and solar-only charge is taking too long."

He thought about it for a moment. The drones could charge in an hour using the sunlight that hit them, but could be back up in minutes using the current generated by the much larger solar arrays of the complex. "I think so. Do you want to test them all at once?"

"We're past that. I want to send them up with the grid."

The super-cooled netting that made up the grid was meant to catch and condense moisture in the air.

"You're going to try to make it rain?"

There had been other efforts. Cloud seeding, static condensers. None of them had been successful on a large scale. The seeding, in fact, had failed completely, despite working perfectly in laboratory conditions. The lack of artificial rain, and their continued reliance on irrigation from groundwater was a running joke in the complex.

"Not yet. We need to test the full flight for a few weeks to see if they can hold the grid steady before we try to cool the grid." Her half-smile told him that there was something she wasn't saying, but before he could ask, she went on. "How long do you think the charging station would take?"

"I suppose you want it somewhere without trees."

The smile widened. "That would probably be for the best, yes."

"I'll get to work on it tomorrow. I'll need to get some parts in from N'Djamena. I think probably …". He did some calculations in his head. "Three days."

Yevgeny forgot all about the missing parts as the sudden rush of work enveloped him. First, he set out the wiring he would need for the charging station – he'd selected a flat, dusty stretch about four hundred meters from the complex – and, despite the irony of it, he made sure the cables were well waterproofed. He set up sixteen posts, well separated from one another. The only thing missing were the special cables that would plug into each of the drones – those were the parts he'd ordered.

The drive to the capital required – to his chagrin – that he borrow one of the buggies. He hated them because he didn't trust them … it was spooky to think that the solar panels could power the vehicle with no fuel, no external power whatsoever. Even after the Transition, rural Russians trusted diesel with their lives … solar was for city folk who weren't at risk of being stranded in the snow a hundred kilometers from anything.

So he put off borrowing the car. Instead, he spent a much longer time than he should have machining the part for Philippa's blender. But there was only so much he could do to a curved tube half the size of his pinkie finger, and he was soon driving along the dusty road.

The surface was sealed with biodegradable oils, ideal for the lightweight, well-sprung buggies, but the trip still took a long time and brought back memories that Yevgeny preferred to suppress. He was a different person when he'd first arrived from Russia, via N'Djamena, along that same road. Then, his head had been full of misconceptions, even if his heart was in the right place.

The sight of an umbrella thorn acacia brought that day back to him in vivid detail. It hadn't even been that long ago. He'd hired a driver to bring him to the complex and, a few kilometers out, he'd seen an African woman walking steadily along the road.

He'd told the man to stop beside her and offered her a lift in tortured French. She'd declined with a smile, in English much better than his French – and also much better than his own English. Then he'd offered her food. She was tall and thin, and he thought she might be underfed. All he'd had was the remains of a hamburger from the McDonald's at the airport.

This had been rejected with a laugh and the explanation that people in Chad tended to eat a much healthier diet … and preferred real meat in their burgers. She'd walked away, leaving him bemused.

He'd been even more bemused when the woman he'd seen walking was introduced to him a few hours later as Dr. Siti Gisemba, the Kenyan Director of the complex – and a legendary figure in her own right, despite being in her early thirties.

Talk about getting off on the wrong foot. The only good of it was that he knew he would never have a chance with her, so he didn't spend too much time dreaming.

Five hours later, Yevgeny returned to the complex. The parts had been waiting for him in the office building that the Green Wall project had in N'Djamena's modern downtown.

He would be able to finish constructing the charging station the following morning, and now he had a few minutes to spare before bicycle time came around. He headed straight for the small compound where retired members of the community lived in airy, beautiful houses surrounded by the living wall itself.

"I'm sorry this took so long," he told Philippa.

The woman just smiled. "I hear you've been busy."

He took the part he'd built and placed it in the open space left by the original. It was a nearly perfect match, but he wasn't satisfied. Philippa watched him fondly while he filed the part until it was a precise match.

"You know," she said, "I never thought you would fit in here. You looked too young, too eager to change things. I thought the rigid structure would get to you and you'd leave after a few months. But you're here to stay, aren't you?"

"What do you mean?"

"Not every young man from … your background … can live with the rules."

"You mean sitting down to lunch at exactly the same time?"

"Of course. That and the fact that you exchange all your working hours for nothing other than room and board. Everyone here would be extremely well paid on the open market."

He shrugged. "I've been on the open market. There's nothing you can buy that compares to living here. I was scared it might not be all that was promised. My main worry was that Africa might be like the old movies. But this … this is paradise."

"If Siti has her way, the whole world will be like this someday. Most of Africa already is, as well as South America and Australia."

He smiled. "Russia … may take a while."

"Maybe less than you think. There are a lot of initiatives already in place. Most of the big cities are getting there. We're actually much more worried about Western Europe and North America."

"They seem to do all right."

"Perhaps, but by keeping up a monetary economy, they are actually slowing their pace of development and falling behind. Their people are doing well, but they're still missing out." She shook her head. "Part of that is the fact that they're afraid to change, of course. But another part is that the environmental groups have grown too radicalized. You don't get harmony like this by beating people over the head and blowing up banks. You don't get it by using unlicensed technology to replace what communities are already using – and causing accidents that kill the very people you're trying to convert. Harmony comes naturally from showing everyone how nice it is ... and by being together. That's the real reason Siti forces us all to be punctual for lunch and dinner." Philippa's eyes twinkled. "She used to really, really hate being tied down for two hours. If it was up to her, she'd work all day without stopping."

"So she does it for us."

"Of course. And we do it for us, as well. And so do you. I've seen you pedaling furiously from miles away to arrive in time to wash before eating. You belong here because you understand ... and even if you didn't understand the reasons behind the insistence until now, you never had to be reminded about the rule, and you never acted as if it was stupid."

He finished adjusting the part and pressed the outer casing back in place. Then he tested the blender and was satisfied to hear a strong, steady whirring.

"That's it. As good as new," he said.

Philippa thanked him and he went off on his ride. After the long, nervous drive in the solar car, he needed to work the kinks out of his system.

But his mind refused to cooperate. There was something, something he'd seen or something he'd heard at Philippa's that had made him uneasy, a feeling that he was missing something important.

He was back in the complex, riding past the habitation module when it hit him.

Of course.

He stopped suddenly, left his bike where it fell and entered the coral-like building. He rushed through the veins of stone that made up the interior of the apartment structure and stopped at the directory. The rooms he was looking for were located on the third floor.

Too impatient to wait for the elevator, Yevgeny sprinted up the steps three at a time. As soon as he located the door, he pounded on it, not bothering to locate the buzzer.

Jennifer answered. Her surprise at finding him looking like he'd just biked for an hour in the heat and then run up the stairs quickly faded to be replaced by an expression of alarm.

She stepped back, turned towards the kitchen and took three steps forward. She tore open a drawer and reached inside.

"Don't," he said.

She stopped and looked back at him.

"Unless you have a gun stashed in there, you won't be able to get rid of me. I grew up in Russia in the Transition. The first thing we learned as kids was how to defend ourselves against someone with a knife. I don't want to have to break your arm."

Jennifer glared at him.

"Besides," he continued. "What are you hoping to gain? A couple of hours? Someone will notice I'm missing. Someone will remember me coming in here. They'll find you soon enough. It's over."

And then she broke down, sat cross-legged on the floor still clutching the knife, and cried.

The two pieces of technology were, as Yevgeny had expected, long gone, but a couple of folders in the apartment turned up blueprints of things still in the works. They were things that Jennifer should never have had access to. Things that she must have taken off the director's desk.

Siti sat down facing her.

"You have no right to violate my privacy this way," Jennifer said, pretending anger. It was obvious, however, that she was actually scared and frightened.

"The folders were on the table. We haven't even searched for anything else. You should let go of the knife."

Jennifer looked at it as if she'd forgotten it was in her hand. She dropped it onto the floor and pushed it away.

"Thank you." Siti gave her a hard look. "Do you want to tell me who you were working for?"

"Would it make any difference?"

"Not really. I won't let you stay no matter who it was."

Jennifer's tears exploded from her once again. Yevgeny's heart broke. He knew the woman had been there for years. Even though she'd been caught red-handed, he was sure the emotion was genuine.

"Is it a corporation?"

Jennifer's sadness disappeared, to be replaced by rage, but it passed quickly. Defeat was the only thing she had left. "What do you take me for?"

"I took you for a loyal member of the community. Now … you tell me."

"I'm going to miss this place. You. Everything. I really do believe. But so many people don't."

"Oh." Siti sounded sad.

It suddenly became clear to Yevgeny that Jennifer must be part of one of the many fringe groups determined to force their lifestyle on people who weren't ready for it, or even particularly interested.

"I'll just pack, then," Jennifer said.

"Yes." Siti turned to go, but stopped. "Wait. Before you go, I have a message for your … people."

"What?" There was defiance in Jennifer's features now. She knew that no one would hurt her. No one would keep her from leaving. That wasn't the way they did things there.

"Tell them that I'm willing to share everything we're doing here. Both what's already been done and what we're developing. I'll give them as much as the lab can produce.

But I have one condition. They have to live here for a year, and see if they can't learn from our methods as well. Maybe if they learn how to teach instead of how to dictate, people will listen to them. Tell them to send an emissary. Two or even ten if they want. You know we can feed as many as they can send." Siti's features hardened. "We'll accept anyone but you."

Now Siti did walk out. Yevgeny followed her; there wasn't really anything for him to do in Jennifer's apartment. He'd already done enough damage.

Out on the path, Siti allowed him to catch up. The woman's stride was much too long for him, and he wasn't going to run after her.

"How did you know?" she said.

"The day we were late for lunch … she pretended she'd been working late. I knew you'd never let that happen. But I only realized it today."

"You're smarter than you look. Are you sure you don't want to go to work in the lab? The offer is still open, you know. I know Hermes says he can use you. And I'm sure you can optimize the drone electronics if they give you access to the codes. I've been having trouble keeping them as steady as I'd like."

"No thanks. I'm all right," he replied.

Two days later, he took a day off. The drone recharging field had been a harder job than he imagined. There'd been a short-circuit somewhere, and it had taken him hours to track it to a cracked cable casing inside the complex itself. But it was done, and drones had been taking off and landing all day. He'd even seen the cooling mesh grid – the element that would, in theory, condense the water in the air – fly at one point. It was as big as a football field, but light enough that the drones could lift it and maneuver.

He chuckled. Siti was doing excellent work, but her obsession for controlling the weather would lead nowhere. Oscar and Philippa, two of the great minds of humanity had beaten their heads against the problem for forty years and never gotten around it. Siti's approach was a bit different, but it depended on too many variables to work. He just hoped the obsession didn't distract her from more fruitful pursuits.

Of course, he could never tell her that directly. The closest he could ever come was to joke with her about it and hope she took the hint.

Even on his days off, the bike ride was sacred. He mounted at exactly six. There was still an hour left until sundown, and he saw that his hopes of Siti relaxing her urge to control the rain were in vain. She was still at it.

The drones, complete with condenser grid, lifted from the charging field as soon as he rode out of the complex. The formation appeared tight enough, with each drone holding its position. Hermes must have rewritten the algorithms.

He watched until the individual drones were almost invisible in the sky, then set his eyes back to the road. Fifteen minutes into his ride, a drop fell on his head. Then another.

Yevgeny looked around. There wasn't a cloud in the sky.

Incredible … Siti's rig was working.

But that couldn't be. She'd said she needed weeks of testing before she would turn it on.

And yet, another look into the sky confirmed it was the only possible explanation. Not one cloud. And now it was raining steadily enough to be annoying.

Well, at least he'd ride out of it in a hundred meters or so. The net wasn't all that big.

Forty-five minutes later, he came to a stop in front of his workshop, soaked to the skin. It had rained on him the entire way.

Siti was waiting for him, her face expressionless.

"You made it rain on me all the way," he said.

"Yes," she replied.

"That was …"

Siti finally couldn't control herself any longer and burst out laughing. "It was what you deserved. That was what it was. You never believed."

He was about to retort, but caught himself and lowered his eyes. "No. I didn't."

"Do you believe now?"

"Do I have any choice? The impossible can happen."

"Yes. It can."

Was that an opening? No. It couldn't be.

But if it was, he would never forgive himself. "You owe me dinner for this," he said.

"Not dinner. Dinner is a communal affair. You know that." His heart sank. Just like that, in a second, she'd shot him down.

She let the silence continue for another two heartbeats, and then she smiled. "But if you can get your hands on a bottle of something, I'd be up for a few drinks on the lab terrace afterwards."

"I thought the lab closed after dark."

Her smile broadened. "I have a key."

He watched her walk off, admiring, as he always did, her perfectly straight posture. Then he snapped out of it. Dinner was in twenty minutes. He needed to change out of the wet clothes ... and where in the world was he going to get a bottle of anything good on such short notice?

Yevgeny sprang into motion.

Lizard Skin

Lucie Lukačovičová

When the world is burning,
Fired within, yet turning...
Ebenezer Jones

THEY GLARED at him. They glared with all the pain, anger and powerlessness that they felt.

They did not perceive him as a cop. They did not perceive him even as a human. They saw him as a vulture, which came to harm them, to feast on their misfortune and loss.

Vassudev Harwalkar concluded he could do nothing about it. He kept walking through the camp of volunteer workers in the direction where he anticipated the beach, hidden in darkness. The volunteers had a few campfires, carefully enclosed in a way that abided by all the security measures. They did not need them really; they had heaters and lamps running on solar energy accumulated during the hot Goan day. Vassudev recognized the campfires as some kind of message or statement. But he had no idea what it was saying.

He slowly passed by a board sign with an inscription: *Ran Ltd. Hired Property – Authorized Personnel Only!*

The sand on the edge of the camp was dotted with small lamps and candles. Among them there were statuettes of Hindu deities, miniatures of Christian saints, crosses, pieces of paper with quotations from Quran written in calligraphy and other religious symbols, which Vassudev couldn't recognize in the flickering light.

There were people praying or meditating or simply mourning silently, sharing their common sorrow – at the same time never leaving the candles unattended.

As Vassudev passed them by, nobody said a word, there was only hostile silence. He noticed a thin girl with a myna bird on her shoulder. She was staring into the distance, glassy eyed.

Vassudev walked on.

When he left the camp behind, he switched on a heavy flashlight.

Only then he saw it. Of course, he had been watching the news on the Viral-Net. But to see the beach with his own eyes was something different.

The black coating of crude oil was stretching in the darkness. Sea and sand seemed to be smothered under it. It gave the landscape a nightmarish feel, like endless film of black blood spilled from the bowels of a damaged tanker. Like a sick second skin covering everything around.

The work of the volunteers trying to clean it had stopped and was not allowed to continue until the accident – that occurred during their activity – was thoroughly investigated.

"Good evening – Mr. Harwalkar, I presume," said a voice nearby.

Vassudev turned around slowly.

He saw a tall young man, European in appearance and speech. He was wearing glasses and had longer dark hair tied at the nape of his neck.

"I am Meru Woods, the local IT expert," he introduced himself. "I am one of the few employees of the company, not a volunteer. I can show you around."

"Where is Mrs. Ran?" Vassudev asked. He took off his electronic service spectacles and left them above his forehead, so he could look the man directly in the eye. "I need her assistance and testimony as the owner and director – if the investigation is to proceed properly."

"She is in the hospital with her injured daughter." Woods was looking at him seriously and strangely enough without any enmity. "Please, follow me. I will explain everything I can."

* * *

Burning to death.

Vassudev shivered. That was happening in front of his eyes on the screen with the security camera footage: a young man, whose clothes and hair caught fire, was staggering over the dunes. There was no sound, so the screaming was left to Vassudev's imagination. A girl ran to him, trying to put out the flames with her sweatshirt, struggling to make the burning man drop and roll. But she was not strong enough. Others came running, extinguishing the fire with sand and a carbon dioxide extinguisher.

The young man was lying motionless. The girl was sitting beside him, staring at her burnt hands, probably going into shock. Somebody was checking if the unfortunate victim is breathing, another girl – with a myna bird on her shoulder – brought the first aid kit, a tall blond young man was obviously calling the ambulance.

Woods paused the footage.

"Are there any other records of the incident?" Vassudev asked quietly. "This one does not show how the fire started."

Woods shook his head.

"The girl, the one who tried to put out the flames...?" Vassudev pointed at the screen.

"That is Ranveig. Mrs. Ran's daughter."

Vassudev lifted his eyes and looked at the logo of Ran Ltd. hanging on the opposite wall. It depicted a stylized woman with fins, partly covered with scales – like some kind of mermaid. She was holding a net. "What kind of person is Mrs. Ran?"

"Very ... determined," Woods answered thoughtfully. "She's familiar with international judicial procedure, with details about oil and oil companies, as well as operation of fishing companies and their ecological impacts."

"Did she study it in her homeland? I have read somewhere she comes from Denmark."

"She is ... self-taught. The hard way."

"What do you mean?"

"Her husband abandoned her and their daughter. He left them with nothing and did everything possible to avoid paying alimony. She travelled quite a lot to find a way to support herself and give Ranveig a decent education and all. Finally she got a good job in a fishing company. Then an oil spill disaster occurred in the area and the fishing company went bust. Mrs. Ran then began to work for some non-profit organizations and later founded her own company for cleaning oil spills – Ran Ltd."

"Ranveig must have harsh childhood experience," Vassudev remarked.

"Ranveig has only her mother and loves her very much. Have you seen the uninhabited modular house in the camp? It's for Ranveig; in case she would need some space for herself. But she never sleeps there, never lives there. She always resides in the headquarters with Mrs. Ran. I used to think that she would be willing to put her hand into fire for her mother and her mother's enterprise. And ... she did."

Vassudev stared out of the window into the darkness before asking: "Do you think Mrs. Ran could have omitted some security measures? Perhaps she was trying to save some money?"

"No. She would never do that." Woods turned to another screen. It showed a live footage from the parking lot near the beach. There were parked vans of different media companies: big international ones, one local Goan, one specialized in ecology from Mumbai and some others, indistinguishable in the weak streetlight. They looked like huge beasts, sleeping in the gloom of the night. Like futuristic predators made of metal and electronics, just waiting for the dawn.

"Some of them want to destroy us, serving our competition," Woods said. "Because there are other companies able to handle oil spills – using chemical dispersants which further harm the environment. Some of the media are trying to make us all martyrs of our cause, because Ran's organization of volunteers providing manual cleaning is unique. For us who work here it is all horrible and unnerving. I know why you came here at night, officer. You wanted to avoid the media as badly as we all do."

Vassudev gazed again at Ran's logo on the wall as if it could give him some answers.

"I would not blame you if you were trying to protect her," he said slowly. "Without her you would lose your job and ..."

Woods laughed: "Sir, I am an IT expert and a technician. I can find a job anywhere on this little planet."

"If you are not protecting your employer, what is it that you want, Mr. Woods?"

"I want the truth. Although I know that the truth usually bites and burns."

A Tesla car stopped on a side road by the dunes. It was far enough from the parking lot, but quite near the temporary modular building which served as headquarters for the oil cleaning operations, housing sensitive technology and providing shelter for the employees.

The car was a heavy jeep type, now at night running on accumulated solar energy. The vehicle was expensive, but it was often used in difficult terrain. Its sides bore traces of mud, sand and dust.

The driver stepped out. She was tall, her fair hair reaching her waist, looking like a soft halo around her head. She wore black trousers and a long-sleeved colourful blouse resembling an Indian *kurta*. Around her hips she had a solid black belt with different holsters and casings for some technical and electronic equipment.

Vassudev went to meet her. *She could be a visionary, a manager or a Viral-Net celebrity,* he thought. *Or ... a cult leader.*

"Good evening, Mrs. Ran."

"Good evening, officer," she answered, adding the customary Indian greeting: *"Namaste."*

Her expression was polite but her eyes were watchful.

She turned to a girl about nineteen years old, who was sitting quietly in the car.

"Go to the infirmary," Ran told her. "I will handle this."

The girl nodded, got out carefully and headed for the camp. He recognized her from the footage.

"That's Ranveig, my daughter," Ran said. "She insisted she can't stay at the hospital, so she signed out."

Her clothes were quite similar to her mother's; so was her appearance, pale and fair-haired. She wore special medical gloves to cover her burnt hands. She kept glancing over her shoulder as if she was a small child, anxiously looking at her mother. But Ran didn't turn around.

Vassudev and Ran were walking together back to the modular house, a cleverly designed structure, which could be easily dismantled and transported.

"Ran is a goddess of the sea," he said suddenly before they reached the door.

She lifted an eyebrow. "I see you are well versed in Scandinavian mythology."

"Actually I am not. You have that information on your Viral-Net site," he admitted.

She smiled but the smile didn't reach her eyes.

"Why does the mermaid on your logo hold a net?" he wanted to know. "Why not a conch, a fish or something like that?"

"We use special nets to stop the oil from spreading at sea," Ran answered.

They entered the building and sat down at the table in a small kitchen, while Woods withdrew to the surveillance room.

"Why are you conducting the investigation alone?" asked Ran, while she poured some coffee into her cup.

"My partner is currently on sick leave," Vassudev shrugged.

It was not exactly true that he was on his own. He had a team and a good one. But it was composed of people working behind the scenes, at computer stations and in laboratories.

"I see. Let's be honest, nobody wants to investigate this case. No matter what you find out, the reporters of Viral-Net will try to tear you apart to get some sensational news," she stated.

He watched her sipping hot coffee.

"What can you tell me about the accident and the local security measures?" he addressed the theme which was inevitable. "I want the facts, but also your opinion, Mrs. Ran."

"Meru Woods showed you the footage, I suppose. Then I am sure you know that the first response of my people could hardly be better. My volunteers have health and safety courses and trainings on regular basis. It proved effective now, even though the victim of this accident could not be saved." She lowered her eyes to her cup.

"I heard that you used advanced technology to protect your workers," he said.

"We can show it all to you in the morning." Her voice sounded tired. "But that is not the real issue. The crude oil, which everybody fears ... was not the cause of this tragedy."

"What was it then?"

"I am sure your colleagues who performed the autopsy of the victim could confirm my words. The substance, which caught fire, was a mixture of gasoline and motor oil. Somebody obviously decided, that when we already had an environmental catastrophe here, one barrel of highly flammable chemicals more or less means no difference. Somebody simply poured out some gallons of hazardous waste behind the dunes, so he could get rid of it easily." She gritted her teeth. "Such behaviour is nothing new. Things like this had happened before, on other sites. We had always informed the local authorities, but nobody had done anything about it."

"You withheld information about the flammable waste from the media," he said, slightly surprised. "How did you manage?"

"They don't dare trespass on the site and camp. The signboards work better than a fence. They know I am eager to sue and I have powerful friends here in India. The reporters fear me enough. And none of my people would speak to them." She made a wry face. "If the reporters had any brains, they would know that crude oil, especially this one here – causing Class B contamination – doesn't ignite in the open air so easily. It's not like in the movies where you see the burning oil wells or drilling rigs. And those who had the expertise obviously didn't have the balls to mention it."

"Some of the media are definitely on your side," Vassudev remarked.

The look she gave him was hard as stone: "I have lost one of the volunteers who are like family to me. I nearly lost my daughter. I am in danger of losing my company, because my enemies could label my methods of work as life-threatening. What I would tell one reporter, others would buy from him and distort to their liking. I won't allow anyone to profit on the suffering of all of us here!"

Vassudev woke up just before dawn. The first thing he remembered was sound of waves.

He had accepted Ran's offer to spend the night in the modular house. He got up from a stretcher underneath the window to see the sky getting pale over the ocean.

As the darkness dispersed, he had to admit, that the view was no better. The dark coating on the sand and sea. Deadly silence disturbed only by the muffled whisper of the waves. No tiny crabs running sideways to find shelter. No brahmini kites circling in the mercilessly blue sky.

Vassudev found a vegetarian breakfast on the table in the kitchen and a set of working clothes Ran had promised him. There was also a note: 'Nikki will show you around and explain everything. R.'

He ate and dressed quickly. Soon somebody knocked on the door and Vassudev answered it.

"Good morning, I am Nikki," said the thin girl he had seen yesterday.

"Good morning, good morning," said the myna bird on her shoulder, imitating her voice very well.

"Nice to meet you, I am Vassudev Harwalkar, officer in charge of investigation of the Candolim Beach incident."

She was tanned, perhaps of Philippine descent, dark haired and eyed, with a certain unrelenting melancholy in her expression. She wore a T-shirt and a sarong, hair in braids, a bit like a Goan hippie from an era quite long gone.

She just smiled sadly: "I'll show you the place, please follow me."

"What's the bird's name?" he asked, as they were walking to another modular building, which looked like a small storage house.

"Name?" said the myna bird imitating Vassudev.

"Hal," answered the girl. "His name's Hal."

"Hal," asserted the bird.

"Its talking skills are unbelievable," Vassudev observed. "It seems your myna bird is an avid English speaker."

"I tried to teach him some words in Filipino, Cebuano and Bikol, but he seems to be utterly unpatriotic and reacts best to English," she shrugged.

Vassudev watched the bird. The yellow and dark feathers brought some distant memories to him. He cleared his throat: "Listen, myna birds are endangered species, how come you have one as a pet? I thought you were an 'eco' yourself?"

Nikki shook her head: "Hippies, otaku, hipsters, gothics, ecos. You really need to label everything, don't you? Perhaps because when you give something a name, it doesn't seem so threatening anymore?"

She stopped for a moment, turning in the direction of the volunteers' camp. He followed her gaze to see tents, sheds, miniature modular houses, silhouettes moving in the early morning light.

He wanted to tell Nikki that he didn't feel threatened by a barely adult girl or a few pseudo-hippies. He could arrest some of them without any trouble. Most of them were nearly kids and there was no way they could stand their ground against an experienced cop.

But he knew this would not work well. For one thing he was sure that Ran would instantly send in her lawyers and the media would jump at it like a shiver of sharks in feeding frenzy. But what was more important: these people already mistrusted the system. That's why they were here, taking ecological matters into their own hands; literally, while cleaning the beach. And he did not want to push them further, to make their anger and disillusion even worse. Even if others did so in the past and would do so in the future.

They got moving again, this time in silence.

Nikki opened the door with a chip in her bracelet.

"Here," she said. "That place which looks like a hygienic station is important. You put on the protective specs and spray your body with the protective emulsion. You wait till it dries and reacts with the uppermost layer of your skin and the residues of dead skin which are peeling off. It creates something like a second skin. The outcome is fully natural; it's like your body itself grows an extra protective layer. Something it already has, but better and stronger, at the same time flexible. Better than plastic. It allows your body to breathe, because it doesn't cover the pores; that's why we still wear other protective gear and clothing. It would not be healthy to spend too much time in it, but we have strictly given the time for which we work."

"Can't it be harmful when you put too much of the emulsion on?"

"It reacts immediately on the surface – so no matter how much you put on, it can't affect the deeper skin layers," she assured him. "After the shift we take a shower and peel it off like reptiles do. We call it lizard skin and we all wear it while working with the oil. Class B substances are not as toxic as Class A, but still …"

"Was the victim of the incident wearing it?" Vassudev asked softly.

Nikki hesitated for a few seconds.

"No," she answered then. "He was not on duty." She sighed. "I'll wait outside."

"We're the only ones here, the traces are not disturbed. And the continuation of the salvaging work has been prohibited," Nikki stated, when Vassudev emerged to the sunlight again. She didn't seem to expect any answer but the impossibility to continue with the cleaning of the beach obviously troubled her. She must have used another modular station to get her own lizard skin, because she looked visibly paler now except the areas around her eyes.

Vassudev felt a strange tingling sensation from the protective layer he was now wearing.

"Feeling not exactly in your skin?" She gave him that sad smile of hers. "You will get used to it quickly. Here," she handed him an inhalator. "You spray this into your mouth. It enhances the production of mucus that will absorb the harmful substances in the air. It will protect your lungs and breathing system. It is safe and thoroughly tested; it only enhances what your body is already doing naturally."

He did as she instructed him. "And how do you get rid of it?"

"Well, we simply cough and spit it out; either with help of another aerosol or naturally when it loses its absorbing qualities. That indicates that the contamination is already too high. It looks slightly disgusting. White mucus with black webs and clusters. But you will also get used to it."

"Will you show me where the accident occurred?"

"Yes, sir," she nodded. "And please keep the specs with you in case you would need to get closer to the spill."

She motioned in the direction of the dunes, away from the sea, and they set out.

"So, how did you get the bird?" Vassudev returned to the former topic. He needed to know more about Nikki's opinions and thoughts to understand how things worked here.

"My father is a scientist, he works in a de-extinction lab on the Philippines," she explained.

"Is he a genetics engineer?"

"Yes. The myna birds are endangered." She actually seemed quite pleased that he knew about it. "The subspecies *Gracula religiosa palawanensis* is even native to the Philippines. But because of their ability to imitate sounds, especially human speech, people wanted them as pets. But in captivity they mostly didn't reproduce. The demand was so massive, they nearly got extinct. They were caught and shipped away illegally and there was no end to it. So my father founded a project with the help of the De-extinction Institute and they clone and sell myna birds legally. The clones are carefully bred so that their desired ability of imitation is greater, they are healthy, free of parasites and not too expensive. Since then, the mynas living in the wild are safe. The poachers lost interest, because their sales have dropped dramatically. Hal is a clone. My dad gave him to me."

"Can I pat it?"

"You know how to handle birds?"

"I..." he hesitated. "I had one as a pet myself when I was a child, the common myna, the Indian species. They were plentiful around our village. We called them *peetanetra*: one with yellow eyes."

"You sound somehow sad about it," Nikki gave him an unreadable glance.

"Well, my *peetanetra* died. One of the neighbour's boys poisoned her."

"You think somebody would ... ?"

"I don't just think. I even managed to prove it," he said quietly. "The boy was punished but that couldn't bring her back."

"You felt the calling to be a cop already then, didn't you?"

Vassudev nodded slightly. He looked at Hal inquiringly.

"I think you should know that Hal is … different," Nikki frowned, obviously worried. "He could bite you."

"Bite me?"

"Look closer," she suggested.

Vassudev did. "Oh my God!" He involuntarily flinched a bit. "What's that?"

"I told you he was a clone."

"That thing's got teeth in its beak!"

"Well, yes. While still a foetus, his jaw was injected with DNA of mammals and … Put simply, his genes were given the order to activate the sequence 'grow teeth'. Hal is one of the successful experiments which were meant to be released to the public. But the market proved too conservative and nobody wanted them. So my family took him in."

"Oh, I see." Vassudev breathed out and shook his head.

"Of course I will leave him in a cage. I'm not allowed to have him with me on duty."

"Grow teeth!" said the myna bird cheerfully.

Vassudev was staring at the ditch in the ground, bordered by police tape and marked with identification stickers. If he had not seen the tape it would be damn easy to fall in. The edges were steep and unstable; small stones, sand and dirt were crumbling down. Inside there was the waste that Ran had told him about. The hole itself wasn't too deep and there was not enough liquid to drown; only perhaps if a person fell really unfortunately. Yet this was the flammable trap which took away one young life.

Vassudev put on the standard police spectacles, containing a visualizing app. The program scanned his whereabouts, locked the stickers and projected a view formed by all the visual documentation taken on spot just after the incident. He could see exactly how the place looked like when his colleagues had arrived.

He noticed that at one side the rim was torn down. Now it was not so much visible anymore, as the edges kept crumbling due to the hot and dry weather. By winking and gazing at the inner screens of the glasses he requested more information. The specs kept track of the movement and narrowing of his pupils and responded immediately.

According to the data uploaded by his colleagues from the analytic department, there were traces of the flammable mixture on the crumbled side, then in a line of footprints, in wake of somebody, who was walking away – in the direction of the camp – while drenched in the liquid.

Vassudev followed the footprints to find himself on the top of the dune.

The victim must have caught fire in the middle of this short route, according to all evidence. Then the young man stumbled ahead in shock and pain, over the dune, to the view of the cameras and his friends who rushed to his aid. And they left behind a chaotic net of traces all over the place as they were running around, trying to save him and to find out what had happened.

Vassudev glanced at Nikki. Her expression became inscrutable, as if she couldn't care less about what had happened. Somehow she closed herself up.

"You didn't take any security measures so nobody would fall in?" he asked.

"You didn't," the myna bird repeated and Vassudev wondered if his voice really sounded so reproachfully.

"No. Because we didn't know this was here." Nikki gave him a long look, keeping her unreadable melancholy calm. "We did check the vicinity of the camp including this place in the morning and there was nothing. In the afternoon of the same day there was a deadly accident."

"No cameras of yours?" he continued.

"No. As Meru Woods and Mrs. Ran could have told you, we are not able guard the whole surroundings. And we shouldn't have to." It was no accusation, only a statement.

"Is it common for the volunteers to just walk around?" he asked.

"The work is demanding. We are all here for a week already, since the crisis started. Nobody left so far. But cleaning the oil, knowing that more is probably still pouring out of the tanker, and seeing the smothered wildlife we could not save, that is hard," she explained, unmoved. "Everybody has some ways to cope with it. Stargazing, long walks, listening to or playing music, writing a diary. So it was not unlikely somebody would venture this way. It was a game of chance – if somebody would spot the hole first, or fall into it."

"I don't mean to harm you in any way. But I have to know." He had the feeling he was reassuring more himself than her.

She stood by his side, expressionless. "Yes. Certainly. I understand that."

Vassudev nodded. Now he had a pretty clear picture of what had happened. Except for one tiny but important detail. How did the liquid catch fire?

"I understand that," said the myna bird in Nikki's hollow voice as the sun touched the horizon.

Even that toothy flying son of a dinosaur acknowledged that Vassudev needed some rest.

After a long day on the site he was sure he would never volunteer for such a work. Dirty, tough going and depressing were the words on his mind. Perhaps it would be better with more people around but there was only him and Nikki with her eyes dark as the oil.

Whenever he got near the camp, practically all the volunteers kept ignoring and avoiding him. The absence of the uniform mitigated their enmity but still he was a stranger in their midst.

There was no doubt that those people were doing a good and well-organized job. The security rules were strict, the system elaborate. Regardless of modern machinery available on the shore, the most important was the manual work and human factor – the presence of real people who were able to handle the crippled environment most gently. To scrub the still living shells, to wash the half-dead birds and nurse them back to health and so on.

After peeling off the lizard skin and getting rid of the protective mucus full of something what looked like disgusting black threads, Vassudev politely refused Nikki's offer to sleep over in the modular guest house.

He bade her goodnight. She left for the camp and he walked to his car. He was tired and no wiser than after the inspection of the place of the accident.

He couldn't get rid of a lingering thought: *How much is Nikki alike to her myna bird? She looks familiar and harmless but could she actually have sharp teeth?*

Then a sudden outburst of laughter was heard at the parking lot. There was a large square painted on the concrete covering the ground. In each corner stood a massive and ugly ashtray and in the square a group of young people were chatting and laughing.

So, that's the smoking area for Ran's volunteers, Vassudev realized. As he came nearer, he saw a man wearing a DOCU News cap retreating quickly to the safety of his van, followed by yet another wave of laughter and insulting comments.

A tall young man, blond and blue-eyed, an electronic cigarette in his hand, stood in the centre of the volunteers' group. He was stripped to the waist, wearing only plain black trousers in contrast to beautifully coloured and patterned clothing of the others. *Like a raven among parrots,* Vassudev thought.

The blond was elegantly muscular, like a large beast of prey, on his smooth chest he was sporting a wide vertical stripe of tattooed ornaments which went from his collar bones and disappeared beneath the belt. It depicted some occult symbols. Viking runes, as the database in Vassudev's spectacles explained.

He had his fingernails painted black and an ornamental tattoo of a serpent, which matched the Nordic style of the runes, on his temple and around one eye.

Vassudev remembered he saw him on the security footage.

Suppressing his fatigue, he could start asking questions like "Where were you at the time of the accident?", but that would instantly earn him their enmity.

In the moment he stepped over the line into the square, everybody turned to him.

"So you're the cop," the blond said, raising an eyebrow.

"So you're the guy who kept his cool and called the ambulance," Vassudev replied.

Then the young man smiled and offered his hand: "Sigurd's the name. I am from Iceland."

"Vassudev." Then he looked around the quiet parking lot. "You managed to mock away the DOCU reporter?" He wanted to be sure of what he had seen.

311

Sigurd nodded: "He's a jerk. All of them are. But this one even pretended to be a smoker to have an excuse to contaminate this place with his foul presence."

"I used to be a smoker but I managed to stop," Vassudev confessed. He did not comment on the fact that most of the young people present were actually not smoking and obviously just socializing. A few even had nicotine band-aids with a fashionable 'No Smoking' sign, displaying proudly how they were kicking the habit.

"Aren't you tempted?" One of the girls asked and offered him an expensive-looking clove cigarette. She was a natural red-head, but obviously had undergone a treatment to change her skin colour. Now she was black as ebony. She was scarcely clad in a thin sarong. Vassudev couldn't stop thinking what her parents must have said to this – and that they most probably were not exactly enchanted. He noticed the badges pinned to the sarong. They were all logos of different international anti-racism organizations. Her smile bore a hint of something flirtatious.

"Well, who would not be?" Vassudev answered. "But this time I'll resist. Though I am afraid that it will not take long before I start smoking again. I guess the media will weaken my nerves soon enough – in the moment they will descend on me like a tsunami wave."

He looked at Sigurd inquiringly.

"Why are you actually here?"

"So I can tell my friends at home that I was here and boast about it."

"I think you are not," Vassudev narrowed his eyes. "If you only wanted to talk about it, you would stay for two, three days and then go. It would be enough. It wouldn't mean too much hard work. No one can make you stay if you don't want to anyway. Am I right?"

"Damn, you are good," Sigurd admitted. "But in any case my reasons are pretty shallow."

In the meantime the red-head took a cigarette, distractedly looking for a lighter.

"May I?" Sigurd asked courteously.

When she leaned to him, a cigarette at her lips, he just snapped his fingers to produce a spark and a small flame.

"How did you—" Vassudev started, then he realized it. "You have this nail polish for the cool kids, the fire-breathing performers or wealthy managers who smoke like a chimney." It was a fashionable thing. The polish reacted with human nails in such a way that it allowed to create small flames by friction.

"You think it will be deemed hazardous and banned any time soon?" Sigurd said provocatively.

"I don't know. But while working on the beach, this lizard skin doesn't cover your nails, or does it?" The cop returned the provocation.

Silence fell.

"First, we're all wearing gloves on the site. Second, the crude oil doesn't catch fire as easily as you would think." Sigurd's voice was full of contempt. "And third, I'm not stupid."

The ebony red-head gave Vassudev a cold look: "'Night, officer. It was nice to meet you."

As Vassudev was getting near to his car, he noticed a group of people coming towards him. Reporters.

He sighed and smoothly changed direction with the skill of a street savvy man who knows how not to meet somebody he doesn't want to.

He returned to the outskirts of the camp where the reporters dared not follow. Ran certainly had some trick up her sleeve to sue the hell out of them if they would. The inscription proclaiming 'Authorized Personnel Only' confirmed his assumptions.

Thinking about Sigurd's remark, he understood now what all the fires and candles meant: We are not idiots; we are not small children; we can handle fire.

He rubbed his eyes and decided to go back to Meru's office to get a coffee before driving home. Meru welcomed him as if the hour of the day or night meant nothing to him. He offered Vassudev a comfortable chair and coffee.

"What do you think about Nikki?" The detective sat down and exhaled slowly. He couldn't stop thinking about the case.

Meru handed him the cup. "She's as grief-stricken as the rest of us, but she's very resilient. A tough-as-nails girl who does what needs to be done. That's why Ran sent her to show you around and she agreed. Plus she's a Philippines national and her father is a scientist of some renown. If you would arrest her, things would get internationally ugly for you." It was not a malicious remark and it was also utterly true.

"But I am not limited to people whom Mrs. Ran sends. Perhaps I should talk to the volunteers who are local? Goan or at least Indian?" Vassudev mused. "You know them. What do you think?"

"I think they will not cooperate. They are scared. They would not say a word and run to Ran to get them a lawyer."

"What are they afraid of?"

"That somebody would blame them for what had happened. They fear that they are easy prey. Foreigners don't feel so threatened."

"Sigurd didn't seem to feel threatened at all," Vassudev made a wry face.

"Ah, Sigurd. He's a collector of strong experience and a fan of *gálgahúmor*, Icelandic black humour. And a bit of a poseur."

"What do you mean?"

Meru just gestured to the window, towards a miniature modular house outside, which had its door full of pictures and stickers. After zooming in, it was possible to see they were photos of dead animals. Most of them with quotes from songs or nursery rhymes – like "I believe I can fly" written on a picture of a dead seagull covered in crude oil.

All the shelters in the camp were adorned in some way. It was obviously part of the volunteers' culture: to make a place feel like home, to express individuality.

Sigurd has his image and works on it methodically, Vassudev thought. *This photographic parade of misery was not easy to make. Even Sigurd's trick of conjuring a flame needs constant upkeep.*

The nail polish works a bit like two-part epoxy. First he has to apply a chemical which slightly corrodes the nail, then another one which embeds itself in the nail to the desired effect. Also he needs to use different substances for his thumb and middle finger, so they can work as a match and friction strip. Not to mention keeping the rest of the nails nicely painted black with an ordinary polish to have them all the same colour. That is not done in five minutes. He must spend a lot of time and effort to keep his coolness factor high.

"Are you a bit knowledgeable in finances?" Vassudev changed the subject. "Ran Ltd. must make massive profits, don't you think? Mrs. Ran just sends out the call and volunteers from all over the world flock to her aid, asking no payment. What about that?"

"It's not so easy. She has built a network of tried and trusted people. They have to have some skill and training. And any money that is not spent to keep the whole enterprise going is spent on lawsuits."

"Really?" Vassudev asked uncertainly.

"Ran sues the oil companies. And of course they try to sue her in return – for everything and anything. See, many of the oil spills happen because the corporations don't give a damn about security measures. The tankers are outdated, the equipment malfunctions because of lack of maintenance. The ships have no sufficient crew. And well, then shipwrecks happen."

"She really has the nerve," Vassudev had to admit.

"It's the favourite imagery of David fighting Goliath; the small against the gigantic. Therefore it gets some positive attention in the media."

Vassudev slowly put down his empty cup.

"How usual or unusual is it to have a lighter with you?" he asked suddenly out of the blue.

"Normally it's just the smokers plus sometimes their close friends. And people who are ramblers or survivalists. In other words, it was not common at all. Of course, now there are many more – to light the candles." Woods raised an eyebrow. "Why are you asking? What are you implying?"

"A mixture of gasoline and motor oil will not ignite by itself. Not by sunshine only be it as hot as it may. Not without a spark."

For a moment there was silence, disturbed only by the humming of the AC unit.

"Do you think that Sigurd would be able to kill somebody? In a fit of anger? Because of hurt pride?" Vassudev asked.

Meru Woods didn't respond. He kept watching the candles and lanterns outside and sighed: "I think that that's not a question for somebody like me. But perhaps I could entrust you something else, a little secret, which you would find very useful."

The town of Betalbatim clad in darkness was gliding past Vassudev. From time to time there was an abrupt movement in the air as the fruit bats fluttered by, like huge butterflies of the night.

Vassudev was looking from the window of his car, now that he didn't need to occupy himself with driving. He was glad for Meru's little secret, as it was the knowledge of a nearly invisible pathway hidden among palms and cashew trees. The volunteers used it to move around the camp and avoid the reporters.

He was reading and re-reading the words he had heard today on the screens of his spectacles, as the program which recorded the dialogues converted them into text straight away. The written word always provided another point of view.

He also replayed the videos of what he had seen; including the footage from the accident. Now he was able to recognize some of the participants of the horrible theatre. There were three people, who came from blind angles of the surveillance system. None of them was on duty in that moment, none had the working clothes on. Ranveig. Sigurd. Nikki.

Vassudev put the spectacles down. Weariness was getting the better of him.

Slowly another autonomously driven car overtook him. He caught a glance of an Indian woman inside; she was dressed in a dark blue saree, her head resting on her shoulder, a child sleeping in her arms. Thanks to quite easily available chemical procedures she had unbelievably fair skin. The child was the colour of precious smooth dark teak wood.

Although science advanced constantly, human vanity remained the same. Since the chemical skin treatment was reasonably accessible, Caucasians often flaunted skin like flawless bronze with no need of sun tan; and many Asians were white as milk.

Vassudev closed his eyes. The peaceful picture of mother and child floated in his mind.

He had no family of his own. He was about thirty, tall and sinewy and quite attractive, but his work always meant more to him than human closeness. Nobody was waiting for him at home. His parents were dead, other family members were estranged. It was quite unusual for India, but Vassudev never felt it as any kind of crushing wrong.

It was all quiet. He could hear only the purr of the machine.

It was interesting how self-sufficient and close-knit the volunteers were. Like a family – now struck by a horrible loss.

The policeman looked back at his service glasses. The beautiful image disappeared, replaced by the vision of a young man's charred and scorched body.

The next morning, Vassudev entered the infirmary when he knew Ran would not be there. She was spending a lot of time by her daughter's side, leaving only to handle the most pressing matters. She was coping with the situation without blinking an eye, a cool-headed manager to the bone.

Ranveig was lying on the bed. She was pale, her platinum-blonde hair seemed nearly white. Her eyes were sunken and feverishly shiny. Both her hands were bandaged.

"*Namaste*," she whispered.

"Good morning. I am Vassudev Harwalkar, officer in charge of investigation of the Candolim Beach incident. We met briefly at the dunes at night."

"How can I help you?" she asked softly.

"Is there anything you remember before the accident? Where were you exactly? Was somebody with you? Or in your view? When did you notice that something was happening? Anything could be useful information." He vocalized the questions slowly and considerately, so she could pick any of them which she would be able to answer.

For a moment she looked past him, searching her memory.

"No, I am sorry." Her voice was shaking. "I recall clearly only the horrible smell. The screaming. The heat. The shock, oh, how it is burning ..." She swallowed. "I did all I could. I have reached my limits. But ..." She fell silent.

"But it did not work?"

She nodded slightly: "Sometimes nothing works. But family has to be protected at any cost; even if it is hard to earn their acceptance."

He was not sure what she meant. But the close ties within the volunteer community were obvious.

"Do you have any idea about who could possibly want to harm your friend?" Vassudev asked in a low voice. He had an unsettling feeling, the source of which he could not determine.

"N-no. I don't know." Her eyes filled with tears.

There was nothing else he could do.

The core of a crime is always the motive. Pay attention to the motive, understand the circumstances and you have a chance to find the culprit.

Various thoughts were spinning in Vassudev's mind whilst he was sitting in the surveillance centre, sipping tea. *Maybe I am looking at it from a wrong angle. There are still two more people who don't have an alibi: Meru Woods and Mrs. Ran.*

The technician was in the computer room in the time of the accident and a few people saw him there as he had asked for coffee and sandwiches.

But Mrs. Ran was a different case altogether. She was ready to do anything to protect the company, the concept, the lifestyle she created. Anything including murder – if somebody was somehow in her way? He looked at the logo once more. The sea goddess holding a net.

Suddenly there was some commotion outside.

When Vassudev stepped out he found most of the volunteers standing on the dunes, looking at the sea. He recognized Nikki and joined her.

"What's going on?" He gazed at the grey horizon and the cloudy sky but couldn't see anything.

"The forecast speaks of bad and windy weather," the girl answered.

All faces around him were tense. There was a storm in the air.

Suddenly it dawned on him. *The storm! It could destroy their nets, their equipment and their work. And they are not allowed to do anything about it, not allowed to touch anything because of the investigation.*

The red-haired girl with ebony skin started sobbing quietly.

Vassudev swallowed. *Actually I could give them the permission. I have that special authority, if I declare this situation as a state of emergency. But I would have to answer for that to my superiors. To take responsibility for whatever goes wrong at this site, for whichever clues get lost.*

Vassudev glanced around. Nobody was looking at him. He heard light footsteps on the sand and turned around.

It was Ran. Their eyes met. *She knows.* He expected her to try to persuade him. He didn't want to look into her face, so he kept examining the hairnet which kept her hair in place.

Ran said nothing.

"Grow teeth," Hal said but somehow it sounded mournful.

The wind from the ocean blew stronger.

"What shall we do now?" Ran asked quietly.

"We shall do what can be done," Vassudev answered. He straightened his back; his words were clearly to be heard: "I declare this an emergency situation! We are allowed to do the necessary to prevent our work from being destroyed by the storm! We will put on the lizard skins and get the job here done!"

"We?" Ran asked raising her eyebrows.

"Nikki taught me how to handle things here. I can help."

"Hell yes!" Sigurd shouted.

"Hell yes!" repeated Hal, fluttering on Nikki's shoulder.

Other voices were heard: "We will!", "Let's get moving!"

Ran lifted her head, her eyes sharp, her words relentless: "Go for the nets! Before the wind gets too strong! All hands on site!"

Everybody got moving. They knew the drill; everyone had his place and his assigned role. Ran nodded to Vassudev: "All right then. Come along!"

Vassudev was resting at the headquarters. He was tired – and glad for spare dry clothes that Meru lent him. Hot tea never tasted so good. The storm was raging outside but all nets, tents and shelters were secured. He suddenly felt calm and accepted and everything was good.

Nikki came quietly in and folded her umbrella, Hal on her shoulder again.

This time she smiled. It was a thankful smile which reflected in her dark eyes.

"The bird is suddenly so quiet," he noted.

"Sometimes he's not in the mood for talking," the girl answered. She let the bird sit on Vassudev's shoulder. He hummed a melody and Hal repeated it.

"My *peetanetra* used to do that. To repeat songs rather than words," he explained. "Somehow she remembered them better. Did you teach Hal to sing?"

Nikki's face brightened. She took her Viral-Net transmitter from her belt and turned it on. First tones of a song filled the air.

"*I'm not feeling in my skin, I am dying from within!*" sang a starlet, whose name Vassudev didn't recall. Her passionate voice was resonating from the speaker. "*Save me, save me, no one else can save me!*"

Nikki turned the music off – and Hal continued without falter: "*In this net of delirium! Feverish, fearing the next turn! Touch me, save me!*" The bird managed to imitate not only the voice, but also the instruments.

"This is my favourite song. I let Hal listen to it from time to time so he could learn it whole," Nikki whispered. Despite the melancholy in her face, her eyes seemed shiny.

The myna bird went on with the performance paying no attention to the people around: "*I am dying … Jeg ville ønske det var dig der brændte! Save me! Save me!*"

"What?!" Nikki, who was swaying to the rhythm, snapped out of it.

Hal fell silent at the disturbance. The voice, which the bird imitated in the middle of the song, was not singing, not in English and it didn't belong to the starlet. There was something sinister in the intonation.

"What was that?" Meru shook his head.

"I have no idea." Nikki gave some treat to the myna bird and tried humming: "*I am dying ...*" Obviously hoping to encourage Hal to repeat what he just said.

But Hal didn't respond, perhaps scared off by the tense atmosphere in the room.

Vassudev activated a translation program in his spectacles. He had the sentence recorded as everything that had happened so far. He focused the computing capacity on extracting the words from the background noise. And he really had to marvel at the skills of the genetically enhanced myna bird.

The language was identified as Danish. The program offered the translation in form of text which appeared at the lower rim of the spectacles: "*I wish it would be you who will burn.*"

Vassudev also recognized the voice, his suspicion confirmed by the match of recorded sound samples. It was Ranveig.

It took some time before Vassudev managed to get the list of times and dates when the transmitter played the song 'My Skin'.

The storm passed and everything was strangely calm.

"Hal must have heard someone saying that in the middle of the song. Most likely straight to him," Nikki sighed. Then she pointed on one of the dates on the small screen of the transmitter. "And this is the day when I let Ranveig for a while alone in my tent. I put the music on for Hal to listen to. It was the day of the accident. Around noon, that is before anything happened."

Meru and Nikki still had no idea what was the meaning of the sentence, but were able to affirm it was Ranveig. The technician was visibly tense, the girl closed herself into her expressionless shell again.

In that moment an e-message flashed at the rim of Vassudev's glasses. It was from his colleagues: "We caught the chap who illegally dumped the waste. When he saw the possible charges, got scared senseless and fully cooperated."

Vassudev opened the enclosed documents. When he saw the picture of the offender, he winced. It wasn't some desperate motorbike hobo as the cop had expected. It was a businessman in a quite expensive looking suit. Just too lazy and greedy to get rid of the waste in the proper way. But what was interesting, he insisted that he dumped the gasoline in the morning, before sunrise. The evidence from traffic cameras and systems confirmed this.

"Nikki? You told me that you have checked the surroundings in the morning. It seems not to be true," he turned to the Filipina girl.

"We did," Meru said firmly. "I'll have a look at the logs."

For a while there was silence.

"The place was checked by Ranveig and she reported nothing. That is strange," Meru announced.

"She could be tired, perhaps she didn't do it properly. It is not so difficult to miss that ditch," Vassudev said. "The possibility of human failure is always present."

"Ranveig took the checking shifts quite often. And she was damn good at it," Meru said, going through the logs.

Vassudev gazed at the company logo, absent-minded. *What could the sentence in Danish imply? Was she cursing the bird while getting ready to kill someone? Would Ranveig harm one of the volunteers? They were her family she wanted to protect!*

For a moment he remembered the exhausting work at the onset of the storm. *It meant so much to all of them.*

"Was the victim causing any trouble? On the site? In the working team?" Vassudev inquired.

"Nothing what I know about," the technician answered. "He seemed perfectly ordinary."

"I really would need to have a look into Ranveig's room here. But I haven't got the search warrant." Vassudev bit his lip.

"You can. I can allow it," Meru stated calmly.

"How?"

"I have no such authority over the volunteer's camp, but I have it for the headquarters. It is in my contract. And

I will gladly repay your courtesy which saved our work. Let's go."

Ranveig had more of a nook than a proper room. It looked very austere and uncosy. With only bare necessities, some materials and propagation items of the company, even the sleeping bag had the logo on it.

"Are you sure this is it?" he asked bleakly.

"Yes. She has nothing else," Meru nodded.

Vassudev looked through the things carefully, gloves on. There was no beer, no cigarettes, not even a piece of chocolate. It felt somehow empty. Then his eyes fell on a pair of working boots.

"When was the last time she wore these?" he asked. "These aren't the boots she had on during the incident."

"I don't know," said Nikki who was standing aside. "I don't remember."

"But we can have a look at the video again," Meru suggested.

Vassudev sighed. Then he skilfully wrapped the boots into a special isolating foil. The police courier will have to deliver them to the lab as soon as possible.

Vassudev was skipping through the security tapes.

Meru was trying to be helpful and Nikki was sitting in the corner "talking" with Hal.

The footage showed that Ranveig had indeed been wearing the boots he found – she had them on in the morning. Later in the afternoon she put on a different pair.

"Here," Vassudev said suddenly. "Pause it."

Ranveig was talking with the victim. There was something strange in her posture although he was not able to pinpoint it. The timer was showing fifty minutes before the accident.

"Can you zoom in a bit?" Vassudev asked.

"Well, I can but it will be no good." Meru shook his head. "The security cameras have only certain resolution. It will not help you to extract any details."

They played with the picture for a while but to no avail. Vassudev sat back, giving himself time to think.

"There's something strange about her hands," he said, looking on the screenshot again.

"You mean Ranveig?" Nikki lifted her head. "Now that you mention it … I think I saw Ranveig in the afternoon before the accident. She had the lizard skin but only on her hands. They were this unnatural pale shade. It is not possible to see it on the camera, because the colour doesn't stand out enough."

Meru frowned: "That's strange. She was not on duty. And why would she forget to peel the lizard skin off completely?"

"Could the lizard skin protect from fire?" Vassudev narrowed his eyes.

"Nah. For a few seconds perhaps. Then it would burn away like a normal skin," Nikki shook her head.

"You mean she was expeting to put her hands into fire? That's nonsense. And she knows the lizard skin wouldn't help her."

"We can confirm it," Meru suggested, "as all the work has stopped, the ecological envelopes with disposed lizard skins have not been not taken away yet."

In the small hours of the night Meru prepared some strong tea and coffee. Nikki was dozing off on a chair. Hal was cheerfully singing 'My Skin', which was slowly starting to get on Vassudev's nerves. *Could Ranveig just wish to roast the bird for this?*

On the table, wrapped in a foil, was a lizard skin. It was well peeled off – and the hands and forearms were missing.

Vassudev was thinking about taking the skin to the lab – to confirm it was Ranveig's – and driving home, calling it a day. But something kept bugging him. Some realization which kept narrowly eluding him. Ranveig had no reason not to abide by the rules. So why wouldn't she?

"What are the properties and advantages of the lizard skin again?" he asked.

"It protects against weak acids and certain types of toxic materials. It's very washable. It keeps no skin grease or anything." Meru started enumerating automatically.

"And therefore it doesn't make fingerprints," Vassudev stated.

"To use it as gloves? But what would Ranveig want to touch without leaving fingerprints? That doesn't make any sense." The technician gestured, confused. "And there's no need to hold her hands apart from her body like she does on the screenshot anyway! The lizard skin was already applied and dry ..."

Nikki squinted at them sleepily as they were subconsciously talking louder.

"Dry?" she repeated bleakly.

"Yes," Vassudev started to explain. "Wait! It's not about the lizard skin! She's holding her hands like somebody who has applied nail polish and is waiting for it to get dry." He frowned. "I think we should wake up Sigurd and ask him something."

The Icelander made a sulky face when Nikki shook his shoulder. Till now he was happily asleep in his modular house which he obviously didn't feel the need to lock.

"What the—" he hissed.

"Your nail polish, Sigurd. Where is it?" the girl asked urgently.

"Of course you can borrow it. But couldn't you wait till morning?" he yawned. "It's there in the small box, like always." He waved his hand and turned on a small lamp.

Vassudev sneaked in, gloves on hands, and looked into the box. There was the whole manicure set. A few nail polishes: black, glow-in-the-dark, icy metallic blue ... but not the spark-generating one.

"Hey, what's the cop doing here?" Sigurd sat up.

"I'll explain later," Nikki whispered. "Just tell me if you have lent the polish to someone in last few days."

"Nope. Nobody asked for it." Sigurd shook his head. "If somebody took it without permission I will be really pissed. I don't keep it locked up, but I want people to be polite and ask!"

"Here. I got it." Vassudev fished the nail polish from a bigger box which stood next to the small one and had the same pattern of frozen kittens on it. He put it into a small foil bag.

"*Helvítis bjáni!*" Sigurd swore. "What's going on?!"

"I'll explain later," Nikki repeated, while Vassudev got out of the door.

He could faintly hear the girl's and the Icelander's muffled conversation.

"What do you expect to find? Fingerprints?" asked Meru, who had been waiting outside.

"Specifically no fingerprints except for Sigurd's." Vassudev frowned. "The problem is that this stuff burns away when your nails burn away. You can't prove anyone had it on if his fingers are turned to charcoal."

"You really think … ?" Meru started uncertainly.

A small icon appeared on Vassudev's glasses, indicating an e-message. He focused his gaze on it to open it. It was from the analysis lab: 'On the soles of the boots there was sand matching the accident location and traces of the waste from the ditch.'

"She was there," Vassudev muttered.

His thoughts were racing. *She was there in the morning, near enough to the ditch, but she didn't report it. Not reporting it would endanger all the volunteers. So ... it was not them whom she considered family. It was somebody else whose acceptance and attention she wanted!*

"Sir?" Meru watched him inquiringly.

"Wait for Nikki and then go get some rest, both of you. You more than deserve it. I just need to check something."

Ran was standing at the doorstep of the infirmary, her phone in hand.

"Yes, I will bring her for the surgery as agreed. Yes. Thank you." She hung up. There were traces of weariness on her face, but not of desolation. She did what had to be done.

"Good evening," Vassudev greeted her. "I need to talk to Ranveig."

"She fell asleep for a while," she said but not in a harsh tone. "Don't wake her up, please. She has to undergo skin transplantation and will need all her strength. I can answer any questions."

"Mrs. Ran ..." He fell silent, looking at her thoughtfully.

"What happened?" She tilted her head.

"It was no accident," he said slowly. "We need your help and cooperation."

"You mean that the company will be freed from the accusations of negligence?" Ran straightened her back.

"Well, yes ..." He didn't expect this turn of the conversation.

"Then the company will survive." She exhaled.

He hesitated then decided to take the risk: "Mrs. Ran, I am afraid your daughter did it. I presume that she didn't feel accepted by you; she didn't feel close enough to you. She must have suffered some kind of mental breakdown and she just wanted to destroy everything that kept you away from her. With her hands injured she didn't have to work with the nets and oil anymore and still she would have your full attention."

Ran froze: "I suppose you are reasonably sure if you are telling me."

He nodded.

"Then what will you tell the media? Will somebody be able to claim that volunteer work on the oil-spills induces madness? How will you handle the arrest of a badly burnt girl? If you do things quietly you won't get any glory for solving such a difficult case. Will you be able to proceed in a way which would spare Ranveig from further mental harm and at the same time free the company from the accusation of negligence? The choice is yours now."

He stared at her, unable to comprehend her cold-blooded reaction: "You are not going to persuade me?"

"What should I tell you? I always kept an eye on all of my volunteers and their well-being. But my daughter proved to be my blind spot. I will break down and cry later. It will have to wait."

"So what shall you do now?" he wanted to know.

She said nothing, the silence dragged on.

Vassudev turned around and headed for his car. He felt he wasn't going to get any answer and had his own decisions to make.

Then he heard her voice: "I will go to the hospital with Ranveig. I will give her my skin for transplantation, the skin from my back."

He stopped.

"Why?" he asked without looking at her. "There are excellent synthetic skin grafts available, aren't there?"

"I know. But it's not the same. Not for her. Like this I will be always with her, always holding her hands. She will feel it."

Have Space Bike, Will Travel

Ingrid Garcia

HIGH EARTH orbit. A place where virtual particles pop in and out of existence, unheard by anybody, while disturbed by cosmic radiation, solar flares and astronauts chasing a wayward satellite.

"You all know how to perform the Reverse Umbrella," Yo-Sung Lee says over the radio, "now who wants to be the pusher? It'll be quite close to the Van Allen belt."

Tameka signals assent, which surprises Yo-Sung, who says, "I know it's strange for me to say so, but, like me, you're the most junior member."

"Exactly," Tameka says, "the one with the lowest amount of accumulated radiation. We checked that."

"Good thinking." Yo-Sung has to agree. "So I guess you've also worked out the brakers and the catcher?"

Patrice and Paddy Ukai put their still-unexpanded cushioning nets forward and José waves his grappling mechanism. "Almost as much fun as hacking into the

Pentagon," Paddy Ukai says to weary smiles from the rest of the team.

"Why the hell am I leading you, then?" Yo-Sung says, only half-joking.

Because you hate it." Patrice's smile easily radiates through his helmet. "Which makes you a great boss," Tameka says as the rest silently nod.

Back on Earth, Yo-Sung moved around in a wheelchair. Inflicted with a rare type of balancing disorder, she couldn't stand – sometimes even sit – upright without falling over. The genetically inherited condition afflicted her neural system, her brain and her inner ear. The condition was so rare and complex that no implant nor pharmaceutical medicines had been developed for it. Many doctors argued for research funding, only to be turned down by pharmaceutical companies that didn't see enough return on investment. Not that her parents would have been able to afford such a treatment, anyway.

Like many a hyperactive mind in a disabled body, she was restless. A South Korean geek girl devouring manga, sci-fi and literature in no particular order. Her brown eyes, curly hair and slightly above average height would've made her one amongst her peers if it wasn't for her constant fear of falling down, her flittering eyes always looking for a handhold and her refusal to take her superior's advice for granted. A brilliant student gaining her physics PhD with honours, while the loan put her in deep debt. She liked to fiddle, electronics were dirt cheap, and open-source software easily available.

So she developed balancing crutches filled with accelerometers, fast servomotors, and fine-grained GPS sensors. She wrote a self-learning algorithm that would teach the crutches to teach her how to stand up, and – eventually – walk.

Of course, modern wheelchairs were quite affordable as the price of electronics had continued to come down, and they were improved with intelligent actuators, through which they could cross thresholds, climb stairs and overcome other obstacles. Even a central actuator, rising to get your head level with standing people. Still, it wasn't the same as walking, as in the wheelchair your muscles atrophied. Not that there was anything wrong with Yo-Sung's muscles, they just needed regular exercise. Unfortunately, the exercises flat on the floor or in the safety of a net just bored her to tears.

Her balancing crutches only corrected her movements. She still had to do most of the work herself, which was good for maintaining her muscle strength.

Initially, it wasn't easy, as the self-learning algorithm made mistakes and over-compensations, causing her to fall over many times. She had the cuts and bruises to show for it. But gradually the software got the gist of it and kept improving. Step by step, she could stand up with her crutches, walk with them, and even found a way to run, in a hop-step-jump kind of way, with them. The software integrated so well that she could take special classes in self-defence: jujitsu, taekwondo and karate. She became an expert, and a foolish mugger had the cuts and bruises to show for it.

Yet her mind remained restless. At night, she looked up to space and found a different way to use her balancing crutches.

The wayward satellite comes in at an oblique angle, its apogee just short of touching the inner Van Allen belt. While it's dangerously close to that invisible hard radiation zone, it's also the point where its speed is lowest and thus easiest to pick up. The radiation in and near the Van Allen belt wreaks havoc with remote control signals, so using drones is out of the question. Human intervention is needed, and this is where ClimateTrack's salvage team – home base, Space Station Zebra – comes in.

The team moves to their positions while checking the rogue satellite's GPS signal one final time. Even if that fails, its projected orbit is now known. While they might seem a motley crew at first sight, their abilities match their functions. Some of these abilities work best in zero gravity, while some work everywhere. For example, riding a bike on Earth is something you never unlearn as the force of gravity is always downwards, while riding a space bike means the rider determines in which direction her energy is directed. The pedalling remains natural, while the orientation and manoeuvring in three dimensions are new skills.

Similarly, some people are better at approaching a moving target, while others excel at estimating where those targets will be. Some do not get spacesick, while others suppress it, using medicine if necessary, to be able to work in this new frontier. Some skills are useless on Earth, while precious in orbit, while some are universal. Hence, some are catchers, while others are pushers. It all comes down to the right mix. Most are players, one is the coach. All of them want to succeed, to win.

Pedalling gently, Patrice and Paddy Ukai manoeuvre to the planned braking points – in line with the trajectory in which Tameka will push the expensive machine – extending their cushioning nets. "It's like phishing a phisher," Paddy Ukai says. He's a fine team member, but doesn't know when to shut up.

José moves on his space bike right behind them, his multiple grappling hook armed and ready. Unlike a unicycle, a space bike does not have a wheel but rather a double pair of exhaust pipes that are split from a single pipe connected to the place where the main gear of a normal bike would be. Instead of a main gear, at the hub of a space bike's pedals an ion generator is located whose power depends on the energy of the biker's pedalling. The double exhaust has a double function. If the double exhaust has the smallest possible angle, it provides the most thrust. However, if the angle of the double exhaust is increased, while both exhaust pipes rotate as well – standard for Yo-Sung's bikes – they can provide a makeshift protection shield at the cost of the resultant thrust.

Tameka bikes to the push position, reversing the position of her space bike's double exhausts in the direction of the Van Allen belt, pedalling hard so that the double exhaust's Reverse Umbrella configuration provides an impromptu radiation shield, her long push pole at the ready.

"Satellite incoming in two minutes," Yo-Sung says on the central channel.

In a salvage operation like this, timing and teamwork are everything that stands between failure and success. The satellite, even at apogee, moves very fast, close to one point five kilometres per second. From a pre-calculated angle, Tameka speeds towards the satellite's highest point in orbit, greatly increasing the angle of her Reverse Umbrella, pedalling with all her might. Tracking software projects the point where she must hit the satellite on the inside of her helmet, but most of her aim is guided by instinct through intense training sessions.

An inaudible clunk as the composite deflection material of the push pole's business end meets the metal of the satellite's hull, exactly at the right momentum. The satellite is pushed from its apogee, greatly reduced in speed, towards the waiting cushioning nets of Patrice and Paddy Ukai. They only need to make minimal corrections to position themselves in the satellite's new trajectory.

It's not the first time that Yo-Sung has wondered how such a diverse group of specialists – a high tech entrepreneur, a system analyst, an exobiologist, an aerodynamicist and even an infamous hacker – still form such a good team. They're certainly motivated, living the dream of being in space. José quit his well-paying job as an aerodynamicist at Boeing to catch old satellites rather than launching new ones. On top of that, his strong arms liberated him from his wheelchair, here in space. Paddy Ukai, an infamous hacker looking for novel opportunities in the new frontier. Tameka left her lab full of specimens in the hope of finding truly extraterrestrial ones up there. And in space, her arthritis disappeared as if by magic. Patrice wanted to expand his system-analysing capabilities into higher realms. Yo-Sung, whose modified balancing crutches became space bikes, found both a new opportunity and a great new environment for the disabled body with the restless mind.

The satellite breaks through the cushioning nets, which transform most of its kinetic energy into heat, burning up in the process. The sacrificial lambs. Let their sacrifice not be in vain, Yo-Sung thinks. She sighs with relief when José's grappling mechanism locks on.

Home free, she thinks exultantly over the cheers of the rest of the team. While it's not the first successful salvage operation with her space bikes, it was the first one with *her* bikes with *her* in charge.

"Congratulations." Magdalena Asunción, Space Station Zebra's manager, pushes a coca leaf towards Yo-Sung. "That went *very* well. Using your bikes should greatly reduce the risks of future operations."

"I'm very sorry," Yo-Sung pushes the expensive leaf back, gently, "but I can't take stimulants because of my condition. I'll stick with my jasmine tea."

"It's me who should apologise, as I shouldn't assume." The slender, auburn woman of Incan descent takes a bow, not an easy feat in zero gravity. "The state you slide into when you command a team? That's not a condition in my book, but an asset. A great one, at that."

"I didn't mean that." The petite yet voluptuous Asian woman returns the bow, without fear of falling over. "That's my martial arts training. I have a balancing disorder, and stimulants, I found out to my dismay, worsen it."

"So sorry to hear that." Asunción puts the coca leaf in her mouth, and starts chewing. "Surely they can treat it, in this day and age?"

"There are many balancing disorders." Yo-Sung sticks her straw in her jasmine tea globule and takes a quick sip. "Mine is one of the rarest. No treatment available."

"How does that affect you here in space, if I may ask?"

"Not at all. Since I have no native sense of up or down, I feel fine in any position in zero gravity."

"I see." The Peruvian woman squints slightly. "Is that why you don't get space sick?"

"I suppose so."

343

"But how do you cope down there?" A slender finger points to the blue globe beneath.

"With my specially designed balancing sticks," Yo-Sung says, quickly hiding a gleeful smile behind her hand, "which were the predecessors of my space bikes."

"That is awesome."

Space Station Zebra is the centre of operations for the Chaos satellites in Earth orbit. The so-called Chaos satellites track the tell-tale signals of initial changes that can cause extreme weather events such as hurricanes, floods and droughts, trying to anticipate the worst impacts of a climate-changed Earth. The Chaos satellites need to be launched into very peculiar, so-called 'Butterfly-Wing' orbits for optimal performance. This is extremely difficult, and sometimes fails. Space Station Zebra's salvage team tries to pick up these very expensive machines. Mostly they use remote-controlled probes to do the dirty work, but for the most complex operations direct human intervention is necessary: teams like the one Yo-Sung is training in the use of her space bikes.

Part of the high risk, and appeal, of their heroics is that their ion thrusters only have a limited range. Underestimate your thruster's power reserve and you could become a lost satellite yourself. Drift off into a Van Allen belt and the hard radiation will wreak havoc with your oxygen deprived body. Yo-Sung developed a thruster with a longer range, using an extra power source: yourself.

Her space bike is a long stick with a saddle on one end, pedals in the middle and two separate ion exhausts at the other end. Through a generator in the hub, pedalling produces an ion stream that can be aimed in all directions through the double exhaust, enabling the space biker to go down without directing the ion thrust beam through her. Using the astronaut as an energy provider.

"While I'm happy to help your company regaining lost satellites," Yo-Sung says, "I fail to see how that would help the people down there."

"We call it accessing the future," Asunción says, "all the weather and climate information that our Chaos satellites pick up, together with measurements on the ground, are fed into a supercomputer. The computer software expands the Lyapunov coefficient into an algorithm that predicts the onset of extreme weather events. So far, it gets it right almost ninety-eight percent of the time, five days in advance."

"Which gives people on Earth some time to prepare for the worst," Yo-Sung says, "But while this saves many lives in the short run, it is basically fighting symptoms, not addressing the root cause."

"Climate change is a hellishly complicated problem." Asunción lets out a weary sigh.

"Exacerbated by pollution, deforestation, ocean acidification and biodiversity loss, to mention just the most obvious ones," Yo-Sung says. "But we can't let the immense complexity of the problem stop us: it's our planetary livelihood at stake."

345

"Which is the problem of the problem. There seems to be no easy solution that can win general approval, that a majority of the people, and the movers and shakers, can get behind."

"We should, and can be more intelligent than that. We are nine billion people, each of us unique and intelligent in our own way. We should be able to try out many different approaches at the same time, and by trial and error improve on the ones that work."

"I don't see it happening quite that fast." Asunción opens her arms, palms up. "Even if we at ClimateTrack try very hard to contribute in our own little way."

"I think that already more is happening than we are aware of. There are many, many people looking for solutions in ways both big and small. Entrepreneurs, inventors, scientists, engineers, even artists who try to inspire people towards thinking constructively. And strange people who help provide a framework for their communities to work in new and exciting ways."

"It might be too little, too late." The Peruvian woman removes the chewed coca leaf from her mouth. "Although there are, of course, GeoShield's solar reflector and PowerMate's atmospheric dust injection projects."

"Madness," Yo-Sung says as Asunción blinks at the ferocity of the South Korean's reply, "It is utter folly to think that such a complex problem can be solved with simple technological panacea."

Word is spreading fast, even for this space age, and quite a few companies are interested in testing Yo-

Sung's space bikes. After receiving permission from Asunción – ClimateTrack sponsored her trip – she gives demonstrations of the space bike to managers of other companies and even governments. While she's not really a natural saleswoman, her deeds count for much more than her words, as her demonstrations of the space bike's capabilities easily convince the majority of to place initial orders, together with training for their personnel, and often themselves.

"You'll be busy when you get back down," Asunción squeezes Yo-Sung's shoulder affectionately. "Do remember that we found you first, paying for your space elevator trip. We get the first batch."

"Of course you do," Yo-Sung says, repressing her reflex to withdraw, not quite used to being seen as other than a freak, "but I'll need time to set up production facilities."

"That's fine, we have your training set. Until they get their own, everybody will envy us." A vibrating ping sounds from Asunción's smart jewellery. She reads the message, then faces Yo-Sung. "Talk of the devil. Another query."

"Who?"

"GeoShield." Asunción reads from the message. "They want a demonstration, after which they determine if your space bikes can be modified for their robot builders."

This shocks Yo-Sung into silence, if only for a few seconds. "Tell them I'm not interested."

"They're a huge company, funded by a large consortium and," Asunción says, pausing for effect, "the USA and China."

"I don't care," Yo-Sung says, shaking her head, vehemently, "what they're doing is wrong."

"Should we do nothing, then?" Asunción says. "Our data clearly show that the planet is going to hell in a handbasket. Violent typhoons, elongated droughts in one place and intense floods in another are already happening, and getting worse. We have to act *now*."

"Not if GeoShield's huge solar reflectors are only fighting symptoms, not addressing the root cause," Yo-Sung says, barely refraining from shouting, "Carbon emissions are still not curbed. This money is better spent introducing carbon negative energy generation, greener lifestyles and reforestation projects."

"That's not what the powers-that-be decided, I'm sorry to say," the Peruvian woman says, raising her hands. "And if they do bite, we're talking about a potentially huge order. A *lot* of money."

"I'd rather stay poor than become rich from something that is utterly wrong."

"The ethics are strong in this one," Asunción says, raising her eyes.

"I can't help it," Yo-Sung says, "what I do is who I am."

"Of all the people I've met in my life," Asunción says, looking Yo-Sung straight in the eyes, "you have the sharpest mind. By far."

Yo-Sung blushes, fiercely, not quite knowing how to take that compliment.

"A great mind," Asunción approaches Yo-Sung, takes her hands, "but do you know that you're a very attractive woman, as well?"

Yo-Sung feels red hot, and not just from her intense blushing. "Nobody ever said that to me."

Asunción takes her in her arms, and kisses her on the cheek. "I fancied you the moment you set foot on board," she says, softly.

Yo-Sung waves her hands helplessly, then makes up her mind and returns the embrace. "Please be gentle, I have no experience. With my balancing disorder, sex is just too dangerous, too awkward on Earth."

"But not here in space." Asunción's kisses descend on Yo-Sung's neck, then she softly bites her ear.

"I'm afraid," Yo-Sung says, then lets out a sigh, "but also excited."

"Only one way to find out," Asunción says, "in my cabin."

Ever since the space elevator was operational, things have become much busier in Earth orbit, on the Moon and beyond. Many opportunities – both in space and on Earth – arose, and by trial and error it was found that baseline humans were not always the best choice for space operations. Despite fervent exercising and expensive supplements, bone and muscle deterioration in a gravity-free environment limited the time normal humans could remain in space, and return to Earth without ill effects. Large space stations could produce artificial gravity by rotating quickly, but transporting mass from the surface was still costly. Cargo berths were in high demand at the space elevator, which also needed to earn back its investment, so the utmost majority of space craft were small with no artificial gravity.

Through trial and error, long-haul astronauts soon were those already physically disabled, who didn't miss the gravity well that caused them pain, anyway.

On top of that, not many people – normal or otherwise – could stand the psychological pressure and inevitable boredom of being alone in a cramped vessel for months on end. People with autism or Asperger's syndrome were much better suited for that. Their relentless focus made them fine candidates for long-haul expeditions. They thrived in a tight regimen they could implement upon themselves – with terabytes of specific knowledge they could explore at will on the ship's computers.

Ironically, economic forces – not compassion nor forced hiring quota – drove this. A lost or malfunctioning spacecraft meant a huge investment gone down the drain, and physical and mental treatments to get normal people back to, well, baseline were expensive, as well.

The mentally and physically disabled astronauts even had a union called CiT – *Contradictio in Terminis* – and proudly referred to themselves as 'crippled autists FTW'.

Seeing how well these 'long-haulers' coped, several healthy space aficionados were trying to genetically engineer themselves to their condition. Like the long-haulers they'd eventually become, they didn't want to go back to Earth. They wanted to live and die in space.

"With your balancing disorder," Asunción says, "did you ever dream of becoming a long-hauler?"

"Not really," Yo-Sung says, caressing Asunción's bald scalp, realizing its practicality, but not quite ready yet to cut her own long curls. "I love Earth too much."

"Well, you can see it from here, too."

"Seeing things from orbit is no match for seeing our natural marvels up close and personal."

"But when you go back, you'll be all... handicapped, again."

"I'm fine. I've got my balancing crutches."

"I'm not saying this just because I hate to see you leave, which I do," says Asunción, groping for the right words, "but I think your space bike company will do well, very well. Over time you'll make enough money to have an implant developed for your condition."

"I don't want to be cured," says Yo-Sung, eyeing Asunción with a fierce stare, "this is part of what I am."

"It's a disability. It limits your movements, destroys your quality of life." Asunción says, on the verge of tears. "I take pity on people like you."

"I don't want your pity." Her eyes turn a fiery hazel. "I want you to accept me as I am."

Urgent breaking news

A QR-66 surface-to-space missile is heading for the space elevator, evading all efforts to intercept it. This is the latest type of intelligent missiles from the U.S. Space Force, designed to outsmart all current anti-missile systems.

The Pentagon denies any involvement with the missile's trajectory, saying the QR-66 is out of control, possibly hacked by a terrorist group. So far, the stray missile has escaped all efforts to destroy it, both by human pilots and automated interception systems.

With nothing standing between it and the space elevator, countries located on the equator are taking emergency measures, evacuating people from the possible impact areas of the huge, disintegrating beanstalk.

In the meantime, Yo-Sung and the salvage team are testing one of her experimental space bikes. "This special model," Yo-Sung says, "has a 'burst' mode for high acceleration, and an 'extreme clamp' mode with a hyper-conducting magnet."

While they are testing the experimental bike's capabilities, the news of the missile's launch against the space elevator hits. Yo-Sung quickly checks the missile's projected trajectory. "We can try to intercept it, if we move fast," she says.

"But how?" Tameka says, "Our equipment is meant for satellites, not missiles."

"I'll think of something," says Yo-Sung, her sense of urgency spiking. "Let's go."

The missile has the latest, the best, the most advanced electronics and software. But Yo-Sung eats, drinks and breathes that stuff. Her space bikes are a generation ahead of everything on the market, and have successfully withstood all the tests and usage the salvage team could throw against them.

The only subject she doesn't feel one hundred per cent up-to-date with is software. Then she remembers the profiles of her team members.

"Paddy," she says, "did you not win the Pan-Pacific hackathon in Melbourne, last year?"

"And I would have gone for the World Championship if this job hadn't come up," Paddy Ukai says. "Why?"

"I'll need your expertise. Please stay in contact with me through the space suit radio. I must use my space bike's radio for the missile."

Such a missile must have a secret access point, so that it can be recalled or destroyed at the last possible moment. A remote kill switch: the French Exocet had it, the American cruise and Minuteman missiles had it, even the Russian SS-18 Satan had it. If she could only find that access point, and then, with Paddy's help, hack the missile's software.

It has to be through a certain radio frequency, one that is hopefully also available on her space bike's radio. Her mind races. Her radio's transmitter is weak, its range is limited. She needs to be close, very close.

But the missile goes fast, much faster than her space bike can possibly move. Yet she needs to be close enough to do the hack.

"Patrice and José, can you throw the cushioning nets in the missile's path?"

"Yes ma'am, but they won't stop this monster."

"As long as they slow it down. Every little thing helps."

"Tameka and Paddy Ukai, I need to be on a parallel trajectory to the missile, and as close as possible, after Patrice and José slow it down." Yo-Sung's talking fast now, hoping the others understand. "Can you go in a pre-trajectory with your push poles, and then transfer as much of your momentum to me? I need all the speed I can get."

"We can," Tameka and Paddy Ukai acknowledge, "but it's gonna hurt."

"We have to save the space elevator, or many others will get more than just hurt. Do it."

"Yes ma'am," they say, while casting an anxious look.

Tameka and Paddy Ukai take a quick one-hundred-and-eighty degree turn, then run a course parallel to the projected missile's. Pedalling with all their might, yet staying perfectly side by side, they aim the business end of their push poles straight at the waiting Yo-Sung, approaching her like an arrow whose aim is perfectly true.

The pain will be intense, more than a normal human being could withstand. But Yo-Sung, when she re-learned how to walk with her balancing crutches on Earth, has gone through much more. She uses the intense pain as

354

a fierce focusing point to get as close to the missile as needed, speeding up with all her might.

In the meantime, Patrice and José both set new records as they manage to get their cushioning nets in front of a machine that moves faster than any stray satellite ever caught. The missile rips through their nets like a red-hot knife through butter, but still it slows down, almost imperceptibly.

Yo-Sung is far ahead, but the missile catches up fast.

This is immensely difficult, close to impossible. Yet she tries, carefully timing the experimental burst mode that burns up ninety percent of the stored electric energy. The acceleration is intense, well over ten G. Any normal human being would have fainted, but Yo-Sung somehow bites through the pain and stays conscious. She gets into spitting distance of the onrushing missile and switches on the hyper-conducting magnet of her experimental space bike. Another sharp acceleration, another mountain of pain...

But then, she's electromagnetically clamped to the missile. Now to get access to its control system. It's not a job for her, but for Paddy Ukai. "Paddy, are you there?"

"Ready and waiting, ma'am."

"Do you have video?" she asks. "And do you see my space bike's monitor?"

"Yes on both counts. Here are my instructions."

Following Paddy Ukai's instructions, even if she doesn't understand half of them, Yo-Sung finds the connecting frequency. Her fingers type on a virtual keyboard with blinding speed, barely keeping up with Paddy's voice commands which are so fast that the others only hear one high-frequency blur. Together they push Yo-Sung's space bike radio to the very limits.

There must be a way in.

If they fail, the missile will hit the space elevator. If its explosion cuts the triple-redundant carbon nanotube band, the top part of the space elevator will lash into space, its probability of hitting something extremely low.

But the bottom part will lash around the equator, marking it with a path of total destruction ten metres wide. They cannot let that happen.

Space Station Zebra's being close to the space elevator – at the launch of the missile – was sheer luck. GeoShield's proximity to the space elevator, though, is planned.

Paddy Ukai unleashes all the crazy hacks he's ever tried, and more.

Paddy Ukai gives her commands that she didn't know even existed. Crazy things that should be impossible, insane, ungraspable.

They are *in*.

"How do I reprogram the course?" In the corner of her eyes, the space elevator is approaching, fast.

"Go to the 'target location module', and overwrite the original co-ordinates," Paddy says, utterly focused.

"But which co-ordinates do I replace it with?"

"Co-ordinates of a place where the warhead can explode without causing damage."

Yo-sung thinks hard, then says, "I know just the place." As Yo-Sung accesses the future orbit of the missile, she is all too aware that a small change in its initial trajectory will have huge effects on its final destination. She feels like a butterfly when she gets into the missile's target location module, flapping her wings as she makes the changes.

Then Yo-Sung unclamps the hyper-conducting magnet, pushes herself off the missile, and pedals away as fast as she can.

The missile, now out of Yo-Sung's radio range, keeps on its way towards the space elevator. Dodging the last interception attempts, then back at it. Has their effort been in vain?

No, there is an almost imperceptibly subtle curve to its trajectory. It's veering off course, ever so slightly.

The world holds its collective breath as the missile goes off track, missing the space elevator by a few hundred metres, not exploding in its vicinity. Swaying further off course, increasingly wildly, sweeping in a broad curve towards the partly finished panels of GeoShield's solar reflector. Hitting the largest panel head-on, then exploding, turning most of the project and its robot builders into radioactive cinders.

Epilogue

"Like it or not," the interviewer says, "you are now a celebrity. What are your plans?"

357

"How many people are watching this?" Yo-Sung Lee asks.

"Six billion, give or take a few hundred million. Why?" The interviewer dislikes a dodged question.

"I want to set up a massive diversity resource centre," Yo-Sung faces the camera, and the world, with eyes wide open, "and reach out to everybody. The rich, the middle class, the poor. The disabled, the unprivileged, the marginalised. But also the workers, the movers and the shakers.

"First we will set up a resource pool for ideas, strategies and out-of-the-box approaches. Then we will implement prototypes, field tests and small-scale real implementations of the most promising ones. Cross-referencing, cross-pollinating and cross-examining along the way, using diversity as a resource, an inspiration and an end goal. Attack the death of a thousand cuts with the imagination of a thousand-and-one nights, applying a thousand-and-two solutions. We can do this: we are multitudes, we are marvellous, we are momentous.

"ClimateTrack, Unicef and the International Recycling Co-operative have already donated initial funds, with other companies, NGOs and institutions to be announced. Crowd sourcing campaign to follow. Check out Optimisfits on the web."

"We will access our future, and then change it for the better."

The Lighthouse Keeper

Andrew Dana Hudson

BAST WAS heading up to the Lighthouse roof, to wipe down the glass, to check the wiring, to clear leaves from the wind pipes, to polish the mirrors, to manage the nesting birds, to oil the hinges, to go through familiar motions that kept his hands busy and his mind unfixed on anything in particular, when his heart stopped working.

Sprawled on the moss floor of the atrium, Bast thought the clawing knot in his chest was just the wind knocked out of him. But then he noticed someone was thumping their palms on his breast. A stranger's lips blew air into his mouth. They were saving his life. His eyes were fluttering, and the sun seemed shattered by crystal arches and the kaleidoscope tower, engulfing him in spiking color. Yellow and red jackets gathered around, the noon chimes began to play. Amidst the fear and relief, Bast felt impatient with the whole affair. Why don't you just leave me alone? He thought. I've got work to do.

But they didn't, and the next thing Bast knew he was tucked into his cottage, well-meaning acquaintances bustling to fill his pantry. This was more company than he'd had in a while. The days that followed were the longest he'd spent off his routine in years. He felt like a lump. Confined to bed by a beneficent kit of monitors and regenerative pumps, Bast itched to return to his rounds. He fretted about the scratches and dents ham-fisted substitutes might be leaving on the objects of his care. The installations were durable, but Bast was a perfectionist.

"You wouldn't let just anyone wipe down the Mona Lisa!" Bast complained.

"The Mona Lisa isn't bulletproof," his nurse replied. "And neither are you. Now stop getting worked up!"

No, his carers weren't having it, and they soon began prodding him to indulge, at long last, the thought of retirement.

"We've got some very good candidates," Terry said, days later. "You put this off too long, mate."

"I can't have some intern bungling around," Bast objected. "I'm right in the middle of renovating the foreshore mosaic. That's two hundred megawatts a week we're losing until that's done."

"Apprentice," Terry corrected. "And not from this bed you aren't." Terry tapped their long nails on the headboard behind Bast's back. Bast had argued with the district curator about this before, but this time Terry seemed determined.

"I need to be able to focus," Bast said. "It's delicate work."

"Perfect for young hands."

"Not ones that don't know what they're doing. Look I've got notes, you've got schematics. When I die someone can figure everything out."

"Someone, eh?" Terry said. "What happened to the Mona Lisa thing?"

Bast didn't say anything. Rain smacked horizontal against the windows. First storm of the year and first in a long while. As much as had been done to curtail climate change, the winds still seemed to get harder every season. Bast sighed to think about the leaves and tree branches piling up under fog nets.

Terry sighed, and Bast could see them changing tactics. "Even if that were true – which, ask the curator in Darebin about the right mess they had when their keeper drank himself into the bay – even with perfect notes, people will want to know that their power plants are in good hands. You're a fixture of the community, Bast! They'll have my arse if I hand the Lighthouse over to someone without your stamp of approval."

Bast hated feeling like just another prideful geezer, but the flattery got the better of him. And, as the rain continued the next day and the next, he reluctantly admitted that his heavy lungs were glad to not be trudging through the steamy streets. Might be okay to at least have some help. But who would appreciate St. Kilda's collection as much as he did?

A week later the nurses unstrapped their machines and pronounced his heart as good as they were going to get it. As he laced up his boots to get back to work, he was so distracted by the to-do list spiraling through his head that he almost forgot the apprentice was coming.

Amelia waited politely outside his front gate, fingering his garden boxes, which looked limp after the week of storms. She was stocky where he was thin, tan where he burned, wore glasses but no headphones. Bast tried to imagine what he could possibly have in common with this child.

"Alright then, I've got a lot to do," Bast said by way of greeting. "So just you watch, and do as I say, and save your questions a few days 'til after I've caught up."

"You need storm nets for these waratahs," Amelia said, trying to straighten one of the flowers. "They tighten closed when the wind picks up. I can bring some if you like."

Bast harrumphed and started walking down Peel to Chapel. Here people lounged in the street grass, waiting for the tram or the Sandringham train. It was already hot, and the busy tram was late, so a few commuters took calls in the shade of the Windsor power plant – a great trapezoidal shard lifted over the train station by supports painted like beanstalks. Black photovoltaics, a decade young, covered the top. The underside was a technicolor cloudscape, sparkling with LEDs.

Bast pulled rags and cleaner from a hidden closet, then eyed the beanstalk. The nurses hadn't said no ladders, but he was already winded from the short walk. He handed the rag to Amelia.

"Soft circles, six per spray," he said, demonstrating the technique. "You'll want to peel off the birdshit, otherwise it'll streak. Have a go, eh?"

Bast sent Amelia up through a locked panel in the clouds. Then he found a perch on Chapel Street and sat down to watch her wash a month's worth of grime off the photovoltaics. A little dirt didn't decrease their output, but Bast loved seeing his reflection in clean, shiny solar. He half-hoped to see signs of distress, to hear excuses or stupid questions. But Amelia scrubbed gamely away, and he felt a pang of shame at his standoffishness.

"How old are you, anyway?" Bast called.

"Nineteen last Friday," Amelia said. "How old are you?"

"Stopped counting," Bast said. Then, feeling he should at least offer advice if he wasn't helping, added: "You do this work, I suggest you do the same. No sense in marking anniversaries like, 'thirty years trimming hedges, twenty years tightening screws.'"

Amelia seemed to mull this over. She climbed down, and Bast had Amelia watch the underside for dead LEDs while he logged into the dashboard. The trapezoid had been running a smidge low in his absence, but still provided a good portion of the neighborhood's power.

They worked their way down towards the bay, stopping to tidy up the piezoelectric jungle gym at Alma Park and the botanical garden's meter-wide refraction globes, which rested like raindrops in giant, aluminum lotus flowers. Each installation was unique, and so required a unique regime of monthly care, which existed now for Bast as muscle memory. Usually he went about the work automatically, his mind logging parts that were showing wear and thinking of the craftspeople he'd need to seek out to fix them. It was oddly exhausting to now sit back and explain what his hands did automatically.

It was already noon when they rounded on the marina, and the chimes of the Lighthouse drifted to them down the parade. Bast wanted to tell himself that Amelia's presence slowed him down, but truth was he was the slow one. His breath went short after a few stairs, and his back ached from too many days in bed. He eyed the glass tower poking over the low rooftops, and felt his heart start to thump louder.

"Oi, fancy some lunch?" he asked. "Chimes don't sound too off. We can hit the big boy in the arvo."

Amelia looked surprised but nodded vigorously, so they walked across the street to a cafe, squeezing past sweaty cyclists to order waffles and smashed avocado on toast. Bast knew everyone, but he was surprised to see the barista wave at Amelia, who popped off to chat.

"Where are you from, anyway?" Bast asked when she returned. Terry had gushed to him over her interview, but he didn't remember much else.

"Down Bentleigh East," Amelia said, shaking pepper onto her toast. "But I spent most of my break days in St. Kilda. Love the beach, you know. Four years, life-saving certified!"

Bast swallowed down his bite of waffle. He remembered the yellow and red jackets. "Were you there? At the Lighthouse, I mean. When my heart ..."

Amelia looked guilty, but he wasn't sure what for. "No. I heard about it though. But I'd already been applying to the curator for months, honest!"

It occurred to Bast that, as he'd been keeper in St. Kilda for most of his life, his taking ill might have meant a scramble of people keen to replace him. He wasn't surprised; the keeper job paid good wages, guaranteed forever by the Lighthouse charter, and the work was there as long as he wanted it. It wasn't glamorous, but in the gentle long tail at the end of industrial expansion, Bast believed that maintenance was the best and realest work around.

"Aye, no worries. Just, see if you still want the gig after this week, right?" Suddenly Bast felt very tired. He felt the Lighthouse in the distance. "Actually, let's knock off for the day. That okay with you?"

"Uh, yes," Amelia said, and they washed their dishes and left.

The next week they swept grass clippings off the solar hills of Albert Park golf course, and checked for leaks in each solar balloon that hovered over Albert Park Lake. Then they gave a proper tune up to the wind turbine that mirrored the 600-year-old Corroboree Tree. Amelia learned fast, Bast had to admit, and she knew when to check with him about a loose screw or bit of rust. Soon he gave up his ban on questions and let her pry from him the history of each artwork and its service to the city.

The week after that he took her down towards Elwood, where a few blocks had taken on the spirit of Venice in anticipation of rising seas. They snagged a share-boat at Milton and Broadway and paddled down the extended canals to Elster Creek, and over to the Bay. There a Korean sculptor was building a dike that would power a desalination plant with the creeping pressure of the tides. Each year the municipal curators found new spots for artists to set up power-giving installations, letting the roots of civilization erupt into beautiful view.

"You're avoiding the Lighthouse, aren't you?" Amelia said the next week.

"Lighten off," Bast grumbled. "I'm working my way up to it."

At the end of the month, he had Amelia collect their equipment from around the neighborhood and lug it to his house for a cleaning. It had been a four-season day that settled on sweltering summer, but they set up their buckets on his front patio anyway. Tool care was his favorite Friday night, set to beer and music. As much as he longed for the solitude of this ritual, however, it didn't feel right to box Amelia out of this part of the job.

"So where are all your cats?" Amelia asked.

"No cats. I don't like cats." Bast knew where this was going.

"You're called 'Bast,' and you don't have cats?" Amelia sounded genuinely shocked.

"It's just a name," Bast said. "Doesn't mean anything. What does your name mean?"

"Industrious," Amelia said promptly.

Bast harrumphed, but handed her a tinny.

"Why don't you like cats?" Amelia asked.

"Why don't you want to go to school?" Bast deflected.

"I am going to school," she said. "Apprenticeship, right? I'm supposed to learn from you!"

"I mean to learn something proper. History or painting or cooking. Something that will make you sound smart at parties."

"I already sound smart at parties," Amelia said. And it was true: she had a quick wit when she wanted, Bast had learned.

"Well," Bast considered, "the parties are easier at your age. Wait until you're me, and Terry drags you to a fancy reception with ambassadors and visiting mayors and all, and you've spent your life going round and round the same ten kilometers. Hard to feel clever then, let me tell ya."

Amelia waved her beer at the neighborhood around his garden. "You crack up the latte guy every day. Everyone knows you! Who cares what some foreigner thinks?"

"Ta, yeah, not me, I suppose," he said. "Just want you to know what you're getting into."

They washed and oiled the tools. Like the installations he tended, many of them were one-of-a-kind, fabbed for a particular task on a particular sculpture. Bast knew each object by heart: a deep, ungeneralizable knowledge that came only through endless hours of handling and use. He knew which extra-long screwdriver he'd need to open the angel at Victoria Gardens, and which specially curved shears best trimmed the topiary figures dancing around the airwells at Fawkner Park. He knew how much force each scraper needed to dig the most dirt out from the seams between solar panels. He knew which parts of each blade dulled first, and how frayed a mop could get before it stopped being useful on textured glass over crystalline silicon.

After a month of pointing and directing, it felt good to sit and let his hands move through the familiar rhymes, honed over years: inspect, wipe, wash, dry, oil, wipe, stow. Amelia watched, amazed, as Bast's rags danced over the tools in efficient swipes. They finished as the sun went down. Bast got them more beers. As he handed Amelia a can, the streetlights pulsed on.

"You ever notice that those things look a bit brighter on Fridays than they do on Mondays?" Amelia mused. Bast was pleased.

"Well, tonight they are brighter," he said. "The infrared solar cells around here make a bit of charge just from the moonlight, the stars, the heat of the Earth – long as they're clean and tuned up. At night the grid switches to the big battery on Coode Island, so the local solars dump their juice into the nearby streetlights. But month by month the panels pick up a nice layer of grime, and the lights dim, just a bit. Then a keeper makes their rounds and … pop! Bright as you please."

"That was us?" Amelia said.

"Well, we're the keepers around here, so," Bast said, "that was us."

Amelia pondered this in silence for a few minutes. Then she spoke up. "Can I ask you a question?"

"Alright, have a go."

"How come you never married?" she asked. It wasn't the question Bast expected.

"I was married," he said. "Early days of this job. Nice girl from Camberwell."

"What happened?"

"She moved to Brisbane. When we hitched up, she said she wanted to stay here, but then she didn't. Still surprised she picked Brisbane though, of all places."

"You didn't go after her?" Amelia asked. Then, sarcastic: "In movies you're supposed to go after her."

"Well, I had the Lighthouse." Bast swigged his beer. "Actually, she's the one who called me Bast. Said I was like a cat. Bred to hang around, keep the rats off, but not much else. Couldn't train me, she said, bit of a joke. I kind of liked the name, so I kept it. Fewer people had heard of me that way. Better than being sad Eddie whose wife ran off."

"Bast is a sun deity, too. I looked it up," Amelia said. "That's something you could use at a party."

"You know, I just might."

"So can we do the Lighthouse next week?" Amelia asked.

Bast crumpled his beer can, binned it in the recycling. "I guess we better," he said.

Monday morning they did the carbon capture prayer wheels at the Balaclava Station bridge, and the solar Serra on the lawn at Labassa mansion. Then they walked up towards Jacka Boulevard, past the amusement park with its pressed-wooden rides, and the ancient theater.

The Lighthouse was clear and iridescent, like a cathedral built at the World's Fair. Despite being made of transparent solar panels, it was, still, recognizably a lighthouse. A cylindrical tower, a hundred meters tall, rose from one corner of an open building Bast called 'the barn.' There park-goers and tourists wandered in to see the exhibits, chew sack lunches, or meet friends before heading to the beach. Atop the barn was a vast fog net, a sail that pulled fresh water from the wet bay wind.

Bast had been made keeper when it was built back in the '20s, and yet, forty years on, he still found new things to admire. For a few years he had traced its swooping lines, then noted how the prism pillars pulled rainbow colors from the light. He watched the water trickle down from the sail and drip from the ceiling onto the mossy earth. He spent a decade listening to the chimes – ethereal tones, six times a day. They reminded him sometimes of a Tibetan singing bowl, sometimes of beer bottles clinking in the wind.

Then, for a long time, he watched the people. Watched how they kicked off their shoes to ground themselves before touching the pillars. How they opened their mouths to catch droplets, or found a dry spot to sit and read, or napped while charging their phones at educational outlets. He waited for the moment when they looked up to take in the electric magic that turned sunlight into music and air conditioning and tram travel.

Now he looked at the Lighthouse with something new: trepidation. His chest tensed at the memory, and he thought of how close he'd happened to brush against death in this place. But then Bast glanced at Amelia and realized she'd probably been looking at this place for years, too. He'd seen the Lighthouse built, but she'd grown up with it. He wondered what she'd noticed. Then Amelia, right on cue, pointed at the far corner.

"When I was a tot my oldies used to drop me off there during farmer's market," she said. "I'd do drawings of the prism colors, try to hand them out to people. I guess I was kinda the unofficial Sunday tour guide. You know, sometimes the chimes lined up with church bells from up Acland Street, and everyone would just stop and let the whole place vibrate like a tuning fork."

Bast hardly ever came to the Lighthouse on Sundays, when it was busiest.

"I like to think we built some good things, my generation," Bast said. "Not me, of course. But I do my part. Don't want it to become some dusty ruin, like I grew up in. Just, sometimes I worry that young folks are gonna see this stuff as in their way."

"Well, not me. I like it." Amelia shrugged. "But that's why we take care of things, eh? So the next folks can have a choice about it. They can tear it down, build their own thing. But if we do this right, they can still keep it, if they want."

Suddenly Bast desperately wanted Amelia to take the job. He wanted to give her the beauty he'd seen in the Lighthouse, and the dozens of other works of public whimsy that gifted the city with water and power. He unlocked the ladder and waved Amelia on.

"Up we go," Bast said.

They climbed into the tower. Amelia first, then Bast. Once in the tower the chatter of the barn faded, and Bast was left with no sound but the humming of the wind, the patter of their climb, and the engulfing drumbeat of his heart. He gripped each rung tight, eyes on Amelia's shoes. He took long, deliberate breaths. He tried not to think about the illumination that had pierced his half-conscious eyes, that had seemed to want to pull him up.

It was a bright, noon day, and the sunlight swam straight down into the cylinder. What didn't charge the solar panels was bounced into the barn prisms by relay mirrors. The whole apparatus shifted with the swaying of the sail, and so the interior of the barn danced with rainbows and fairy lights. But inside the tower itself, where few but the keeper got to see, the sun was like fireworks in a funhouse. Against his better judgment, Bast closed his eyes and climbed by feel. Then Amelia's strong hand grabbed his arm and pulled him out onto the barn's glass roof. A chilly antarctic breeze whipped at their hair. Amelia was grinning, and waved at a little girl, staring up at them from the barn below.

"Tried to sneak up here once," she said. "But me mum wouldn't let me pry the lock. Suppose you'd've had to fix that."

"All in a day's work," Bast said. "Come on."

Together they wiped down the glass and checked the wiring. They cleared leaves from the wind pipes that made the Lighthouse sing and polished the tower's mirrors. They oiled the hinges of the sail and gently shooed away nesting birds. It wasn't a lot to do, but it was work that needed doing. Renewable didn't mean free. Someone had to be there to do the renewing.

The work was less automatic with Amelia there, but Bast found a different kind of rhythm in his explanations. He talked her through walking on the slanted glass, which swaths got dirty first, how to spot a tile that might come loose in a few weeks. Knowledge that was hard to capture in schematics.

When they finished, Amelia began to descend to the barn. But Bast stopped her.

"You wanna see the top, don't ya?" he said, and he showed her the second ladder, rising to the lantern room.

The climb up was long and dizzy-making; Bast didn't make it often. More than once he had to stop and lock his arms in the ladder to catch his breath. When he reached the lantern room, Amelia was leaning out to peer at the Melbourne skyline.

"This never gets old, does it?" she asked.

"Oh, it does," he said. "But you can get old with it."

Down below the wind pipes opened, and the pulsing tone of chimes bubbled up from the barn. At the center of the lantern room a beacon the size of a jackfruit flashed out at the bay – a nod to the works that communities build in service to a bigger world. Around them the city crawled with trams and trains, bikes and electric skateboards. Each roof burst with greenery, or glinted with postage-stamps of black solar, drinking the sun. Could this last forever? Bast wondered. He couldn't think why not. Amelia moved back to the ladder, looked at him.

"You can stay here a while, if you like," she said. "I can finish the work."

The Spider and the Stars

D.K. Mok

DEL'S CHILDHOOD, like many others, was woven from enchanted tales. Every night, as the warmth of the day radiated back through the glass water-wall of her bedroom, Del curled up with her plush quokka and listened, enthralled, as her mother spun wondrous stories.

These were never stories of dragons and fairies, mermaids and centaurs. No, these were stories of fierce young women with flocks of tree-planting drones, firing seeds into the barren sands and rolling back the desert. Or tales of ravenous locusts sweeping across the land in suffocating plagues, and the farmers who responded by cultivating carnivorous wheat.

But tonight, there had been no story. Del waited in bed until even Quokka's genial features seemed to furrow with impatience.

"Wait here," whispered Del. She was almost five, and therefore officially allowed to negotiate the terms of Bedtime. Stories were a requirement under Article Three, since she had fulfilled the conditions of Article Two: specifically, the Brushing of Teeth.

She trod softly towards the sound of voices in the kitchen. Her mother sounded uncharacteristically frustrated; her father, uncharacteristically chipper.

"It's their loss," he was saying. "There'll be other competitions—"

"Not like the Solaria Grande Exhibition." Her mother's voice was thick with disappointment. "It'll be twenty years before it comes this way again—"

"So we'll travel to the next one—"

"With all this gear? What if the truck overturns? The last thing we need is a hysterical headline like *Mutant Bugs on Rampage!* It's hard enough getting people not to gag at the word 'entomophagy'—"

"Maybe we shouldn't use that word next time. How about 'alternative protein'?"

There was a soul-crushing sigh. "People won't eat spiders because they have too many legs, but they'll happily eat crabs. They won't eat shea caterpillars because they're too gooey, but they'll slurp down oysters. Gram for gram, insect protein is cheaper, healthier and more sustainable than red meat. To make a single beef patty, it takes two thousand litres of water. To make the same amount of cricket flour, you need a moist towelette and a tolerance for swarms—"

"I know. And *that's* why you'll make this work. You don't need some fancy prize. You have your passion, and your entomology degree. And you have me and my winning way with a hot wok and spices—"

"And me," Del blurted from the doorway. "I'll help you look after the bugs."

"Oh, Del, daughter of mine ..." Her mother scooped her up like a rugby ball, the comforting scent of ripe apricots and jasmine lingering in her mother's thick brown hair. "Am I late for story time?"

As the cicadas bleated their one-note love songs from the eucalypts outside, Del settled onto her sleeping mat, the straw cool against her skin. She slid her night terrarium a little closer, the bioluminescent mushrooms and glow-worms suffusing the room with a gentle blue-green radiance.

"Can I have a story about ogres?" Del's playmates at preschool had terrified each other with stories of child-guzzling ogres, and Del wondered if the ogre had considered eating cricket damper and jam instead.

"Hmm ... I don't know many stories about ogres. Oh, wait, there is one very special ogre – the ogre-faced spider, *Deinopis ravida*. A huntress of the night who stalks her prey with a silken net, with eyes so keen and clever she can see the galaxy Andromeda."

And it was in this moment – her mind filled beyond capacity with this wordless, moonlit image of a stargazing spider – that Del chose her destiny.

Ten Years Later

It had rained all summer, and the water tanks were overflowing, but the local frogs kept the mosquitoes at bay. Even so, citronella candles lined the backyard deck, adding their fragrant glow to the festive solar fairy lights. Del wove through the convivial crowd, carrying one last platter of crispy garlic tortilla chips, setting it down between the creamy mango curry and the crunchy lime and chilli beer snacks.

Del glimpsed her mother in lively conversation with the mayor, while her father manned the barbecue, an aroma like chargrilled prawns and capsicum infusing the balmy air. On the bandstand, a woman on an electric oud was trying to drown out an enthusiastic accordionist, and Del's temples twinged.

Her work done, she slipped quietly into an adjoining paddock and down a wide stone stairwell that descended into the earth. The wall console blinked as it recognised her wrist-chip, and she passed through the airlock, entering a sprawling underground chamber. The humid air smelled of fresh oats and loam, and the room was almost entirely dark. Dim red guide-strips marked the floor, and overhead, the ceiling was studded with thousands of pinprick lights.

Countless rows of two-metre tall racks stretched into the distance, each filled with shallow drawers constructed from corn-starch plastic. A ventilation gap separated each drawer from its neighbour, so that the room resembled a cross between a bakery and library. Large signs were affixed to the end of each row, along with smaller labels on each drawer:

CRICKETS (ACHETA DOMESTICUS)

MEALWORMS (TENEBRIO MOLITOR)

SILKWORMS (BOMBYX MORI)

Del's father had been right. They hadn't needed some fancy prize to realize her mother's vision; just a few years, a new marketing angle, an environmental emergency, and a gutful of hard work. A faint flush of pride warmed Del as she surveyed the tidy insect farm, her mother's colourful logo printed on every crate and carton.

KOUMI'S ORGANIC FOODS: DELICIOUS SUSTAINABLE PROTEIN

Overcoming people's aversion to creepy crawlies had been their greatest challenge, until they realized that cultural attitudes weren't an obstacle, but an asset. If most people hadn't cared when their corn chips were made from palm oil and the tears of orangutans, why would they care now that their cheese-powder fix was made from sustainably farmed, gluten-free crickets? As long as it looked and tasted like a corn chip, most people didn't care where it came from.

Lilana Koumi's banquet parties had become a thing of local legend. They'd started as sales and networking events for potential clients, but as the business prospered, they'd become an annual victory celebration for the family. And it was true, no one really cared that the tortilla chips were made from cricket flour, or that the mango curry included pepper-roasted termite puree, or that the beer snacks consisted of deep-fried, salt-and-pepper grasshoppers. Everything was delicious, and almost nothing looked like bugs.

Del walked down the softly lit aisle, the chorus of *chirrups* washing over her. While most of the crickets' songs were probably entomological booty-calls, she couldn't help imagining that some were wistful odes to waving grass and summer rain. She lifted the mesh of a passing drawer and tossed in a few pieces of carrot. The facility had automated feeding systems, but Del still liked to drop them extra snacks.

The underground chamber was naturally climate-controlled, and the lights were powered by biogas from the nearby cheese factory. And while Del knew it was only her imagination, she sometimes thought the light smelled faintly of cheddar.

At the far end of the subterranean shed, through a small, plain door, lay Del's realm. It had been intended as a supply closet, but Del had begged her mother for the cosy space.

You have a big lab in the warehouse upstairs, Del had said. *Let this be mine.*

And so it was.

Tanks and terrariums and trays and aquariums crammed the small space, brimming with grasses and ferns and multi-legged residents. Giant water bugs paddled lazily, while peacock spiders danced their nervous rhumbas. Charts covered the walls, and boxes of slides were neatly arranged around a scuffed microscope. Stern signs were prominently attached to every insect residence: NOT FOR EATING!

Del reached into a leafy terrarium and gently lifted out a delicate, caramel-coloured spider about the size of a dime. The ogre-faced spider scurried up Del's arm and perched on her shoulder, staring at her with limpid black eyes.

"Hello, Artemis," Del smiled. "Ready to go stargazing again?"

Artemis continued to stare, and, not for the first time, Del wondered if deciphering the expression on a tiny arachnid face was like trying to read a poem inked onto a grain of rice.

While Del's mother spent much of her time researching the nutritional value of insects, Del had become fascinated by the engineering marvel of termite mounds and the dazzling aerodynamics of dragonflies' wings. Her mind sprouted with possibilities, imagining how this knowledge might transform her own world. She envisioned gigantic skyscrapers with convection ventilation systems, requiring no artificial heating or cooling, and agile drones flying through dense jungles in urgent search-and-rescue missions.

Often, as Del peered down her microscope, Artemis would keep her company, ambling thoughtfully across Del's pages of notes, or hanging upside-down from a potted fern, occasionally waving a leg as though in encouragement. Or perhaps telling her to hurry up so they could go outside.

Del conducted a routine check of the room's filters and meshes, double-checking the seals on a tall cylindrical terrarium. Inside, the fire ants were forming another tower, climbing determinedly on top of one another to create a sturdy latticework that resembled an Eiffel Tower of ants. They seemed to do this every time they outgrew their existing home, but Del wondered how high they might go if left unchecked, and if, perhaps, somewhere in that seething lattice, there was a fire ant who longed to reach the clouds.

She would have to get them a larger tank.

Back outside, Del found a quiet spot by the jacarandas, the fallen purple blooms already wilting into potpourri. From her perch, Artemis turned her gaze towards the sky.

Someone coughed from the shadows.

"Hey, am I interrupting?"

A teenage boy with light brown skin and an easy smile stood holding a rustic wooden plate. Del returned the smile.

"Hey, Ziad. Thanks for coming."

Ziad's family ran a busy bakery in town. They were vegetarians, but they came to every banquet, bearing pastries and warm wishes.

"Well, Dad loves a good party. I saw you were frantically busy, as usual. I thought you might be hungry."

He offered the unfamiliar plate, which seemed to bear a delicate sculptural work of contemporary art.

"Wow," said Del. "That looks like it belongs in a gallery."

Ziad beamed. "It's a kangaroo grass sable with lemon myrtle ice cream, quandong tart and a sweet potato twill."

Just as meat had become a luxury in an increasingly arid world, so too, thirsty crops like rice and wheat were beginning to attract concern. Those with foresight were turning to plants like kangaroo grass and saltbush, which required no irrigation, no synthetic fertilisers and no pesticides. Unfortunately, the palate of the masses was yet to be convinced.

Del took a bite of the warm, buttery pastry and tried not to salivate as the tangy quandong jam hit her tastebuds.

"It tastes like a perfect day. I'm sure you'll have your own patisserie in no time."

"Not just a patisserie. It'll have its own garden, its own farm, with heirloom vegetables and heritage fruits and exciting new varieties of grains and berries and honeys." He sighed. "Or, at least, that's the dream."

"Maybe this'll help." Del bumped her wrist-chip gently against his, and a holographic screen blinked into life between them. An ornate certificate shimmered briefly before being replaced by a page of dense disclaimers. Finally, a large title *swooshed* into view:

WELCOME TO CRISPR FOR BEGINNERS.

PLEASE EDIT GENES RESPONSIBLY.

Ziad's wide-eyed expression made him look almost like a human version of Artemis. "You got a CRISPR kit?"

"*We* got a CRISPR kit. Don't get too excited; it's just the student version with a vial of *Drosophila*, but we can share the equipment. Now you can make your pest-resistant chives ..."

"And you can make your flame-resistant moths!"

They grinned at each other as bogong moths fluttered through the sultry air, and Artemis gazed at the stars.

Another Ten Years Later

In the canopy of the scrubland, perched on ten-metre stilts, there nestled a sleek cabin of photovoltaic glass and reclaimed timber. In the eaves, elderly spiders knitted cobwebs, while on the roof, corellas rode the spinning ventilators, cackling uproariously.

Within the airy sunlit rooms, Del rushed from bench to shelf, flicking items off a holographic list that hovered to her right. She slotted one last carefully sealed terrarium into her trolley case before plucking a pristine flyer from her corkboard.

THE SOLARIA GRANDE EXHIBITION AND PRIZE

INNOVATORS, VISIONARIES, INVENTORS, ENTREPRENEURS, ACTIVISTS

COMING TO TERRARIUM CITY

Del pressed the flyer to her chest. Terrarium City was only twelve hours away by levitation train. Her mother's experience at the exhibition had been less than heartening, but her descriptions of the magnificent halls and cosmopolitan crowd had ignited Del's imagination. And while Del loved her cabin in the canopy, and her job at the local Community Knowledge Centre, she longed to venture beyond the red dust and scribbly gum trees of her home town. Far beyond.

A quiet *pitter-patter* announced the arrival of her housemate. A tawny spider the size of a Labrador skittered into the room, clutching a ruffled net of cobweb silk between her forelegs. At the sight of the trolley case, her huge black eyes shone with worried disapproval.

Del clipped the case shut. "Sorry, Devana. I wish I could bring you with me, but I just know someone's going to panic and try to squish you."

Devana was a distant daughter of Artemis, and the benefactor of Del's years of tinkering with CRISPR. However, the more Del probed the cryptic genome of insects and arachnids, and the more she studied their complex behaviours, the less inclined she felt to modify them, and the more she longed to understand their strange and alluring worlds.

Del withdrew a translucent golden pod from a warming cabinet and tossed it to Devana, who snatched it from the air and sank her fangs through the soft gel skin, greedily drinking up the bottlebrush nectar. It had taken Del almost a year to devise this latest formulation, but Devana seemed to find it palatable, and it gave her carapace a healthy sheen.

"Be good," said Del. "Make sure the cockatoos don't chew my house to sawdust while I'm away."

"Everything will be here when you get back," said a voice from the foyer. Del's mother leaned against the gently curving doorframe, an insulated lunchbox in one hand. "Your father sends his love, and dumplings. Vegetarian."

It had been a wrenching decision for Del, many years ago, when she'd excised meat from her diet, including insect protein. But having spent so much time with her tiny companions, having seen their rich, complex lives filled with as much hope, tragedy and delight as her own, in the end, it had hardly been a decision at all. The choice had wounded her parents, but they understood. Or, at least, they said they did.

"All the filters have been changed," said Del. "The cabinet is full of nectar pods. You don't have to do anything with the incubators, but if the fire-ants start building again—"

"It'll be fine. Just enjoy yourself, and remember, the prize doesn't matter."

"I know." Del tucked the flyer into her jacket, her stomach suddenly fluttering. "It's just ... what if they laugh at me?"

"Then it'll be a family tradition. My dearest Del, daughter of mine, they can laugh at us, but they can't stop us."

Del's mother drew her into a hug, and for a brief moment, it was twenty summers ago, when the days smelled of ripe apricots and jasmine.

As Del walked down the leafy track away from her cabin, she turned to see Devana standing on the roof, waving her forelegs. Whether in farewell or in the hopes of netting an unwary cockatoo, Del couldn't be sure, but she waved back.

Ziad was already waiting for her at the levitation station, his two storage drones following him obediently. Their sleek cylindrical forms made them look like a pair of patisserie refrigerators moonlighting as henchmen. As Del jogged over with her luggage, Ziad gave her an excited grin.

"Ready to transform the world with your entomology research?"

"We'll see. Ready to make incremental but meaningful change with your climate-resilient crops and nutritionally responsible, mind-blowing desserts?"

"I have two tower-cases of pastries, puddings and cakes, so whatever happens, I'll be having a good time."

The station was a curving sandstone platform, partially enclosed by lofty timber beams and tinted skylights. Even in the baking summer heat, the angular design of the roof drew cool air in from the surrounding native gardens and exhaled warm air through the ceiling vents. A bell-like tone signalled the arrival of the train, and Del watched with anxious delight as it snaked across the sand.

Affectionately known as the Wyrm, the silver, serpentine locomotive glided a metre above the trackless ground. It was guided by GPS and location beacons stationed every kilometre along its path, and powered by a crucible of geomagnetism, photovoltaics, and lightning in a bottle.

The interior was part Orient Express, part Star Trek, with panoramic windows on every side. Del and Ziad settled into an economy booth, sipping ginger tea and practising their presentations. But the changing landscape outside kept tugging at Del's attention: there were towns, just like hers, speckled with solar arrays and water tanks. But there were also villages floating on inland seas, their bustling markets a crowd of floating tea houses and creaking junks with patchwork sails. There were forests of typhoon turbines ready to capture the rage of mighty storms, and enormous greenhouses in the desert, flanked by desalination plants powered by the sun.

As the terrain outside grew more arid – the parched earth puckering into shingles – an oasis slowly rose on the horizon. A gigantic dome of glass – a garden city in a bell jar, infused with greenery and flecked with iridescent butterflies and scarlet macaws.

Terrarium City.

Terrarium City Exhibition Centre was an enormous labyrinth of adjoining halls, and the registration foyer resembled a fusion of intergalactic spaceport and overgrown conservatory. Climbing roses spiralled up the stone columns, reaching towards a ceiling that was little more than a glassy frame for the sky. Full-grown figs towered around them, their roots sinking deep into the floor, and it was hard to tell where the carpet stopped and the moss began.

At a registration booth wreathed in delicate pink mandevillas, Del and Ziad finally received their convention passes.

Ziad quietly pumped a fist. "Yes! I'm in Meadow Hall. That's supposed to be one of the fun ones. How about you?"

Del looked at her pass. "I'm in Tundra Hall."

"Uh, I'm sure that's fun too. I'll come visit your booth."

Del glanced at the sprawling map overhead. "No, that's all right. It makes sense that they'd situate the live exhibits far away from the food exhibits."

As it turned out, Del's neighbouring booth was technically a food exhibit.

"Hi, I'm Xiaren Appelhof," said an angular woman with rosy cheeks and a smile like a flash of steel. "Distributed biogas generation. You?"

"Del Koumi. Entomological research." She tried not to stare at the tall, complicated tanks lining Xiaren's booth. They resembled a more militant version of Ziad's storage drones.

Xiaren followed her gaze. "Ah, I see you've noticed my portable domestic biogas system. Normally, biogas harvesting systems require thousands of tonnes of cheese to create a commercially viable amount of whey for anaerobic digestion. My system utilises less than twenty kilos of cheese, and generates enough gas for heating and cooking in a typical home. I call it the *Fromagerie 5000!*"

Xiaren swung open a panel in the tank to reveal five shelves of ripening cheeses surrounded by gurgling pipes and humming canisters. Del rocked back on her heels, the intense smell of gorgonzola hitting her with almost physical force.

"That's ... powerful."

"I've specially cultivated the microorganisms to generate vastly more biogas than normal. And the cheese tastes amazing."

Xiaren cut a gooey wedge from a creamy blue and offered it to Del, who, after a moment's hesitation, took a bite. Notes of chilli and lychee simmered beneath the pungent flavour, and her eyes watered.

"This would make an insanely good pasta sauce." She gave herself a moment for the sparkles to disappear from her vision. "So, why did you go into cheese?"

Xiaren shrugged. "My hometown isn't overly fond of dairy, but we needed clean energy. And in my mind, gas is gas, whether it's happening inside a cow or a star. Or a round of cheese."

Del looked at the racks of peaceful cheeses, and wondered if they knew they had the heart of stars.

Over the next four days, she and Xiaren bonded over rice-paper rolls and grilled cheese sandwiches, listening to each other delivering their spiels to the curious visitors who streamed endlessly through the halls. Some people seemed interested in Del's collection of giant phasmids and burrowing cockroaches. Less so in her infographics, research papers and posters of 'fun facts'.

"Koumi?" said one middle-aged man, studying her information screen as it hovered over his wrist-chip. "Any relation to Lilana?"

"That's my mother."

The man's smile broadened. "I saw her presentation nearly twenty years ago. She knew her stuff. Generous, too. My pitch for a café run by homeless ex-cons sank at the panel, but your mum gave me a cricket flour starter kit and a recipe for butterscotch pancakes. It's still a bestseller at the café now. I was so tickled when I saw her Caramelised Onion Protein Bars in my local supermarket a few years back. Tell your mother, 'Irvine says hi'."

However, not every visitor was as supportive as Irvine. Del's stand elicited as many 'ew's as Xiaren's elicited 'phew's. Many potential investors scurried past, eyes averted, handkerchiefs over their noses. By the time Del's convention pass flashed with her presentation alert, she was feeling less than buoyed by the public's reaction.

"Hey," said Xiaren. "It doesn't matter what people say. What matters is what you do about it. I'm sure your bugs think you're awesome."

Del made her way through the seething crowd, clutching a single terrarium. Every exhibitor was granted one ninety-second pitch slot with minimal props. If the panel wanted more information, they'd investigate your online portfolio, and, if you were lucky, they'd visit your booth.

She took a slight detour through Meadow Hall, marvelling at the glittering lights, colourful holograms and delicious aromas. One stand billowed gently with cumulus clouds, while another promised neural-implant learning modules.

She finally spotted Ziad's booth. His glistening displays of pastries had tempted a large crowd, and he was enthusiastically describing the carbon footprint of a regular egg tart, compared to the carbon footprint of his regeneratively farmed eggs and macadamia butter pastry egg tarts. Del noted, with considerable satisfaction, that Ziad's onlookers included a significant number of snappily dressed proxy droids, favoured by professional investors who wanted to inspect potential ventures without leaving the house. Del glimpsed one or two faceports that seemed to show the bleary expression of someone who was probably still in their pyjamas.

Del's pass flashed more urgently, and she hurried the rest of the way to Galaxy Hall. The cavernous theatre was almost pitch-black, lit only by twinkling beads of lights on the ceiling and softly coruscating guide-strips on the floor. The hall was largely empty – most people preferred to watch the presentations on their displays, but Del's heart still stuck in her throat as she walked down the aisle and onto the stage.

Her courage almost failed her as she saw the panel of five judges seated near the front. Metres away from her sat Solaria Grande, her brown skin dusted with holographic flecks, her frohawk teased with grey and threaded with light-emitting filaments. Cybernetic contacts made her irises a sigil of golden circuitry, and she looked every inch the ecological goddess who'd forced the desert into retreat. Her seed-planting drones had strafed the land with precisely mapped grasslands, scrub and forests. Her educational programs and support networks had empowered communities to manage the natural regeneration of dormant vegetation systems.

Del felt her voice evaporating as those golden eyes fixed onto her.

"Adelie Koumi," said Solaria Grande. "What do you have for us?"

With shaking hands, Del set the covered terrarium onto the presentation table. "Dung ..." Her voice cracked, and the silence seemed to swallow her. She took a slow, deep breath, and imagined she could see Andromeda. "Dung beetles navigate by the stars. Bogong moths migrate thousands of kilometres by starlight. We still know so little about insects and their relationship with the constellations, yet they could hold the key to our off-world aspirations.

"Our ability to colonise other planets hinges upon how well we can recreate functioning ecosystems. How can we do that without the pollinators and the decomposers? Without the complex web of organisms that sustains life on Earth? If we intend to make our home on other worlds, that home will need insects.

"Furthermore, space radiation remains one of our biggest obstacles to interstellar travel. However, tardigrade cells contain a protein that protects DNA from radiation damage, and not only could this protein allow humans to travel beyond the safety of our planet, it could also have implications for protecting us against cancers, radiation therapy, and cellular degeneration.

"Another challenge is developing resilient materials that can withstand physical and radioactive assault, but remain sufficiently lightweight and versatile for launch and operational needs. However, I've experimented with the proteins in spider silk, and I believe there are potential applications in the development of self-healing spaceships, habitats and safety lines.

"Finally, orbital junk poses a threat not only to space travel, but to the safety of our satellites and space stations. I've been studying the movement of spiders in zero-gravity, and I believe that automated arachnoid robots and mesh snares could play a key role in the retrieval of dangerous orbital refuse.

"Now, I don't have a product to sell or a business to implement. What I'm hoping to do is spark interest, encourage collaborations, spur research. What I'm proposing is a space station dedicated to the study of invertebrate organisms in non-terrestrial environments. Because when we eventually journey to the stars, I believe our tiny colleagues not only deserve to, but essentially must, come with us."

Del pulled the cloth from the terrarium to reveal a zero-gravity chamber containing a model spaceship surrounded by tiny floating balls of aluminium foil. She flashed a laser pointer across the porthole of the ship, and an ogre-faced spider excitedly scurried out. It launched into a gently swimming motion through the weightless space and proceeded to collect the nectar-daubed foil with a silken snare.

It wasn't a product, or a service, or a design. It was probably rather silly.

But it was memorable.

She finally dared to look at the panel, whose expressions ranged from bemused to stony.

"Thank you," said Grande. "Please enjoy the rest of the exhibition."

With a mixture of embarrassment and elation, Del left the stage. As she walked past the panel, she thought she caught a flicker of a smile on Grande's lips, but it might have been a trick of the starlight.

On the final day of the exhibition, hardly anyone came through Tundra Hall. It would seem that word had spread, and a consensus had been reached that there was little to see here.

"I'm sure it has nothing to do with your presentation," said Xiaren. "It was cute. I mean interesting. Hardly anyone said it was weird."

"Uh, thanks …"

A familiar figure trotted over. "Actually, it was slightly weird. But also very cool." Ziad graciously set down a tray laden with eclairs, baklava, mochi, and raspberry strudels.

Del struggled, and failed, to keep her mood in a trench. "They're about to announce the winner. Shouldn't you be networking in the Investor's Lounge?"

"My details are online," he replied. "And I saw this irresistible presentation about these incredible exploding cheeses."

Xiaren sighed. "No one was hurt. And I've figured out the problem."

As Ziad sampled Xiaren's tasting plate, Del started on an eclair, interrupted only by an impatient '*Ahem*'.

A heavy-set woman with brown skin and scarlet-lacquered nails stood before Del's booth, arms crossed, wearing an expression like someone who spends her day maintaining a polite tone of voice while suppressing a category-five rage-hurricane.

"Are you the one who wants to build rocketships for spiders?"

"Well …" Del wondered if she were about to be subjected to another rant about scientists and taxpayer money. She reached for her 'Fun Facts About Science' leaflet, complete with a helpful infographic about the 90% return on investment. "Well, yes, but I have this leaflet—"

"My Jada has something to say to you." The woman clearly had no time for infographics. She nudged her charge.

Del peered over the counter, and a small girl with a vigorous puff of brown hair thrust a large piece of paper towards her. The crayon drawing depicted a shuttle sloshing with spiders, and a puff-haired girl sitting at the controls, smiling like the sun.

"Jada wants to pilot one of your ships when she grows up," said the woman. "Shuttling spiders into space to keep the planet safe."

The girl nodded vigorously, thrusting the picture towards Del again as though presenting her CV. Del tenderly accepted it, not mentioning that free-range probably wasn't the best way to transport a colony of spiders.

"Thank you. I'll keep you in mind."

The girl saluted ferociously before marching away with her mother.

"That was also weird," said Ziad. "But adorable."

A chord of music rippled from the front of the hall, accompanied by a mesmerising aurora. The stage suffused with light, coalescing into a holographic broadcast of the closing ceremony concurrently taking place in Celebration Hall. The convener thanked all the attendees, and a series of guests gave stirring speeches about innovation and persistence. But everyone was waiting for the final speaker, and the final announcement.

Solaria Grande was resplendent in an emerald suit that appeared to generate its own micro-ecosystem, seeming to ripple with grass one moment and shimmer with moss the next.

"The prize is not about the prestige," she declared, "although it has launched careers and established reputations. The prize is not about the money, although it has seeded ambitious projects and turned dreams into flourishing businesses. The prize is what you brought here with you. The prize is what you take away. The prize is what you've shared with all the people who passed through those doors. But that's not what most of you came here for, is it? So, without further ado—"

In the breathless silence of the hall, Del, Ziad and Xiaren linked hands, grinning with the inexpressible joy of being *here* and *now*, on the cusp of something extraordinary, no matter what came next.

"—the winner of the Solaria Grande Exhibition Prize is—"

Another Thirty Years Later

The shuttle docked with barely a bump, and Del released the armrests of her business-class seat. She'd made this trip countless times now, but that final *click* of the docking clamps always sent electric shivers to the very tips of her fingers. She brought her face close to the passenger-side window, her nose almost touching the cold, transparent matrix.

In the dizzying expanse of space, the station hung in the star-dusted void. It resembled a complicated molecule, with large glassy nodes interconnected via semi-rigid passageways. Its surface rippled with tiny photovoltaic scales, all turning to lap up the passing sun. In the half-light of space, it looked almost like a slumbering snake, curling itself into Celtic knots.

A coppery octobot jetted gracefully past, trailing a net of captured space debris. Del watched with a faint ache of pride as it climbed in through a station hatch and disappeared with its haul.

Del passed through decontamination and stepped into the arrival hall. She'd imagined, once, that space would be all chrome and glass and pulsing lights. Clinical, synthetic, easy to clean. But, back on Earth, past efforts to eliminate germs and bugs from human habitations had led to an explosion in allergies, inflammatory diseases and decimated microbiomes. Successful, long-term space exploration would not – could not – be a sterile venture, and what humanity needed now was a sandpit to experiment in.

Throughout the hall, aluminium trusses were laced with lilac wisteria, and mesh walls brimmed with ferns and bromeliads, forming an avenue of vertical gardens. Despite the softly humming filtration systems, the scent of orange blossom and pear tarts wafted from the nearby cafés. Del's mouth twitched into a smile – as it always did – at the sleek sign emblazoned over the entrance arch.

TERRARIUM SPACE STATION

Del had few rituals, but this one she had maintained for twelve years, since the day of her first visit. She made her way to the Summer Arboretum, past aromatic lemon trees and velvety bushes of French lavender. In a small grove, curtained off by bottlebrush, there stood a little bronze statue of an ogre-faced spider holding a small moon aloft in her forelegs.

DEDICATED TO ARTEMIS, WHOSE CHILDREN REACHED THE STARS

Del gazed up at the large circular skylight, the cloud-dappled Earth a delicate sphere hanging in the darkness, and wondered what Artemis would have made of this.

"Del! I only just saw your name on the arrival logs." A lean young woman with a short mane of curly brown hair walked across the flowering grasses, her navy flight suit marked with the epaulettes of a captain. "Why didn't you tell us you were coming?"

"Jada! I thought you weren't due back for another week."

"We had a biomechanics team from Astroviva scheduled to arrive yesterday, so I thought I'd come back early. They're trying to design an asteroid rover with variable terrain mobility, emergency aerial capabilities, flexible anchoring technology, and a compact folding solar array."

"Peacock spiders," said Del automatically, and Jada grinned.

"They're with the arachnology team as we speak."

"You've been busy. I saw the new Phasmid and Mantis Habitat Pods on the inflight preview."

"Yes, those opened last month. I don't think the stick insects have realized it's zero-g yet, and I don't think the mantids care. Oh, and in other exciting news – it's still under wraps, but we're planning to build a Cephalo Pod. Because who doesn't want to see octopuses in space?"

Del's heart somersaulted in anticipation as she imagined the mischief an octopus might get up to in space. "Save me a ticket to the opening."

"Will do. So, are you here for work or pleasure this time?"

"It's always a bit of both. But I'm meeting an old friend here later."

"Let me know if you need anything. And say 'hi' to your folks for me."

"I will."

Del visited the various research pods, listening as each scientist enthused about their latest project. It was hard to imagine that, thirty years ago, all she had was a room full of bugs and a dream. As it turned out, others had shared that dream.

In the end, the Solaria Grande Prize had gone to a non-profit organisation that coordinated teams of teachers, librarians, and androids, sending them out in nimble airships to help communities build, equip, and staff schools for girls in remote regions.

But Del's wobbly video of a weightless spider gripping a wad of aluminium had captured the imagination of a few people out there, some of whom had looked into Del's projects and reached out to her, and to each other.

And, like a colony of spiders, the web of connections had grown until it was strong enough to catch an elephant. Or launch a space station.

Later that night, Del enjoyed dinner at one of the station's restaurants – spicy eggplant stew and mango pancakes – before she made her way back to the Summer Arboretum. The dome had drifted into its nocturnal cycle, the lights dimmed so that only moonlight shone through the skylights. Del strolled the gentle slopes, and from a distant pod, disoriented crickets sang odes to memories of 'up' and 'down'.

"Hi, Del. I brought you something."

Del turned to see Ziad standing beside a sandstone water feature, holding a plate of something that resembled a swirl of light.

Del laughed, wrapping her friend in a warm embrace. "How was your flight?"

"Terrifying. I refer to the ticket price, not the journey."

Del winced. "Space tourism is still in its infancy—"

"You mean poorly regulated monopolies are still gouging consumers."

"Speaking of monopolies, how's Xiaren?"

"She's well. Still irritated every time the press calls her a 'biofuels magnate'."

"Ah, she'll always be a fromager at heart."

Ziad smiled, his gaze coming to rest on the tiny statue of a spider and her moon. "Well, we all managed to follow our hearts, didn't we?"

Del considered this. "I think, perhaps, we followed the science and the necessity. And our hearts just didn't allow us to give up."

A breeze stirred in the microclimate of the arboretum, and Del could almost taste the smoky summers of long ago. She and Ziad stood side by side, watching the Earth swirl gently with the seasons.

From up here, all of humanity was little more than a microcosm, every living speck indistinguishable from any other. And yet, if you looked closer, you'd see the breathtaking complexity of every single soul; you'd see new stories constantly unfolding, new journeys constantly beginning.

Somewhere, down there, a pair of ambitious teenagers shared their hopes beneath a gibbous moon.

Somewhere, down there, a campfire burned beneath a sky streaked with galaxies, and a moth fluttered, unscathed, through the flames.

And somewhere, down there, an ogre-faced spider watched a strange star moving across the midnight sky, and dreamed.

About the Authors

Jerri Jerreat's writing, from Anishinaabe & Haudenosaunee territory, appears in *Grist/Fix: Climate Fiction 2022*, *Fairlight Books stories*, *Flyway: Journal of Writing & Environment*, *Yale Review Online*, *Onyx Publications*, *Alluvian*, *Every Day Fiction*, *Fictive Dreams*, *Feminine Collective*, *The New Quarterly*, as well as in anthologies such as *Solarpunk Creatures*; *Glass and Gardens Solarpunk Winters*; *Solarpunk Summers*. She directs an award-winning solarpunk festival: Youth Imagine The Future.

Ken Liu (http://kenliu.name), winner of the Nebula, Hugo, and World Fantasy awards, is the author of the *Dandelion Dynasty*, a silkpunk epic fantasy series (starting with *The Grace of Kings*), as well as *The Paper Menagerie and Other Stories* and *The Hidden Girl and Other Stories*.

Thomas Badlan has wanted to be a writer for as long as he can remember. He studied Creative Writing at the University of Derby in the UK and currently works as a Teaching Assistant in a Manchester High School. He is also a long-standing member of Manchester's Monday Night Writer's Group. He has had five previous stories published by World Weaver Press, Improbable Press, Ab Terra Books, Future Fiction and Eibonvale Press.

Ciro Faienza is a filmmaker, writer, artist, actor and Hugo-nominated editor. His short story 'Jae's Solution' was a top finalist in PRI's 3-Minute Futures contest. His work has been anthologized and translated in multiple languages, including an Italian best-of-the-year volume. He lives in Massachussets. Find him online at postmedium.blog.

Brenda Cooper is a technology professional, a writer and a futurist. Brenda holds an MFA from Stonecoast and is an Imaginary College Fellow at the Center for Science and the Imagination, CSI, at Arizona State University. Brenda is also a member of the Brain Trust for the Biodiversity and Conservation domain at XPrize. Her novel-length fiction has won two Endeavour awards and been shortlisted for the Philip K. Dick Award. Brenda's most recent work includes short stories published in *Seattle Magazine*, *Anthropocene Magazine* and *Slate*. Brenda is the IT Director for Lease Crutcher Lewis, a Seattle construction company. She lives in Woodinville, Washington with her wife, five dogs and three bicycles. See more at brenda-cooper.com.

Renan Bernardo is a Nebula finalist science fiction and fantasy writer from Brazil. His fiction has appeared in *Reactor* (Tor.com), *Apex Magazine*, *PodCastle*, *Escape Pod* and others. His writing scope is broad, from secondary world fantasy to dark science fiction, but he enjoys the intersection of climate narratives with science, technology and the human relations inherent to it. His solarpunk/cli-fi short fiction collection, *Different Kinds of Defiance*, was published by Android Press in 2024.

Jennifer Lee Rossman (they/them) is a queer, disabled and autistic author and editor from the land of carousels and Rod Serling. Their work has been featured in dozens of anthologies, and their reincarnation thriller novel *Blue Incarnations* is now available. Find more of their work on their website jenniferleerossman.blogspot.com and follow them on Twitter @ JenLRossman.

Francesco Verso (Bologna, 1973) is a multiple-award-winning Science Fiction writer and editor (three Europe Awards, two Urania Awards, two Italy Awards, one Golden Dragon Award and one Galaxy Award). He has published: *Antidoti umani*, *e-Doll*, *Nexhuman*, *Bloodbusters, Zendroide, Futurespotting* and *The Roamers* (made of *The Pulldogs* and *No/Mad/Land*). *Nexhuman* and *Bloodbusters* have been published in the UK and in China. *The Roamers* was published by Flame Tree Press in May 2023 and will be out in France in 2025. A promoter of World SF and solarpunk, he also works as editor and publisher of *Future Fiction*, a multicultural project dedicated to scouting and publishing the best SF in translation from more than 40 countries and 14 languages. From 2019 he's the Honorary Director of the Fishing Fortress Science Fiction Academy of Chongqing. He may be found at www.futurefiction.org.

Sarena Ulibarri lives, writes and plants trees in the American Southwest. Her solarpunk novella *Another Life* was published by Stelliform Press in 2023, and *Steel Tree* (a science fiction retelling of *The Nutcracker*) was published by Android Press. Her short stories have appeared in magazines such as *Lightspeed*, *DreamForge* and *Solarpunk Magazine*. As an anthologist, she curated *Glass and Gardens: Solarpunk Summers* and *Glass and Gardens: Solarpunk Winters* and co-edited *Multispecies Cities* and *Solarpunk Creatures*.

Gustavo Bondoni is a novelist and short story writer with over four hundred stories published in fifteen countries, in seven languages. He is a member of Codex and a Full Member of SFWA. He has published six science fiction novels including one trilogy, four monster books, a dark military fantasy and a thriller. His short fiction is collected in *Pale Reflection* (2020), *Off the Beaten Path* (2019), *Tenth Orbit and Other Faraway Places* (2010) and *Virtuoso and Other Stories* (2011). His website is at gustavobondoni.com.

Lucie Lukačovičová is a writer, translator and creative writing teacher. She comes from the Czech Republic but lived for some time in Angola, Cuba and India. She received her master's degree in Librarianship and Cultural Anthropology at the Charles University. She has published over 100 short stories and seven novels in Czech. She has also published texts in Chinese, German, Romanian, Italian, Portuguese and Kannada.

Her English stories have been published in the anthologies *Life Beyond Us*, *Bright Mirror* and others.

Ingrid Garcia is still selling wines in a vintage wine shop in the south of Spain as her dream of becoming a full-time writer is extremely slow to take off. She's been published in *F&SF*, *Eighteen: Stories of Mischief & Mayhem*, *Ride the Starwind* and *Sword and Sonnet*, amongst others. Like many others, she's working on her first novel.

Andrew Dana Hudson is a speculative fiction writer, sustainability researcher and futurist. He is the author of *Our Shared Storm: A* Novel *of Five Climate Futures*, as well as many stories and essays appearing in publications such as *Slate*, *Jacobin*, *Vice*, *Lightspeed*, *Analog*, and more. His writing, particularly his essay 'On the Political Dimensions of Solarpunk', has helped theorize the solarpunk genre.

D.K. Mok is a fantasy and science fiction author whose work includes the novels *Squid's Grief* and *Hunt for Valamon*, and the collection *The Heart of the Labyrinth and Other Stories*. DK has been shortlisted for seven Aurealis Awards, three Ditmars, and three Washington Science Fiction Association Small Press Awards. DK is based in Sydney, Australia, and her favourite fossil deposit is the Burgess Shale. Find out more at www.dkmok.com.

About Future Fiction

Future Fiction is a small press and cultural association created by Francesco Verso to promote an interdisciplinary approach to the idea of the future: in 10 years it has published the best science fiction in the world, from 14 languages and 35 countries, with authors like Ian McDonald, Liu Cixin, Vandana Singh, Chen Qiufan and Ken Liu, winning the Best Publisher Award from the European SF Society in 2019 and a Galaxy Award in 2023.

With the ambition to map the other 'tomorrows' declined by many cultures, Future Fiction organizes workshops, conferences and conventions in Europe, Latin America and China on issues related to anticipation and speculation, with essays, novels, short stories and anthologies – in printed, audiobook and comic format. Over the years, the project has become an excellent content aggregator and a place of discovery for anyone who sees in the future not only upcoming dystopias and unlikely apocalypses but also an analysis and entertainment tool to find an orientation amongst the incredible transformations that are impacting humanity at all levels, from Capitalocene to biopolitics and nanotechnology, from AI, Big Data and aging population, to climate change and solarpunk.

Acknowledgments

413

Beyond & Within

THE FLAME TREE Beyond & Within short story collections bring together tales of myth and imagination by modern and contemporary writers, carefully selected by anthologists, and sometimes featuring short stories and fiction from a single author. Overall, the series presents a wide range of diverse and inclusive voices, often writing folkloric-inflected short fiction, but always with an emphasis on the supernatural, science fiction, the mysterious and the speculative. The books themselves are gorgeous, with foiled covers, printed edges and published only in hardcover editions, offering a lifetime of reading pleasure.

FLAME TREE FICTION

A wide range of new and classic fiction, from myth to modern stories, with tales from the distant past to the far future, including short story anthologies, Collector's Editions, Collectable Classics, Gothic Fantasy collections and Epic Tales of mythology and folklore.

•

Available at all good bookstores, and online at flametreepublishing.com